MONSTERS WITHIN MEN

TJ ROSE

CONTENTS

AUTHOR'S NOTE

Welcome! *Monsters within Men* is a dystopian post-apocalyptic MM romance, suitable only for adult readers. Although dark at points, at its core, the novel explores the transformative nature of love and the light it can bring, even in the midst of darkness.

Content warnings:

- (consensual) explicit sexual content

- grief & depression

- self-harm & suicide attempts (not graphically described)

- death of side characters

For any further guidance on these content warnings, please contact me at tjroseauthor@gmail.com, and I will assist you.

This novel is written in British English.

"Hope is the thing with feathers that perches in the soul."

Emily Dickinson

NOAH

It had only just gone ten o'clock, but Noah was running for his life yet again.

Gunshots rattled through the air, sending birds scattering in every direction. Clearly his squad hadn't taken the slightest bit of notice of his directive to conserve bullets in the briefing this morning.

The audio feed on his combat helmet crackled before Splat's voice barked into his ear, "Forrest, what the hell are you doing in the bloody *maze*? And watch your six!"

He pivoted on his heel, running backwards as fast as he dared as he unloaded several bolts from his crossbow at the cluster of monsters chasing him.

Fuck it, he thought, and swapped to his rifle.

Today's mission was only meant to be a covert supply run. A scouting report suggested there could be stashes of tinned food awaiting them in the restaurant of Lightwater Amusement Park. *In and out*, they'd said. *You'll be back for lunch*, they'd said.

Activating the drone-cam view on his VisorX's interior display, he watched himself run from above through the overgrown hedge maze. *Two lefts, then a right...*

Hungry snarls snapped him back to the scene in front of him: three more typeAs, who'd fought their way through the thick shrubbery of the hedge maze, were barrelling towards him.

"I can't shoot *and* figure my way out," he shouted into his mic.

He heard Splat sigh dramatically, as if it pained him to help his commanding officer out of a life and death situation.

"Keep going straight. Walsh and Sanders are by the exit, waiting for you. Next left," Splat instructed, and Noah followed his directions, shooting two typeAs smack-bang in the middle of their foreheads. Noah grinned—Habib was going to be jealous of his body count.

"Left. Then right..."

When Noah burst out of the oppressively dim light of the maze, several types—latecomers to Noah's trail of followers—were still hot on his tail.

"Feckin' hell, LT, you're a popular one today," Aoife said, raising her rifle in the relaxed, languid way she knew annoyed him. The chest piece of her combat suit was splattered with so much gore, he could barely see the hard black material.

"Can you just—"

"I'm on it." Meredith unloaded three rounds, hitting all three of her marks. Noah would have whistled in approval if he had any breath left.

Aoife waved her rifle in the air. "That's not on, not even giving me the chance."

"You snooze, you lose, bitch."

"Sitrep? Where's everyone else?" Noah said, more to snap them back to attention than anything—he was already flicking through the drone's feeds.

Aoife nodded to the west. "Over by the rollercoaster."

Marching in formation with Noah leading, the trio crossed the long-abandoned park with haste.

A minor explosion sounded in the near distance, small wisps of smoke trailing into the sky.

"Splat?" Noah increased his pace. "What's going on over there?"

"Nothing much. Things were just getting a little boring, so I thought I'd spice it up."

"What have I said about—"

Noah cut himself off, staring at a typeB that pressed its face against a chain-link fence. "Go on. I'll be there in a second," he said to Aoife and Meredith.

He clocked them glancing at each other, hesitating for a millisecond too long before they followed his order.

When the women passed the entrance to the log flume ride, Noah took a step towards the fence. He surveyed the typeB as it lunged for him, forcing its clawed fingers through the small gaps, creating a loud, harsh clanging sound as it threw itself against the metal. A human man once, but no longer. Now it was only a vehicle for the virus that had devoured him.

Noah stared at the creature.

It stared back.

Familiarity hit him like a punch to the gut; the all-consuming heavy net of his grief threatened to drag him under. *Khyan.*

It wasn't the clumps of golden hair that stubbornly clung to the type's scalp that reminded him of his dead boyfriend, nor was it its slight, skinny frame. It certainly wasn't its grey scaley skin, adorned with weeping sores. It was, of course, its green, green eyes. Khyan's *enchanted wood* eyes. Noah had stared into them for hours at a time, while he ran his—

"LT? What are you doing?"

He turned to find Habib and Vitt staring at him. Aoife and Meredith must have sounded the alarm. *Traitors.* Covered in blood and grime and God-knows-what-else, they aimed their rifles through the bars of the carriage, where the type had resorted to gnawing at the metal with its teeth.

"Wait!"

He half-stepped towards it, but Vitt caught his arm.

"Noah," she said, using that soft voice she'd used on him for the last eighteen months whenever she felt sorry for him. "That's *not* him. Wasn't ever him. You know that, right?"

"Of course I do."

Get your shit together, Lieutenant.

Without further fanfare, Habib lifted his crossbow and shot a bolt through its brain. The clanging ceased.

A familiar ache of grief squeezed Noah's heart as he dragged his eyes away from the twitching body on the ground.

Habib gestured behind him. "King has requested we rejoin his group near the merry-go-round. They're swamped."

"Let's go then," said Noah, pushing past them to lead the way.

For a moment, the crunching of broken glass underfoot was the only sound as they passed an array of carnival games and concession stands—blue paint almost entirely peeled away—and faded posters advertising prizes long gone. The one roller coaster Lightwater Amusement Park boasted, once towering high, was now slumped and broken, its carriages scattered on the ground like broken bones.

Overgrown weeds threatened to trip them on every step, but finally the rest of the squadron came into view, next to the carousel. He scanned the perimeter. Eight soldiers in total, scattered across the fairground, but all up and standing at least. Breathing a sigh of relief at every member of his flock being alive and accounted for, he raised his crossbow in the air to take down an incoming typeA.

Crawling between two creepy-looking pink horses, it scampered on its hind legs and knees, desperate to get to the blood it smelled. Noah unloaded a bolt, and then another one. Down it went, tumbling over its deformed body, a child doing a forward roll.

Savannah waved at him. His eyes shot straight to the blood on her gloves.

"Who's bleeding? Blue tape it, pronto," he snapped.

He stepped towards her, but was interrupted by a panicked voice screaming, "Forrest!" and then, "Noah!"

He didn't need his interface notification to identify it as Sam's voice. Their newest recruit sounded even younger than his sixteen years. The adrenaline coursing through his blood had him turning and instinctively running in the correct direction before he even looked at the map overlay on his screen.

Why had Sam left formation? Noah gritted his teeth. Now wasn't the time.

Noah charged towards Sam, where three typeBs had corralled the young man—*child*—into a corner created by the ticket booth and a brick wall. Sam raised his rifle and fired a round, and then another, into the nearest type's brain. It dropped like a stone. Then came the telltale click of an empty clip.

Though he should have been focussed on his attacker, Sam glanced past the remaining monster to look at Noah. Trusting him to save him. Noah unshouldered his rifle and took down another type within the space of a blink. There was still one more, however, and it lurched towards Sam, who let loose a scream that consumed Noah's soul.

But then Wolf was there, acting every bit the beast he was named after. Lunging towards the type, the German shepherd latched his sharp canines onto the type's neck, spraying dark blood everywhere as he tore through its carotid arteries.

"Good job, boy," Noah said, reaching Sam at last. He scratched Wolf's ears quickly so nobody would see him petting the canine unit. He looked up to find Sam cradling his torso like he couldn't believe he was alive. "Jackson, I told you to reserve your bull—"

A type fell from the sky.

No, not the sky, from the roof of the ticket booth.

It lunged towards Sam, jumping onto his body sideways to clamp its legs around his thigh, a monkey clinging to a swaying tree. With its agile, sharply pointed claws, a parody of the human hands they once were, the type slashed at Sam's body.

"Get it off me," Sam screeched, turning this way and that, pushing the type's face by the jaw with his gloved hand.

Savannah materialised to Noah's left. "Stay still!"

Sam did not stay still.

Noah raised his rifle, attempted to aim. "Sam, we can't shoot unless you stop moving!"

Finding the hard, black shell of Sam's combat suit a difficult material to penetrate, the type began to grope wildly at his helmet.

Sam screamed.

The scars on Noah's fragile heart burst at the seam.

He dropped his rifle and lunged towards Sam. If he couldn't get a clear shot, he'd pry the type off him if it was the last thing he did.

He knew he was too late the moment Sam's helmet fell to the ground with a sickening *thud*. The type had its sharp fangs embedded in Sam's neck before Noah could do more than watch, mere centimetres away. Behind him, his squad cried out as some of them unloaded several rounds into the type in last-minute desperation. The type slumped to the ground, taking Sam with it. Pushing the creature off Sam, Noah collapsed, cradling the boy in his arms.

"Forrest," Habib said, his voice etched with a warning. But Habib needn't have worried. Sam would bleed out before any chance of him turning—the type had taken a sizeable chunk out of his jugular. Thick, bright-red blood oozed out of Sam's neck, drenching Noah's thighs.

"LT," croaked Sam in a whisper, his eyes already glazing over. "I'm... sorry."

Noah stroked his hair. It was all he could do now. "Shh. You did well, Sam. We're all so proud of you. Your dad is proud of you, too. Close your eyes. Rest."

Sam, the loyal soldier he'd been since he'd joined them a handful of months ago, followed Noah's orders. The squad formed a protective circle around them as they silently watched Sam's breathing become more and more shallow. And then, with one final shudder, Sam breathed his last.

Habib and Vitt stepped towards Noah in unison, dragging him to his feet.

"Time to pop smoke," Habib said. "Splat and Shun will bag the body."

Noah shook them off and took three steps away from his group of soldiers, each of them likely eyeing him, watching him for any signs of impending breakdown. He forcefully closed his eyes and widened his jaw to its utmost extent, silently screaming.

The mission ended how it was always going to end.

Another body bag.
Another failure to keep his flock safe.
Another tally mark seared into his heart.

NOAH

"Captain wants to see you at Command, Noah."

Noah, slumped against a tree stump, looked up in alarm to see Vitt peering down at him. He'd dozed off and now the dying embers of the fire in the middle of the clearing hinted at a late hour.

"What? Now?" he said, his voice gravelly from disuse. He shook his head and rose to his feet, checking his wristband to find it was almost eleven p.m.

Vitt only shrugged in response as she threw herself to the ground nearby. Noah was in his usual spot near the bonfire—the furthest stump from the path back to the compound. It *had* been a long day, but he chided himself for falling asleep outside so easily.

"I better go quickly then," he said, brushing himself down. Thin cedar shavings covered his clothes—from his latest whittling project, a small crow, wings slightly unfurled, as if it was about to take flight.

"Good luck," Vitt called after him as he made his way to the path. "I hope the bitch is in a good mood." Noah turned back to glare at her, raising his finger to his lips. He glanced around, praying nobody else was lurking nearby, ready to report her for insubordination. Luckily, it was a cold autumnal evening, so they were alone at the meeting space. If they weren't asleep, the rest of the regiment would be showering, eating a late dinner, or enjoying their free time relaxing in one of the communal spaces.

Noah and Vitt were the only members of their squad who enjoyed the peace and quiet the garden offered at this time of night. However, until an hour ago, all eight remaining members of Squad E gathered together for Sam's ceremony, once again toasting to a life cut far too short. *Don't think about that now,* Noah urged himself, as the wave of guilt and despair that had plagued him since Sam's death washed over him once again.

A nest of serpents writhed within his stomach at the thought of meeting the captain at such an odd hour. What was wrong? Were they finally demoting him? Was he about to be bundled into the back of a van, thrown out into the streets of London? Who would he be, if not the CO of Squad E?

Noah sprinted down the forest path to enter the main compound—Command Headquarters was on the other side of the barracks, and the captain did not enjoy being kept waiting.

Even at the late hour, with October's first chill setting in, the streets were still abuzz with activity. He spotted Aoife and Habib playing football against two members of a different squad. They'd set up four metal buckets as goals in the cramped space between two dormitory buildings. The ball made an almighty crashing sound as it bounced off the thin metal sheets of the corrugated walls. Noah, wanting to get to his destination in haste, waved while jogging by. This prompted a confused glance from Habib.

"Apparently I'm needed at the Headshed," Noah shouted over, picking up his pace.

He took a moment to compose himself before turning the final corner. Words from his uncle echoed in his mind: *Leadership is thirty percent talent, seventy percent performance.* He took the final few steps, taking a deep breath and straightening his spine, before nodding to the two guards stationed outside HQ.

The building, three stories of gleaming glass, was easily the most imposing on the site. Being mostly composed of carbon sheet steel—built hastily, ten years ago—the dormitory blocks looked like slums in comparison. Noah took the stairs two at a time to reach Murphy's personal office, then knocked twice.

"Enter."

Noah immediately saluted the older woman, dressed in her navy-blue uniform. Golden rank pins adorned the black band on her right shoulder like constellations. Like usual, Noah's eyes naturally came to rest on her chin, but he forced his head up to meet her gaze when he said, "Captain."

Captain Murphy gave a tiny nod of her head, indicating that he should relax and sit down in front of the vast oak desk that dominated the room. The captain gave him a tight-lipped smile across the expanse of space between them.

He couldn't help but glance down at the built-in screen that encompassed most of the desk, which displayed multiple open documents. A few were personnel files with unsmiling ID photographs. Behind the captain, a wall was alive with animated maps of areas with red dots, and a collection of schedules and rotas. His eye was drawn to the bottom left, where photographs of typeBs, all lying dead in grotesque inhuman positions, encircled a small line of text that read—

Captain Murphy powered down the displays with a click of her finger. Noah's eyes shot straight back at her, focussing on a few strands of greying blonde hair that had escaped the woman's usually flawlessly tight bun.

"Lieutenant Forrest. How have you been?" she said.

Noah opened his mouth to reply—

"How was Samuel Jackson's service? I heard the fireworks earlier."

Sixteen small fireworks. One for every year of his life. And like his life, the display was over in a heartbeat.

"I'm well, ma'am."

"Jackson was a good soldier. I know you thought highly of him."

"Yes, ma'am."

Murphy tapped her fingers restlessly on the desk. "Some of the other lieutenants have mentioned they are concerned about you, Noah." Noah squirmed at the use of his first name. It had not gone unnoticed among his comrades that Noah often seemed to get preferential treatment from the captain. "You understand that Jackson's death was unavoidable, and that Squad E could have done nothing differently?"

Noah closed his eyes to hide the tears that threatened to fall. He replayed the moments that had tormented him over the last thirty hours: Sam's eyelids fluttering closed, Meredith trying to stifle her quiet sobs on the drive home, Splat punching the wall so hard he split his knuckle.

"Yes, ma'am," he finally replied, exhaling a slow, shaky breath. *But I might have got there quicker if I wasn't too busy staring at a typeB that reminded me of my dead boyfriend.*

"It may not seem like it, but you *are* doing well, Noah. I was saying this to your uncle the other day. You've only been leading Squad E for a short time, but look how far you've come. I know the other lieutenants don't go easy on you. They likely feel threatened that you've made it so far at such a young age. But what is most clear is that you've won the respect of your team." Respect was a strong word. They liked him, certainly. Trusted him to lead them to success? Doubtful.

"Thank you, ma'am." When would this be over?

"Actually, the reason I've called you here today is because you have two new members joining you tonight. There was some sort of incident earlier that delayed the collection team, so they're getting dropped off around one dark thirty this morning. You'll need to meet them at the gate to support check in."

He felt himself tense and wrestled for composure. "Tonight? Two of them?" They lost Sam only a day ago and now they were to add more green fodder to the mix?

"Your squad needed to be topped up. Don't worry, I've marked you out of active duty for two months of basic training." Noah inwardly groaned. His squad would *not* be happy about that. "You'll need to send half of Squad E to border patrol every day." *Even worse.* "The extra training time will be beneficial for the rest of your squad as well." This was standard Murphy. Praising in one breath, then suggesting incompetence with the other.

"Understood, ma'am."

"Right. Off you go then, Forrest. I'll share the documents of the new recruits with you shortly." She paused for a moment, seeming to choose her words carefully. "Intel says that at least one of them could be... fairly resistant to joining us. They're conscripts. It would serve you well to make a solid impression of your leadership to them. It is always easier to do that with new people."

Noah read between the lines of her words and fought against the heat burning on his cheeks. The current Squad E formed from an amalgamation of people he'd known in some capacity for years. They would always respect his leadership to his face. However, he was younger than lots of them, and he'd known most of them as friends beforehand. It made for a far less than traditional dynamic between them all.

"Your uncle sends his regards, by the way. He said he would stop by and check in," the captain continued.

Noah forced himself to smile as he nodded and left the building. His uncle, Chief of Defence for all the regiments currently serving across the city, often made empty promises to see him. That suited Noah perfectly. Their shared surname had only caused him grief so far.

Checking his wristband, he headed straight to the gate to await the new members of Squad E. *Please, no more teenagers.* As the entire military force haemorrhaged casualties, more and more ill-suited new recruits popped up in the barracks. Years ago, a captain requesting that new recruits were operation-ready within two months would have been ludicrous, but now it was standard proce-dure.

Noah's wristband lit up with an incoming notification, and he tapped it to bring up the information on his new comrades. A young woman's profile flashed onto the screen. In her ID photo, she wore the barest hint of a smile, as if she was trying to suppress a laugh. Scrolling down to her birth date, Noah saw she'd recently turned twenty-five. Noah swiped to the next picture. Male, his wide blue eyes giving him a slightly wild, crazed look. He looked far younger in his photo than the stated age of twenty-two. He'd be twenty-three in just a couple of months. But the question was, would he live until twenty-four?

As he settled down to wait for the transit van, fireworks exploded faintly in the distance. Another service for another dead soldier. He looked up to see small bright flashes of green, pink and white streaking the sky. He pretended that he would not count them, but it was futile.

Twenty-eight pops.

Twenty-eight years lived, and now, nothing.

Twenty-eight. The same age as Noah himself.

ZEKE

They came for him on a Tuesday evening.

At almost the exact moment the clock hit five minutes to midnight, Zeke knew the game was up. He couldn't resist twitching the curtain back at the sound of a rumbling growl of a van. Two figures, shrouded in darkness, took the steps two at a time on their journey to the front door of his apartment block. Seconds later, the sharp, piercing tone of the doorbell shrieked through his apartment. He considered not answering. What would they do? Break down the door? Drag him from his house kicking and screaming? It rang again, two buzzes this time, the second longer than the first, declaring, *We're not going anywhere.*

"Hello?" he said, after dragging himself to the door, cursing himself for the pathetic whimper that came out.

"Bates! Nice to meet you finally. Are you coming down or are we coming up?" came a booming male voice through the speaker system. There was a long pause. Hand shaking, he pressed the door release button, unlatched his front door, and crossed the room to sit on his windowsill.

He gazed out at the glittering city landscape before him, trying to soak in the view one last time. In the far distance, the shadowy outline of the London Eye stood dark and still. A decade had passed since its last slow circular rotation, but Zeke always thought he would see it move again if he stared at it long enough. Far closer was the illuminated sign of the tube station nearest to his house, its bright glow serving only a reminder of when builders blocked every station with concrete brick nine layers deep. Why was it even lit up? What a waste of electricity.

It didn't take long for the men to climb the two stories to his apartment. They didn't bother with knocking—they slipped inside and closed the door behind them without making a sound. He appraised his guests. One, a large bald man, wore a tight, friendly smile, while his shorter partner's face was blank and unreadable.

"Mr Bates! The man himself, at last! I would introduce us, but I think you know who we are," said the bald man. He took a seat on Zeke's armchair and lay back, sprawling his arms behind his head.

"You're the people that have been harassing me every hour for almost two weeks now."

Derrick Brown was the name left at the end of the messages. Was that his real name? Or the one he used when he was dragging people from their beds in the middle of the night?

"I'm surprised to find you here, to be honest. I thought you might have made this difficult for everyone by hiding out somewhere."

Zeke turned to face the window again and placed his palm on the glass. "I didn't need to hide because I've had to decline the offer. I've already filed the meaningful employment clause paperwork."

"That option was inapplicable to you the moment you ceased to be meaningfully employed, Mr Bates."

"I work at Oakfield Institute. I'm a junior researcher there. My employer—"

"Was no longer your employer as of fourteen days ago. I am aware you were a research *assistant*. I'm sure you were very good at it. Sadly, you're now unemployed. That makes you eligible for conscription under the Fifty-Two Amendment."

"He's just gone away somewhere. He's coming back," Zeke whispered into the window. His breath caught on the glass, obscuring his view.

Behind him, Derrick gave a sharp laugh. "I can reassure you he certainly isn't. Right now, *Doctor,*"—he said the word with a sneer—"Albert Harding is sitting in a cell down at Blackhouse Regional."

Zeke spun around to face them. "The *prison*?"

The other man spoke at last. "My mate took him in 'bout two days back now. Put up a right performance. I heard they had to taser him to get him in the vehicle."

"But... why? What has he *done*?" Zeke was becoming more and more frenzied, but he was past caring about appearances.

A few weeks ago, when Zeke turned up to work to find the laboratory door locked, he'd known something was wrong. That feeling was only compounded when two police officers turned up at his flat that evening, asking a series of very guarded questions. But he'd thought Doctor Harding had gone missing, or potentially experienced a nervous breakdown due to the stress of the job. Never once did he imagine he'd been *arrested*. Were his colleagues aware of this development?

Derrick smiled then abruptly sat forward, causing Zeke to flinch. "None of my business, that. Right, time to get this show on the road. Are you walking out of here with us or are we waking up the neighbours?" he said, conversationally.

"Look, there's really no point in me going there," he began, forcing himself to sound as steady and reasonable as possible. He would not beg. He would not beg. He would not— "Just listen for a second! I would make a goddamn awful soldier. I've never killed anything in my life. I'm happy to do anything else. I can cook, I can clean—"

"Bring it up with your superiors when we get there, kid. I'm just the messenger." Derrick rose from the chair and straightened his back with an audible click. "You have five minutes to pack your stuff before we're out of here."

Once he'd thrown a handful of possessions into a small bag, Zeke walked without protest to the van, flanked by the two men as if he might make a run for it at any moment.

Derrick slid open the door while pulling back his coat to rest his hand lazily on a gun in his belt, as if daring him to run. Zeke didn't run. He wasn't stupid enough to think he would get even fifty steps before Derrick caught up to him. And in what direction would he even run? For the last two years, the research lab and his small studio flat had been his entire world.

Derrick prodded his back, and he stepped into the dark abyss of the vehicle. "I forgot to mention," Derrick said, slamming the door. "I've got a friend for you."

A small, feminine face framed by thick black braids peered over at him in the darkness. The woman, a handful of years older than him, wore a thick black coat thrown over her body like a blanket. "Alright?" she asked, squinting her dark eyes at him. "You too, huh?"

He wasn't sure what to say, so stared out of the tinted glass instead.

"I'm Francesca. Frankie." The girl was persistent.

"Zeke."

"How long did you manage to avoid them?"

"Two weeks."

"Two *weeks*?" Frankie chuckled. "I've been sofa surfing for months," she said, a hint of pride in her voice. "Ah well. I guess I couldn't put it off forever. I was a pastry chef up until July. Heaven's Drizzle? Heard of it?" When Zeke didn't reply, she pressed on. "Usual story. Business grew slow. Who can afford to spend ration stamps on dessert? They let half the workforce go. What did you do, anyway?"

Zeke groaned and rested his head against the windowpane. The van picked up speed, and he saw familiar landmarks whiz by. "Do you know where we're going, exactly?" he asked instead.

"An eastern regiment. Avantis Compound. Do you think we'll end up in the same team?"

"Probably not." *Hopefully not,* Zeke thought with an inward groan. She was even chattier than Zaya. *Zaya.* The thought of his twin sister spiralled his mind into an even more depressed slump. She'd be fine in London without him—it would be him that would struggle with not seeing her every other day.

Zeke opened up his contacts on his wristband and slipped his headphones into his ears, preparing to call Zaya. But his throat constricted painfully, and hot tears blurred his vision. He couldn't call her like this—she'd just worry more.

Frankie wittered on and on, filling the long journey with meandering, one-sided conversation until Zeke pretended to be asleep. The peace didn't last for more than thirty minutes, however. The van jerked him upright when the vehicle halted.

"We must be here!" Frankie practically squeaked.

"You've been acting like you're actually excited to get here," he spat out before he could catch himself.

Frankie shot him a taken-aback look. "Well, there's not much choice really, other than to make the most of it, right? At least we'll be doing our part to help."

There wasn't time for Zeke to reply before Derrick swung the backdoor of the van open and gestured for them to jump out. They found themselves in a large underground parking garage filled with military vehicles.

"You were due almost an hour ago," said a voice, dripping with annoyance. "I was just about to leave."

Zeke glanced over. Standing in front of the van was a tired-looking young man in a thick black coat. He ran a hand through his long, dark hair, tied back into a ponytail. The tanned skin of his face did nothing to hide the dark circles under his eyes. Looking from Zeke to Frankie, he sighed.

"Sadly for you, neither of these two were particularly enthusiastic about their journey with me tonight," Derek said, already walking back to the passenger seat. "Enjoy!"

The van screeched out of the parking lot, pausing only to be waved through the gate by armed guards. Zeke glanced at Frankie, who'd moved closer to him, her arm just brushing his. "Bates and Fleming?" Zeke blinked at the man. "Those are your names, yes?" he snapped. He spoke with the slightest hint of an accent Zeke struggled to place.

Zeke was just about to speak when Frankie saved them with, "Yes, that's us." He couldn't help feeling annoyed at the sprightly tone of her voice. What was her deal?

"Great. I'm Lieutenant Noah Forrest. I'm your new commanding officer."

NOAH

He looks even younger than his picture, Noah couldn't help thinking, staring at the new boy. Zeke Bates looked as exhausted as Noah felt. His dishevelled, dark blonde hair fell over thick-rimmed black glasses. This, along with his round cheeks, gave Noah the faint impression of a baby squirrel.

Bates rubbed at angry, red indents on his face, likely from lying against the van window. He scowled before crossing his arms in front of him and shooting daggers at Noah. Remembering Murphy's advice about setting a strong first impression, Noah braced for battle.

"I want to talk to your superior," the young man demanded, his voice audibly shaking.

"I am the only superior you're going to get access to, Bates," he snapped with as much force as he could muster. "And you will address me as sir." It had the desired effect: the recruit's mouth dropped open before slamming shut again. He continued to stare openly at Noah, like he was waiting for a different answer.

Francesca Fleming stepped forward. "Nice to meet you, sir. I'm Frankie." She offered out her hand and Noah shook it.

"Follow me, please." Noah started walking, praying they would follow with no argument.

The pair trailed after him as he led them out of the garage and through the many winding paths that would lead to the admin office, which adjoined the small hospital.

Repeatedly glancing back to verify their continued presence, he observed Zeke Bates, his gaze locked on the ground, kicking up dirt as he walked.

In contrast, Frankie held her head up, eyes darting around, absorbing all of her surroundings. "So, Zeke and I are staying together?" she asked, as they made their last turn. "Sir," she added.

Noah wanted to kick himself. What on earth possessed him to tell them to address him as sir outside of the field? His team were going to tear him apart laughing at him tomorrow. Other lieutenants ran their squads more formally, but Noah had adopted a relaxed approach to the hierarchical system. It often earned him some raised eyebrows from the other lieutenants.

"You're both joining Squad E. We're a direct combat unit. There are seven others you'll meet tomorrow."

"Great!" said Frankie. At least *she* was being enthusiastic. Her high energy meant she'd fit in perfectly with the rest of the squad. "Where are you from, sir? South America?"

Noah locked eyes with her, surprised. He'd been fluent in English for so long it always surprised him when people identified the trace of his accent immediately. "My mother was born in Brazil. But I'm from the Netherlands, originally. I was one of the last out when Rotterdam fell five years ago."

"Wow. Sorry. That must have been tough."

Understatement of the century. "It seems like a lifetime ago now."

Martha was the administrator on duty for on-boarding that night, and she made quick work of ushering them through when they arrived at reception. He apologised for the late hour, which earned them all a biscuit from a secret tin under her desk.

It took being asked three times for Zeke to hand over all his electronic devices to be stored in the locker room. Frankie resorted to ripping his electronic wristband from his arm and going through his pockets while Noah rummaged through his bag. At first, it seemed like all Zeke brought were three books and some underwear, until something bright orange tumbled to the ground. It was a small soft toy—a fox with a fluffy tail and big round eyes that seemed to gaze at Noah with love and affection. Several patches of worn-out fur showed its age.

Patches of red spread over Zeke's face and neck like spilt ink as he snatched the toy out of Noah's hand and stuffed it back into his bag. "It's special to me," he mumbled, not meeting Noah's eye.

Before Noah had time to reply, Martha was trying to remove Zeke's glasses and Zeke was shouting, "Hey!" and batting her hand away. "They're prescription!" he snapped, and Martha crinkled her eyebrows.

"Non-electronic?"

"Yes," he replied. When Martha raised her eyebrow, Zeke removed his glasses and passed them to her. After careful inspection, she handed them back.

"You'll probably want to wear contacts here. Or talk to a doctor about sorting your eyesight," Noah said.

Zeke fixed his eyes on an empty spot on the opposite wall, gripping the side of the chair until his knuckles went white.

"I'm going to insert your microchips now," Martha said, pushing Frankie's sleeve up and wiping her arm with an antiseptic cloth. When she picked up a small scalpel, Zeke catapulted out of his chair. Frankie's head snapped towards him, her braids whipping around her face.

"S-sorry," Zeke stammered. "I'm not great with blood."

Well, that's just fucking perfect.

Martha looked like she was trying to suppress a laugh. She turned back to Frankie, who barely blinked as Martha made a small incision and inserted the minuscule rice-shaped chip.

"You're up, Bates," Martha said, forcing Zeke to turn away from the wall. He slumped back in his chair, looking pale.

Frankie laughed. "Shall I hold your hand?"

Zeke grimaced through the entire procedure, squeezing his eyes shut until Martha told him it was over.

"Fantastic. Your IDs have been reclassified and assigned to these." Martha passed them new wristbands—the generic expanding screen style issued to every military personnel. "Read and sign here, please." Martha offered them a small, black fingerprint scanner, connected to a screen displaying a document in a tiny font. Frankie skimmed through it and pressed her index finger onto the scanner. Zeke set out reading it properly before swiftly giving up, scrolling to the bottom and jamming his finger into the machine like he was trying to break it.

"You should read that first," Noah said.

"What's the point?"

After several more minutes of typing out various information, Martha gave Zeke and Frankie their own standard-issue navy-blue uniform, a pillowcase and bed sheet, tablet, earbuds, a metal water bottle, and a mug.

"You'd best keep an eye on that one, love," Martha whispered to Noah as they left, nodding to Zeke.

Noah threw her a look that he hoped said, *Tell me about it.*

"I didn't realise I was joining a prison camp, *sir*," Zeke muttered under his breath as he trailed after Noah.

Noah froze. "What was that?"

"You heard me. We're not allowed any communication with our friends and family? That's it until you post my body back to them in bits and pieces? Unless I'm completely devoured and there's nothing left of me, of course."

Noah pretended he hadn't heard the last two sentences. "You're welcome to contact them using your new devices through the proper channels, following the guidelines in the documentation you've been sent. Anyone is free to call whoever they like. Habib calls his wife and child every evening," Noah said, increasing his pace as they approached the door to their dormitory block. It was now beyond late; they only had four hours of sleep ahead of them at most. Even less if this new kid wanted to waste the entire night arguing with him. He ushered them through the door.

"This is us, Beech block. Keep it down now. Everyone is asleep. Wake up is at six a.m. every day. Squad E usually runs together before breakfast. What are your average mile times?"

"Erm... I usually measure my level of fitness in amount of breaks I need walking up a hill," Frankie whispered as they passed many doors, noisy snoring escaping through their cracks. They came to a staircase and began to climb. "I'm down to just two breaks now, though."

Noah wished he hadn't asked. This was going to be a long eight weeks.

They arrived at the women's quarters, Noah gesturing towards an orange door marked '173'. "Flemings, you're in here with the other four Squad E women. The men are up a floor. The girls will look after you if you need anything in the morning." Beside him, Zeke tensed and looked at Frankie before grabbing her arm.

"It's all okay, Zeke," Frankie said, and reached over to hug him tightly. "I'll see you tomorrow."

"So you're aware from the beginning, relationships between comrades are very much discouraged." As soon as the words left his mouth, Noah wanted to pick them up and shove them back in. The girl had only *hugged* Zeke and here he was, acting like he was about to write them up.

"Jesus Christ," Zeke said, his voice dripping with resentment.

"Don't worry," Frankie said, winking as she slipped into the room. "He hasn't bought me dinner yet."

He didn't bother to attempt any more conversation as they continued to the next floor. When they arrived at Noah's personal bedroom, he stopped, unable to stand Zeke's company for the last few steps.

"This is me. Carry on ten doors down and you'll see two hundred and eighty-seven. Try not to wake the others up." Habib did not look kindly on any interruptions to his eight hours.

"Is there any way I could talk to someone tomorrow?" Zeke stepped in front of Noah's door. "Sir," he added, looking pained. "I need to explain that... that I'm happy to do anything for my term here. Clean. Cook. Admin work. Medical assistant. But I will be literally useless on the battlefield. A liability. My degree is in human biology. I was a research assistant before, maybe I could support someone here? If you could just look into it..."

Zeke adopted a pleading expression, and Noah tore his eyes away from the depths of despair in his blue eyes before he started feeling sorry for him. He could only imagine the captain's reaction if he went to her with this tomorrow morning.

"Your role has been decided, Bates. There are no 'research teams' out here. You clearly passed the background health and intelligence tests to be assigned to this squad. I suggest you get over yourself. Your life isn't worth any more than anyone else's." Noah removed Zeke's arm from its position blocking the doorway and pushed him aside. "You have four hours of sleep available to you. I suggest you doss down, as tomorrow is clearly going to be a tough day for everyone."

"Yes, *sir*," Zeke spat, his face a perfect blank mask. He turned and stomped down the corridor.

Inside his room, Noah threw himself on his bed, fully clothed. As he shut his eyes, he prayed tomorrow would never come.

ZEKE

A wet, slimy sensation on his cheek, coupled with hot, wet breath, woke Zeke out of his sleep. It was pitch black. He kicked and flailed in his panic, throwing his blanket to the floor. Immediately, a collection of snickering laughs came from the other side of the dormitory. Last night, he'd stumbled blindly around in the room before he'd passed out in the nearest empty bed, thankfully a bottom bunk.

The culprits of the laughter flicked the lights on and two men, older than Zeke, revealed themselves. The pair wore matching running gear: black, tight-fitting trousers with a bright blue stripe down each leg.

"Morning sunshine," one said cheerfully. Zeke was forced to tilt his head almost back to his pillow to take in the whole shape of the man speaking to him. He was imposingly tall, with dark brown skin and a thick black beard. "I'm Habib. And you're late for breakfast."

"Cameron King," said the second man. He was at least a foot shorter than his friend, and far less muscular, which made Zeke feel marginally more reassured. "Most people call me Splat though. We let you sleep until seven, by the way. Thank us later."

Cameron—Splat?—began throwing Zeke the uniform he'd left in a puddle on the floor last night. "This all needs to go in your drawer," he continued, sliding out a wide drawer from under the mattress Zeke was currently on. Whatever he saw did not please him. "Aww, hell no! Luo has dumped all his shit in a *third* drawer. I've had it with that guy." Splat lifted the drawer up and tipped the entire contents on the bed opposite. "We literally gave him a whole spare drawer. He doesn't need *three.*"

"Did something... lick me a second ago?" Zeke asked.

"That was Wolf. Our canine support unit. Didn't Noah have him with him yesterday?" Habib stripped down to his underwear, forcing Zeke to avert his eyes. "Wolf!" he called. A large German shepherd—brown aside from a fluffy white patch on his chest—appeared from behind the corner of Zeke's bed and charged at Habib, running circles around him while pushing his body against him. "We use the dogs in direct combat and to scout ahead. They have enhanced olfactory capabilities."

The dog cocked his head to one side, as if listening to something Zeke couldn't hear, before bounding off out of the room.

Splat shook his head. "Noah called him back to him again. He likes to pretend that Wolf is just *his* dog. Anyway, want a wet? Bring your mug to breakfast."

The jovial atmosphere and deafening noise of the canteen threw Zeke off balance when he entered, trailing behind Splat and Habib like a lost puppy. At least thirty long tables stood in an array that stretched the length of the massive hall. At the far side of the entrance, kitchen staff were standing behind a hatch, supervising soldiers serving themselves breakfast. Men and women jostled each other forward in the long queue, laughing and smiling. To the left of the serving area was a large digital monitor that appeared to display some sort of leaderboard.

"What's that?" Zeke asked.

"Squad rankings." Habib scanned the room until he found who he was looking for, then ushered Splat and Zeke towards a table in the right-hand corner.

Zeke took a closer look at the board. It listed twenty different squads in order of points. Squad E, the number 131 written beside them, was a handful of places up from the bottom.

"What, like this is some sort of game?"

"It's a game we're going to lose, now that you've benched us for the next two months."

"What do the points correlate to?"

"Each typeA or typeB kill is a point, man. It's as simple as that. It resets every quarter."

Arriving at the table, he felt his anxiety lessen slightly at the sight of Frankie, who was sitting in between two women. "Vitt Bianco. Call me Vitt," one said in a thick Italian accent, offering him her hand as he sat opposite her. "This is Meredith." She gestured to the girl on the other side of Frankie, who greeted him through a mouthful of food. He began to frantically run over the list of names in his head, cataloguing them. *Splat, short and loud. Habib, tall and scary. Vitt, too-white teeth.*

His gaze lingered for too long on Meredith's light blonde hair, which was styled in tight twin braids underneath the patterned bandana. *Meredith, headband girl.* Her eyes met his with a questioning look.

"Sorry... I was just thinking how much my twin sister would love your headband." The words filled his stomach with acid. When was he going to have time to contact Zaya? Did she even know he was gone? Why hadn't he mustered the energy to message her in the van?

"You have a sister?" said Frankie. "How did I not know that?"

"Because we met literally eight hours ago?"

Frankie laughed and threw him a cereal bar and an apple. "Aoife said to grab these for you. Her and Savannah are queuing again."

Frankie waved over to the line, and two girls waved back. They were both equally pale, but one, a full head shorter than the other, had bright auburn hair, accentuated by the taller girl's dark locks.

"Have you seen Noah?" Splat asked.

"He's taken Wolf to Alice again," Vitt replied. "She's our canine specialist, Zeke."

Habib groaned. "I wish he'd fuss over our injuries as much as he does for that damned dog."

"Calm down. He's here now." Vitt's brown eyes lit up, and her smile widened as she attracted the attention of Lieutenant Forrest.

Zeke's heart sank. He was in no rush to see him again after his embarrassing outburst last night. But their commanding officer jogged over to their table, with the dog close by. Perching opposite him, on the edge of the bench, Noah caught the two plums Vitt threw him. He blew her a kiss in return.

Savannah and Aoife slid in next to Noah and unloaded a small pile of warm bread rolls into the middle. The two girls introduced themselves, and the squad dug into the bread. Zeke dutifully took one, but he wasn't hungry. Nerves surrounding the day ahead circled his stomach like angry piranhas.

He wasn't in the mood to make conversation, but luckily for him, Frankie was. She set about interrogating the others about how long they'd been in the East

Regiment for, and where they'd come from originally. He learned that most of the squad—Savannah, Luo, Splat, Habib and Meredith—were born in England. They had already heard yesterday about their commanding officer, Noah Forrest, being one of the last out of the Netherlands when it collapsed, but others also had interesting stories to tell. The Italian military sent Vitt and others over as part of a trade deal for resources six years ago. Aoife snuck onto a ferry from Ireland and walked most of the way to London before begging to enlist in exchange for citizenship. She'd been wise to do so: eight months later, Belfast went radio silent.

"What did you do in London, Zeke?" Meredith asked, her doll-like blue eyes boring into him.

His mouth ran dry as everyone's eyes flickered over to him. "I worked in a research lab." When this didn't sound like enough detail, he added, "I wanted to go into medicine, but my aversion to blood held me back."

Habib's snicker was audible even over the loud clattering of cutlery and plates. "Sounds like the army will be a perfect fit, then." He smiled over at him, but there was little warmth in his expression.

"So, are they close to finding a cure?" Meredith said.

He gritted his teeth. Zaya's friends asked him this almost every time he hung out with them. "Not really my department."

Savannah eyed him for a moment before changing the subject. "Who's on mug duty then?"

"It's Luo's turn," said Splat, evident annoyance in his voice. Was he still angry about the drawer situation? "Where is he?"

"One guess, like," said Aoife, grimacing, at the same time as Vitt said, "Off-piste."

Splat jumped up as he scanned the room, his eyes landing on a table three across from them.

"Boss, are you going to go get him, or should I?"

"It's not against the rules to eat with a different squad, Splat." Noah sighed, as if he were tired of repeating himself.

"It is when it's Squad C," Splat muttered in reply.

Something caught Vitt's eye, and she leaned across the table. "Noah. Don't react, but Newman is on his way over and he has an especially punchable look about him today."

"How're we doing today, Squad E?" the intruder said from behind him, slapping Zeke hard on the back and almost choking him on a mouthful of water.

"Fresh blood, aye? Shame you guys won't be out and about with us for a while, though." His large frame pushed against Zeke as he reached forward to shake Frankie's hand. "Tobias Newman," he said. "If you get bored with these losers, there's a spot open in Squad C."

"Fuck off, Newman," Habib said, with a bored expression.

"Woah there, no need for language. I was just being polite. I like to make new friends." He brought his hands down to rest on Zeke's shoulders and squeezed. "What's up with this one, then? Nervous is he?"

Zeke felt his face heat and surged forward, trying to wriggle his way out of the other man's grip. Gone was yesterday evening's bravado. *Say something,* he urged himself, but his traitorous mouth remained clamped shut. Tobias squeezed harder. "Seems like a sweet kid, though. Careful not to lose this one."

A loud metal bang erupted from the end of the table. Noah had slammed his metal mug down so hard a few droplets of liquid splatted over the table. "Remove your hands from him or I swear to God Newman—"

"Relax, relax."

Tobias's firm grip relinquished its prey. "Always a pleasure, Squad E. Enjoy your break from the front line." His laugh faded as he moved away from the table.

"And send back Luo," Noah shouted after him.

After a moment of tense silence, Zeke, face still burning and eyes firmly planted to the table, asked, "Who was that?"

"*Un grandissimo stronzo,*" Vitt muttered. She looked at the piece of bread in her hand with disgust. "He's the CO of Squad C, can you believe? He's a joke of a lieutenant."

"His squad is now third though," Splat said, pointing up at the leaderboard. The rest of the squad let out noises of shock and protest as they craned their necks to view the scores.

"Stop staring," Noah said, his eyes on his food. "How many times have I told you to ignore that stupid thing?"

"Shall I go and get Luo?" Habib shot glowering looks toward Squad C's table.

"In a moment." Noah raised his hand and Habib sat down. He stood up and each of the squad members turned towards him. "Right then. The first five to do patrol duty are Hab, Meredith, Savannah, Luo and Aoife." There was a collective groan around the table. "We'll swap around each day."

A bell sounded and all around them, people started moving. Zeke caught Frankie's eye, not bothering to conceal his nerves. Frankie caught his arm as they trailed out of the canteen, giving it a squeeze.

"We'll warm up with some basic fitness drills," Noah said. He stood, flanked by Splat and Vitt, in a small outdoor training field. Lines on the ground formed a track, and wooden beams, bars and hurdles were clustered in the middle of the oval.

Zeke's stomach clenched with nerves. It was as if he'd been transported back seven years to school and was about to be dragged through a sports lesson. Physical exercise had never been his forte, as his comrades were about to discover. Many a time he'd hidden himself in the corner of a library with a book, choosing to face the wrath of the attendance officer rather than the humiliation of the football pitch.

"You'll need to lose the glasses now."

Noah's voice refocussed his attention. Wishing for the millionth time that he could get over his squeamishness about touching his eyes to wear contact lenses, he removed his glasses and placed them on a nearby bench. Behind Noah, the world slipped into a haze of green and brown.

"Let's get on with it then," Frankie said, rising to her feet. She bounced on her feet before lunging into leg stretches, her braids swinging in the air.

They started with five minutes of suicides—some sort of fresh hell involving sprinting to progressively further lines—with Wolf chasing after them, nipping at their heels. After, he collapsed next to Frankie, his breathing hard and laboured. He twisted onto his back to see Splat roll his eyes while subtly shaking his head.

"On your feet, both of you," Noah said. "You think you're going to sit down whenever you like in the field?" Noah stepped towards him and offered him a hand, but Zeke ignored it, pushing himself to his feet. He wouldn't let these smug arseholes win.

"Are you ready for the Bianco Special?" Noah said, his mouth slightly smirking.

Vitt gave him a sidelong glance. "Are you sure they're up to that, Noah? I don't want to write them off for the rest of the day."

"I guess we'll find out."

They trailed after Vitt, who led them to a wide-open patch of grass. Zeke forced his heart rate to steady by taking long, deep breaths. He could do this. He would shatter their low expectations of him.

The 'Bianco Special' started with fifty squats. Splat shouted at him three times that he was doing them wrong, coming beside him to nudge his legs and back into position. He almost let out a cry of relief when the trio concluded they should stop at thirty for today. They went into twenty forward lunges on each side, followed by twenty-five push-ups. Frankie collapsed beside him at number nineteen with a low moan.

Vitt lightly kicked her. "Six more!" she said. Vitt, already finished with her own set, joined Frankie on the ground to complete her remaining ones with her. Zeke was so tired by twenty-three he cheated on the last two, barely raising himself two inches from the ground. He glanced up at Noah, waiting to be reprimanded. But whatever Noah saw in his face seemed to placate him.

"Two minute water break," Splat said, throwing Frankie and Zeke their bottles.

Zeke struggled with unscrewing the lid, unable to control his shaky hands. He dropped the bottle onto the ground. Stared at it. Shut his eyes.

"Here." Cold metal was pressed into his hand. His water bottle. Zeke opened his eyes to find Noah's face looking at him with concern. The man seemed to wrestle with something before finding his voice. "The bars are next."

Over the next forty minutes, Zeke and Frankie endured set after set of crawls, rushes, a hideous exercise called 'bicycle crunches' and side planks. Every time Zeke fell, Frankie picked him up, and he did the same for her.

Eventually, when he was drenched in sweat and Frankie looked like she was about to cry, Noah announced, "Last set before cooldown!"

The final round of torture was to be 'squat thrusts' and it horrified Zeke to discover they involved alternating between squats and push-ups.

"How many?" he asked, his voice barely audible.

"Twenty!" said Vitt.

Zeke and Frankie groaned, but Splat chuckled. "If you think this is bad, wait until you try my workout tomorrow," he said, jumping straight down to begin his reps.

Just twenty more. He imagined Splat's gleeful grin and Noah's disappointed expression if he gave up now. He bent down into a squat to begin. Fire shot up his leg in protest, but he ignored it. Squat. Push up. Repeat. *Fifteen*. Beads of sweat dripped from his nose. Squat. Push up. Repeat.

A wave of nausea hit him as he pushed down for his seventeenth rep. A strange sensation came over him. All his aches and pains faded away. There was only his heartbeat and the voices of the others—faint in the distance, as if they'd moved away from him. Blackness seeped the edges of his vision and he found that he'd curled into a ball. Cold. So very cold. He shivered as he felt himself violently retch onto the grass—thick, sour tasting bile spilled from his lips.

He turned on his side and closed his eyes.

ZEKE

"Stop, Splat. That isn't helpful."

Zeke lay still, his eyes clamped shut. He had no inclination to open them. He would just lay here and wait to die. Better than being ripped apart by monsters when they sent him out in a few months' time. Better than facing Noah and the others. He'd told Noah yesterday he wasn't cut out to be a soldier. Why hadn't he listened?

"Aww, boss, come on. You're going easy on him," Splat replied. What had Splat planned on doing before Noah stopped him? But Splat could piss all over him and leave him here to rot for all he currently cared. "They've only got eight weeks before we're back out there."

"I'm aware," Noah snapped.

"Sorry, boss," he mumbled. Footsteps walked away from them.

A gentle hand rested on his arm and shook him lightly. "Bates?" came Noah's voice, directly into his ear. Zeke didn't move. "Zeke, if you don't sit up in five seconds, I'm calling for medical support. Unless you want the embarrassment of being carried all the way back on a stretcher, I suggest you open your eyes."

Zeke cracked open his left eye just a millimetre. Noah was squatting in front of him, his arms folded. When Noah clocked he was looking at him, he gently pulled him up into a sitting position.

"Hey," he said softly, his hand still resting on Zeke's arm. "You did really well there. Don't tell him I told you, but Splat bailed out halfway through his first time through that." His voice dropped to a whisper, and he winked conspiratorially.

A part of Zeke wanted to smile, laugh, to let Noah pull him up. Let him walk him back to the others waiting on the bench. Let him shape him into a member of his squad, become friends with everyone, and share in their inside jokes and secret smiles. Instead, Zeke pushed Noah off him with all his strength that remained. Shakily, he got to his feet and walked away towards the others without looking back.

When he reached them, Vitt and Splat smiled at him, looking slightly guilty. He threw himself on the bench, mortification sweeping over him in waves.

"Let's have an early lunch," Vitt suggested to Noah, who'd trailed behind him.

"New record," Splat said, laughing and tapping his wristband. "She only made it to eleven without demanding food."

Despite the early hour, Noah seemed to agree with her—he tipped out five brown paper bags from a rucksack, placing them all in the middle.

"Mystery bag time!" Vitt said to Frankie and Zeke. "Good luck to you both."

The others scrambled to grab a bag, leaving Zeke with the last one. The group opened them simultaneously to a chorus of cheers and groans. Without talking, Noah, Splat and Vitt began throwing various items of food and drink at each other to swap them. Noah came to sit beside Zeke on the bench, already chewing on some dried fruit.

"No more worrying about ration stamps, at least," Noah said. "The food here isn't bad. Especially the dinners." He peeked into Zeke's lunch bag. "You've got a mystery fish sandwich. Do you like fish?"

"Not really." Zeke kept his eyes trained on a blurry rock in the distance.

Noah rummaged through his own bag and showed Zeke his sandwich. "Want to swap? I've got cheese."

"No, thanks." Abruptly, Zeke jumped up, leaving Noah to sit next to Frankie on the grass. He ate his bland mix of food while Frankie merrily chatted his ear off, energy evidently revived. He quickly learned all about the feud between her two roommates, her childhood pet rabbit and her favourite recipe for lemon drizzle cake.

"What's your favourite cake?" she asked Zeke, who'd been mostly silent for the entire conversation.

He blinked. "We used to make these delicious peanut butter brownies when we were little. I haven't eaten peanut butter in years," he said, a wave of nostalgia punching him in the gut.

"I don't think anybody has had peanut butter in years. But I'll bring everyone back some goodies when I next visit the bakery. If it's still there by then..." Frankie trailed off, likely wondering how long it would be before pastry chef joined the long list of obsolete jobs, under train drivers and flight attendants.

But her suggestion of returning to London made him sit upright. "Are we allowed to leave when we're not fighting? We don't work every day, right?" He fought to keep the alarm out of his voice.

"So, we all get roughly every seventh day as a rest day together," Vitt said. She eyed a brown, rectangular shaped item in Noah's hand that could possibly pass as cake. He sighed, snapped it in half and threw it to her.

"We usually get the same day of the week off for about a month before it changes. Ours is currently Fridays. But we're not allowed to leave the Avantis boundary. We're technically still 'on duty' and expected to suit up if required. So, importantly, we can go out the night before, but we can't be so hungover we can't shoot a gun the next day."

"So we're never to leave for a whole day?" Desperation crept in.

"We're allowed one day a month off," explained Splat, through a mouthful of food. "They're pre-scheduled in advance and you can't specify them. Sometimes people will swap with you, but Noah has to approve everything."

"My sister and I... our birthday is on the fifth of December. We normally spend it together." Zeke regretted the words instantly. Nobody was going to grant him any favours when all he'd done so far was snap at everybody and faint on the ground.

Noah flicked through the calendar on his wristband. "Nobody from Squad E is off that day. Sorry." He sounded genuinely apologetic, causing a sudden wave of guilt within Zeke—all Noah had been so far was fair and kind, and all Zeke had been was a whiny brat. What would Zaya say if she had seen his behaviour so far? *Do you actually want any friends, Zeke? Because this is a very funny way of going about it.*

Frankie nudged him with her shoulder. "Don't worry, we can throw you a party."

Zeke's head whipped towards her at breakneck speed. "Please don't," he said, and the others all laughed.

"As long as there's cake involved," said Vitt. "Noah, if I see you feed one more crust to Wolf, I'm going to tell Doctor Herbert on you and you'll be in trouble for starving yourself again."

Noah ran his hands through Wolf's scruff, and the dog leaned happily into him. "You literally just stole half my dessert." Noah stood, stretched, and the others instantly copied him.

Despite his body's protests, Zeke bolted to his feet, determined to embrace whatever was in store for them next.

"Right, ten more laps then," Noah said. He only lasted a few beats before bursting out laughing—their expressions must have been quite the sight. "Just kidding."

Zeke thanked his lucky stars that the first part of the afternoon involved lots of sitting in a dark classroom. This was much more his cup of tea. Splat and Vitt headed off elsewhere, leaving Noah to walk Frankie and Zeke through a long list of information. They sat through protocols, codes, fire drills, compound breach drills, medical check-up schedules, and disciplinary procedures. Frankie's eyes drifted closed on more than one occasion, and Zeke covertly tried to nudge his elbow into her ribs.

Noah brought up a detailed map onto the screen. "This is London, obviously," he said, tapping the middle of the map, an eggplant shape, shaded blue. It covered the residential districts Zeke knew well from living in various accommodations over the last few years, but it also bulged up into a large patch of the north, where the agricultural district was. Noah then tapped the area that circled the perimeter of the city area, shaded red. It was five times larger than that of the blue. "And this... this is the war zone."

He looked over at them. What was Noah searching for with his piercing gaze? "We're Eighth East Regiment. There are thirty-seven other army bases on the perimeter of the border." Noah tapped along all the thick dots along the edge, where blue met red. "Our regiment handles this section of the border. About ten klicks long. Kilometres. When we're not guarding the border, we're sent out in the field, usually around here." Noah swept his hand in a vague direction over the right of the map.

"What will we be doing exactly when we 'head out', sir?" asked Francesca. Zeke wished she hadn't. He didn't want to know what horrors awaited them when they left the relative safety of the compound.

Noah hesitated. "All sorts of missions. But let's not worry about that yet." He swiped the map off the screen at the same time as Vitt and Splat entered the room. "Come for a refresher?"

"We wanted to watch Professor Forrest in front of a class," Splat quipped, earning a glare from Noah.

Noah swiped the screen to the next image.

Frankie jumped back in her chair, raising her hand to her mouth. A high definition photograph of a dead typeA, on a metal table, filled the screen. A gaping hole in its head alluded to a gunshot wound. Its lips, twisted up into the ghost of a smile, were the only human thing about it. The monster's purplish arms, positioned above its head, made it seem like the monster was begging for mercy. The arms bulged grotesquely at odd angles but even more disturbing still was the clots of gore clinging to a shredded, bloated stomach.

Zeke's own stomach clenched at the sight of the dried blood, but he forced himself to not look away. After all, he'd be seeing sights a lot worse than this during his time here.

Noah zoomed in on its head. Clumps of missing hair near its forehead revealed a blotchy, scaly scalp. Looking closely, they could see the tips of a row of sharp fangs protruding out from its lips.

"TypeA," Noah said to his silent audience.

"Jesus Christ," Frankie said, her eyes saucer-wide.

Noah shot her an incredulous look. "Have you never seen one before?"

"Yeah, of course I have. It's just..." Frankie was rendered speechless for once.

"I've seen them. In real life I mean," Zeke said. "We got to dissect loads in my lab." That was a slight lie. He'd come across two dead typeAs in his years at Oakfield and only to watch people far more senior than him interact with them.

"Great!" said Noah, too enthusiastic. "Do you want to give us a brief rundown on their physiology?"

This guy was taking his role far too seriously now.

Zeke turned to face Frankie as if he was just speaking to her. "TypeA is the name for the beast-like version of the mutants, who exhibit primitive behaviour. They have limited executive functioning and therefore lack the ability to think logically. However, their body mass is often up to forty percent bigger than their average human counterparts. In optimal conditions, they routinely reach twenty kilometres per hour. As well as a completely new set of teeth—" he gestured to the screen, and Noah zoomed into the mouth, "—typeAs also experience phenomenally quick muscle growth in every area of their body. Their metabolism changes as well, but we probably don't need to go into that?" Zeke looked at Noah.

"Thank you, Bates."

Zeke's traitorous stomach fluttered with pride.

Noah clicked forward on his presentation to bring up a table on the screen which listed typeA attributes. "Like Zeke said, they rely on base-driven instincts. We often take strategic advantage of this. They tend to crawl on hands and feet, though they are adept climbers. There's certainly something about them that makes them feel more animal than human."

"Unlike typeBs?" Frankie asked. Noah brought up a second photograph. This time, the body on the metal table was slightly more recognisably person-shaped.

"Bates?"

"The evolved strain of the Rapid Onset Neurotransmutation Syndrome virus, that developed six years ago, produces a slightly more huid physique. They lack the bulbous growths that are seen in typeAs, and only develop about twenty percent more muscle mass." Zeke cringed at himself. He sounded like a walking scientific journal.

"So are they easier to kill?" asked Noah, his gaze boring into Zeke.

"Fuck no," said Splat. "They're still physically incredibly strong, and they possess a great deal more of intelligence."

Noah nodded. "TypeBs have enough self-restraint to bite their victim without eating so much of their flesh they die. They seem to understand the importance of allowing the victim to develop into another typeB. They can also perform simple cognitive tasks, like twisting door knobs."

"Some can even talk, right?" Frankie asked, eyes wide.

"Sort of. Baby-like babbling, I guess." Vitt leaned back in her chair, chewing a strand of her long, brown hair, looking thoughtful. "But there's not really much time to strike up conversation with them. Although we hardly need to ask them about their favourite drink." She cackled to herself like it was the most hilarious thing in the world.

Noah ran his hand through his hair and sighed. As if on cue, Wolf trotted over to him and sat on his haunches. "It's almost five. Time for his run. I'll meet you guys in the showers."

With a single flick of his wrist, Noah commanded Wolf to follow him out of the room.

"You've survived day one," said Vitt, clapping Zeke on the back.

And only fainted once, Zeke added. *Great work.*

They bumped into the other five members of Squad E outside the shower block. After grabbing their 'off duty' clothes, Splat made them walk all the way to the bathroom on the fourth floor. Apparently, it was way quieter and only used by a few squads. A man they hadn't met yet was standing with Savannah, Aoife, Habib and Meredith. Zeke guessed it could only be the infamous Luo, who'd caused Splat to become enraged twice this morning. Luo, taller than Splat but not a patch on Habib, was Asian, with short dark hair, a shaven face and a friendly smile.

"Nice to meet you. You look exhausted," Luo said, as they entered the male bathroom. Luo reached out to shake his hand, and Zeke froze for a moment, shocked by the shiny gleam of his bionic right arm. Its cool fingers gripped Zeke's with flawless dexterity.

"Are you going to eat with *us* this evening, Luo?" Splat asked, with obvious malice.

"Chill out, man," he replied. "If you're so desperate for my attention, there are more attractive ways to seduce me."

Splat whipped him with his t-shirt.

Zeke's eyes magnetised to a large patch of dark brown, textured skin on Splat's chest that reminded him of tree bark. A burn scar?

Unlike the others, Zeke waited until he was in his shower cubicle to remove any items of clothing. As soon as he locked the door, he sat down and peeled each item off, groaning through the stabbing pain caused by having to bend in certain directions. He remained sat on the floor for his shower, resting his head against the icy wall. How had he only been in this place for less than twenty-four hours? It already felt like a lifetime. He listened to the sounds of Squad E showering, chatting, changing, and then finally leaving. Once dressed, he leaned against the door, praying nobody would think to wait for him.

Soon, the only sound he could hear was a voice he thought was Habib's, humming a song under his breath.

"Oh, hey, Noah."

"Where's everybody else?"

"Fire pit. Were you running Wolf?"

"Yep." Noah said, then groaned. "I think I've hurt my hamstring again."

"Are you going to go ask Doctor Herbert to check it out?" There was a teasing tone to Habib's voice now. "A *physical* examination?"

"Shut up."

"Nobody would blame you if you went for it, man. If anyone needs some release, it's you. It's been far too long since you've got any."

"You are far too invested in my love life," replied Noah, but not unkindly. Zeke squirmed. What would they think if they noticed he was still in here? Would they think he was deliberately eavesdropping?

"Seriously though. It's been over twelve months since—"

"It's been eighteen," Noah quietly interjected.

"Nobody would think badly of you. That's all I'm saying."

There was a long, uncomfortable pause. Finally, Habib cleared his throat. "Sometimes I think you're punishing yourself for not letting Splat and Meredith get together. That was the right call, you know."

"I'm not," said Noah, irritated.

"Anyway," Habib said. "New topic. What do we think of the newbies, then?" Zeke considered putting his fingers in his ears, unsure of if he could handle what was about to come out of Noah's mouth. "Splat just told me the kid was rude to you today."

"He's not a kid, Hab."

"Sounds like he's acting like one. Actually, he reminds me of a puppy. Scared and hiding under the sofa. But if he's being a dick to you... Want me to impart some words of wisdom on him?"

Zeke's heart thudded. What would that entail?

Noah sighed. "Both of them are doing their best, under the circumstances. We literally ripped them from their lives against their will yesterday. We can't blame them for not jumping for joy at being thrust into a job they didn't sign up for."

"Well, someone needs to replace the numbers. We're bleeding out."

"Talking of the fresh blood, did someone walk Zeke to the fire? He might not know we hang there before dinner."

"I'm sure the puppy's fine," Habib said, and Zeke imagined him rolling his eyes. "He's not a kid, remember? You're going soft in your old age. Don't let Newman catch you being nice. He was talking shit about you again to Squad C, according to Luo."

"I wish he'd stop eating with them."

"He's just trying to chat up their girls. Every member of K has already shot him down, so he's had to jump ship. Although, now that Frankie is here..."

After a few more minutes of idle talk, their voices finally drifted past Zeke, down towards the exit. Breathing a sigh of relief, he dragged himself out of the shower cubicle.

Slipping inside the dormitory, Zeke found it empty. Overjoyed at the prospect of being alone, he set about organising the drawer Splat cleared for him earlier. He considered opening one of the books he'd brought before deciding he was far too tired.

He thumbed through one of the books he'd brought, a battered paperback that Zaya had passed on to him because it had a dragon on the front. She knew him so well.

Zaya. He needed to contact her. His sister knew that the military had summoned him two weeks ago. Had she guessed he'd finally been dragged here? She would be fuming that it had taken so long to contact her.

After fiddling with the small tablet he'd been given, it didn't take long to discover that it was connected to an internal intranet with extremely limited capacity. It surprised him to see he could still send emails, although he'd been given a new address to use. Where to begin? What to say? Zaya seemed so far away from him right now that she may as well be on a different planet.

They came for me. I'm at the Eighth East Regiment base. I'm okay. No idea when I can see you. Apparently Oakfield Lab has completely shut down? I need to talk to someone else from work to find out what happened. Oliver or Rebecca. They took my wristband so I don't have anyone's numbers. Yours is the only email I ever memorised. Love you. Z.

How many people would read it before Zaya received it? Would it even actually be sent? His eyes grew heavy. He was more than happy to miss dinner. His social battery was thoroughly depleted and he needed to catch up from the sleep he missed the night before. As he closed his eyes, the image of the typeB, lying dead on a table, floated out of the depths of his mind. But now, it wore his own features.

NOAH

The atmosphere around the fire pit was light-hearted as Noah reached it, taking up his usual spot against the stubby tree trunk, with Wolf resting by his feet. Squad E generally congregated there each day before dinner. Today, several members of other squads joined them around the fire, jostling each other for the best position—near the flames, but away from the eye-watering smoke being blown by wind that would mischievously change direction. Tree trunks and rocks encircled the warm bonfire in the centre. To the north, a small shed slumped precariously to the right, as if tired from a long day's work. Behind the shed, a small allotment grew a handful of vegetables and herbs.

Aoife entertained them by strumming various snippets of songs on her acoustic guitar, her dark-auburn hair spilling forward, obscuring her face.

Savannah rested her head on Meredith's lap, her eyes drawn tight in concentration. Meredith hovered one open palm an inch or two over Savannah's heart, performing Reiki on her. She'd tried it a few times with Noah in the past, but he'd always ended up bursting out laughing. Meredith used her other hand to take long drags on a pen filled with violet liquid, blowing the thick vapour away from Savannah's face. She threw it to Splat without looking at him.

"This got anything good in it today?" he asked.

"I certainly hope not," said Noah, although he knew full well he could trust his team to follow regulations. The systematic drug testing was usually enough of a repellent. "Has anyone seen Zeke?" Noah lowered his voice so it wouldn't reach Habib on the other side of the circle. Zeke's absence annoyed him. Why hadn't the others made sure he followed them down? He wouldn't learn to gel with them as a group unless he spent time with them.

"He wasn't in the room when I was there ten minutes ago," said Luo.

Everyone else shook their heads, all seeming unfazed apart from Frankie. "I'm worried about him as well. Shall I ring him?" she asked.

Noah nodded. He'd be more likely to pick up for her. When her call went unanswered, he said, "Maybe we should check medical."

"That seems like a pretty extreme reaction," said Splat. "He's probably just walking around somewhere. Getting a feel of the place."

"If he's feeling anything like me, he isn't deliberately walking anywhere," said Frankie, groaning as she stretched out her legs. "But I'll go look for him with you, Noah, if you want?"

"Tomorrow's workout is going to be interesting with you two," said Vitt. She was lying on her stomach, arranging dead leaves into a pattern. "Want to play a few games?" she asked, producing Avalanche Blitz from her rucksack. She tipped out the twelve ceramic hexagon counters and shuffled the cards.

Noah shook his head; he couldn't stop worrying about Zeke's whereabouts. Last night's first icy exchanges now felt like a lifetime ago. Zeke had been incredibly rude, but how much of that was just his fear taking hold of him? Noah had been so sure he was going to have an unpleasant day training Zeke today, but then he'd tried so hard, pushing his body to the limit and then listening intently to everything Noah said. As the day progressed, Noah had found himself warming to the young man more and more. It wasn't Zeke's fault he'd been conscripted into the military. Now it was Noah's job to keep him safe.

But where was he now? What if he'd taken off in a vain attempt at escape? "I'm going to go look for him."

A voice piped up from across the fire pit. "You looking for your new boy?" said Krish from Squad K. "I saw him sitting with Tobias and most of C on the picnic benches near Willow block."

"What? What's he doing with them?" Noah said, rising to his feet, but Krish only shrugged and went back to his conversation.

Without being asked, Vitt jumped up to join Noah, and after reassuring Frankie she should stay to rest her legs, they walked around the circle to collect Habib. He was video calling his wife, but it was his five-year-old daughter, Adeela, who filled the screen, her dark curls a perfect replica of his. At the mention of Tobias Newman, Habib waved goodbye and was ready to go within seconds. They set off, cutting through the supplies warehouse to shave off minutes of their journey.

Once there, it was easy enough to spot Squad C amongst the crowds of people: Tobias Newman was standing on a bench, holding court to those gathered around them. When he spotted Noah, flanked by Vitt and Habib, storming towards him, he unleashed a wicked smile.

"Don't go off-piste," hissed Vitt in Noah's ear as they approached.

"Well, this is a pleasure," Tobias said, jumping down from the bench.

"Newman," Noah said, and nodded. Two of Newman's most loyal followers, Brandon Penn and David Reeves, had Zeke sandwiched between them. Noah tried to read Zeke's expression, but Tobias stepped towards him, obscuring his view. Now he was here, he felt slightly silly demanding Zeke's release, as if he were a toy Tobias had stolen. How would this look to the many other squads gathered around the tables? Quite possibly, Zeke was even enjoying his evening with Squad C.

"We came to check on Zeke," Vitt said, after it became clear Noah wasn't going to.

"He's great. He's having a barrel of laughs with us."

Habib cracked his knuckles. Out of all of them, he was always the first to let Tobias wind him up. "He doesn't look happy to me."

Tobias turned, and the table fell silent. He addressed Zeke directly. "Noah is concerned we've abducted you. Are you having a good time with us?"

Zeke's mouth dropped open, his face seven shades of scarlet. "Sure," he eventually mumbled, eyes cast down.

A surge of rage bubbled up within Noah at Zeke's mortification. Zeke had already had a tough start to the day and now was being tormented by Tobias. Noah gave one sharp nod to Habib.

"Alright, that's enough," said Habib, leaping into action. He marched around the table and several people shrank back from his massive frame.

Brandon Penn threw his arm around Zeke's shoulder as if they were old friends. "Come on, he only just got here."

Habib ignored Penn and hooked an arm under Zeke's other shoulder to yank him up, before pushing him back to Noah and Vitt. A small round of snickers circulated, and Zeke's chin dipped downwards. Noah turned to leave, biting his lip. Had he just made this ten times worse for everyone?

"You're welcome back anytime, Zeke," Tobias called after them as they left. "Let me know if they're causing you any trouble."

They marched through the streets, back towards the fire pit.

"Was that really necessary?" Zeke asked.

"Why were you with them?" Noah shot back. He was walking far in front of the other three, as if he could run away from the whole embarrassing situation.

"Tobias caught me on the way to the bathroom. He... *invited* me to join them outside."

"Probably to piss off Noah," said Vitt. Noah turned and caught her eye, raising his eyebrows. "Oh, sorry. I'm sure they do actually want to get to know you, Zeke."

"Thanks," said Zeke with a hint of sarcasm, then sighed. "To be fair, Tobias did spend most of the time shit-talking Noah."

Habib scoffed. "I'm sure he did. What did Newman say?"

Noah grimaced, tensing his body.

"A load of stuff about Noah only becoming lieutenant because of his famous general uncle, mainly. And also—" Zeke paused, glancing at Noah.

"Spit it out."

"He was also mocking the way you are with Wolf, saying you treated him like a pet."

Vitt let out a manic giggle, but Habib stopped walking. "That fucker. I'm not letting him talk shit about you to all of those squads." He turned around and started walking back, turning Noah's blood cold.

"Wait, Habib, stop," Noah said, rushing after him and grabbing his arm. "Please. You'll just make it worse. He'll just use it as another example of my incompetence as a leader."

Habib wavered.

"Remember what happened last time you punched him, Hab," said Vitt.

"It was great. The fucker had a black eye for a week."

Noah sighed. "You spent twenty-four hours away in the Hole for instigating that fight. You came back with two broken ribs and said it was the worst day of your life," he said, eyeing him.

Habib sighed and ruffled Noah's hair before pulling on his ponytail. "Fine. You win. Let's go back."

When they returned to the clearing, Frankie greeted Zeke with a massive hug, as if he'd just been rescued from a den of angry lions. Which, perhaps, was semi-accurate. "We're on the eight-thirty dinner serving today," Frankie said, pulling him down next to her.

Noah almost returned to his usual stump before faltering, sitting down on the other side of Zeke, on the damp earth. Wolf joined them, and Noah ran his hands through his thick fur, feeling calmer now. Zeke seemed at least slightly happier back with Squad E. He hoped.

"Why does Tobias hate Squad E so much?" Zeke asked.

Splat looked up from gazing into the fire. "Lots of the guys have massive authority issues with the refugee soldiers. Which is stupid, because our military is a third foreign blood at this point. Plus, Noah has been here for years, so he needs to get over it."

"Newman's jealous, obviously," said Vitt, reshuffling the cards from earlier. "He was the youngest lieutenant until Noah beat his record by three years. Also, we love Noah." She blew him a kiss. "Mostly. But Tobias rules his squad by fear, not mutual respect."

Noah smiled at her. Whenever he was feeling low, Vitt was always there to cheerlead him on.

When Zeke seemed poised to ask more, Noah changed the topic, lowering his voice to say, "Well done for today. You did great."

Suspicion clouded Zeke's face, but he mumbled, "Thanks," before giving Noah the tiniest hint of a smile. "I also wanted to say sorry about yesterday. And this morning. I'm not usually... like that." Zeke stared at Noah intently, his blue eyes wide, like he desperately wanted Noah to believe him.

"Don't worry about it. I'm sure this is all a bit of a shock." Noah waved his hand in the air before gently tapping Zeke's knee. "This can't be easy for you."

Zeke nodded. "And thanks for rescuing me from Tobias. He really is a shithead."

Noah roared with laughter and grinned at Zeke until he reddened and dropped his gaze. But Noah kept studying him. Zeke was undeniably cute in the warm firelight: dishevelled blonde hair, glasses askew, lips twitching upwards into a smile he was trying to suppress.

"Anytime," Noah said, and before he could stop himself, reached out to ruffle Zeke's hair.

The next day began like most did for Squad E. Meredith, Savannah, and Aoife completed their morning yoga in the training field, while the others went for a pre-breakfast run. Relief coursed through Noah when he saw Habib escorting Zeke to the track. Zeke followed at a slower pace, massaging his legs, but it pleased Noah that he was participating. The sooner Zeke adapted to his new life, the happier he would be. Often, the only solace the soldiers got came from their team.

Noah sent Wolf back to keep Zeke company, the dog happily trotting beside him, nudging him when Zeke slowed down. After three laps, Noah blew the whistle, and they headed to the showers.

After breakfast, Noah sent Squad E off to the sentinel duty, keeping Meredith and Aoife to assist him. They led the way back to the training field. Zeke and Frankie looked far from ecstatic at seeing it again and the lighter session Noah led them through resulted in the pair of them panting after a few minutes.

"Okay, I think you two are going to have to have extra physical training before dinner each day," Noah said, as Frankie and Zeke collapsed on each other during a water break.

Frankie groaned.

"You'll be thanking him when you're legging it for your life," said Aoife. "And don't we do that at least twice a week?"

"That's because you charge into the danger, Aoife, rather than away from it," said Meredith, smacking Aoife on her arm. "When we head out, please do not follow her at any time. She has a death wish."

"We're focussing on weapons this morning," Noah said, steering the conversation away from death.

Zeke stilled.

"Have either of you ever held a gun?"

"What do you think?" Zeke raised his eyebrow.

"Does caramelizing sugar using a blowtorch count?" asked Frankie.

Noah sighed. "Follow me to the shooting range."

Ten minutes later, Noah stood facing the others, the field of practice targets behind him. He'd trained so many soldiers by now, his spiel practically fell out of his mouth.

"We stick to crossbows wherever possible, to help meet our bullet restriction quota, as well as not wanting to attract any further types with the noise." Noah waved his own crossbow in the air, twanging on the fibreglass bow. "Five bolts before reload. But when things go south,"—*as they always undoubtedly do*—"we swap out."

After a detailed rundown of the four different firearms in standard use, Meredith and Aoife demonstrated their use. Alongside him, they were Squad E's best shooters. "Everyone has a combat pistol strapped to their belts at all times," he said, as the two women modelled shooting the head of every cardboard target that popped up behind a metal railing. Their audience cheered.

"Bates, Fleming, let's go."

Noah led them over to bullseye targets. Frankie impressed him by hitting yellow three times in a row on her first round. Zeke handled the gun like it was a poisonous snake. He stared at it, flicking the safety on and off repeatedly. Raising it to the target, he pulled the trigger, squeezing his eyes and stumbling back from the recoil. Noah tried not to laugh at his expression. The shot went wide.

"Try again."

This time, the round clipped the side of the target before sailing off into the forest behind.

"I told you I'd be useless," Zeke said, as his third attempt went even more off-track.

"Here," said Noah. "You're not positioning your leg like I showed you." He came behind him and kicked his right leg out. Then he placed his hands on Zeke's arms, feeling him go rigid. "Turn this way. Pistol up. Look through the viewfinder." He rested a finger under Zeke's chin, tilting it upwards. "Fire."

The bullet flew through the air, landing on the outer ring of blue. Noah stayed behind him, pushing his body up to press against Zeke's. His head only came up to Noah's mouth, making it easy for Noah to wrap his arms under Zeke's, lifting him into the perfect position.

Zeke fired off more shots. Three blues. Two inner-circle yellows.

"I think I've got it now," Zeke muttered, shaking him off.

Noah moved over to support Frankie, but Meredith had already corrected her aim and she was now hitting the bullseye almost half the time.

"Ready for moving targets?" Meredith asked.

"No!" said Zeke, but Meredith was already going to set up the machine. Frankie and Zeke spent the next twenty minutes attempting to hit moving blobs of cardboard, Zeke missing far more than he hit.

"You'll like the next gun, Zeke," Meredith said.

Aoife considered him. "I'm thinking a semi-automatic sniper might be just the thing to test his mettle."

As it turned out, Zeke did have much more luck with the sniper, beating Frankie easily, although Noah thought she might have been deliberately shooting wide at points. He took his time lining up the shot and hit the bullseye three times in a row. Zeke looked pleased with himself: a small grin carved its way onto his face.

Next, Noah grabbed the burst rifles out of the box and explained that they would be Zeke and Frankie's primary firearm before throwing them over.

"Can you... show me again?" Zeke asked, eyes trained on the targets as he held the rifle.

Noah hid his surprise. "Sure. Just let me know when you want me to stop." Noah reached around Zeke again, drawing him into him. His mouth brushed against Zeke's ear as he instructed him on how to hold it. "When we press the trigger, there's going to be an even bigger kick back this time. Don't panic, I'll hold you." Zeke closed his eyes. "Eyes open," Noah laughed, nudging him with his chin.

Zeke mustered up the courage to pull the trigger. Noah felt him immediately attempt to let go, but he held Zeke's hand in place for two seconds, spraying the area in front of them.

Zeke cheered. "I did it!"

Noah had done most of the work, but he squeezed him in celebration, anyway. "Let's go again."

Noah remained behind Zeke for a few more rounds. His body was soft and warm, and Noah relished the soft sounds of joy he made when he hit a target. He'd happily stand behind him all day. The thought alarmed him. Maybe Habib was right yesterday and it really *had* been too long.

He dragged himself away, shaking his head slightly in an attempt to squash his salacious thoughts. Zeke was surprisingly lovely, but he was his CO.

"You're on your own now."

Zeke fired off a few more rounds solo, spraying the targets with glee.

Noah called the women back over to them.

"You both need to get your rifle reload time down to three seconds." Noah swapped the detachable box magazine—displaying effortless grace that could only come with a decade's worth of experience.

When Noah began timing Zeke and Frankie, Zeke's hands began to shake again, and he dropped the entire rifle on the ground several times in his attempt to keep up with Frankie's score.

Trying not to sigh, Noah called it a day. Zeke was clearly done with firearms training. "We've used the ammo pretty liberally today, but in the field, we have to conserve as many rounds as possible. That's why we try to stick with the crossbows, and all carry these as well."

Noah unsheathed his knife from his belt and held it up. Its long, twenty centimetre, razor-sharp blade gleamed in the light. The tan leather handle, worn from its excessive use over the last few years, was a familiar weight in his hand. He spun it around in a circle, using his fingers, before passing it to Frankie.

"In any scenario where a type has been demobilized, always finish them with a slash to the neck. Habib and Splat will show off by practically decapitating them, but the rest of us are more sensible."

"Most of the time," said Meredith.

Both of the new recruits stared at the knife in Frankie's hand in awe and fear.

"And Splat is in charge of the bombs? Do we ever get to do that?" Frankie asked.

Aoife roared. "I love this one! Leave it to Splat. You don't want to be getting anywhere near his bomb tech. It's his baby, and he'll blow *you* up if you try to interfere."

"What's after lunch?" asked Zeke.

"Motorbikes," Noah replied, silently amused by their look of horror.

ZEKE

I t was almost half-past five when they eventually stopped for the day. The motorbikes were a wild ride. First, Frankie and Zeke rode pillion behind Aoife and Noah as they showed them the dirt track and the controls. He'd clung onto Noah for dear life as he jumped over a platform, suspending them in mid-air for what felt like minutes. Noah's entire body had shaken with suppressed laughter as Zeke shouted for him to slow down.

After Noah was sure Zeke wouldn't kill them, they'd swapped over. Zeke was shaky at first, tipping the massive motorbike over and almost being buried by the machine—but Noah had been there to save him. The tyre rim scraped his leg, but not wanting to look weak as Frankie whizzed around, he got straight back in the saddle. Noah had slipped behind him and gently guided him with his knees. When Zeke insisted on travelling at ten miles per hour, Noah had lunged over at him, forcing his fingers to push down on the handle.

"Great job today! Let's go shower. Zeke, try not to get lost today on the way to the fire pit," said Noah, once they'd parked the motorbikes in the underground garage.

Zeke rolled his eyes. He'd learned his lesson. If he saw Tobias Newman in the corridor this evening, he would turn and run. The thirty minutes he'd spent in Newman's company yesterday were the lowest point of his day, including Vitt's workout.

"That was so fun today," Frankie said, slipping her arm around his shoulder. Zeke was quickly getting used to her constant physical affection. At least he had *one* friend here. And she was right—today *was* better. However, tomorrow they began physical combat drills. In the words of Meredith, 'a.k.a. how to not get eaten'. He was already dreading his lack of muscle strength showing him up again.

He stopped Noah outside of a shower cubicle. Noah stared at him, wide-eyed, until Zeke found the eye contact so intense that he looked away.

"Can you show me where the weight room is after this?" Zeke said.

"Of course." Noah looked pleased, and Zeke wrestled with conflicting emotions. Look at him now, becoming a perfect little soldier within days of arriving. *But what choice do I have?*

By the time he came out, he'd made Noah wait so long for him that the others arrived back from patrol duty. Habib, Luo and Splat stripped instantly and wore only loose towels as they crowded around Noah on the seats. Noah's damp hair, usually pulled back, cascaded down his face to his shoulders. Zeke hadn't realised how long it was.

"It was a tough shift." Habib was sitting with his head in his hands. "We had three attempted breaches within twenty minutes. As soon as we handed over to the next squad, we heard shouts. The typeAs are just relentless at the minute. They're happy to throw themselves at the walls, again and again."

Eventually, Noah gestured for Zeke to follow him to the gym.

"Will we mainly be assigned at the border, once we're trained?" Zeke asked, mostly to fill the void.

"Yes, unless Squad E is allocated a specific mission."

"Is guarding the wall dangerous?"

"Not usually. Many more soldiers die on the assignments beyond. You'll like sentinel duty, though. There's way more sitting and sniping involved," Noah said, glancing over at him with a small smile.

After turning several corners, a small single-story building came into view, noticeable for its design: swirls of interlocking coloured paint splashes covered the white facade. It gave it an almost childish appearance.

"What's that room?"

"That's Fusion. It's our multicultural faith hub. Aoife and Habib use it regularly, if you're interested."

They kept walking until they hit the gym. At first, the building looked identical to the corrugated metal exterior of the dormitory blocks, but then, looking through a window, Zeke noticed lines of exercise equipment. Soldiers occupied most of them, running and cycling with sweaty determination. They looked seriously athletic.

"Shall I... come in with you?" Noah said, after an awkward pause.

"No, no, that's fine," said Zeke. Although the thought of Noah leaving him alone panicked him, he didn't want to take up even more of Noah's time. Or have Noah watch him failing to lift the lightest weight. "But... I wasn't actually paying attention to where we are. Where's the fire pit from here?"

"Keep walking west. If you're lost at any point, though, you can always call Wolf. The dogs all have hearing implants in. Listen, here's Wolf's whistle." Noah placed his fingers in his mouth, and let loose a piercing whistle in a simple tune. A silence stretched out, and Zeke was sure that nothing was going to happen. But then Wolf bounded round the corner, licking Noah's hand in greeting.

"Naughty boy, you know you're not supposed to lick me," Noah said, scratching his head. Zeke was starting to understand where Tobias was coming from.

"I'll leave him here with you, then he can lead you to us later." Noah knelt by Wolf, addressing him directly. "Click your fingers twice so he knows to stay with you."

When Zeke did so, Wolf came to sit by him, looking up at him with large, brown eyes. "Later, click three times or just say my name. He should get the message to come find us. Ring me if you need anything."

Noah looked hesitant to leave them, so he waved and headed inside the building. He crept around the edge of the room to not attract attention. The intensity of the surrounding people was intimidating. The soldiers kept any chatter to a minimum as they pushed their bodies to go faster and harder.

He sat on a sponge mat for a while near some weights, unsure of where to begin. Tentatively trying the smallest dumbbells, it surprised him to find he could lift them. He quickly discarded them, however, laying against the wall instead.

Wolf trotted over and lay his head on Zeke's lap. He scratched the dog's ears as he looked around him. There was no way he was ever going to get to the level of the soldiers on the machines, who were practically machines themselves. He looked up at them reverently. How long did it take to get their strong, toned muscles? He didn't have long before they threw him in front of ravenous beasts who would tear him apart in seconds.

A familiar face materialised before him, blocking his view. Splat. He looked confused—probably because Zeke was the only one in the gym sitting down against a wall. "What are you doing? You know Wolf can't be in here, right?"

"I was lifting some weights."

"Uh-huh. What happened?"

Suspicion seeped through him. "Did Noah send you to keep an eye on me?"

"What? No, I was just walking to the armoury when I saw you through the window." He paused for a moment. "There's a reason we usually train new cadets out in the training field, rather than in this gym. Namely, so they don't start comparing themselves to people that have dedicated their lives to pushing their bodies to the limit."

Splat shifted on his feet. "Why don't you come with me? I can show you my demolition kit. You can help me take inventory. I can even show you how to calibrate the devices. Nobody else has ever had any interest, so it'll be good to talk to someone who can understand the difference between C-4 and Semtex."

Shouting erupted from outside of the building. As if a spell had been broken, people jumped from their machines and filed out, concern and fear peppering their voices.

Splat froze, his eyebrows furrowed. "Come on."

They hurried out behind the others, Wolf hot on their tail. The closer they got to the commotion, the louder the shouting—and the wailing—became. Someone, a woman, was uncontrollably sobbing. It was a gut-wrenching sound of almost inhuman proportion. They pushed their way to the front of the crowd that had gathered near the gate, where Zeke had first entered the compound a few nights ago. It was hard to see the woman at first, as five others—her squad mates?—were huddled around her. They stroked her hair and squeezed her arms as she howled.

"Should we be here?" said Zeke, raising his voice so Splat could hear.

He felt hands on his shoulders and turned to see Noah and Vitt, with the others behind them. Frankie moved to stand beside Zeke, slipping one arm through his.

"They're all... dead..." the woman screeched out. Zeke's view of her cleared. Rather than the navy uniforms soldiers were required to wear around the barracks, she wore the black combat gear worn outside of the compound. Her helmet rested on her lap and a splatter of blood covered her left cheek. Her whole body trembled as she clutched her knees to her chest, rocking back and forth.

Splat, standing behind him, gasped. "That's Sandhurst! She's in the squad that came on after us at the wall." The sound of a heavy engine drew closer as a small pickup truck came out of the garage gate. It was hard to see inside, but Zeke could make out body shapes under white cloth. The sight of the truck further distressed the crying woman, who beat her fists against the ground.

"Enough!"

A silence fell. All eyes turned to lock on to the speaker. The voice belonged to an older lady, coarse grey hair tied up in a high bun. She wore a style of military suit Zeke hadn't seen yet, heavily decorated with sparkling gold pins.

"Captain Murphy," Noah breathed into his ear, tickling him.

"Officer Sandhurst," she said to the woman on the ground, who'd stopped moving to stare at her. "I understand that you're upset. But in the chaos and confusion at the border, you, and now the members of your squad, have breached protocol. I need everyone to step away from Sandhurst immediately." A ripple of murmurs circulated through the crowd. Sandhurst's companions let go of her, leaving her alone on the ground in a crumpled ball. Someone immediately ushered all five of them into the back of a van.

Captain Murphy marched across the tarmac to talk to the pickup truck driver. From the look on the captain's face, what they said did not impress her. The truck hastily backed up into the darkness of the garage.

Zeke looked around. It seemed as if the entire regiment was now here—a turbulent sea of people stretching all the way back as far as he could see. Another scream burst out from somewhere in the crowd. Everyone's eyes shot to Sandhurst. Rocking back and forth in her ball, the woman was moving so fast it almost looked like she was vibrating. Her head started snapping up and down, flying back further and further each time. What was happening? Was she fitting?

Someone yanked Zeke's arm backwards so hard it almost ripped from its socket.

"Stay behind me," Noah hissed into his ear, stepping in front of him and unsheathing his dagger from his belt.

But Zeke was in no mood to be pushed around. "Why? What's happening?"

There was no need for Noah to answer. In a flash of movement, Sandhurst was on her feet, crouched in a hungry, predatory pose. She heaved once, twice and then thick, clumpy, dark-red gore exploded from her mouth onto the concrete. A sickening wave of revulsion pulsated through Zeke as light-headedness took hold of him at the sight of the blood. *Please, not here. Not in front of everyone.*

"Permission to shoot, Captain?" shouted the officer closest to Captain Murphy. But Murphy didn't have time to give the affirmative order before Sandhurst flung herself into the crowd. If the soldiers were on edge before, they were hysterical now. Hundreds of terrified souls surged backwards, scrambling to get away from her.

An all-out stampede began. Zeke felt himself get ripped apart from Frankie as he floated in the sea of panicked unarmed officers fleeing for their lives. He heard round after round being emptied as an alarm shrieked. Three long beeps followed by a pause. The lockdown alarm?

A body tumbled into Zeke, hard, causing him to stumble over something—a rock? A human body?—and trip, sending him flying. He landed painfully on his wrist, scraping it against the side of the pavement. The hot sting told him he'd torn the skin. That was bad. That was very bad. The last thing you wanted when faced with a bloodthirsty nightmare was the scent of blood on you. Even more so when you were prone to fainting at a single droplet of it.

Don't look. Don't look. Don't look.

He urged himself up onto his hands and knees, but within seconds a kick to his stomach sent him flying onto his back.

Crack!

His jaw shut with a snap as his head hit the ground. Bright fireworks exploded behind his eyes and metal clanging filled his ears.

Just like yesterday, the edges of his vision faded. Distantly, he had a thought that if he fell unconscious here, that would be the end of him. At least he wouldn't be awake when the type reached him. What would they do with his body? Would Frankie, at least, be sad? What about the others? Likely they'd be relieved. He shuffled onto his side and saw legs scurrying by him. So many legs, like an enormous centipede...

"What are you doing?" a voice roared in his ear. Someone pulled him roughly to his feet and shook him like a rag doll. *Noah.*

He collapsed against him, gesturing to his bleeding head. Blood poured down his neck, the sensation of it enough to cause waves of nausea to bubble up inside him. Noah's crazed eyes darted down Zeke's body, assessing him. After a moment's hesitation, he bent down and threw Zeke's arms around his neck. "Hold on," he said, sliding Zeke's legs off the ground with an effortless sweep of his arm.

Zeke squeezed his arms together around Noah's neck. He felt the vibrations of Noah's heavy footsteps as he sprinted down the road.

"I'm probably getting blood all over you," he said, mortified, even in the state he was.

"It's okay, we're almost there. Do you think you can walk now?"

Wriggling in response, Zeke jumped down and let Noah guide him the rest of the way towards the dormitory building.

"Why is he covered in blood?" the guard at the door shouted, raising his gun to block the way.

"He's fine, he's just banged his head. Let us through," Noah demanded, pushing the guard's gun up and Zeke underneath.

The guard grabbed Zeke and inspected his head. Then he rolled up Zeke's sleeves, running his hands over the flesh to check for wounds. Eventually satisfied, he nodded. "It's lockdown. You know what to do."

He half-walked, half-crawled up the many flights of stairs between the entrance and their dorm room. Eventually, Noah slipped his arm through his, supporting him in the final few steps. Noah's body warmth gently eased the residual panic racing through Zeke.

"Are you okay? You're shaking like a leaf," Noah said, abruptly halting them and lifting Zeke's chin up with gentle fingers. He met Noah's gaze, and his eyes were aglow with sincere concern.

Zeke nodded. "It's just the adrenaline flood. I'll be okay in a second. Where are the others?"

"Hopefully in here. I left them when I noticed you weren't with us."

It felt like a sensible time to thank Noah, but Zeke couldn't quite form the words. Noah had left everyone else to run back to save him. He'd run back *towards* the newly mutated type, risking his life. For him. Any last shred of resentment Zeke felt towards Noah faded away, replaced with awe and admiration.

Noah opened the door to the men's dormitory and ushered Zeke inside. Squad E crowded the dark room with far more bodies than it usually held. Outside of the window, red lights flashed in time with the lockdown alarm, casting them all in crimson shadows.

"Is everyone here? Girls, why aren't you in your room?" said Noah, scanning the room.

Zeke collapsed on his bed, and Frankie gravitated towards him.

"We were worried about you two. We'll head down in a minute," said Vitt.

Frankie found a towel and pressed it to his scalp, rubbing small circles on his back. "What happened Noah? Is he okay?"

"He's fine. The type didn't get anywhere near him. But we need to get him to the hospital."

"If it's just a head bump, I doubt they'll want to deal with that right now," said Habib, sliding a first-aid kit from a tall shelf. "I'll patch him up."

"I'm okay," Zeke groaned. He squeezed his eyes shut, knowing the second he saw his own blood, it would be game over. "Just give me a second."

"What happened?" Frankie demanded, shaking him with some force, and Zeke opened his eyes to see Noah guiding Frankie away from him.

"Someone pushed me over. Then I got kicked a few times. Then I hit my head. That's all."

"*That's all*?" repeated Frankie. "Christ. Thank God you're alive."

Habib pulled Zeke from this lower bunk bed, dragging him to the floor and twisting him onto his front. He tipped icy water onto the throbbing patch of skull at the back of his head, causing Zeke to suck in a breath.

"Ouch!"

"Stay still, I'm trying to clean it. Meredith, pass me the alcohol. Noah, hold his legs down so he doesn't kick me." Habib was enjoying this far too much.

He felt a heavy weight press his legs to the floor. "It's fine. Let me sit up," Zeke said, struggling against them. Habib emptied more cold liquid onto his head. This time, the contact with his laceration burned like holy fire. "Fuck!"

Meredith flashed a bright light over Zeke. "He might need stitches, Hab."

"Nah, it's just a scratch," said Luo, sounding bored with the entire ordeal.

"It's not just a scratch, Luo," snapped Noah. "He was barely conscious when I found him."

After several long agonising wipes with a sterile cloth, Meredith declared he would, indeed, need stitches. But first, Habib had to cut a—supposedly small—chunk of his hair off. After far too many scissor sounds than Zeke was comfortable with, Habib rummaged in the first-aid kit beside Zeke's head before pulling out a rectangular pad with surgical string zig-zagging across it. "This will only hurt for a second," he said.

Zeke bit down on his hand to spare him the embarrassment of screaming when Habib threaded the needle through and pulled the tab, pulling his scalp together. He then wrapped several layers of bandages around the entire circumference of Zeke's head. Finally, he released Zeke.

"Now *that* is a look," said Frankie.

Zeke scowled at her.

There was a knock at the door. "Register."

Noah opened the door. "Squad E, all present."

"Why are the ladies up here?" came the reply.

"The *ladies* were assisting in first-aid," said Noah. "But they're on their way down now."

When the five women filed out, promising to ring them from their room, Noah headed over to sit on the unused sixth bunk. "Wow."

"That's an understatement," Splat said.

Zeke looked between the other men. "So... is this a typical everyday event or...?"

Noah snorted. "I've never seen anything like that before. I mean, I've seen people turn, sure. In the field. Never before in the compound, though. Early symptoms of turning always kick in within an hour of contact with RONS, so it would be hard to make it back here in time undetected. But what I can't get over about today, is how hundreds of highly trained soldiers let their panic turn the situation into a complete bloodbath."

"The captain... she said something about a breach in procedure?"

Habib turned to Zeke, scratching his thick beard. "Sounded like there was chaos when Sandhurst's squad was taken down. She must have been bitten but they didn't catch it. Somehow hitched a lift back to compound rather than going to the isolation booths to be checked."

"Someone is going to have to do *a lot* of paperwork," said Luo.

"Jesus, Luo, at least four people are dead," snapped Splat, throwing a pillow at him down from his top bunk. "That's not funny."

"It's way more than four," said Noah. "I saw loads of bodies on the ground when I went back for Zeke. I think everyone got a little trigger-happy."

Zeke walked over to the window, shifting the curtain. Outside was deserted, apart from two armed guards patrolling the streets. The crisis seemed to be over. For now. He turned and went over to Noah, aware of eyes following him crossing the room.

"Thanks," he said quietly. "I owe you one."

"I'll remember that. I'm sure you'll have plenty of opportunity to fire-man-carry *me* out of danger in a few weeks," he said with a wink.

"I wouldn't count on that," Habib said. "Dude can barely lift twenty kilograms."

Roars of laughter exploded from the other five men as Zeke went to lie down on his bunk.

"Shh, Vitt is ringing," Noah said, holding up his tablet. "Hello? What's the latest?" He pressed the screen a few times before turning the tablet towards the group. Vitt's face filled the screen.

"Good news is, the streets are all clear," she said. "Bad news, obviously apart from the casualties, is that dinner is in our rooms tonight."

"We won't find out what happened until tomorrow then," said Splat.

"Oh, third bad news," Vitt continued, "Murphy is calling a 'lessons learned' crisis meeting tomorrow with all the lieutenants. To be fair, that's only bad news for Noah."

"Great," Noah said.

"Shall I take over training for the morning?"

How were they all now acting so normal, as if the events from earlier were a minor inconvenience, a bump in the road? Zeke was still reeling, replaying the harrowing screams of the infected woman again and again in his mind.

"Zeke might need a day off strenuous exercise. See how you guys do. I'll join as soon as I can." Noah ended the call, tossing the tablet across the bed. "I'm going to stay here tonight."

"Yeah? Need us to cuddle the bad dreams away?" Luo said, snickering.

"I think it's best to stay close. Let me know if your head gets worse, Zeke. First though, I'm going to see if they'll let me go see if Wolf's okay." Zeke sat up with a jolt, realising for the first time that Wolf was missing. Wolf, who'd been Zeke's responsibility.

"Relax Noah, I saw Alice call all the dogs back into the barn as we headed inside," said Habib. "But I am proud that it took you a solid ten minutes before you turned your attention back to Wolf."

Noah fell back down on the bed. "If you were as cute as him, I would care about you, too."

It was many hours later, almost nine-fifteen, when dinner arrived. Zeke's head throbbed as Noah tipped each of the bags out to create a mound of food on the floorboards. Five out of the six sandwiches, wrapped in brown paper, had 'fish' written on them in a messy scrawl. One read 'cheese'. Seconds before the others dived into the middle, Noah grabbed the cheese sandwich and threw it at Zeke's chest. He caught it, mouth ajar in surprise.

"Hey!" grumbled Splat.

"If you almost die tomorrow, you can have the cheese sandwich," Noah said, as his wristband vibrated with an incoming message. "They're releasing Zeke and I from the room so I can take him to medical."

"I'm honestly fine," said Zeke. The last thing he wanted right now was more medical attention.

"What's wrong with my stitching?" asked Habib.

"Nothing, I just want it properly checked out, that's all."

Habib snorted. "Oh yeah? Is Doctor Herbert on duty tonight, by any chance?"

"Come on, we'll eat on the way," Noah said, standing to wait by the door. He clearly wasn't taking no for an answer.

The medical block was in a state of disarray when they entered. Zeke was far from the only one injured in the stampede. Every seat in the waiting room was occupied, with many people sprawled out on the floor.

"I don't think I need to be here," Zeke said, his gaze fixed on a man whose arm was contorted in a disturbing manner.

"I'll feel happier once we've quickly checked you over," Noah replied, pushing him firmly past the desk and down a narrow corridor. Two double doors proclaimed: Sunflower Ward, Psychiatric Unit. Zeke blinked as Noah rang the buzzer. Why were they going *there*?

"I've called in a favour," Noah whispered. "Leo is going to slot you in now, on his break."

Zeke glanced at Noah, overwhelmed yet touched at his determination to take care of him. Noah flashed him a quick grin, causing Zeke to dart his eyes away and walk quicker to the examination room.

When they reached Doctor Herbert's door, it swung open, revealing a small examination room, one wall decorated with swirling pastel colours. A tall man in his early thirties ushered them inside. Dark red patches stained the sleeve of his white coat. He was clearly exhausted, but his face broke into a soft smile at the sight of Noah.

"Hey, you," Doctor Herbert said. "It's a shame it took someone getting injured for you to make time to come see me." He beamed at Noah, who grinned guiltily back, and Zeke instantly felt uncomfortable.

"Sorry. Thanks for this. Have they roped you into dealing with the chaos out front?" he asked, gesturing at the blood on his sleeve.

"It's been a mad one."

Doctor Herbert nodded Zeke over to lie on the bed. He inspected the stitches on his scalp, took his blood pressure and flashed a bright pen torch in his eyes. By the time the doctor scanned the circumference of his head with a paddle, Zeke had grown uneasy from the quiet and was eager to be out of there. Finally, Doctor Herbert put down the machine. He said, "Be right back," before drawing a curtain around the bed, leaving Zeke lying there to continue his ordeal.

The doctor spoke to Noah in soft, hushed tones, too quiet for Zeke to hear. Their conversation droned on and on. When Noah laughed—his 'throw back his head and roar' laugh that Zeke was already growing to know and love—he gritted his teeth. Zeke leaped down from the bed, smashing his feet against the floor with a bang.

Noah pulled the curtain back. "Sorry Zeke. Leo says you're all good. Hab did alright after all. We'd better go. I'm sure you're super busy, Leo."

"Never too busy for you," Herbert said, and Zeke fought back a groan. "Let me know when your next rest day is, and we'll sort something."

They left the building through a back entrance and hurried back to Beech block. "Sorry for leaving you behind the curtain like that," Noah said. "It was rude of us."

"It's fine," Zeke mumbled, relieved to be out of there.

Hours later, when all the others were snoring loudly, Zeke tossed and turned. Images of the woman spasming uncontrollably looped around his mind. He could not let that be him. He needed to talk to Doctor Harding and find out why he was arrested. He needed to get back to his real life at Oakfield Institute.

Remembering he'd emailed Zaya, he opened up his tablet to find a reply from her dated two a.m. That couldn't be right. Zaya was rarely up past ten. They must be screening all incoming emails and approving them at odd hours.

Zeke! I'm so sorry. I'm going to be lost without you. Are you okay? Can they really make you fight them if you don't want to? Tell them about the time you broke your little finger punching the wall. That should help your case. In all seriousness, what can I do? I've got Rebecca and Oliver's details for you. I'll attach them in a second, as well as my number. It would be great to hear your voice. I'm sure we'll see each other soon. All my love, Z. x.

NOAH

All around him, lieutenants shifted nervously in their seats. The captain had entered the room without smiling. After saluting her, they all waited in pensive silence for her to reach the lectern of the small auditorium. Each stomp of her boots sent a fresh wave of dread through Noah. Five other captains video linked in to hear the report, their mouths set in grim lines as their heads floated over Captain Murphy on a screen.

"Yesterday afternoon, I witnessed some of the most shambolic, abysmal failings I have ever seen in my thirty-year career," Murphy began, and Noah already wanted to hang his head like a scolded child. "Before we go into detail, I want to share with you the final body count."

Another screen to the right of the podium came to life. It displayed twelve portrait photographs of officers, Sandhurst among them. Noah recognised most of them. Had spoken to many of them personally over the years. A ripple circulated around the audience.

"Twelve lives. Twelve of our brothers and sisters. Twelve less of us to fight our enemy. Most of them perfectly avoidable deaths." All eyes locked on Murphy's as she scanned the room, making eye contact with each of them. Then, Murphy's gaze flickered to the side as someone entered the hall.

"Welcome, General. Lieutenants, Commander Nathaniel Forrest wanted to attend this meeting personally." Noah's stomach twisted as he joined the others in standing to salute their Chief of Defence, dressed in his heavily decorated uniform. He gave Noah a tiny nod on the way to stand behind Murphy. Noah closed his eyes, inwardly groaning. If his uncle had travelled to get here, he wouldn't leave without first seeing Noah. Ever since he'd been made CO seven months ago, he'd found spending time with him more difficult. He always felt like he needed to prove something to him. Like he was letting down the family name.

"As you were," his uncle commanded, prompting another flurry of movement.

"Failing one," Murphy began, "started at the border. After a particularly eventful afternoon, Squad W entered duty on the third rotation. They were assigned Belhus Woods to Thames Chase. Command tasked Lieutenant James with following up a disturbance at South Ockendon Wind Farm. He sent four officers over the wall to investigate, and they located several clusters of types."

Murphy brought up a video feed. Sandhurst and three others were in close combat with types. TypeAs, judging by their crouched stances. Blindsided, Sandhurst's body was quickly knocked to the ground. The monstrosity climbed on top of her, gnawing her thigh with its mouth. The feed continued, showing Sandhurst's typeA being struck down by a swarm of bullets. The monster lay on the concrete, blood framing its grotesquely bulbous head. When Sandhurst rose to her knees, Murphy paused the video and zoomed in on her thigh. The image, although grainy, clearly showed a small rip in the black fabric of her suit.

"Failing one. This image takes us unquestionably over the threshold for Isolation Protocol. Unfortunately, the code never came. The monitoring team, faced with reviewing many feeds at once, did not identify Sandhurst's laceration."

Another murmur bounced around the audience. Some sounded relieved, as if they thought everyone else was off the hook. Noah knew better.

"I'll spare you the rest of the footage. More typeAs take down the other three squad members before Sandhurst demobilises them. Let's fast forward."

The display changed to a blurry picture of Sandhurst getting into a transport van. "Failing two and three. Sandhurst calls in a triple CD. A collection team set off to collect the three bodies and met her twelve minutes later. We have no video record of this part of the afternoon, as the team have stated there were no combat helmets left in the box within the station. In debriefing, each member of the team was adamant they followed protocol and completed the required medical checks that allowed Sandhurst to be permitted back over the wall. They are liars, or incompetent fools." The captain, a slither of rage seeping into her calm composure, paused. *Liars, incompetent, or perhaps doing their very best in the most challenging job of their life,* thought Noah.

"Failing four. Sandhurst is now over the wall. Within minutes, she is assigned transport to bring her back to Avantis. This is footage from the inside of the van, approximately forty-five minutes after Sandhurst's initial contact with the RONS virus. As we know, infected victims almost always display symptoms indicating they're about to turn within the first hour. The driver of the van, despite having full access to this feed, took no action."

Sandhurst came back onto the screen. This time, she was sitting in the back of a van, hugging her arms around herself as she shook her head and rocked. Occasionally, her mouth would twist with anguish as she cried out. The video played on. At first, Noah wasn't sure what they were looking for. But then he spotted it. Her eyes. They were flicking up and down. Her body seized. The van jumped, possibly going over a rough surface. Sandhurst's head flew back and smashed into the headrest. She seemed to recover, returning to her miserable grief by clawing at her hair.

For a fleeting moment, Noah was transported back to the day of Khyan's death, and the darkness that engulfed him. He had little memory of his behaviour, but felt a rush of gratitude towards his friends, for whom it must have been a truly horrific experience.

"The van reached the compound and Sandhurst jumped out of the vehicle, breezing straight through the checkpoint without being stopped. Her distressed state seemingly confused the pair on duty, who didn't stop the crying woman running determinedly past them. Failing five."

"And finally,"—Noah sighed in relief—"failing six. Every single one of you stood there, some with your entire squads, gaping and ogling for several minutes, doing absolutely nothing to intervene. Rather than move everybody along, you helped create the crowd that turned into a stampede that turned into a blood-bath."

He tried to look at the faces of the other lieutenants around him without turning his head. Did they look as guilty as he now felt? To be fair, he'd arrived later than most. But it was only after Sandhurst started showing signs of infection that he'd started pulling his team away.

"General Forrest is now going to spend the next two hours analysing each of these failings, and produce recommendation documentation."

Noah caught the slight tensing of Murphy's face as she handed over to his uncle. Ultimately, it was she who would take most of the fallout for their regiment's failures. He could only imagine the meeting that took place before this one.

Predictably, two hours turned into three. By the end, Noah was fighting to stifle yawns. When the captain finally dismissed them, Noah filed out with the rest, half-hoping that his uncle would somehow be too busy to speak to him. He'd only taken about seven steps outside of the building, however, before someone grabbed his arm.

"*Neef*," his uncle said, his warm and friendly voice making Noah feel awful.

"General Forrest," he replied, saluting him.

"Oh, stop all that." His uncle pulled him over to stand on the side, out of the flow of the foot traffic. "We're the only family each of us has left. I think we deserve a little familiarity, don't you?"

He pulled his face into a smile. "I'm sorry you had to come today. This is really embarrassing for Eighth East."

His uncle clapped him on the back. "It was a good opportunity to see you, though. It's been too long. Murphy tells me you've been doing really well. I'm glad. I knew you had it in you. I knew stepping up would be the perfect distraction for you after..." His uncle waved his hands in the air, seemingly unwilling to finish his sentence.

"Khyan?"

"Yes."

Noah turned away, closing the subject. "Shall we grab a quick brew?"

"Let's."

His uncle found a table in the corner of the dining hall. The kitchen left a tank of boiling water out for anyone to help themselves, and Noah prepared their drinks. When he returned, his uncle was looking unusually sombre.

"There's a particular reason I'm glad to be able to talk to you today, Noah."

"Oh? Why's that?" A hundred scenarios flashed across his mind, each more anxiety-inducing than the last.

"Before I continue, know that everything I say in this conversation is highly confidential." His uncle leaned forwards, dropping his voice even lower. "I mean it, Noah. This is between us."

Noah glanced around the dining hall, but there was nobody within earshot. What was going on? He clasped his hands together in his lap, digging his nails into his skin. Icy dread settled over him.

"In my role as Chief of Defence, I am privy to certain information." The older man took off his cap, revealing a balding head. "I'm just going to jump straight to it. Things are looking bad, Noah. Really bad. Everybody is putting on a brave face so as to not cause mass hysteria, but the shit is going to hit the fan. We've got six months. Maybe less. All our infrastructure is collapsing."

He stared at him, dumbfounded. "Like what? What do you mean?"

"We've done incredibly well to sustain some semblance of normal life in the remaining cities over the last decade. But there are things we're running out of. Things we can't make enough of, quickly enough—"

"Like ammunition?"

His uncle seemed to lose his patience. "No, Noah, not just that. Everything. *Everything*. The tiny mechanisms used in the electronic shutter gates. Button cell batteries. Small pins needed to create new firearms. And yes, ammunition too. We've scavenged and made do for years now, but our supply options are running out. Food supplies are scarce as well. We still import a lot from Birmingham, but they've drawn up new contracts offering us twenty percent less from June. But worst of all is the economy—"

Noah had heard enough. He stood up, leaving his drink untouched. "I need to go. My squad needs me."

"Sit down, Noah." His voice slipped back into the authoritarian tone he'd used in Noah's childhood, when he was misbehaving with his brothers. "Please."

He remained standing, arms folded.

"The economy is about to crawl to a standstill. Dozens of small businesses are going under every month. We're reaching a point where very soon, money will become obsolete."

"So?" On some level, he was aware he was beginning to sound child-like and idiotic. "Maybe a money-free society is a good thing. Didn't they used to say money was the root of all evil?"

His uncle sighed. "You were all so young when the world fell apart. I think we forget that sometimes."

"I was almost an adult."

"Hardly," his uncle said, but with a hint of a smile. "Have you been into the city recently? I think you should go soon. Take a walk around. Have some fun. It might be your last chance."

"Before what?" he whispered.

His uncle tapped his fingers on the table. He reached in and took out a small brown package from his coat. "I know how committed you are to this job, Noah. It makes me so proud to see. But if there ever comes a time when you need to escape, I want you to have... options."

"If London falls, we'll be evacuated somewhere else, right? Just like Rotter-dam."

Noah worked hard to repress most memories of that awful night, when the city he'd grown up in fell. One image however, always refused to be squashed. Him with his uncle's arm around his shoulder, in a cargo helicopter, looking down at hundreds of terrified faces. Their arms reaching up towards them, as if the helicopter was a lost balloon they could grab on to.

"Maybe. Maybe not." General Forrest looked tired as he slid the parcel over the table. "Within that box are several keys and detailed instructions on the whereabouts of a yacht. It's in a garage in Leigh-on-Sea, not too far from here. It should be in good working order. It's self-powered with a backup generator."

"But... where would I even go?" He laughed, a manic note to it, and pushed the parcel back across the table.

"There are some ideas in the notes I've written for you."

"Uncle Nathan, this is *insane*."

The general jumped up, crossing the space to cup one side of Noah's face with his hand.

"I promised your mother I would look after you. This is me doing the very last thing I can do to help. If you won't take it for me, take it for her."

Noah's heart lurched at the mention of his mother. For a moment, the familiar feeling of utter loneliness that haunted his dreams consumed him. He'd lost so many people over the last decade. His parents. Siblings. Friends. Lovers. And now, it seemed he was on the precipice of losing many more. Possibly everyone. Sighing, he pocketed the parcel.

"Good lad. Now, let's walk over and see this squad of yours. I've rather missed Bianco."

When Noah and his uncle entered the classroom, Vitt was sitting cross-legged on top of the desk at the front, her head tipped back in laughter. At the sight of the unannounced guests, she fell backwards and half-fell off the desk. Everyone else in the room—Zeke, Luo and Frankie—turned to stand and salute General Forrest. He waved their hands down.

"You must be the two new recruits I've just heard so much about," he said, walking over to shake their hands. "It is a pleasure to have you with us. Thank you in advance for your dedication to your duty and your service."

Noah cringed, lingering behind his uncle.

"We've been working them hard, sir," Vitt said.

"I'm sure you have been, Bianco. Now, do me a favour and look after my nephew here? He could use a bit of fun, I think. When's your next rest day?"

"Day after tomorrow," Luo said. "But we rarely have *fun* on them." He shot Noah a pointed look.

"I'll be working through it, with Zeke and Frankie." Noah had already resigned himself to his fate of losing his day off when he woke up this morning to Zeke's wound bleeding through his bandage. If he was to prepare them for what was to come, he was going to need every last second.

"Nonsense!" said his uncle, giving him a playful slap on the back. "Bianco, I put you personally in charge of dragging Lieutenant Forrest into the city tomorrow night."

"On it," Vitt said, saluting.

"Sweet!" Luo said. "Thanks, sir."

"Absolutely not." Seeing Vitt's disappointed face, he groaned, and finally added, "Maybe right at the end of their basic, in December."

His uncle's voice turned deadly serious to say, "We never know how much time we have left. It's important to grab life by the balls while you still can."

Frankie and Zeke, both conspicuously quiet since their entrance, gave each other an indecipherable look.

A few minutes later, Noah's uncle made his excuses to leave, and Noah immediately announced lunch, sensing a less than productive energy in the room. Noah chose a seat next to Zeke, passing him a cheese sandwich mystery bag.

Noah nudged Zeke with his knee. "From tomorrow, I'm going to get Splat to start showing you how all the demolition stuff works. We normally have one expert per squad, but two definitely won't hurt. I think you'll be really good at it."

Zeke tipped his head to one side, a tiny blush on his pale cheeks. "Thanks. I really want to be as useful in some way, considering... well... you know..." Zeke broke off, shoving his cheese sandwich into his mouth. "But anyway, thanks, I'll try my best."

"You'll be blowing stuff up in no time, firestarter."

Noah bit the inside of his cheek. Why did that line sound incredibly flirtatious, now that it was out of his mouth? In lieu of a better plan, he jumped up and headed over to talk to Vitt, resisting every impulse to look back at Zeke.

That night, the entire compound lined the streets to watch the fireworks, in honour of the lives taken the day before. Noah tried to count them, but lost track after 250 bursts of light streaked through the sky.

ZEKE

Time warped as the next few weeks raced past. Early morning runs with the squad, Wolf nipping at his heels. Target practice, drills, VR simulations. Endless mystery bags. Habib, next to him, shouting in his ear. Frankie, pulling him up off of the ground when he was tired. Noah, smiling at him no matter how many times he failed a drill. Vitt at the fire pit, passing him one mug of steaming tea, and then another. Late night informal sessions with Splat, learning about explosives, blast radius calculations, and controlled detonation techniques.

Rinse and repeat.

Zeke was present for every session and complied without comment. However, during evenings spent around the fire, he daydreamed of his life back in London, or of Doctor Harding arriving at the gate, demanding his star student back.

Often, he would find himself looking over at Frankie belly-laughing with the others, her head tipped back, eyes alive with delight. She was the missing piece to their puzzle, whereas his hard, bitter edges allowed little space for the others to connect with him. Squad E was impossibly close, often speaking in the shared language that could only be the product of a group spending sixteen hours a day with each other. Yet he often felt like an alien in their presence.

His only two solaces were Frankie and Noah. Frankie was determined to be an absolute ray-of-sunshine at any given moment, which he pretended irritated him while secretly depending on it. She'd even resorted to tickling him out of a bad mood once, to his horror. And then there was Noah, who treated him with respect and kindness he didn't deserve, after how he'd acted towards him at the beginning. Noah, who fell back to walk with him when he got tired, and repoured Zeke's coffee for him even when it wasn't his 'mug duty'.

Most of the squad spent their rest days relaxing, playing games or sports. However, Noah forced Zeke and Frankie to continue to train with him, although he did release them a few hours early. "You'll thank me when you're not dead," he repeatedly said, which did nothing for Zeke's confidence. On these days, he would go back to the dormitory to sleep for a precious few extra hours before Splat came to drag him to dinner.

On one such rest day, about four weeks in, Noah interrupted his routine. Zeke had just exited the shower cubicle, wearing only a towel, when Noah pounced on him.

He'd half-expected Noah to insist on dragging him back to the mat-lined hall where they conducted close-combat drills. He'd failed rather badly earlier in the day, 'dying' three times in a row.

Instead Noah stared at him for a heartbeat, eyes gazing past Zeke's shoulder. He cleared his throat. "Are you free to walk somewhere before dinner? I found something I think you might like."

Time stilled for a moment.

"I guess?" was all Zeke managed in his confusion.

He immediately regretted his hesitant response; Noah's face fell and his posture sagged.

"That sounds great!" He winced at himself. Now he sounded far too enthusiastic. "I'll just... get dressed first, if that's okay."

Noah laughed and agreed to meet him outside the building in ten minutes.

Zeke pulled on his clothes in a rush, heart pounding at the idea of spending time alone with Noah. Over the few weeks, he'd grown more and more awestruck by the man. Noah led his team with relentless loyalty and love. He was beyond patient with Zeke's shortcomings, showing him things again and again. He often found himself simply staring at him, wondering how the hell he managed to do such a demanding job and still stay standing.

You don't need to be nervous about going on a bloody walk, he told himself as he took the final steps to the front door, where Noah waited. *This isn't a date. It can't be.*

Noah smiled, then eyed his tatty brown jacket. "I can help you order a waterproof coat, if that one has reached the end of its lifespan."

"It's fine." Zeke zipped it up to prove it, grimacing when the zip caught twice in the material. "Where are we going, then?"

Noah led him towards the path to the fire pit at first, before veering off to the left. A small opening in the dense foliage—that surrounded the entire Avantis compound—revealed a narrow path winding its way into the heart of the woods.

"I always run Wolf up this way. Not sure if anyone else comes here."

"Why isn't Wolf here now?"

Noah threw him a mysterious smile, and Zeke's curiosity at what this bizarre trip was about to entail spiked. Noah continuously glanced at the brass watch he wore above his wristband. It appeared to double as a compass.

"Nice watch."

"My father gave it to me. The week before he died."

Zeke had a sudden urge to reach out to grab Noah's hand, to run his fingers over the watch. He pushed his hands into his pockets instead.

After five more minutes of walking, Noah stopped and pointed. Hidden at the base of a gnarled, ancient tree was a small, unobtrusive hole in the ground. A soft breeze rustled the leaves above, as if to invite them to come and take a closer look.

"Is that... a fox den?"

"Yep. I saw them here yesterday."

"But how did you...?" Zeke trailed off, remembering Noah saw his fox toy the night he arrived. Hopefully, the others hadn't told Noah that he cuddled it every night as he fell asleep.

Noah glanced at him, seeming to want to gauge his reaction. "I realised on the way, I should have probably checked that you actually like foxes before marching you all the way out here."

Zeke laughed. "Luckily for you, I do indeed like foxes. It's sort of a thing I have with Zaya."

"Okay. That's good." Noah shuffled on the spot, seeming uncomfortable. "Well, we're a bit early. Let's go crouch over there and keep quiet."

The long, spiky grass was uncomfortable and damp to sit on, but Zeke didn't mind. He was overwhelmingly struck with gratitude at Noah's thoughtfulness—so much so that he felt even shyer than usual as they sat side by side, facing the fox den. Noah's knee was just grazing his own; they were so close he could smell the faint smell of bonfire that always followed him, even when he hadn't been to the fire pit that day. He fought back images of him resting his head on Noah's lap and pinched himself to refocus. This ever-growing infatuation with his CO was beginning to be a problem. A *surprising* problem.

Back in London, Zeke dated a few girls, mostly people Zaya set him up with. He hadn't gotten very far with any of them. He'd just never felt that connection, that supposed magical spark that others spoke about. But he'd never even considered dating a guy. Never even looked twice at them.

But was that completely true? What about Oliver, his partner in crime at the lab where they'd worked? He'd enjoyed getting him to laugh, and they were spending increasing amounts of time together before Oakfield shut...

"So, what's the deal with your love of foxes? I thought most Londoners think they're pests?"

Zeke blinked. "Zaya and I aren't from London. We're from Rye—a small town near the coast in Kent. They evacuated us there a month after the outbreak reached stage three." He hadn't thought about Rye in such a long time, and it was an unwelcome punch to the gut to be reminded of it. "It was a crazy time."

Noah, likely noticing his discomfort, said, "You don't have to tell me about it. Unless you want to."

Zeke paused, wondering if to continue. Post-RONS virus, everyone had *their story*. His wasn't one he ever told. But for some reason, tonight he was in a sharing mood.

"After they announced stage three, we stayed locked up in our house for weeks. They kept promising our area was next on the list for evacuation, but nothing ever materialised. We boarded up all the doors and windows, so couldn't see outside, but we could hear... we could hear..."

Zeke closed his eyes as if it would stop the sounds from looping around his brain. Oh, the *screaming*.

A warm hand on his thigh brought him back to reality. A hand that started to move up and down his leg in a comforting motion. "You're okay now," Noah whispered.

Zeke forced himself to continue. "Anyway, we ran out of food two weeks in. We'd been rationing, obviously, but food supplies had been fairly scarce up to that point, so we were running low from the beginning. My dad, after seeing Zaya faint for the third time, said he was leaving the house to find help. He never came back."

Noah squeezed Zeke's leg, and Zeke let his head drop onto Noah's shoulder.

"You can probably guess what happened next. Our mum gave it forty-eight hours before she completely lost it. She had a complete meltdown. By this point, all of us were severely malnourished—I remember Mum could barely walk—but still she removed the wooden boards on the door, told us she loved us, then went to look for him. Zaya and I barely functioned after that. We knew our parents were dead, but were too sick to even grieve for them. We just... lay on the floor together. It was another three days before the evacuation order eventually came through."

An image Zeke had never been able to forget fought its way to the surface: Zaya's face, gaunt and shaking, taking unsteady breaths as she turned up the volume on the TV, which was broadcasting an emergency channel.

"We had thought they'd pick us up at our door," Zeke said. "But they said we all had to get to a rendezvous point. I grabbed a few photographs from upstairs so we were all ready to go, but when I went back to Zaya, she was on the floor. Her eyes were shut and she wouldn't wake up, even when I shouted her name and shook her. She felt so cold."

Zeke's voice cracked on the last word, and Noah's arm snaked around his waist to pull him towards him. Zeke resisted for a moment before letting himself melt fully into him. He hadn't ever recounted this story, not to anyone, and the emotional intensity of reliving it was surprising him.

Noah brushed his fingertips over Zeke's arm, so softly Zeke wasn't sure if he was imagining it. "What did you do?"

"Well, you're going to find this hard to believe," Zeke said, trying to inject some light back into the conversation. "But I ended up carrying her. The whole way."

"You're joking."

"Hey!" Zeke said, lightly slapping Noah, who started laughing before stopping himself.

"Sorry. But that's incredible, Zeke. Especially when you were only twelve and were in a similar condition to Zaya yourself."

Zeke shrugged. "At that point, Zaya was my entire world. I would have rather been eaten by types than leave her behind. But it was a difficult journey. My only weapon was a random kitchen knife. I had to carry Zaya three miles to the meeting point."

"Did you see any types?"

"Yes. Luckily, there were loads of bodies on the street that they were fighting over. There was one close call, though. We had about a mile left of our journey when a type jumped out of an alley. He was recently turned, middle-aged, a bit of a belly. He was wearing this red Coca-Cola t-shirt. I remember it because it had blood all over it, a different shade of red to the material. Anyway, I dropped Zaya and just froze. I just stared at his red t-shirt as he took a step towards me and sniffed the air. I thought it was all over then. I said all my goodbyes in my head. But then someone else screamed nearby, maybe down an adjacent road or something, and he took off. I can't even describe how terrified I was, I was literally shaking with fear. I was tempted to just give up. I thought I couldn't take another single step. But I kept thinking that if I didn't continue, Zaya would die. So I picked her back up and carried on. And when I reached the military trucks, I collapsed onto the ground with her and begged someone to help her."

There was a slight pause before Noah said quietly, "Thank you for telling me all that, Zeke. You were very brave. Zaya is so lucky to have you in her life."

"Well, all we have left is each other now."

Noah's face twisted. "Same with me and Uncle Nathan. He's all I've got left."

A silence full of ghosts choked the space between them.

Zeke inhaled a deep lungful of air and reluctantly shuffled out of Noah's embrace, before his brain could misinterpret Noah's kind-hearted comfort for something else. "Anyway... let's go back to the foxes. Our parents got us a matching pair of that fox toy you saw in my bag one Christmas. Zaya and I used to steal food from the cupboards to go feed this little family of foxes that lived opposite our house. Mum used to go nuts, said it was encouraging them not to hunt naturally or something. I think she was just annoyed about the food going missing." Zeke laughed, lost for a moment in the handful of happy childhood memories he still had left.

"Talking of stealing food..."

The light was fading as dusk set in, but Noah's bright grin was clearly visible as he opened his rucksack. He took out a brown paper bag, tilting it towards Zeke to reveal a handful of apple slices and slabs of the synthetic meat fondly known as facon.

"So you can feed them," Noah said, his eyes twinkling.

Stunned into silence, a warm, fuzzy feeling invaded Zeke's chest.

"Noah... This... This is very kind of you."

Noah ducked his head. "I wanted to cheer you up. I know you still don't want to be here, and I appreciate the effort you've been making. And Frankie, of course," he added quickly. "Besides, I like foxes too. None of the others appreciate the outdoors as much as me. I could use a walking and bird-watching partner."

The sound of the quiet rustling of dried leaves spared him from replying. Both their heads snapped forwards. Zeke drew in a sharp breath before holding very still. A small fox, probably under a year old, took two cautious steps out of the den, freezing when it saw them in their not-so-covert hiding place. After a moment, the young creature, its sleek, orange coat lightly speckled with mud, fully emerged from the den with a playful bounce in its step, its sharp eyes taking in the surroundings with curious interest.

"Go on," hissed Noah into his ear, his mouth's proximity sending a shiver down Zeke's entire body.

Moving at a snail's pace, Zeke crept towards the fox, pausing when he was a few feet away to throw the contents onto the ground. At first, the fox jumped back, leaning on its haunches and flattening its ears. But upon smelling the food, the fox lunged forward, grabbing the facon and moving away to chew and swallow it in the corner of the clearing.

Zeke glanced back at Noah to see that he was taking pictures on his wristband.

"You can send these to Zaya. Show her we're not completely torturing you here." Noah's low voice didn't bother the young fox, who snatched up the rest of the food, greedily gobbling it down. Noah laughed. "Hey, you were meant to save half of that for your friend!"

A surge of bravery shot through Zeke as he said, "We'll have to come back again with more," before shooting Noah a smile.

"Sure, but you're helping me steal the food from the kitchen next time. Then, at least if we're caught, we go down together."

"Deal."

That night, Zeke lay in his bed, awake long after the others were snoring. A sense of determination and purpose settled over him. When Noah had called him brave earlier, it sparked something within him. Something that begged to burn bright. He was going to try as hard as he could to become the soldier that Noah needed him to be. That Squad E needed him to be. That London needed him to be.

For the first time since Zeke arrived, he didn't drift off to sleep with his usual feelings of exhaustion, dread, and loneliness. When he slept, he dreamt of two foxes in a moonlit forest, brushing up against one another as they ran.

NOAH

Noah studied Zeke from across the fire pit. It was only the two of them now—the drop in temperature earlier had sent everyone else hurrying back inside.

Zeke had fallen asleep half an hour ago. His languid strokes through Wolf's fur had become slower and slower until his arm flopped lifelessly over the dog's snoring frame. Noah was supposed to be finishing a whittling project, a raven mid-flight, but he couldn't tear his eyes away from Zeke. He looked so beautifully relaxed like this—it made a pleasant change from his usual look of fear or disappointment in himself.

Noah should really wake him up and make him go to bed. Tomorrow would be yet another long day for him. But somehow, he couldn't bring himself to break the moment: the sight of Zeke draped over Wolf; the dying light from the fire's embers casting harsh shadows across his youthful face.

This was the first time Noah had allowed himself to be alone with Zeke since the outing to feed the foxes, weeks ago now. He had enjoyed spending time with Zeke very much. Too much. Noah had only intended to get to know Zeke a little more, to further help him adjust to military life. But being alone with him stirred feelings in Noah that he thought he wasn't capable of feeling anymore, ever since Khyan died. Zeke's story of survival, his excitement at the fox, the way he had leaned into Noah...

Noah crossed the space, moving quietly to sit next to Zeke and Wolf, entangled together. The synchronised rise and fall of their chests made him smile until he noticed a faint bruise on Zeke's forehead, likely from when Habib threw him across the room earlier during close-combat training. Each time Habib came for him, Noah's arms had twitched with the urge to jump in front of Zeke, to protect him.

But Zeke had surprised him with how he'd soared back up again and again, teeth gritted in determination. In fact, Zeke surprised him with every day that passed.

He surprised him when he turned up ten minutes early to training.

He surprised him when he asked each member of the squad question after question about their personal lives.

He surprised him when he overheard Zeke talking candidly to his sister during their morning voice calls on the walk to breakfast, the depth of his laugh ocean-deep.

He especially surprised him when he blushed bright-red whenever Noah caught his eye.

He ever so carefully brushed Zeke's hair away from his face. He stirred, moving his arm so it rested on Noah's. Then he gripped it tightly and mumbled something under his breath. Was he dreaming? Of what?

Noah really should wake him up.

Ten more minutes. Ten more minutes of stolen peace.

He tried to pull his arm away, but it only caused Zeke to grip it even tighter.

Something inside him crumbled.

He became consumed by the desire to gather him into his arms, to keep him by his side, to shield him from the world, to…

Was Zeke the glue for his cracked heart that he hadn't even known he wanted?

But it didn't matter. He wouldn't get to find out.

He had one very important job to do: lead Squad E.

And that didn't involve him catching feelings for his newest recruit.

Did it?

ZEKE

Z eke could scarcely believe it when the two-month mark came hurtling into view. The others were overjoyed—partly because their field assignments would begin again, partly because nobody had forgotten Noah's promise of a night in the city. Zeke tried to wrangle free of it one night at dinner—the prospect of an evening alone with his books made him want to cry with joy—but Vitt laughed and threatened to drag him there in handcuffs.

Then he realised that this could be possibly his only opportunity to see Zaya. The night before the visit, he rang his sister from his bed. He'd spoken to her a few times already, keeping the conversation light and brief—fully aware that every call connected via his wristband was likely to have silent listeners lurking in the background.

"Hey Zee," said Zaya, answering almost immediately. Noises of angry shouting in the background burst out from the speaker.

"What's going on?"

"Oh, just more riots. They're still protesting the rationing bill that's going to the vote next week. How are you?"

"I'm okay. We're heading to the city tomorrow night to go to some nightclub the others like. There's no way I'll be allowed to leave my squad, but if you come meet us, I could slip away for a bit."

"You're allowed to come into the city?" Happiness entwined with shock coloured her voice.

"Just for the evening. We have a rest day the following day. It's my last day of training tomorrow."

"And then they'll send you out to fight types? Fuck. Do you feel ready?"

The sound of Zaya's voice, calm yet laced with worry, gently peeled back the armour he'd built around himself. "You should see me, Zaya, I'm utterly useless still."

"Are you still a scrawny short-ass?"

"I have at least five percent more muscle mass, but yes. Don't worry, I think you'll recognise me."

"I'm so excited to see you! Oh, Becca finally replied to me."

"She did?"

Ever since Zaya sent him Becca's details weeks ago, he'd tried several times to contact her. But despite his best efforts, she hadn't replied to any messages or picked up his calls.

"Yep. She said she'd been *busy.*" What was Zaya trying to say? "I can ask if she'll join us tomorrow?"

"Yes, that sounds—"

At that moment, the door flew open, and Splat and Luo entered. Their angry tones suggested they were arguing once again.

"I've got to go. I'll ring later with the details of where we'll be."

Turning off the device, he turned his attention to Splat and Luo.

"Oh! Sorry Zeke. We thought you were fireside," said Splat, sitting down next to him and slapping his leg. "You did great today! You crushed that last drill!"

Zeke blinked at him. Was he lying just to boost his confidence? Regardless, the praise seeped into him, and a small smile found its way onto his lips.

"You guys! You made it!" said Meredith at breakfast the next morning. She beamed at Zeke, pushing food towards him. The bread she offered smelt fresh and buttery. He miserably spooned on a healthy amount of strawberry jam; the prospect of being sent out to the war zone in forty-eight hours made him feel sick to his stomach.

"We've still got to make it through today," Frankie said.

Noah, sitting on Meredith's right, allowed Wolf to sit on the bench next to him, his arm around his neck, causing Habib to glower at him. "So, are you ready for the test?" he asked, looking at Zeke.

"What?" he spat, dropping his bread.

Vitt burst out laughing. "He's kidding. Shut up, you ass."

"We're just going to go over a few final things today. And we'll finally go and collect your combat suits." Noah fed Wolf the crust of his toast. "Until the last six months, we had always trained new recruits in them from the start, but we've been having... supply issues."

"More importantly, we're still going out tonight, right?" asked Savannah.

"*Yes*," Vitt replied, glaring at Noah. He put his hands up in mock defeat.

Noah had posted the rest of the squad at the border, so it was just him who escorted Zeke and Frankie to the armoury. Up to this point, Zeke had avoided the armoury, which, located just to the left of the main gate, stored their suits, weapons, and other equipment in between assignments.

Although most of the buildings that made up the barracks were purpose-built—cheaply and efficiently—the armoury was one of the few exceptions. A small manor house in a previous life, thick ivy climbed half of the exterior wall, creeping all the way to the front entrance: a set of heavy wooden double doors, flanked by two guards. The guards greeted Noah warmly, scanned their chips, and sent them through.

The inside of the house was devoid of any remnants of the past. They walked through many empty corridors to reach a door that read 'Stephen Benefici'.

"Hello?" Noah called as he opened the door. The smell of gunpowder and oil hit them. An older man with a thick grey beard and stern eyes sat at a workbench, fiddling with a deconstructed rifle. The man sighed.

"Sorry Stephen. These two start active duty tomorrow. They need the full gear I ordered."

Stephen rose to his feet. "Let's see what we've got then."

"While I'm here, Spla— Sorry, *Cameron* King wanted me to chase up the request he put in for a new undersuit. His is starting to show less elasticity. Looking slightly stretched in places."

Stephen grunted. "I sent him a message this morning saying it's a no go. I just don't have enough TPU at the minute. We've got a lot more new recruits that need them first."

Zeke's brain cycled to place the acronym. "Are those the 3D printed thermoplastic polyurethane undersuits?" Splat had described them to him the other day.

Noah nodded. "Each soldier is assigned a set."

Stephen already had all of their measurements—every soldier was subjected to a weekly medical checkup—but double checked them anyway before disappearing into another part of the manor house. Noah left with him to collect his own gear from his locker upstairs and reappeared shortly, with Stephen dragging a wooden cart behind him. Besides suits, it contained two VisorX helmets—these at least they'd practised with many times before.

"We need to apply blocker and suit up within four minutes in case of emergency scenarios," explained Noah. "I'll run you through it, then the pair of you can have a go."

Zeke saw Noah half-dressed in the changing room most days, but struggled not to avert his eyes as he effortlessly stepped out of his uniform, leaving it in a messy heap on the floor. He grabbed from the side a bottle of blocker: a notoriously unpleasant sticky gel, mostly translucent with a blue tinge, that soldiers covered themselves in before entering the field.

Noah sprayed the blocker all over his skin, detailing how much to use while he rubbed it into his muscular chest. In theory, applying blocker to every inch of your skin would minimise your smell and pheromones, making attracting types less likely.

Zeke watched Noah knead it into the firm muscles of his abdomen. What would the smooth skin feel like, if it were his fingers on Noah instead? As he studied Noah rubbing the blocker in deep circles, his heartbeat increased as blood rushed to a place it really shouldn't be going. He resisted breathing a sigh of relief when Noah finally began pulling on his tightly fitting undersuit, the black fabric clinging to his frame.

Noah moved on to demonstrating how to position the knee and shoulder pads, followed by the chest piece, moving so quickly Zeke found it difficult to keep up, his brain still examining his deeply inappropriate reaction.

Noah pulled on a pair of dark boots and laced them up to cover a large portion of his thigh. Finally, he slipped on his own helmet: a shiny black headpiece with a clear visor, which would protect every inch of his face. He grinned at them and bowed when Frankie clapped. "Three minutes forty seconds," he said, waving his wristband at them. "You need to be speedy, but make sure everything fits properly and is tight. The last thing you want is to give them any chinks in your armour to utilise." *Utilise—meaning eat your fucking flesh.*

"Your turn!" said Noah, throwing him the bottle.

Opening it, the scent of eucalyptus awoke a forest of memories in him, washing over him like a drug. Earlier that year, he helped run trials on various batches of the substance in the lab. An image of Oliver squirting the stuff in Zeke's hair to make Becca laugh caused a painful stab of nostalgia to erupt in him.

Frankie's laugh brought him back to the present. She had started removing her clothes from where she was standing, but Zeke went to a corner of the room to strip to his underwear, and then applied the cold goo to his legs. A slight tingling sensation rippled across his skin, but the substance absorbed quickly. Which brand of blocker did the unmarked bottle contain? Some were far more effective than others in the blind trials assigned to his lab.

"Ninety seconds so far!" Noah shouted at them. Zeke pulled on his custom-made undersuit so quickly he sent his glasses flying across the room. Noah grabbed them before he could, putting them to one side. When he reached the chest piece, Noah had to come over and turn it around, as it was on backwards. Noah's warning of thirty seconds remaining only made him panic further, and he fumbled with the shoulder pads, dropping them to the floor. Noah gave up on his countdown, picked up the equipment, and showed him how to put them on again.

"Sorry," mumbled Zeke, heat rushing to his cheeks. Frankie was sitting on a stool by the workbench, fully kitted out and looking extremely professional.

"These are a bit of a nightmare to learn at first." Noah pulled the pads taut. He picked Zeke's helmet off from the floor and handed him his glasses before gently placing the helmet on his head for him.

"Fantastic job!" Noah said to them, presumably aimed at Frankie, as Zeke had fucked it up. Again. "Let's double check your VisorXs are connecting properly." Noah powered on the helmets remotely from a tablet.

Zeke's display panel burst to life. His view of the room through the visor was now bordered by red text presenting data. Over the last few weeks, he'd mastered how to navigate the interface to access a multitude of displays: the location of other squad members, heat maps, night vision mode, camera feeds. This, at least, he was good at.

"I still can't get over how cool this is," said Frankie.

Noah laughed in delight. "I'll remind you that you said that. They can be cumbersome to wear for ten hours straight."

Zeke silently stared out of a window. The thought of wearing this suit out of the compound in a couple of days had his brain fighting for oxygen.

"Are you okay, Zeke?" Frankie walked over and pressed the latch under his chin to release his helmet. She pulled it off and forced his head up to look at her. "You are going to be fine. Not only because you are now a kick-arse super soldier, but because you've got me and the rest of Squad E to look out for you. Noah won't let anything happen to us."

Looking directly into her dark eyes, he became overwhelmed by her concern. He bit back a half-formed snarky reply and said, "Thanks. I couldn't have made it through the last two months without you." It was true—every time he'd felt low, she'd done her best to get him back on his feet, and he'd done the same for her. He was proud to call her his friend.

Frankie flashed him a grin, displaying her brilliant-white teeth.

Noah looked at them with a complicated expression on his face. Was he running through all the ways Zeke was going to get them all killed? "Last stop is our lockers. Change back, then I'll lead the way."

Noah guided them to the second floor, a wide-open space housing hundreds of thin slithers of steel lockers.

"HR have already set up your bands to open yours," he said, gesturing to two beside each other.

Zeke swiped his wristband over the sensor on the handle to release the lock. At the base of the interior locker, there was a port that matched the shape of his helmet—a charging dock. Above it, something shiny and silver hung from a small rail.

"What's this?" said Frankie. He turned to find her holding an identical object in her hands.

"Dog tags," Noah said quietly, apologetic. "They're pretty antiquated now. We've used chips for the last twenty years. I guess it's a bit of an ode to the past. Plus, they're still sometimes necessary to identify a body where the chip is... missing."

"Torn from the soldier's flesh, you mean?" said Zeke. Noah and Frankie said nothing else, so he turned back to his locker and lifted the plaque on the metal chain: Zeke Bates, ED 263-742-251.

As he hung up his gear, a sense of finality struck him. This was it: the day after tomorrow, he'd be putting on this outfit, and heading into the field. But first, at least, was their trip into the city, and seeing Zaya at last.

Later, Habib grabbed Zeke in the corridor, on his way back from showering. "Can I talk to you for a second?" he said, steering him away from the dorm room into a quiet side-corridor.

"What is it?"

Habib stepped closer, forcing him to look up to meet his eye. "I just wanted to see if we were going to get any funny business on our little trip out tonight."

Zeke took a step sideways to reclaim his space, but Habib only followed, crowding him against the wall. Zeke wanted to tell him to fuck off, but, in truth, Habib still terrified him. Habib coached him daily on weight training, and he'd been supportive, despite pushing him to his absolute limit. But Zeke always felt uncomfortable when it was just the two of them. He knew he hadn't yet earned Habib's approval, but what it would take to get it, he had no clue.

"What funny business?"

"Noah doesn't seem to think you're a flight risk. He thinks you're not stupid enough. Luo, on the other hand, has five mug duties resting on it." Habib shuffled even closer to him, his low voice deadly calm but laced with warning.

"And what about you?" Zeke fought to keep his voice calm.

"I'm not sure," Habib said, running his fingers through his thick beard. "That's why I wanted to warn you that if you try to make any trouble for Noah, there will be consequences."

"What's it to you guys, anyway? They'll just replace me with someone else. Someone far better than me."

Habib's face pulled itself into a sneer. "Pull yourself together, Zeke. Let me make myself crystal clear. I'm coming along for the first hour, before I go to see my family for the evening. But if you go walkies, it will reflect badly on Noah and badly on Squad E. So unless you want a visit to the Hole, I suggest you stick very, very close. Because make no mistake—if you do try to run, they will find you."

How did Habib expect him to want to be here if he was going to randomly attack him like this? A pulse of humiliation swept through him. Hot tears prickled behind his eyes, and he blinked rapidly to push them back. The last thing he wanted to do was to cry in front of Habib.

"Hey," came a voice. Turning, he found Frankie's concerned face.

"Back off, Habib. He's not going anywhere. Although I wouldn't blame him, if that's the way you've been talking to him behind our backs."

Habib shrugged. "He can be your charge tonight, then."

"He doesn't need a babysitter," she hissed, grabbing Zeke's arm. "Come on, Zeke."

He shook free of her grasp, but followed her down the corridor.

"I didn't know they were treating you like that," she said.

"Not all of them. Only Habib really, but it was just a few comments until just then."

"I'm going to tell Noah he was being super aggressive."

"What's the point? Noah probably put him up to it," he said, although he didn't believe it.

Frankie narrowed her eyes to give Zeke an incredulous look. "I doubt that. You may not have noticed this, but Noah's a bit of a softie at heart. We definitely got lucky to be assigned to him."

Frankie delivered him to his room, making him promise to tell her if Habib was rude to him again. Sighing, he lay on his bottom bunk, fingering the knots in the wood above. Habib's sudden aggression had shaken him. Where had it come from? But what he'd said to Zaya earlier was true—despite Squad E's best efforts, he *was* a liability—a liability who'd made it clear that if he could leave, he would in a heartbeat.

The entrance of the others into their room interrupted his self-pity parade. Splat pushed Noah through the door, with the others following close behind.

"We've dragged Noah to our room in case he got lost on the way to the gate," Splat explained, with a wink. "Luo and I spent the last thirty minutes trying to find him. He was hiding out with Alice and the dogs."

"I was returning Wolf for the evening." Noah shrugged Splat off him.

"So, boys, are we suiting up or what?" Luo sprawled on the floor half-naked, organising numerous huge piles of clothes. Zeke finally understood why he needed two drawers.

"What do you mean?" asked Zeke.

"Ignore him," said Noah. "He likes to wear his military uniform into the city to attract more attention, but the rest of us don't stoop to his level." Noah threw Luo's shoe at his head.

"Aww, come on. You know it works best when we do it together."

"To be fair, Noah, you did promise me you wouldn't brood in the corner for the entire night this time, and at least scope out the scene," said Habib.

Noah's eyes widened. "I did not!"

"We'll see."

Zeke shuffled through his drawer. As his brain had been scrambled the night of his enforced conscription, he'd only brought the clothes he arrived in. He wore them every evening after he showered, often washing and drying them overnight. As he reached for them, Splat interrupted him.

"Nope," he said, slamming Zeke's drawer back under the bed. "No way in hell. You may be content to wear your one outfit until you die, but the rest of us are sick of it. You're borrowing something of mine. We're about the same size."

Zeke raised his eyebrows. Splat was by far the shortest of the group, close to Zeke. But although he'd definitely gained some muscle definition in the last few weeks, the comparison was still laughable.

"It'll be fine," said Splat, throwing various clothes at Zeke's face. "Do you have any other shoes?"

His well-loved black trainers sat waiting for him next to his drawer, their laces fraying. "I'm wearing these," he said. Splat grimaced but said nothing. Zeke selected a periwinkle-blue linen button-down shirt and a pair of dark jeans, throwing the rest back over to Splat.

"You look great!" said Luo, after he dressed. "You can totally wingman me tonight... unless we're flying in opposite directions?"

He sensed all ears in the room turn to him and cringed. It didn't take a genius to work out that his sexuality was obviously under speculation. Over the last few weeks, several of Squad E questioned him on his dating life back in the city, receiving limited information back. "I'm not *flying* in any direction tonight," he replied.

"Okay, but if you *were* to be flying—"

"Enough Luo."

Although delivered quietly, Noah's tone brought Luo to a halt. Zeke was glad to be spared answering him. He didn't actually know which way he was flying anymore. Definitely not in a *straight* line, anyway.

"You can keep those clothes, Zeke." Splat winked at him.

"Thanks." He offered Splat his best attempt at a genuine smile. Out of all the men, Splat made the most effort with him. Luo teased him, Habib pushed him, and Noah... Noah was exceedingly polite, patiently explaining and demonstrating things repeatedly until things finally clicked into place. Noah's excitement at Zeke's smallest inch of progress made him work even harder to impress him.

But since the evening they fed the foxes, Noah had kept Zeke at a professional distance, not seeking out any more opportunities to be alone with him. Had he done something wrong? Had he overshared? Perhaps Noah didn't want to waste time getting to know someone who'd likely get himself killed on his first trip over the border. But most likely, he'd noticed Zeke's embarrassing obsession with him and was drawing a firm boundary between them.

The men continued their individual rituals of getting ready. Noah changed into a patterned oversized cardigan, its sleeves rolled up. He left the top button on his shirt undone, revealing the dip of his collarbone. Zeke shook his head—why was he noticing his CO's *collarbone* of all things? But his eyes drifted upwards to linger on Noah's silky dark hair, thinking of how it looked down after his shower each day, the damp locks clinging to his face and neck.

As if Luo could read his mind, he said, "Put your hair down, Noah. We'll get more attention that way." He tugged at Noah's hairband, but Noah slapped Luo's hand away.

"You're on your own, Luo. Get over it," Noah said, laughing.

"Seems like Aoife is my last resort for wingwoman."

"Didn't she steal away the girl you were chatting up last time?" said Splat. Luo threw a dirty sock at him.

"Are we ready, then?" Habib said at last, giving them all an appraising look.

"We'll have to wait another hour for the girls," Splat said, rolling his eyes.

But, as they headed down the stairs, they found them crowding the corridor outside of their room. Splat wolf-whistled as they approached, much to their disgust. Zeke couldn't help but stare at them. It was disorientating to see all of them out of their uniforms, or the hoodies they wore around the fire pit. Similar smoky eye shadow adorned their eyes, but they opted for a variety of outfits, dressing in a mixture of dresses, skirts, and trousers.

Frankie, in a tight-fitting sequinned black dress, slid her arm through his. "You look nice."

"You guys all look... different," said Zeke.

All the women burst into laughter.

"We last went out about six months ago," said Vitt. "Let us have our fun."

Noah grinned and ruffled her hair. "Come on then. Let's go pretend everything's fine for a few hours."

ZEKE

After a lengthy checking out process, Squad E entered the underground garage where Zeke first arrived, a lifetime ago. It was livelier tonight; many people hovered around parked cars, chatting and vaping. Noah left them huddled in a group to sort out transport.

"Hab doesn't drink, but he's off to see his wife in a bit and will make his own way back. Unless Noah finds someone to lift us back and forth, one of us will have to stay sober," Meredith explained. Most of the people Zeke knew—admittedly Zaya's friends, which skewed the data somewhat—ignored the rule of not drinking when technically controlling a self-driving vehicle. He figured that soldiers must have to be upstanding citizens.

"I'll stay sober," he volunteered.

"No, you won't," said Splat, glaring at him. "This is yours and Frankie's celebration party."

"Is it?" said Frankie, her eyes sparkling.

Across the expansive garage, he spotted Noah engrossed in conversation with a man leaning against a van. Noah's hands gestured wildly, and he wore a wide grin on his face.

"That's right, Noah, turn on the charm," said Savannah under her breath. She sidled up close to Zeke. Her thin jumper tightly hugged her almost skeletal-thin frame, and she'd tied her black hair into its customary ballerina bun. Out of all of them, bar himself, she looked the least like she belonged with the athletic group.

Noah's laughter echoed across the garage, and Zeke's eyes shot back towards him. When he saw Noah resting his hand on the stranger's arm, a flash of annoyance shot through him. God, did this guy really need to be so nice to everyone he spoke to? Pulsating maelstroms of jealousy swirled inside of him. He wanted Noah to be laughing with *him* like that. He wanted to impress Noah, to be rewarded by his big brown eyes lighting up like they did every time Zeke showed the tiniest bit of improvement.

"Jesus, what's taking him so long?" Zeke snapped, when the guy moved so close to Noah that their foreheads were practically touching.

Frankie nudged him. "What's up with you?"

"Chill, he's coming now." Meredith, holding her heels as she walked barefoot, nodded at Noah.

"Brian is good to take us. It's his off day today. He's seeing a friend in the city tonight, and wants to head back by two," said Noah, as he reached them.

"Seems like you had a lot more than that to talk about," Habib said, smirking, further igniting the bundle of fury in Zeke's stomach. *That's enough now*, he told himself. Clearly, the fleeting moments of compassion Noah had showed him were scrambling his brain, rewiring it in idiotic directions.

They headed over to the van. Zeke thought Noah would climb into the front with Brian, but he slipped into the back with him.

"We'll have to share this seat belt. We're one seat short," Noah said.

Don't look too pleased, Zeke warned himself.

Brian got the all-clear from the gate guards and, as the metal shutters rose slowly, a jolt of excitement hit Zeke. He was finally leaving the barracks after eight weeks locked inside. He was on his way to see Zaya!

The forty-five minute journey was torture. At every right-turn, Zeke's body pushed into Noah's, squashing him against the side. Even through clothes, his skin tingled with every contact.

Brian dropped them straight outside of the nightclub that Luo and Splat had chosen. One of the few remaining bars in London's east-side, Club Enigma had been described by Aoife as 'the perfect mix between scatty and swanky', whatever that meant. Zeke could count on two hands the amount of times he'd been to any nightclub, ever.

Frankie claimed his arm in hers as they marched towards the bar. He bit his lip. How was he going to slip away from them to meet Zaya shortly?

When they joined the short queue of loud, cheerful party goers, Luo instantly struck up conversation with the people in front of them, who let them queue jump when they heard they were military. Luo promised to find the two girls inside and gave Zeke a conspiratorial wink. Luo laughed at his eye-roll.

Luo's influence only went so far, however, as his attempt at the counter to blag free entry for them all failed. After such a long time, it felt strange to pay for something as he scanned his wristband.

When he hesitated at the entrance, alarmed at the awfully loud music pumping through the door, Frankie dragged him through the threshold into the club. A large dancefloor, neon lights blazing, took up most of the space. A DJ sat on a circular podium in the middle, headphones on, swaying to the trance-like music. Around the edge, numerous booths lined the walls, fashioned out of repurposed train carriages. His shoes clung to the sticky carpet as they walked over to a free booth, which the ten of them squeezed into.

"They're serving watered-down white wine, or home-brew beer," Luo reported.

"What? That's it? There were way more choices than that last time," said Meredith.

Noah scoffed. "And I bet it's all extortionately expensive."

"So, eight beers it is then?" Splat said, jumping up and Savannah followed to help him with the drinks.

Zeke watched the bartender pull the pints, remembering the various job applications he'd filled in as soon as his conscription letter came. He'd not received a single interview request. None that came through quick enough, anyway.

When Splat and Savannah arrived back shortly after, everyone grabbed a beer, bar Habib and Savannah, who clutched iced water instead.

"I'll say this now, as this will be the last time we're all together before I round you all up at one-thirty," Noah began, shooting Luo and Splat pointed glances. "We're here tonight to celebrate Frankie and Zeke. Although it might not have been the life either of you wanted, we're all proud of the way you've thrown yourself into it. We've only known you for a short time, but you're already a part of the team. Our family. So... cheers," he finished, and everyone clinked their glasses together.

Meredith threw her arm around Frankie and kissed her on the cheek. Splat punched Zeke on the arm. But Zeke stared off into the distance, not meeting anyone's eyes. Noah's speech was certainly true of Frankie, but of himself...? He'd acted so immature at the beginning and had done little to redeem himself since. He sipped his beer miserably, grimacing at the taste.

"And here's to Sam," Meredith said. "Although snatched away from us far too soon, forever in our hearts."

"To Sam!" they all cheered, including Zeke, who felt peculiar about toasting to someone he'd never met. In a month's time, they'd likely be raising drinks to his dead body. What would they say? Average at best?

Within minutes, most of Squad E abandoned their drinks for the dance floor. Luo and Splat headed straight for the two girls they'd met in the queue. When Habib downed his drink and said his goodbyes to head off to see his wife and child, he gave Zeke a sharp nod, which he ignored.

Before long, only Zeke and Noah remained on opposite sides of the booth. Zeke considered following Frankie and the girls, but the feral enthusiasm with which they were dancing put him off. Savannah ran at Aoife, who caught her and lifted her over her head, causing the crowd to go wild, cheering and applauding the pair until they bowed.

Meredith, who'd blown out her hair to create a lion's mane of curls under her golden mandala bandana, kept sneaking looks at Splat chatting up his conquest. Zeke replayed the conversation he'd overheard on his first day, when Habib said Noah had forbid them to get together. What was the story there?

Noah interrupted his daydreaming by shouting over the music, "Not much of a dancer, either, huh?"

"Definitely not."

"What did you do for fun then, before we whisked you away?"

"I worked pretty long hours at the lab. Then we would head to the pier after work and chill for a bit. Sometimes I would stay over at Zaya's."

"I saw some books in your bag," said Noah. "I mean, when we checked you in." He shuffled awkwardly, staring at his drink. "I thought they looked cool. I've read nothing in years."

"I've only read a few pages since I got here. I've been too tired."

"Sorry about that," said Noah, with a hint of a smile. "Hopefully you'll have slightly more time now you've finished training. You could always bring your book to the fire."

"Thanks for your permission," Zeke said. He dug his nail into his hand. Why was he being an utter arse? *Because he's ignored you since he took you to the fox den and listened to you burble on about one of the worst days of your life, making you think you were becoming friends.* "Sorry," he muttered. "You can borrow any of my books if you want to."

Noah drained the rest of his drink.

"Want another one?" Zeke offered, to make amends.

"Nah. I'll just drink theirs. They won't be back for them."

Zeke glanced at his wristband. Thirty minutes to go. "So, don't be mad, but I've organised to meet my sister here in half an hour."

Noah's eyebrows shot up. "Oh? That's... fine. That's great. It'll be good for you to see her."

The tension drained away from Zeke's body.

"You could have gone to see her at her house if you wanted, you know. It's not like Habib has special permission to leave us or anything."

"I wasn't sure I'd be allowed."

Noah stared at him strangely. "What, why?"

"I thought... You might think I was making a run for it or something..." Zeke all but mumbled.

Noah shook his head in disbelief. "Don't be ridiculous." He seemed poised to say more on the topic but then continued, "Where are you meeting her? There's a courtyard upstairs."

"There is?" It would be a relief to get away from the loud music.

"Why don't we go there now? It'll be quieter." Noah grabbed a fresh drink, hopped down from the booth, and looked back at him. He slid out and Noah grabbed his hand, threading his fingers through his. He was momentarily stunned, before realising that Noah only wanted to ensure he didn't get lost as they battled their way through the crowd of dancers.

The revellers pushed and shoved them as they weaved their way through to the opposite wall. Zeke squeezed Noah's hand tightly to make sure someone did not rip them apart, following him up a winding staircase and out into the fresh night air.

The small courtyard boasted an array of bistro tables scattered across a mosaic floor. Violet and white flowers burst from planters that edged the garden. Noah held onto his hand until they found a table in a quiet corner. When he finally let go, Zeke missed the warm comfort it provided.

"You can see the entire city if you stand on the chairs," Noah said, before doing just that. Zeke jumped up to join him, wobbling on the wonky metal stool. London's glittering skyline came into view. Only two months had passed since he last saw it, but he smiled, leaning over the barrier, taking it all in. If he squinted, he could pretend he could see his old apartment. Turning back, he found Noah staring at him.

"What?"

Noah sighed. "I think that's the first time I've seen you smile."

"That's not true. What about when we fed the foxes? Also, I smile every time you let me have the cheese sandwiches."

Noah laughed before jumping down and tugging on Zeke's sleeve, pulling him down to sit. "I meant what I said earlier. You've done so well over the last two months. You're going to be an asset to the team."

He bit back the protests that danced on the tip of his tongue. Noah was lying through his teeth, but only to be kind.

"Thanks. Thanks for all your help. We were lucky to land in your squad," he said, echoing Frankie's words from earlier. "You're a great leader," he added, dropping his gaze to the table. "And a great teacher."

"Can I get that on record?"

"No, and I will deny it was ever said."

Noah chuckled, smiling widely. For the first time, Zeke noticed Noah's chipped canine tooth on his left side. Noah leaned forward, his hands clasped together. A stray strand of hair escaped from its tie and framed his face on one side. Aching to tuck it behind his ear, Zeke busied his hands by applying lip balm from a small red stick. When Noah eyed it, suppressing a smirk—likely at the 'cherry bomb' labelling in glittery font—he explained it was Zaya's.

"So, what's the story there?" Zeke asked, gesturing to Noah's tattoo on the underside of his left wrist. It was a bird—a dove?—its wings spread out in flight. It spanned almost his entire wrist and carried a bluebell in its beak.

Noah unclasped his hands to brush his fingers over the dove. "I got it to help me remember someone I loved very much."

He shouldn't pry; this was personal. But yet, he had to know... Zeke drained the last of his drink. "Your boyfriend?" he said, praying that he wasn't mistaken.

Noah's expression was broken but his voice was matter-of-fact when he replied, "Yes. His name was Khyan. He died well over a year ago. He did the job Alice does now," while tracing the edges of the dove, lost in thought.

"Looking after the dogs?"

Noah pretended to look horrified. "Don't let Alice hear you say that. They're trained military units."

"You don't treat Wolf like a trained military unit."

Noah groaned. "Not you too." He leaned back, stretching in his chair before stifling a yawn.

Liquid courage—or was it stupidity?—coursed through his veins. "So... how're things going with that doctor?" Zeke asked.

Noah's eyes widened. "Was he that obvious?"

"Are you joking? I thought he was going to throw me out the window to put you on the bed."

Noah laughed again, the sound causing Zeke to rise like a helium balloon.

"Oh God. If it makes you feel better, I don't think he'll act like that the next time I see him. I've been avoiding his calls." Noah smiled a lopsided, guilty grin.

Zeke's heart thumped in his chest in time with the heavy bass downstairs. "How come?"

"Leo is great. He was my lead doctor last year when I went through some stuff after Khyan died. Then we became friends. But..." he trailed off, gaze boring into Zeke's eyes, unblinking. "There's nothing there for me."

A chemical reaction erupted within him, and his cheeks flushed with heat. He dropped the intense eye contact to fiddle with his empty glass, racking his brain for a rapid change in conversation.

Luckily, Noah saved him—he coughed, and Zeke looked up to see that his expression was now uncertain as he said, "Can I— Would it be okay if I met your sister in a minute? I'll just introduce myself and then head back downstairs."

"Uhh... sure."

"I don't have to," said Noah, quickly. "I was just thinking it would be... nice."

Noah and Zaya didn't exist in the same universe. What would they make of each other?

His wrist started vibrating. He slipped on his earbuds.

"Hello?"

"Zeke! I'm so sorry. I've been trying to call you, but they've been blocking the signal again. I've just climbed back up to my flat."

"What? I thought you were meeting me here."

Across the table, Noah's eyes crinkled in concern.

"It's the fucking rioters. They've really done it this time. They kicked off so much the police have blocked us all in until morning. Nobody in or out. They've even got some military power in. Obviously, not you."

Zeke climbed up onto his chair again, gazing out across the city in the vague direction of Zaya. So near, yet so far away.

"Zeke?"

"I'm here. I'm just... sad. I really needed to see you."

"Same. I'm sure we can figure something out. Look, I need to go, but Becca is still on her way. She should be on time."

"She is?" Zeke's wristband vibrated, alerting him to another incoming call. It was the number he'd repeatedly tried weeks ago: Rebecca Caldish. "I need to go as well. Love you." Zeke hung up and tapped his wristband to accept the call before telling Becca where to find him.

"I'm so sorry, Zeke." Noah appeared genuinely upset.

He shrugged. "My old colleague is still meeting me."

"Ahh yes, you wanted answers about your old boss being arrested, didn't you?"

"Did I tell you about that?"

"Frankie did." Noah picked a leaf off a nearby plant and twirled it in his fingers. "What sort of work were you doing with him, anyway?"

"We were... it's complicated."

Noah frowned. "I'm not stupid. Try me."

"No, it's not that, it's—" Zeke broke off. Becca was beelining towards them.

"I'll be downstairs if you need anything, keeping the rest of them out of trouble," said Noah, nodding at Becca as he slipped past her.

Zeke jumped up to greet Becca. Although she was only a decade older than him, she seemed to have aged dramatically in the last few months—deep frown lines had etched themselves into her forehead.

"Zeke. I'm sorry about not picking up a few weeks ago. I didn't know who would be listening." Her eyes glanced down at his wristband. She pointed at it and cocked her head to one side.

"I don't think it records audio unless I'm on a call," he said, but powered it down regardless.

"I wouldn't be surprised. How have you been? Are they treating you okay?" Becca reached across the table to touch his arm.

"It's been... an experience. Let's just say I was a lot more useful at Oakfield."

Becca's expression turned sympathetic. "I miss Oakfield too. I was going to apply for other lab jobs, but Ben has gone back to work now while I'm on toddler duty. Speaking of, I only have ten minutes or so with you. Ben is in the car with Poppy. It's way past her bedtime now."

Disappointment shot through him like a knife. He hadn't known how much he needed to see someone from his old life until this moment. "Okay, let's jump straight to it, then. What the fuck happened, Becca?"

He thought back to the day two weeks before the military carted him away in the middle of the night. He'd arrived at Oakfield to find the gate locked, with Becca, Oliver and a handful of other staff standing in the rain, shivering. Eventually, when Doctor Harding—or any of the admin team—failed to pick up any of their calls, they all headed home.

"You know the police arrested him, right?"

"Yes, but what *for*?" His impatience spilled out of him; he'd asked himself this question every day for the last two months.

"The charges against him..." Becca began, then trailed off. "I'm not supposed to know this yet, because they're still building the case. The police came to talk to you that first night he disappeared, right?"

He nodded. "They didn't tell me he'd been arrested though. I only found that out the night I was conscripted. That first night, they just asked loads of random questions. I couldn't answer most of them."

"They came to me, too. But then, a month ago, I was called back in—probably because I was a senior supervisor—and they asked a bunch more questions. They had some serious concerns about things going on behind closed doors."

"What do you mean? Just say it!"

"They arrested him for experimenting on children."

He stared at her. There was no way that was true. He hadn't seen Doctor Harding with any children in all the years he'd been there.

"That's ridiculous," he said. At Becca's emotionless expression, he let out a nervous laugh. "That's great though—they'll find out that he's innocent and release him, right? We can go back there."

Becca switched on the voice she often used when she wanted him to listen to her carefully. "I know this is difficult to hear, Zeke. You and Oliver always looked up to him. We all did. And that's why I need to ask you something. It'll stay just between us."

"What is it?"

He shivered, but not because of the chilly breeze. Somewhere, buried deep within his mind, he knew what she was about to say.

"Did Doctor Harding ever use you as a participant?"

He pursed his lips, looking past her at the skyline view.

"Zeke?"

Don't tell anyone you're helping me out, Zeke. They wouldn't understand.

"What are you not telling me?"

He shook his head. "It's nothing Becca. I just gave him some blood a few times. Oliver did too. Harding couldn't get enough samples from the blood drives. He took it from us after you guys left for the night. We knew it wasn't strictly legal, but it wasn't a big deal." He shrugged, attempting to appear nonchalant.

Becca froze. "Zeke... Please tell me you watched him do it. Tell me you saw him use a vacutainer system rather than a syringe and needle."

However, the expression in Becca's eyes conveyed a silent understanding that rendered his response unnecessary. Of course he hadn't been looking. He'd squeezed his eyes tightly shut the entire time while he faced away—Doctor Harding assuring him he wouldn't see a single drop of blood.

"How did you even know about this?" Zeke whispered.

Becca shook her head. "Something Oliver said ages ago stuck in my brain. We made plans to meet up, but he's not answered any of my calls in weeks."

"He's not answered any of mine, either. But Becca... Doctor Harding would never have harmed any *children*," he said in a hollow whisper.

Becca squeezed his hand. "We just don't know that, Zeke. If he was using you and Oliver as subjects, who knows what he was capable of. They suspect he was smuggling trial drugs out of Oakfield and giving them to others to administer. If you know anything, you need to tell the police."

"I can't believe you think he would ever do that!" His throat tightened. The thought of his tutor, his mentor, the kind old man that would joke around with them every day being demonized didn't sit right with him.

"Stop being so naïve, Zeke," Becca snapped, her face frowning for a moment before softening. "I'm sorry, but I have to go now. I wish I could stay. If we're careful, we can video call in a few days. I'll try again to get hold of Oliver and tell him to—"

"Don't." Acid bubbled in his stomach. How could Becca think this was possible? "If he wants to talk to me, he'll contact me himself. Thank you for coming. It was nice to see you."

"Zeke—" she said, but he'd already left the table, headed for the stairs. He ran down them, two at a time, leaving Becca far behind him. The music pounded in his ears as he reached the dance floor. The crowd was screaming along with a song he didn't know. A snippet of Aoife singing in a drunken, heavy Irish accent made him veer away from the dancers. A hand reached out to grab him—Frankie's? He shrugged it off.

Anger and panic circulated inside of him, threatening to overwhelm him. His feet led him back to the booth they'd sat at earlier to find it was now occupied by strangers. He considered leaving the nightclub, but didn't want to risk seeing Becca again on her way out.

It was so loud. He couldn't think.

Covering his ears with his hands, he slumped against a nearby wall, sank to the floor, and shut his eyes.

"Zeke?"

Hands were shaking him. He opened his eyes. Noah crouched in front of him, face etched with concern. "What's the matter?" he shouted over the music.

"Everything," he replied, finally relenting and bursting into tears.

NOAH

Noah had never been good with tears.

Growing up in a family of marines that believed in tough love, he'd learned from a young age that tears wouldn't get him very far.

But now, Zeke's hysterical sobs shook him to the core.

Grabbing his arm, he pulled him to his feet and pushed him around the edge of the dance floor, then through the corridor and into the street. The bouncers—seeing Zeke's distress—shot him a suspicious look, and he wondered if they would stop them. He typed out a message on his wristband to Frankie. She would be much better placed than him to deal with whatever this was.

He led them around the corner, slowing when the noise of Club Enigma faded. Zeke pulled away from him to slump against the wall, hugging his knees to his chest.

"What happened with Becca?" he asked, sitting beside him.

Silence.

Zeke's body shook. Was he having some sort of breakdown? He tentatively rested his hand on Zeke's back, but pulled back at the sight of Frankie running around the corner. She took one look at Zeke and threw her arms around him, cradling him to her.

"What's going on? Has he taken something?" Frankie said, lifting Zeke's head up to the light.

Zeke half-laughed, half-sobbed in her arms.

"No. Something happened with his old colleague that he met upstairs. He was fine before he met her."

He'd been more than fine. In the courtyard, Zeke looked the happiest and the most relaxed Noah had ever seen him. His pretty blue eyes had lit up every time Noah laughed.

"I guess I'm just realising that I thought... deep down... that they would sort it all out. That it would be a big misunderstanding. That I would be able to go... home," Zeke said, choking out the last word.

The words hit Noah like a slap. Even after everything he'd done to make Zeke feel safe and secure in his squad, he still wanted to go home. Noah's brain couldn't process it, because to him, Squad E was *home*. And now, Squad E wouldn't be the same without Zeke.

"Oh, Zeke," said Frankie, stroking his hair out of his eyes.

Noah raised his wristband. "I'll call Brian and see if he can pick us up early."

"No! Please don't. I don't want to ruin anyone's night. You two should go back inside." Zeke, somewhat calmer now, slumped against the wall, rubbing at his bloodshot eyes. His glasses poked out of his shirt pocket.

Frankie tutted. "Don't be stupid. I was getting tired in there, anyway. Those other girls are crazy."

"Can you tell us what happened, Zeke? What did he get arrested for then?" Noah asked.

Zeke breathed out shakily. "I don't believe it's true. I don't want you guys thinking that's what we were doing there."

"You've never really told us what you even did at Oakfield. What does a research assistant even do?" The wind picked up; a gust of chilly air blew damp leaves at them. One landed on Zeke's head. Noah brushed it off, smoothing down his hair where it had been. In this light, it looked almost strawberry blonde.

Zeke raised his voice to shout over the wind. "We were clinical researchers collecting evidence for multiple studies. Most of the stuff they gave me and Oliver—he was another graduate student like me—to do was super basic. Rebecca was the Senior Associate, and she directed us most of the time. Doctor Harding was in and out. He had a lot of meetings. But when he was around, he was great. He would often spend extra time with Oliver and I, and was eager to help us progress in our careers."

Zeke broke off to rub his arms, shivering. It was too cold to be sitting on the pavement. Noah shuffled closer, pressing his legs to Zeke's.

"Anyway, Rebecca said... she said they arrested him for testing experimental drugs on children." Zeke glanced between them, and Noah didn't try to hide the look of shock surely plastered on his face. *Children*? "I said to her it was ridiculous, but apparently they've got enough evidence to charge him. It sounded like Becca *believes* it," he added, his voice laced with melancholy.

"If you had nothing to do with it, you don't need to feel guilty," Noah said gently, nudging his arm against his. *Stop touching him.* Thank goodness Frankie was here. He'd spent the evening overstepping boundaries and then torturing himself for doing so—he needed no more opportunities.

It was hard to pinpoint the exact moment his grossly inappropriate crush had irreversibly taken hold of him, sinking its teeth deep into his heart. Was it as far back as two months ago, when he'd scooped Zeke out of the stampede, clutched him to his chest, and Zeke looked up at him so trustingly, with those impossibly blue eyes? Was it when he saw Zeke copy him by stealthily feeding Wolf the crusts of his sandwiches? Or was it during combat training last Friday, watching him get up off of the ground again and again, even when he was bleeding?

It certainly didn't help that—ever since the night he saved him—he often caught Zeke outright staring at him, quickly averting his gaze whenever their eyes met. Zeke had almost definitely developed some sort of hero worship, which Noah shouldn't take advantage of. *Wouldn't* take advantage of.

"Noah?"

He snapped back to reality to see Frankie staring at him.

"It's raining. Shall we go inside?"

Small, shiny droplets of water crowned Frankie's braids. He was about to reply when a loud commotion around the corner distracted him.

"Is that Splat shouting?" Noah rose to his feet, tugging at Zeke's sleeve for him to follow, then led the way back towards the club. He already had a pretty good idea of what they were about to face: he would recognise those loud, drunken shouts anywhere.

The first thing he noticed was Splat's bloody lip. He was being physically restrained by Vitt, who pinned both of his arms behind his back. If it were any of the other men, she might have struggled, but Vitt was an inch taller and—apparently—stronger than Splat. Luo was standing ten feet away, arguing with a bouncer, who was blocking his path to Splat. To Noah's horror, he pushed the bouncer, earning him a sharp kick in the stomach.

"Stop!" Noah commanded. He couldn't risk any of them being too injured for duty, or worse: arrested. But, most of all, it was painful to see his two friends with so much animosity in their expressions. To his credit, Luo obeyed, turning and going to slouch on the wall, arms crossed and eyes on the pavement.

"What the hell happened?" he snapped at Vitt, without even a glance at Splat.

"Damned if I know. I saw Splat shove Luo before he punched him back. By the time I reached them, security had thrown them out."

"Get off me!" Splat writhed in her grip.

Vitt glanced behind Noah, to where Frankie and Zeke leaned against a lamp-post, a safe distance away. "What was up with Zeke? Jesus, was there something in the beer this evening?"

Noah waved her question away and grabbed hold of Splat's shirt with two hands. "Vitt will let go of you when you calm down and tell us what happened."

"Luo's a fucking bastard, that's what happened," he spat out, sounding more miserable than furious. "He doesn't even like her. He just enjoys toying with her to wind me up." A shimmer of unshed tears floated in Splat's eyes.

Great, more crying.

Noah said, "Who?" even though he knew there was only one likely candidate for Luo's affections that would have enraged Splat to this level: Meredith. He sighed. "For God's sake. What happened to those two girls you were chatting up?"

"What? That was ages ago."

Noah shook his head. Then, Meredith came storming out of the building, chased by Savannah and Aoife. She took one look at Splat's bloody face, and Luo slouched against the wall, and ran off down the road.

Noah turned to Vitt. "And you wonder why I hate going into the city with this lot?"

"Should we go after them?" asked Frankie, watching the receding figures of the three women.

"Nah. Aoife will drag her back. I don't know why she's got her jumpers in a knot, anyway," said Vitt.

"You mean pyjamas?" replied Noah.

"Same difference."

"Can you go talk to Luo?" *I can't deal with his bullshit right now,* Noah wanted to add. But he couldn't be seen as taking sides.

Vitt sighed, releasing Splat, who fell onto the wet ground.

"You shouldn't let him get to you so much," Noah said, crouching down to meet him at eye level. "You know Meredith would never do anything with him."

Asking Meredith and Splat to back off from each other four months ago was one of the hardest things he'd done as a leader. The pair had hardly been subtle. At first, it was furtive glances across the breakfast table. But it quickly escalated into softly spoken, private conversations on the edge of the fire pit, heads low. Hands lingering casually on arms. Both of them mysteriously absent at dinner.

At least neither of them attempted to deny it when he spoke to them, together, after it couldn't be ignored any longer. He'd tentatively offered to ask Captain Murphy to transfer one of them into a different squad, hoping they didn't take him up on it. They didn't. Even at that point, with Squad E relatively newly formed, the horrified expression on their faces testified that they would sacrifice their fledgling love for the stability of their new family.

But that did little to comfort Noah whenever he saw them shoot wistful glances at each other.

Vitt came back over from talking with Luo, and summarised that as far as Luo was concerned, he was 'just dancing' with Meredith. Splat spat a large gob of bloody saliva onto the ground in disgust.

Noah turned to slip away to ring Brian, praying he wouldn't mind leaving early, because this night was well and truly over. To the side, Zeke shivered in his drenched shirt. Droplets of water covered his glasses, obscuring his eyes.

"Is your coat inside?"

"I forgot it."

He slipped off his own black trench coat and threw it at him. Walking away before Zeke could refuse it, he was already imagining how he'd look in it, with the coat dwarfing his slight frame. He shook his head. What was he playing at? He really should have stuck to one drink.

Nobody wanted to sit next to Luo during the journey home.

Meredith had eventually returned, walking straight past them all on the way to the van, sliding into the back. Brian raised his eyebrows but said nothing. The others piled in, leaving Noah and Luo to take the front. Luo opened his mouth to say something—his account of the evening's events, no doubt—but Noah silenced him with a hand. He'd hear his side of the story tomorrow. He turned the speakers up all the way, blasting music so loud that nobody would even try to talk to him.

His thoughts turned to the following day. He didn't particularly enjoy rest days, even at the best of times. With every other day so action packed and micromanaged, he often spent the day feeling anxious about wasting it, rather than enjoying it. Tomorrow, it would be his job to ensure the feud between Luo and Splat didn't fracture the team, poison the atmosphere and cause everyone's mood to sour.

After parking in the garage, Noah profusely apologised to Brian for the hassle they'd caused in making him cut his night short. As soon as they cleared the checkpoint, Meredith stormed off towards Beech block. Splat stared hard at her receding form, kicking the dirt on the ground.

"Why is *she* so angry?" Splat said.

Vitt laughed and turned to Savannah. "Oh, men."

It started to rain harder; the droplets thundered down in heavy, angry splotches. By the time they reached their floor, Splat stormed ahead, with Luo trailing behind the group, looking forlorn. Noah glanced at Zeke. Without Habib to referee, Zeke was about to have an uncomfortable night's sleep.

"Are you going to be okay with them?" he whispered.

Zeke's eyes widened. "You think they'll go for each other again?"

"No. Yes. Maybe."

Come to my room. You'll be safe there.

"If you hear screaming, please come running," Zeke said.

Zeke paused at Noah's door and his heart stuttered for a beat as Zeke turned to face him. His damp hair, stuck up in messy directions, made him look young and wild. He started to shrug off Noah's coat, which came down to below his knees.

Noah held up his hand. "You can keep it. Yours isn't very thick. And I have several."

Zeke's usual coat was also fraying at the sleeves, and the zip had finally broken.

"No, no, it's fine," Zeke said, trying to push the coat into Noah's arms.

"Honestly, please, take it. You look good in it." The words spilled out of his mouth before he had time to clamp his lips together.

This was a dangerous game.

Zeke flushed scarlet, dropping his eyes. "Thanks," he mumbled.

"Message me if they start fighting and I'll come immediately," Noah said, a small part of him hoping that would be the case.

There was nothing else to say, so Noah nodded and slipped inside his room. He stripped off his soggy outfit, dumping his clothes on the small mountain of laundry in the corner. He lay on his bed, resting a pillow over his head, screaming softly into it.

You're a fucking hypocrite, he told himself, again and again, until he fell asleep.

NOAH

*T**hud.*

   Thud.

Thud.

Noah awoke with a pounding headache, which seemed unfair considering he'd only had three drinks. Eight-thirty a.m. The latest he'd woken up in a long time. Were the others up yet? Not for the first time, he felt a twinge of jealousy towards them for sharing a room. He should be grateful for this coveted private space, but he often found the silence unbearable and hated not knowing where his flock was. Dragging himself out of bed, he resisted knocking on their door and went to collect Wolf.

"You look tired," said Alice, as he approached the kennels. The fresh hay she was throwing on the floor gave the space a summery, earthy smell. Mud splattered her trademark brightly coloured outfit, which always made her look younger than her forty-something years. Her dark eyes twinkled as she said, "I heard there was some drama in the city."

He groaned. "How do you know that?"

"Newman was here a moment ago, gossiping with Penn."

"What? How does *Tobias* know?"

Alice held up her hands and shrugged before whistling Wolf's tune. Often, the dog sensed Noah coming and waited for him at the gate, but not today. He bounded around the corner and charged through his legs, rubbing up against him.

"What was Tobias saying?"

"The usual crap. Don't let him get to you, Noah." She leaned down to stroke Wolf. Alice had a soft spot for the dog and was almost as guilty as Noah for treating him like a pet. "Isn't it your rest day today? What are you up to?"

Dread bubbled up in him. He had no plans beyond suffering through an awkward breakfast. His wristband vibrated. A meeting request from Captain Murphy. Ten a.m.

"Well, that settles that then," he said.

"Have a good day, Noah." She caught his arm as he turned to leave. "Look after yourself, okay?"

He smiled at her, trying to put enough energy behind it to convince her he was fine. He *was* fine. Everything was fine.

Squad E had already nabbed one of their favourite tables, the nearest to the coffee station, by the time he arrived for breakfast. Luo was noticeably absent—where was he? Should he track him down to check on him?

He scanned the faces of his squad. Dark circles and messy hair, but they all seemed in good spirits.

"Alright?" he asked, sliding in next to Meredith.

"Peachy."

Splat was sitting in the opposite corner, as far away from Meredith as possible. He grimaced through his swollen lip as he sipped from his mug. "It was your mug duty, Noah. You owe us double later now."

"How was Adeela?" Noah asked Habib. He envied how refreshed he looked.

"She's great," Habib said, pulling out his tablet to flash Noah a picture of her holding up a drawing.

"Is that supposed to be you?" said Vitt. "It looks more like a pizza."

Noah eyed Zeke, sitting with Splat. They were talking in a low, hushed tone, their heads almost touching. Noah strained his ear to catch what they were saying, but Aoife was slurping water loudly next to him.

"Are Zeke and I with you this morning, Noah?" said Frankie, distracting him from his mission.

He twisted words around on his tongue before finally replying, "No. You'll need all of your energy for day one tomorrow."

"We seriously need to up our game," Habib said, pointing at the leaderboard. "We only racked up forty kills on border duty over the last month. We're now second to bottom."

Noah resisted rolling his eyes. He hated that damn leaderboard. Although he couldn't deny it was certainly motivational. "Murphy wants to see me in a moment. Where are you guys headed today?" he asked, pointedly avoiding looking at Zeke.

"Savannah's going AWOL to run off with her dance crew, so Meredith and I are gonna show Frankie and Zeke the crack with the lake," said Aoife.

"Are Splat and I not invited?" said Habib.

"If you carry the bags." Meredith blew Habib a kiss. "Are you coming, Noah?"

"I guess so," he said, relieved as the structure of his day formed in front of him. "You guys go ahead and hopefully I'll be there by noon."

Noah arrived at Command ten minutes early, after ordering Wolf to stay near the picnic benches to be collected on the way back. He wished the dog was there beside him—a sense of dread settled in his stomach as the guards nodded him through the front door to the building. When he reached Murphy's office, the door was slightly ajar. Two raised voices floated out of it, so he knocked sharply.

"Enter."

He recognised Murphy's guest as a general from a southern regiment. His stony face nodded once at Noah as Noah saluted. The general glanced back at Murphy with a look that suggested their conversation was far from over as he stormed out of the room.

Noah sat down. "Everything okay, ma'am?" he asked, knowing he was crossing the line.

She must have been in a good mood, because she replied, "Just a friendly territory dispute—you know what the South are like. Sounds like they're in trouble, though. They've lost even more personnel this year than we have. We're going to have to take over some of their border next month." Murphy sat up straighter, Noah's cue that the current line of conversation was over. "How are you, Noah? I can't believe it's been two months since we last sat down. How are the two new officers?"

"They're—" he searched for the words, "—trained." That was *technically* true.

"Go on," Murphy prompted.

"We've done our best in the time allotted to us, ma'am. They're not going to win any medals anytime soon, but they should manage not to shoot themselves in the face."

To his surprise, she threw back her head and laughed. If she was in this good of a mood...

It killed him to do it. But he had to try.

"Ma'am, if I may, I have to make a suggestion."

Murphy raised her eyebrows.

Before he could change his mind, he said, "Zeke Bates has done his very best, but his performance in every drill is subpar. He simply isn't direct-combat material. But he's very academic. I think he would do well on the surveillance team. Or even engineering."

The smile dropped from her face like a mask falling to the floor at the end of a performance. "None of those teams have vacancies at present. And frankly, as you know, we need to get bodies out there."

Noah clamped his tongue to the roof of his mouth to resist arguing and dug his fingernails into his wrist, hard. He heard Khyan's voice in his head telling him to stop, and found his dove tattoo, stroking his wrist in gentle circles.

"I'm sure you're selling yourself short, Lieutenant Forrest. Your training seemed very thorough every time I've happened by."

The guy can barely shoot a stationary object from twenty feet away, Noah wanted to say. *Even the thought of being remotely near a type has him in a panic. He'll probably choke the moment he sees one, putting us all in danger. Plus, the thought of him being hurt sends my brain into a frenzy...* "Yes, ma'am."

"Very good. Anyway, I wanted to let you know about a special assignment. Likely in three days' time. Take your new squad members on patrol duty until then. Give them some real war-zone experience. Then, we want you to lead a live capture mission of a specific type implanted with a tracker."

Noah fought back his shock from showing in his expression. A live capture mission? He'd seen a fair few brought in over the years, but had never led such a mission before.

"You did ask for meatier assignments, Forrest. This is it. Unless you'd rather another squad pick it up?"

Habib would kill him.

"No, ma'am. I was just... honoured to be chosen."

"Very good. I'll send out the details this evening."

Noah stood up and pushed his chair in.

"One more thing."

He froze.

"Has... has your uncle been in contact recently?"

His blood ran cold with the memory of their last conversation.

"No, ma'am, not since the conference. Did you... need something?"

Captain Murphy gazed at him with narrowed eyes. What was she searching for? What had his uncle done? Why was she asking *him* about it?

"Very good. You're dismissed."

Noah left the building, heart thumping like a captured baby rabbit. He picked up Wolf and headed straight back to his room. He rummaged through his bottom drawer for a solid minute before he found what he was looking for: the small parcel wrapped in paper his uncle gave him weeks ago, unopened. Toying with the edge, he ripped the corner off of the thin, brown paper, but something stopped him from tearing it all off.

Something had happened with Uncle Nathan, that was for certain. Until he opened this package, he could plead innocent. Laugh off their recent conversation as the ramblings of a tired general. If Murphy found him to have documents and keys to mysterious boats in his drawer, there would surely be consequences. But yet, he could not quite bring himself to throw it in the bin. He pushed his laundry-mountain to one side to pull at a loose skirting board, slipping the package behind it.

Wolf growled quietly and nudged his knee with his head. He wanted to walk. Glancing out the window, he saw the sun was high in the sky, making a welcome change from yesterday's downpour. Time for the lake.

Lightwater Lake was a thirty-minute trek south of Avantis's cluster of buildings, just within the permitted radius for rest days. Noah meandered through the thick forest, now in no hurry to reach Squad E despite his feelings of loneliness earlier. He paused to watch a tornado of Blackcaps burst out of the treeline, taking flight.

Wolf ran ahead several times, unhappy with his slow pace, howling for Noah to catch up. Noah smelt the lake before he saw it: the thick, earthy odour of damp reeds, slightly obscured by the sweet scent of the water-crowfoot flowers that floated along the edges.

His squad was camped on the far side, forcing him to walk all the way around to join them. Despite the early-December chill, the women laid their towels out like they were at the beach. Splat and Zeke sat beside them, sprawled out on the mossy grass. Down the bank, Habib sat on a deck chair on a small jetty, fishing rod in hand. Half of the wooden boards sunk into the lake, making it look like Habib was on a sinking raft. He waved to Noah before casting his eyes back to the bobber.

"Chilly?" he asked, throwing himself down next to Vitt. She and Zeke were the only ones in their coats.

"You know my Italian blood runs cold," Vitt replied.

He turned the conversation away from coats before anyone asked why Zeke was suddenly in Noah's. *Because I'm an absolute fool, that's why.* His heart had tripped a beat seeing him in it again, Zeke's hands grabbing the collar to pull it further around himself.

"Who let Habib bring his rod?"

Splat groaned. "As if we *let* him. We'll be here until midnight now."

"Who's up for Blitz?" Vitt pulled the game out of her yellow anorak. The other three girls grunted in response. They were lying face down on their towels, trying to steal a few more hours of sleep.

The rest of them played a few rounds, with Vitt reigning champion. With the sun warming his back, and the sight of Zeke so relaxed around them all—at last—the tension Noah had held in his body since last night melted away.

As Vitt shuffled the deck in between rounds, a loud whistle came from the jetty. It was their warning whistle: starting high, ending low. Every pair of eyes magnetised to Habib. Noah's gaze shifted past Habib to the far side of the lake, where a group of people emerged from the trees, heading clockwise towards them.

Splat jumped up, frowning. "Oh hell, no."

"What?" said Zeke, squinting through his glasses in confusion.

Noah would recognise that swagger even if Tobias Newman was a thousand miles away from him. Two others from his squad joined him, trailing behind as he charged towards them, a large, dark sack slung over one shoulder.

"What's he doing here?" said Frankie, awoken from her slumber.

"Causing trouble," said Noah. "Whatever you do, don't rise to his bullshit."

"Hopefully Habib stays on his chair then," said Splat.

But Habib had other plans and abandoned his rod to join them. "If they think they're stopping here, they've got another thing coming," he said, his arms folded over his chest.

Zeke curled into a miserable ball, pulling the coat even tighter around him.

"I'll meet them on the path," suggested Noah—anything to avoid Newman terrorising his squad.

"Nah, just sit down and ignore them," said Splat. "They might walk straight past. Let's continue with the game." They gave in to him, rolling the eight dice and pretending to concentrate on their cards.

When the trio were close, Aoife said, "Just leave him to Meredith and me," while rubbing her eyes and letting out a yawn. "He's usually a tad less of an eejit when we're around."

Before anyone could reply, a booming voice shouted down the bank. "Afternoon!" Newman climbed down the hill, closely followed by Brandon Penn and Sebastian Moss, the usual suspects.

The three intruders sat down on the bank, bridging the gap between the previously sleeping girls and the rest of Squad E to form a semi-circle. Tobias flung the sack he was carrying down in front of him.

"Afternoon. I didn't realise you guys were off today," said Meredith, sitting up on her towel, cross-legged.

"We're not," said Newman. "Some plans changed and half of us weren't needed. Kitchen sent us out for some rabbits." He nudged the bag with his foot. Frankie shuffled backwards, wrinkling her face. "You can thank us when you're eating dinner later."

"We will definitely make sure to do that," Vitt said, her voice level and sugar-sweet.

"We were about to head back in a second." Habib was the only one standing, arms crossed.

"Really? Didn't Noah just get here?" said Brandon. "We saw him sit down about twenty minutes ago."

Noah tensed. How long had they been spying on them for? Beside him, Wolf sensed his unease and growled softly, baring a slither of teeth at Squad C.

"Forrest, get your pet under control," snapped Tobias, all earlier pretences dropped. "One day, your indulgence in him will cause someone to get hurt. I, for one, won't hesitate to put him down when that time comes."

As if hiding, the sun went behind a cloud. Squad E all shuffled nervously at the change in tone, eyes snapping over to Noah—naturally deferring to their commanding officer to see how he wanted to play it. Habib, rocking backwards and forwards on the balls of his feet, looked ready to explode. Zeke hid under his coat as if it were a shield.

Noah swallowed back his anger to ask, "Why are you here, Newman?"

"Just wanted to congratulate you on your next assignment. And ask you who you blew to get it." On either side of him, Sebastian and Brandon snickered.

"What the fuck, Tobias?" said Vitt.

Noah planned to inform his squad at dinner, after they'd enjoyed their rest day, and Savannah and Luo rejoined them. How on earth did Tobias know when Noah was only assigned the mission an hour ago?

"What assignment?" Habib's eyes darted between them.

"Jealousy isn't a good look on you, Newman," Noah said, coolly. "I suggest you take it up with Captain Murphy if you have a problem with how she is allocating our assignments."

"I only have a problem with nepotism."

"Then I suggest you share your thoughts with Murphy. I'm sure she'll be fascinated to hear your theories. Unless, of course, she just sees right through you to the asshole you are."

Everybody's eyes widened. He'd put up with Tobias's taunting for so long, he'd likely surprised them with his aggression. But enough was enough. They were a long way from the barracks, and out of range of any camera. If Newman wanted a three-versus-eight fight, he'd get it.

The sound of Habib cracking his knuckles seemed to place the same thought in Newman's mind. Tobias abruptly swung the sack over his shoulder and set off back up the bank, his lackeys following half a second later. Reaching the top, he turned back to say, "I was only concerned for the safety of your squad on such a dangerous assignment, Forrest. You know, with your track record and all."

A thunderclap of ice exploded through Noah. He must have looked ready to charge up the hill because suddenly Vitt was in his ear, whispering, "Leave it Noah, he's not worth it."

"She's right, boss," said Splat.

"I'll see you later, Forrest," Tobias shouted down, waving at them as he disappeared into the treeline.

"Jesus. Feckin'. Christ," said Aoife. "Are you alright, Noah?"

He forced his lips back into his usual easygoing smile. "Sure."

"What's the dangerous assignment he was talking about?" said Zeke, his face ashen.

"I only just found out when I met Murphy earlier. It's not for a few days. She's assigned us a live capture mission."

A chorus of shock, horror, and confused voices rippled through the group.

"Really? Even with these two greenies?" said Habib, his eyebrows furrowed.

"Thanks for the vote of confidence, Habib," said Frankie. "What will we be… live capturing exactly?"

"Most likely a typeB exhibiting a specific behaviour of interest. It's not that uncommon. I've seen a fair few brought in over the years," said Splat. "But the assignments usually fall to the BR troop."

"Black Rangers," Noah said to Zeke. "You might have seen a few around, but they're housed in a separate compound."

"They have swanky golden-lined suits," added Habib.

"Anyway," continued Noah, noting Zeke's miserable face, "let's forget it for now. We'll go through the details in briefing."

The others nodded and tried to resume whatever they were doing before Newman ruined their rest day. It was useless, however—especially for Frankie and Zeke, who quickly left to take a walk around the lake, their lips pressed into hard lines. Noah wanted to join them, to reassure Zeke it was going to be alright. Instead, he went over to the dock with Habib to watch him fish for the next two hours.

He caught nothing.

ZEKE

Zeke entered the armoury shaking with nerves, bile in his throat. He was only an hour away from his first shift on border patrol. Although Frankie was hardly jumping for joy, she was, as usual, keeping it together at least. Giving him a tight smile, she swung open her locker and placed her dog tags around her neck.

Soon after, the others joined her, stripping off their clothes and turning the floor into a sea of navy uniforms. The overwhelming stench of ten people smothering blocker all over their bodies made him want to retch. Noah's eyes studied him as he changed into his combat suit—checking he wasn't putting it all on back to front this time?

Once everyone was fully suited up, carrying helmets in daysacks, Noah inspected Frankie's handiwork. He tightened a few of the straps on her chest piece before giving her a nod. She followed the others out of the locker room as Noah turned to Zeke. He ran his hands up and down the undersuit that covered most of Zeke's skin, appraising it carefully. His caress elicited an exquisite cascade of tingles that served to pleasantly distract him from the impending mission.

All at once, Zeke couldn't take any more of it. "It shouldn't be torn yet. It's brand new."

"You never know. Don't forget your gloves." Noah grabbed Zeke's gloves from his locker. He took Zeke's right hand, placing it on top of his own. Noah gently tugged the gloves on and sealed them to the fabric on Zeke's sleeve, squeezing his hand before letting it drop. They stood still for a moment in the silent room, Noah's gaze drifting upwards to connect with his. The intensity of the moment suffocated him, drying his mouth.

"Thanks," Zeke said eventually, glancing at the stairs. Weren't the others waiting for them?

Spell broken, Noah leapt into action, sweeping their daysacks up from the floor and throwing Zeke his. He turned and charged towards the door, disappearing from Zeke's sight before he'd barely taken a step. Not sure what to make of this erratic behaviour coming from their lieutenant, he pushed it from his mind.

As soon as he reached the double doors of the armoury, Vitt and Habib led the way through the checkpoint into the garage. Splat and Luo carried a large metal box between them containing their equipment. He was glad not to have been asked to carry it. It looked heavy.

"Where's Wolf?" Frankie asked Noah.

"We don't always bring the dogs to duty with us. We don't know how the day will pan out, and they could get stuck at a watchtower by themselves for ages. They typically come on most of the specialized missions though."

They walked deep into the dark garage to a large white transit van. Habib programmed the auto-pilot from the driver's seat, and two bored guards ushered them through the main gates, the metal door inching up agonisingly slowly.

Habib poked his head back with his hands outstretched. "Frankie. Zeke. Your tags please."

Despite being confused, they complied without question, although it took several minutes to drag the tags out from under several layers of clothing and armour. Habib whipped a small army knife from his belt. A disturbing screeching sound echoed through the van as Habib carved something into the back of their tags.

When Habib passed them back, Zeke held his up. One side remained the same, his name and ID number. On the back, however, new lettering was engraved: Squad E - Brothers in Arms, Family for Life. He marvelled at Habib's handiwork in such a small space.

"Hey, what about sisters?" Frankie said.

"*We* don't need a reminder around our necks to remember our loyalty," replied Vitt.

It was a short drive to the border. The road, badly in need of a fresh layer of tarmac, was bumpy; their heads snapped backwards several times a minute. Zeke was almost glad to see the 'Foxburrow Outpost 1km' sign when they eventually arrived. The outpost comprised three single-story red-brick buildings clustered near each other. An old decorative water fountain, rusty with disuse, lay dormant in the middle of them.

Behind the buildings was the famous London Wall: the border that kept the monsters out, and the people safely inside. He'd seen photos of it plenty of times, but the scale of it, now that he was seeing it in the flesh, left him awestruck. Thick coils of concertina wire, the sharp barbs promising to shred any climbers into pieces, sat atop the thirty-foot bricked wall.

Three soldiers met them at the fountain, where several large metal boxes lay. Noah headed over to them while the rest of them stretched out their muscles, returning to inform them, "Night shift was super quiet. Should be a calm day. Squad J relieved F on the Stapleford to Theydon stretch half an hour ago."

Zeke struggled to keep up with what was going on as a flurry of activity erupted. He understood vaguely that Noah was sorting them into pairs and assigning them watch towers. The others, after grabbing weapons from the container, all headed back into the van to be delivered along the line, but Noah grabbed his arm when he made to follow.

"We're going to that tower," Noah said, nodding to a tall metal structure along the wall, within walking distance. Frankie gave Zeke's hand a reassuring squeeze before she waved goodbye as Habib whisked them away to continue up the road. Zeke turned to face Noah, heartbeat spiking as he realised he would be alone again with him. Did Noah want to spend time with him, or was he just babysitting the weakest link?

They followed the wall to reach the tower, and Zeke trailed his fingers across it as they walked. The story was that a team of a thousand workers erected it within seven days, ten long years ago now. Half-memories of seeing footage of the wall being built floated around his mind, but he wasn't sure if they were truly from when he was twelve, or if he'd seen videos since then.

Noah, who'd quickly charged ahead of him, turned around to see where he was. Zeke expected to be told to hurry up, but to his surprise, he walked back towards him, looking up at the wall with reverent eyes.

"I always forget how remarkable the border is," he said. "I've seen it so many times now. Do you want to see something incredible?"

"What is it?"

"Follow me." Noah jogged the rest of the way to the tower, but then ran straight past it, carrying on along the barricade until he came to an enormous metal gate, painted black. "Here." He pointed at the brick wall on the far side of the gate.

Along it, stretching over several metres, was a colossal mural. A breathtakingly beautiful weeping willow tree, its branches swaying to the left, pushed by invisible wind. Zeke stepped closer to examine the plethora of leaves painted an autumnal golden-yellow. He gasped. Every vertical hanging leaf bore a single name.

"It's everyone that helped build the wall."

"Everyone here loves carving stuff into shit, huh?" Zeke said, tracing the name of Yoanna Black with his fingertips.

"Seemingly so. But it's cool, right?" Noah's excited gaze bore into him expectantly.

"Totally. We're lucky they built this as quickly as they did. It must have saved countless lives."

"Speaking of saving lives, we're now two minutes late for handover."

He followed Noah over to the square-shaped tower. Five motorbikes, shrouded in thick black covers, stood to attention at the base. They ran up the spiral staircase that encircled the metal columns that held the structure together. At the top of the stairs, a small room, mostly composed of thick glass, awaited them. Sparsely furnished, it contained only a few desks, chairs and a massive control interface which stretched the length of the far wall.

The two soldiers already stationed there looked fatigued. They didn't waste a second hanging around to talk to them before racing down the stairs.

Zeke sat down in the chair closest to the control panel and stared at the five different monitors that displayed images. Three of them were camera feeds, each of them rotating locations every five seconds. The other two displayed reams of words and numbers.

"This is the data from the motion sensors," Noah explained. "We have hundreds of cameras out in the field, but *thousands* of sensors. If the numbers are high, we usually fly a drone or two over to check it out."

Noah pulled out a flask from his daysack, unscrewing it to take a small sip of steaming tea. "And now for the fun part. We sit, watch, and wait. It's why the others hate duty so much. It can end up ten hours of this," he said, sweeping his arm across the room.

"They would rather be over the wall fighting types?" He raised his eyebrows.

"That's what they signed up to do." Noah flashed him a grin. "They're good at it too."

Zeke stared at the monitor directly in front of him. It was currently displaying a narrow alley. On the left of it, part of a building looked partially destroyed. A shadow darted across the space. The screen flickered to the next image.

"Go back! I think I saw one!" he said, barely containing his excitement. Noah's bellowing laugh made him tear his eyes away from the monitor.

"Zeke, there are literally millions of them out there. That's sort of the point of us being locked in here. Seeing a shadow on one camera isn't a reason to sound the alarm. Now if we see five or more in a ten metre radius, that's a cluster. We call that in."

Zeke swung around in his chair full circle before leaning forward, resting his chin on his hands. The feed flicked through uneventfully.

"Don't the surveillance team watch these cameras? I don't really get the point of waiting around here all day."

"You're sounding suspiciously like Habib and Splat right now," Noah said, amused. "We're here so we're in position to take any action deemed necessary by Command."

Zeke checked the time on his band eight times before they hit the next hour. He filled the silence by asking a series of what he hoped were intelligent-sounding questions.

"So, in that case, would we—"

The ringing of Noah's wristband interrupted them.

"Lieutenant Forrest, this is Officer Stone, acting on behalf of infrastructure. Command has cleared us to assign all of your personnel for a code seven-seven, I repeat, a code seven-seven. Please confirm."

Zeke's eyes locked with Noah's, hoping to see a clue of what was to come. However, Noah's face remained impassive.

"When was the threshold reached?"

"Five minutes, thirty seconds ago. They want it blocked within the hour. You're only a twenty-minute drive. Location is on its way to your dashboard. Do you need anything else from us, sir?"

"That's all. Thanks, Stone." Noah ended the call, and jumped up, repacking the few possessions he carried in his sack.

"What's going on? Are we going over the wall?" Zeke said, his voice an octave higher than usual.

"Yes." Noah didn't look up from his intent scrutiny of the tablet.

"But what are we doing?"

"I need to call the others, Zeke. Hold on."

He tapped three times on his wristband, and within seconds, one person from each of the other watchtowers joined the call.

"Murphy has assigned us an emergency seven-seven."

"You've got to be shitting me. Best. Duty. Ever," came Splat's voice out of Noah's band.

"I want everyone on bikes within five. I'm sending the rendezvous point now."

Zeke's heart stuttered in his chest as panic took hold of him. He grabbed hold of Noah's arm and lightly shook it. "But what's happening?" he almost shouted.

At last, Noah stopped to give him his full attention, expression softening. He dropped his bag to reach for Zeke's other arm, and now held him still in front of him. "Don't worry. You'll just be watching and supporting us on this one," he said, before adding in a softer tone, "You've got this."

After lightly squeezing them, Noah released his arms, picked up both their daysacks, then eased him towards the door by pushing the small of his back. Noah retrieved the weapons they'd left in a box near the bottom step and passed him a crossbow and burst rifle.

Throwing the cover off the closest motorbike, Noah jumped on it and kicked the stand.

"You're driving." Noah scooted backwards to allow space for him to take the handlebar. Zeke stayed frozen in place. "Unless you'd rather shoot?" Noah raised one sceptical eyebrow. "I would prefer to return with most of my limbs attached, however."

Zeke forced himself forward, climbing into the saddle. He steadied his shaking hands by gripping the throttle as hard as he could. Noah's arms snaking around his waist did nothing to calm his nerves. He pressed the ignition key, startling as the vehicle roared to life, the vibrations shaking his whole body. Behind him, Noah slid forward, further closing the space between them. This was going to be a long drive.

"Helmets," Noah shouted over the hum. He placed Zeke's on his head for him, tightening the strap under his chin, before storing both of their daysacks in the saddlebags.

"Let's go." Noah's voice burst through his helmet's in-built speaker. He squeezed Zeke's side for emphasis and pointed at the black gate. Zeke entertained a brief fantasy of twisting the throttle all the way towards him and charging the closed gate at full speed. It would surely be a relatively quick and painless way to die.

Pulling the clutch level while kicking the shifter into first gear, Zeke hesitantly rolled the bike towards the wall. It took another urgent squeeze from Noah to force him to pull on the throttle.

And then they were off.

Noah must have requested the gate to open ahead of time, because the black metal exit was steadily rising in front of them. Just in time, he noticed that there was a holding space within the body of the wall, and slammed on the brakes, sending them skidding.

As soon as they were inside, the interior gate slid back down, locking them in. Absolute darkness enveloped them. He fumbled around to find the bike's lights, but a few seconds later, the gate in front of them rose rapidly upwards, revealing the outside world.

The outside world. He hadn't set foot in it for a decade.

"Go, Zeke!" Noah urged, squeezing him once again with his left hand while pointing forwards with the barrel of his machine gun.

Ready or not, here I come.

Zeke kicked the bike back into life, speeding onto the wide-open carriageway, jaw clenched, eyes set straight ahead. Noah remotely controlled his helmet for him—a map overlay appeared, red arrows pointing out a suggested route.

"Are the types going to be on us straight away?"

"Let me worry about them. You just need to follow the road and ignore everything else."

"But what if—"

"Zeke," Noah said. "Take a breath." Noah's thighs clamped even harder against his, then he withdrew his arm from around Zeke's waist to rub his back in small, slow circles. If Noah was trying to eradicate the types from Zeke's mind, it was working.

They drove straight ahead for a while, Zeke's speed increasing with his confidence. His heart sank, however, when his interface requested they turn off at a junction.

"It's going to get a lot more rough from here on out. I wouldn't try to go much above thirty. Remember what Vitt was talking about the other day—don't blindly follow the AR arrows, trust what your eyes can see."

"How long until we get there?"

"Only about ten minutes. We're almost there," Noah said, even though Zeke knew the difficult part of the journey was yet to begin.

Zeke turned off by taking a sharp left, sending dust flying up beside them. It was instantly clear what Noah meant by 'rough'. Although the road leading up to the wall entry point was well-maintained—it needed to be, with how much it was used—the infrastructure budget only stretched so far. Large portions of tarmac were missing, requiring him to either weave his way around them or risk throwing them off the bike.

The further they travelled, the worse the conditions got. Thick overgrown patches of hedges forced him to swerve several times. Above, trees leered ominously towards them, branches outstretched, ready to snag them.

Finally, they reached the crest of a hill. The remnants of human civilization came into view. Zeke slowed to a halt.

This area hadn't gotten off lightly in the initial round of carpet bombing, a decade ago now. In front of him was a sea of ravaged buildings. Many angrily jutted up towards the slate-grey sky, their edges jagged like half-rotten teeth. Some were reduced to their metal skeletal frames, some ashes and rubble. Looking at it now, he could almost see the smoke, almost hear the reporters narrating over the footage as drone cameras captured it for the first time. He remembered him and Zaya, silently sitting side by side, staring at screens for hours while around them their parents cried, panicked, and screamed at each other.

"It's... quite a sight, isn't it?" Noah said.

"Sorry." Zeke rolled the bike forward, navigating the rough terrain of the downwards slope carefully.

"It's a cloudy day, so expect a fair bit of activity on route from now."

It was at the very base of the hill that he saw the first one. A dark blur of movement to his right, in a side alley.

"Noah..." Zeke croaked out.

"I've got you. Don't even look at them." Noah's reassuring voice trickled into his ear as he squeezed Zeke tightly before letting go, turning his body away from him. Rapid vibrations from Noah's shots buzzed through Zeke, almost throwing him off-balance. The faint echoes of inhuman cries tormented his mind as he sped on, as fast as he dared. The road was now treacherous. Debris seemed to jump out at him from the shadows, threatening to upend them at any moment. A right-turn arrow appeared on his visor. Zeke flicked the indicator.

"Who are you signalling to?" Noah said, laughing. Zeke couldn't fathom how he could be so calm when they were mere inches away from death. "Maybe try indicating left, they might fall for it."

After what was possibly the most terrifying ten minutes of Zeke's life, the distance-to-goal alert ticked down to a hundred metres. They were now on a wide-open road—a dual-carriageway in its previous life. Squad E waited in a small circle ahead, their backs to each other, weapons in position. They'd parked three more motorbikes nearby, as well as a quad bike. Curiously, it was towing a trailer, with what he was fairly sure was a cement mixer in it. Zeke gritted his teeth. He was still clueless as to what a code seven-seven was.

"Alright, listen up. It's about five hundred metres to the drain. Habib and Vitt will pour the cement."

"We're doing what now?" said Zeke, hoping his tone conveyed his annoyance at the lack of information.

"The rest of us will be defending, standard formation. Splat, get the drone feed live."

Splat unlocked a small black box near his feet and began to fiddle with the contents.

Noah ordered them into a ten-men V formation, with Zeke and Frankie at the back, and Habib driving the quad bike on the far right. They set off towards a curve in the road at a cautious pace, eyes scanning to the left of them, where dark overgrown hedges spilled over onto the asphalt. Frankie nudged Zeke with her arm. He could just make out the shape of her smile through her helmet.

Noah, far left of the V, paused, holding up his hand to halt them. "Check out the drone cam before we turn the bend."

Zeke focussed his eyes on the icon on his interface and pressed a button on the side of his helmet. His vision became partially obstructed by a video overlay. Sweeping low in line with the treetops, the drone camera glided slowly, panning in on the pavement. A pavement *teeming* with typeAs. Zeke counted seven—no, eight—of them. Gathered in a small group, they were crouched in their typical animalistic stance, resting on their haunches. Their protruding eyes gazed up at the camera. Several jumped up, snatching their clawed hands into the air, as if the drone was a bubble they were trying to pop. Fanged mouths snarled angrily upwards, and he was thankful there was no audio.

Splat fiddled with the drone's tablet. The camera swung wildly for a brief moment before settling down, zooming in on a dark rectangular hole. Sitting next to it was a drain cover so overgrown with moss, the grates were barely visible.

"There's our target," said Noah.

"Have they come out of there?" Zeke asked.

"Yep." Habib pointed to the machinery in his trailer. "We're here to fuck that plan right up."

"Zeke and Frankie, I want you well back, staying with Splat in the centre of the road."

Splat scoffed. "Aww, how come I'm on babysitting duty?"

"I thought you were excited to challenge Zeke to your drills?" Noah replied. Splat huffed out a resigned breath of air. "I mean it, Splat; I want you three at least a hundred metres away."

"Got it, boss."

"Ready?" Noah asked.

Everyone bar Zeke nodded. Noah started edging forward, and the others followed in formation.

Zeke's stomach somersaulted as they turned the bend and he clutched his crossbow tighter to still his shaking hands.

Upon turning, the slight slope of the road allowed them a good vantage point to view the enemy. Although still a far distance away, the eight shapes were clearly visible—dark, writhing masses that were still jumping up at the drone.

"Number nine incoming!" said Splat, forcing the drone feed back onto their visors. Zeke watched in horror as a ninth typeA clawed its way out of the drain hole to join the fray. The liver spots on its scaly scalp suggested the human was in their late fifties when they'd turned.

"As soon as we start to shoot, they will charge us. Be ready," warned Vitt.

"When are we shooting them?" asked Zeke.

"On the count of twenty steps." Noah raised his gun, and the others copied in a ripple of movement.

They crept forward.

Five.

Four.

Three.

Two.

One.

A burst of noise shattered the quiet afternoon as the squad unloaded bolt after bolt at the cluster of types. Zeke aimed feebly, to at least look the part. He lined up a clear shot of a younger-looking typeA, between its bulging eyes, but it fell before he could pull the trigger.

"All down." Noah's voice was just audible over the racket. "For now," he added, turning to Zeke and Frankie. "The racket we just made will likely draw dozens from the surrounding areas. We need to be quick."

"On it," said Habib, speeding off ahead of them on the quad bike, with Vitt sprinting alongside him.

Zeke experienced a strange compulsion to examine the dead bodies of the types up close, but Splat stopped him by grabbing his wrist, while doing the same to Frankie's. The others left them behind to surround the enormous cement mixer, which was merrily churning as Habib dragged it along.

"Can they really just pour cement down the hole to stop them?" said Zeke.

"Obviously, that's not enough material to block the hole completely. But it's enough to obstruct the passage. Depends on the shape of the drain. Also, it's a special compound mixture. Has tiny shards of glass in, which rips their skin if they try to crawl past it."

Zeke nodded in approval. "Shall we run through the explosives drills?" He was becoming adept at building a range of incendiary bombs under Splat's tutorage, and wanted to impress him by being able to build them equally well in the outside world.

Splat grinned and dropped to his knees to open the large metal box he'd wheeled behind him. The black metal casing snapped over to reveal a plethora of colourful canisters, wires, and small electronic devices. "Okay, show Frankie you can set up a timed-fuse IED."

Zeke started about completing Splat's request, knowing the process by rote by this point, his eyes occasionally darting over to the rest of the squad. Every small noise from the trees spooked him, and a particularly loud gust of wind almost caused him to drop his creation onto the ground.

"Watch this for a second," said Splat, and Zeke looked up as the rest of the team positioned the cement mixer next to the drain. Habib and Vitt dragged it into the final position and tilted it downwards, funnelling the gloopy substance into the gaping hole.

"What's going on with the drone, Splat?" said Frankie.

Zeke's eyes shot up, and he dropped the half-finished bomb back into the kit box. Their drone was bouncing wildly in the air, like a rubber ball on steroids. The blades came dangerously close to hitting Meredith in the face.

"What the hell are you doing, Splat?" Meredith shouted, through the audio feed.

"It's not me!"

"The thing is going to take a finger off if you don't sort it out."

Splat grumbled under his breath as he fiddled with the controls. The drone collided with Savannah's helmet with an audible crack.

"Owww!" she said, jumping backwards.

Zeke tuned in to the drone's camera feed. The panicked faces of Squad E as the drone hurtled towards them would have been hilarious if they weren't in a life-threatening environment.

"Shut it down!" came Noah's startled cry.

"It's glitched! The software has frozen. You need to manually turn it off like I did last time. Sort it out before it damages itself. If we break another one, we're screwed."

"There's no way I'm catching that thing," said Savannah. The drone floated above her head for a few moments before dropping to whack against her helmet again.

"Oh, for fuck's sake." Splat threw down most of his gear. "Stay here," he said, already sprinting away from them.

Frankie, wearing a slight smirk, turned to Zeke. "I can't wait to rewatch this later."

Zeke squinted over at the squad. "What's going on now?"

Noah was in front of Splat, one hand on his hip, one hand gesturing wildly.

"Is he shouting at him?" Frankie replied. "What—" She broke off with a gasp. Beyond the rest of Squad E, a flock of birds flurried away from a nearby tree. Six more typeAs materialised from nowhere. They charged towards the group, arms sprawling out, as if they were about to hug them, not rip their heads off. Noah and the others, distracted by the still misbehaving drone and Noah's argument with Splat, were slow to react. A cacophony of panicked shouts and orders came through the audio feed.

Zeke grabbed Frankie's arm. "Should we shoot?"

"I don't kn—"

A strangled cry replaced Frankie's voice as her arm was ripped from his grasp. Her crossbow tumbled to the ground, landing by his feet. He turned to find Frankie frantically struggling out of the grip of two typeBs. They were working as a team, one on each side, gripping her arms firmly as they dragged her towards the bushes.

Fuck.

"Zeke!" Frankie cried, lurching herself back towards him. Her feet fought for purchase on the stony ground.

Fixed in position, his eyes glued themselves to Frankie's receding body.

"Bates!" came Vitt's urgent voice through the audio feed.

One of the types clawed at Frankie's stomach. It wore a ripped, red Coca-Cola t-shirt. *Just like the one ten years ago.*

Zeke was no longer in the outskirts of London. He was twelve again, frozen in fear on a road in the town he grew up in, Zaya unconscious at his feet, a type coming closer, closer, closer and him doing *nothing, nothing nothing.*

"Bates! Zeke! Shoot them!" Noah's voice commanded him.

But Zeke remained motionless; his body stone-still.

They were almost at the treeline. They clawed at Frankie's helmet—trying to remove it? Adrenaline coursed through him, but it only rooted him further to the spot.

"What the actual fuck, Zeke?" said Habib. His voice was too loud. Why was his voice so loud?

Someone barrelled past him, knocking him to the ground. He sat there, continuing to stare straight ahead. The type on Frankie's left snapped its jaw open, revealing long, infinite lines of sharp fangs.

The last thing he heard before Frankie's body disappeared out of view was the most soul-sickening scream of despair he'd ever heard.

NOAH

"**S**anders and Walker, stay with Bates. Everyone else, follow me."

Noah watched as his squad followed his command instantaneously: Aoife and Savannah leapt into position guarding Zeke, while the rest slipped into formation beside Noah.

He wasted no time diving through the bushes in the general direction the types had dragged Frankie. Thorns caught on the fabric of his suit, slowing him down as he charged forwards, entering a thicket of trees and ferns twice the size of him.

"Two o'clock!" shouted Splat, who'd within the utter carnage somehow fixed the drone. It raced off to the right. "Follow it!"

Dashing through the ferns as quickly as they could muster, they used their rifles to push back particularly aggravating foliage. Noah, not able to see or hear Frankie now, felt sick to his stomach. The types only had a few seconds' head start, so it shouldn't have been this hard to catch them up. The bird's-eye view of the drone cam showed Frankie still being dragged, at breakneck speed, through the undergrowth, her head whacking against foliage as they went.

"Faster! King, are you able to line up the drone gun?"

"Nada. Too risky," replied Splat. "They're about to bang into an old ten-foot wire mesh fence, though. There's our chance."

Noah watched the types slow as they spotted the fence. For a brief second, the pair on either side of Frankie seemed to argue, pulling her in two different directions. The hesitation slowed them, and he finally saw them with his own eyes. Sliding under a particularly prickly fern, he unsheathed his dagger and charged towards the nearest type.

"King, back me up. Everyone else, take down the other one."

Now that they'd caught up with their prey, the dispatch of the two mutants was effortless. Noah slid his dagger through the type's neck like putty, and it instantly released its grip on Frankie. He pushed its forehead backwards to ensure its mouth was secure before sliding the dagger the rest of the way around, severing the neck's connection to the spinal cord. By the time he'd turned around, the other type lay equally motionless on the ground. Luo leered over it with his bionic arm plunged through its stomach, while Vitt conducted a full-body assessment of Frankie.

"Fleming, status report," Noah said.

Frankie was shaking. "I think... I think I'm fine?"

"I'm sure you're far from fine." The look on Habib's face was one Noah recognised as his *I'm not going to let this go* expression.

"No visible suit breaches," reported Vitt, after she finished running her hands over every inch of Frankie's body. "I'll take her vitals every five minutes for the hour."

"My head hurts," Frankie said.

She made to take the helmet off, but Vitt caught her arm. "Let's get you back."

"Is Zeke okay?" Frankie asked.

Habib made a noise of disgust. "He won't be by the time I'm through with him."

"Habib," Noah warned.

"Are you kidding? The idiot just almost cost Frankie her life."

"It's my fault too," Frankie said. "We both should have been looking behind us once Splat left."

"Nah, Frankie, it's my fault," said Splat. He looked down, kicking the ground. "I should have followed orders and stuck with you two."

"We're heading back now," said Noah. "When we reach them, nobody is to berate Bates for his performance. Am I clear?" If Zeke's confidence was low before, he'd surely be a nervous wreck after this. He attempted to glare at Habib through his helmet. "Let's go."

When they burst through the treeline into the road, Noah let out a breath of relief—he'd half-expected Zeke to be curled in a ball on the ground. Instead, he was standing with Aoife and Savannah. Noah headed straight for him, wishing more than anything he could wrap his arms around him, tell him it was okay. Protect his little fledgling from the others, from himself, from the world.

Zeke's eyes remained downcast until he saw Frankie emerging last, supported by Vitt.

"Zeke!" Frankie cried, flinging her arms around him and Noah tried to suppress a smile. Frankie truly was one in a million. "Are you okay?"

"Am *I* okay?" he repeated in a monotone. "Frankie, I'm so sorry. Shit, I'm so, *so* sorry."

"Don't worry." But Frankie's wobbling legs gave out, and she sank to her knees, with Zeke following. She took several deep breaths, inspecting her outstretched arms as if checking she was still alive. "That was... intense. But I'm fine."

"I don't think anything about this is *fine*," Habib snapped, his voice laced with fury.

"Enough," Noah said, using his most authoritative voice as he stepped towards him.

"This is utter bullshit. You can't keep babying him, Noah. He's going to get us all killed," spat Habib.

Zeke surrounded his body with his arms, hugging himself. "He's right," he said, looking so broken Noah almost broke in two himself.

"I'm the one that almost died, Habib, and I'm telling you to back off," said Frankie. She was as close to anger as Noah had ever seen her. "Can't you see how upset he is?"

"You were the one that almost died *this time*," said Habib.

"Drop it, Habib. That's an order. We need to get back and debrief. Everyone, with me." Noah stalked off, leaving little time for the rest of them to arrange themselves in formation. His head pounded from the embarrassment of Habib's open defiance. He'd always enjoyed a relaxed approach to leadership, but the squad usually knew when to draw the line. This time, Habib must be really pissed. As they reached the bikes, Noah snuck a glance at Zeke. The vacant expression he saw there chilled him.

"Are you okay to drive?" Noah asked Zeke quietly.

Zeke gave Noah the tiniest nod and slid into the front position.

"Everyone back to their assigned posts. Once we're there, I'll send over the details for you to record statements."

"Got it, boss," said Splat.

The squad peeled off in different directions. Zeke was slow to start the engine and get the bike moving; Noah resisted the temptation to hurry him along—the last thing they needed now was another ambush.

The journey back was uneventful. Zeke remained stoically silent, and Noah felt the awkward tension rising until its boiling point almost choked him. When they were through the gate with the bike reparked, Noah jumped straight off and headed towards the spiral staircase of the tower. But looking behind him, he saw Zeke hadn't left the bike. He sat there, helmet still on, staring straight ahead.

"Zeke, ar—"

"I need a minute."

"I'm not just going to leave you here in this state."

But when it was clear Zeke wasn't going to move or talk any further to him, he reluctantly walked back up to the tower. Really, he should have ordered Zeke to follow him up. He should shout at him for disobedience. He should shake him and lecture him on how he almost caused someone's death. He pictured Tobias's mocking sneer. *You're about due to lose another one, Forrest.*

Zeke didn't come up after a minute. Nor ten. Noah completed the debrief without him, stating that Zeke was 'unavailable to make his statement' several times before the operator on the other side finally gave up. When it reached thirty minutes, he couldn't wait any longer. He couldn't concentrate, his thoughts haunted by Zeke's harrowed eyes.

He headed back down the stairs, freezing in his tracks when he saw an empty bike. He eventually found him back at the obsolete water fountain.

"Zeke," he said as gently as possible, "we have to remain in our assigned tower." Noah expected him to either ignore him or have a meltdown. Instead, Zeke slowly stood up and headed back, with Noah trailing behind him.

The afternoon passed in mundane tedium. Noah busied himself with observing the feeds and completing admin work. Zeke sat on a chair, staring intently at a monitor.

"Do you want to talk about it?" Noah said, when only five minutes remained before handover. *Please say something. Anything.*

Zeke didn't look at him as he replied, "What's there to say?"

"Forrest. Take a seat."

Captain Murphy sat opposite him on the other side of her expansive table. She'd summoned him to this 'incident follow up' meeting within three minutes of his shift ending. Noah followed her instruction, squirming uncomfortably in his seat.

"Ma'am," he said.

"You've had quite the day." She swung lightly in her chair. "And quite the scare, by the look of it."

"Fortunately, no personnel were seriously injured, ma'am."

"Indeed. You weren't exaggerating the other day when you mentioned Bates was struggling to adapt to his new role."

That was one way to put it. An array of conflicting emotions tore at his heart. Was Murphy about to pull Zeke out of his squad?

"Make sure it doesn't happen again."

And how exactly shall I do that, ma'am?

"It was never my intention that Bates and Fleming would be left alone on their first mission. As you can see from the no—"

"Yes, yes. Cameron King has always been a... quirky one. See that you have no more drone malfunctions."

Noah's cheeks burned as he dropped his gaze, gritting his teeth. "Is that everything, ma'am?"

"Almost. Heard from your uncle recently?"

This again.

"No, ma'am, not since we spoke about him a few days ago." He fought to keep the impatience out of his voice. If they were that concerned about General Forrest, wouldn't they be monitoring Noah's communications, anyway?

Murphy gave him a long, hard stare. "That will be all." She flicked her wrist towards the door and dropped her gaze to the table, bringing the holographic display back to life with a wave of her hand.

Noah scurried out of the room.

After collecting Wolf from Alice, Noah headed over to the mess hall. Squad E was stationed at their usual table in the corner. Noah's heart sank when it became apparent Zeke wasn't with them, although he couldn't say he was surprised. As he slipped in beside Frankie, he said, "How are you doing now?"

"Better." She gave him a tight smile that didn't meet her eyes. "Do you know where Zeke is? The guys lost him as soon as we split up to shower."

Splat cut off his conversation with Savannah. "We didn't 'lose' him, he pissed off. I gave him a massive pep talk about not being too hard on himself, but I don't think he was in a receptive mood."

"I'm sure he'll be here in a few minutes," added Luo.

But he didn't arrive for dinner in a few minutes. Noah made them wait around for almost an hour until the kitchen staff shooed them out of the hall. On the way out, Frankie tried ringing him, which earned her a look from Habib.

Admitting defeat, Noah followed the rest of Squad E over to the fire pit. Clouds were spitting light drizzle, causing the flames to flicker and waiver as it continued its defiant burn. Despite the weather, a handful of officers from other squads huddled around the fire. Noah's team fanned out to claim their usual spots. A stranger on the other side of the clearing caught his eye. She sat alone, swigging from a hip-flask. Her Black Ranger uniform attracted many furtive glances. What was a Ranger doing relaxing around Avantis's unofficial hang-out spot?

"I've got a voice message from my relatives in Canada," Luo abruptly announced, his voice hushed. Everyone's attention immediately focussed on Luo; direct news about other cities always drew a crowd.

"They finally managed to get back to you?" said Meredith.

Luo slipped his headphones in and shut his eyes. Noah felt a pang of jealousy at the outside contact. There was nobody left to leave him voice messages. Nobody apart from his suspiciously absent uncle.

On a whim, he jumped up and trudged through the long grass to the gated allotment patch. He tapped on his wristband to call Uncle Nathan. It rang for an eternity before being cut off. He considered leaving him a voice note, but settled on typing:

Call me back.

He hit send, turning around to head back to the fire. He didn't take a single step, however, before banging into something. The something—someone—started hissing in mumbled German. Turning on his wristband's flashlight to reveal his attacker, he illuminated the pale face of the Black Ranger. Hazy eyes indicated she'd now consumed *many* sips of her hip flask.

"Can I help you?"

"Lieutenant Forrest?"

"Depends who's asking."

The woman—late thirties, likely a career soldier judging by her adorned sleeve—swayed slightly, before collapsing onto the ground. "Want some?" she said, hiccuping, offering him the flask.

He fought to keep the irritation out of his voice. The Black Rangers were supposed to be London's best. Sent on surreptitious missions of high importance, the task force was highly regarded in the community. But Noah didn't think highly of this particular Black Ranger so far. "Can I walk you back to the gate?" he asked, not bothering to hide the annoyance in his voice. He was cold, and wanted to return to the fire, where Zeke would surely have joined them by now.

She waved her hand to gesture for him to sit down. "I'm Leonie Voigt. Your uncle's sent me."

His breath hitched. Leonie Voigt. He recognised that name as one of the most high-profile Black Rangers—she'd done several filmed interviews for mainstream media. "What? Why?" He knelt down next to the woman, shining the flashlight at her face to get a good look at her.

"He says don't bother to message or call. He can't reply." Leonie hiccuped again, which made her laugh. Her manic giggle unsettled him. He wasn't sure whether to catch her as she swung her body backwards to lie on the ground, gazing up at the stars through the thick cloud cover.

"I lost eight of my friends today."

Eight! Heaviness settled over his limbs, a magnet pulling him to the Earth's core.

"I'm sorry to hear that."

"Aren't you going to ask how?" The peculiar woman unscrewed the cap on her flask and poured it vertically into her mouth. Upon discovering it was empty, she threw it a few feet away from them. "They were all banked by typeBs."

Noah blinked. "Banked?"

"Their tracker chips are still active. All eight of them, about fifty miles north of here. Imagine being dragged all that way."

"Why would they drag them fifty miles away?"

Leonie let out a cackling laugh. "I think they've worked out we won't bother sending a rescue mission out beyond twenty miles."

"That's ridiculous. If we had good intel anyone was alive, in captivity, we would—"

More laughter. Still sprawled on the ground, Leonie's body shook as delirious sounding noises spilled out of her.

"You know the real reason we don't rescue anyone in the banks, right?" Leonie jumped to her feet, swinging her arms wildly as she said, "If the typeBs have a nice, steady stream of human blood—and flesh—to snack on, they won't bother rounding up the troops to attempt to breach the city."

He shivered. "How many *banks* are there?"

"Dozens. Hundreds even. Some have a handful of people, some have more. Obviously,"—she paused to squint at him—"Lieutenant Forrest, we never had this conversation. And now, I need to go and find more alcohol." She made to move past him.

"Wait." He grabbed her arm. "What else can you tell me about General Forrest? Is he okay?"

"Oh!" she said, swaying under Noah's grip. "I almost forgot. He said to tell you..." Her eyebrows knitted together in concentration. "*You have everything you need, and you* will *need to use it*. Something like that, anyway."

After composing himself, he returned to his tree stump to find Splat and Aoife crouched close to Luo, concern etched onto their faces.

"What's happened?" said Noah.

Luo shook his head. "The message... was really distorted. I could barely hear over the chaos in the background. They shouted something about loving me and that they were sorry we weren't all together."

A grim silence fell.

"Aww, hell, man," said Splat. He flung his arm around him and squeezed him tight—their spat paused, at least momentarily.

"It'll be okay. It's *Montreal*," said Noah, unconvincingly, even to himself. During the decade-long war, Montreal had often stood out amongst the cities in North America for their resilience and forward-thinking ideas.

"We said that about Houston. They built a fucking fort. Didn't stop them from falling last June," said Luo. He stared at the ground, crestfallen.

"Oh Luo," said Meredith. She went to pat his arm, but stopped herself, throwing Splat a quick glance.

"Ah, don't be worrying about something that might never happen." Aoife jumped to her feet. "Why don't you come with me and we'll walk Savannah to her dance class? We can stop by HQ and see if anyone there has any word."

The three of them meandered off, disappearing into the darkness of the forest path. Vitt started a game of Avalanche Blitz and Noah attempted to half-heartedly play, but his attention was elsewhere. His mind ping-ponged between Zeke, Luo's family in Canada, and his uncle.

Eventually, it grew cold and drizzly around the fire pit, and only Noah, Vitt and Habib remained. Wolf's fur became damp by the time the last of the dying embers sizzled out, sending the final three back through the forest path. When they emerged from the other side, they found Tobias Newman with a gaggle of loyal cronies vaping outside of a nearby doorway.

"Oi, Forrest!" he shouted over.

"Do not engage. Do not engage," hissed Vitt into his ear.

Noah nodded to Tobias once and made to walk past him.

"Heard your pet is up to no good this evening."

His eyes shot down to Wolf, who panted up at him.

"Nah, not that one, the other one. The new kid."

"We're not in the mood this evening, Tobias," said Habib. He put his hand on Noah's back and pushed him towards their building.

But Noah refused to move. "What do you mean?"

Tobias took a long, long drag on his vape before blasting them with an aggressive breath of minty vapour. "Heard he bought a fair few baggies from Old Billy. Planning a party, are you?"

Tobias smirked, for the briefest of seconds, before Noah sent him flying towards the brick wall. The pen he'd been using clattered to the ground as Tobias's face twisted in confused rage, nostrils flaring.

"Where is he?" snarled Noah. Behind Newman, Reeves and Moss shuffled uncomfortably. Noah felt Habib's presence as he moved towards them, stepping into the flickering spotlight. Noah's pulse raced as he pressed his forearm against Tobias's neck. This was more than enough to warrant a disciplinary, but he didn't care.

"Get the fuck off me," said Tobias, writhing against his grip. "I don't know where he is now. Seb just said he saw him."

Noah jerked his head around to Sebastian Moss, raising his eyebrows expectantly. "How does he even know who Old Billy is?" One of the many drivers that ferried supplies to and from the army bases, Billy was notorious for his clandestine side business of supplying drugs to anyone who asked the right questions. Noah ground his teeth almost to the point of pain.

"Chill out, man," Moss replied. "I only saw them make the exchange. That's all. I don't know if he even took them."

"When?"

"About an hour or so. I don't know where he went after that."

Noah released his grip on Tobias and fell back in line with Habib and Vitt.

"Jesus Christ, Forrest," spat Tobias. "Do that again and—"

"—and what?" Noah shouted. "You'll do what, Newman?" Habib and Vitt stared at him, shock plastered on their faces. Vitt hooked her arm through his and guided him away from Tobias and his squad. He felt their eyes on them as they marched away into the inner compound.

"We need to find him."

"You don't think he's planning to..." Vitt trailed off, biting her lip. "Surely not, right?"

"I don't know, Vitt," he said, unable to hold back the bite in his voice. "He's not exactly in the greatest of headspaces right now."

"He's not stupid enough to do that," said Habib.

Noah shook his head. The drizzle permeated most of his layers now, and he shook with cold. Teeth chattering, he jogged towards Beech block. "I can't request Command track his chip without specifying a reason. Let's use that as a last resort. Habib, go check your room. Vitt, go get Frankie. Get her to ring him again. I'm going to see if I can get Wolf to track him."

"In this weather?" said Vitt, wrinkling her nose.

Noah shrugged. Alice worked tirelessly with the canines to enhance their personnel location capabilities. Time to put them to the test.

Vitt and Habib sprinted off. Noah bent down, eye level with Wolf, scratching behind his wet ears. Frantically, he battled the rain to swipe on his wristband, looking for the whistle sounds Alice added the other day. He touched Zeke's name and a series of high-pitched whistles blasted out. Wolf barked twice, staring at him and wagging his tail. They remained watching each other for a long moment. His heart sank.

"Where's Zeke, Wolf?" he said, but the dog only stared at him. He played the whistle again. Nothing.

Just as he was about to admit defeat, Wolf unexpectedly jumped up, cocking his ears and sniffing. He took off into the darkness, with Noah sprinting after him. Wolf tore through the compound, past the mess hall and the dormitory blocks. Noah frowned. Where exactly was Zeke hiding?

Wolf finally came to a stop outside the Fusion building, sitting down and whining softly. Through the transparent door was only darkness. Fusion was never technically shut; it welcomed worshippers to visit any time of day. Noah crept inside, ignoring the sign asking him to take off his shoes. Rain pounded heavily against the ceiling, drowning out his frantic heartbeat. The lights flickered on automatically, illuminating the space in dim light. Scanning the room, he saw plush rugs, four large cupboards, tables...

And a figure shrouded in shadows.

Zeke sat slouched against the wall with his head tilted forward, his hair damp from rain.

Wolf bounded towards him, incessantly barking until Noah touched his head in approval.

"Zeke!" Noah knelt next to him and lifted his chin up, activating his flashlight to get a better look. Even with the bright light, Zeke's eyes remained closed. He pressed two fingers to Zeke's neck, exhaling a shaky breath when he felt a slow pulse and lukewarm skin. "Wake up." He shook Zeke violently by the shoulders. Wolf whined beside him and Zeke made a strange, guttural sound.

Noah dug into the pockets of the coat he'd gifted him until his fingers met plastic. He held up three tiny transparent plastic bags to his light. Empty. Images of smashing Old Billy's face into the side of his van flashed through his mind.

This is your fault. You shouldn't have left his side. You let this happen.

"What have you taken?" Noah shouted, shaking him so hard his head bashed against the wall. "Fuuuuuck!" he screamed, before muffling his mouth with the back of his palm. If someone discovered Zeke like this...

"H-heeey..." Zeke said, sounding like he was talking through a mouth full of stones. "What cha' doin'?"

"What did you take?" His voice, shaking with fury and fear, seemed to focus Zeke, who raised his head to meet his eye. Noah stared into Zeke's blown pupils. Zeke blinked in response. "Jesus fucking Christ, Zeke! Tell me what you took!"

"Just... leave me," Zeke croaked out.

Noah bit back a range of explosive expletives. He wanted to shout at Zeke for being so stupid, so selfish. He wanted to hit him and hug him and hit him all over again. "If I walk you into the medical bay like this, you're going to be written up. They'll send you to the Hole. For months. Are you listening?"

He held the edges of Zeke's coat, pulling him towards him, but Zeke grunted and pushed Noah off of him. For a fleeting moment, Noah contemplated shoving his fingers down Zeke's throat, but decided against it: he was out of his depth here. "Listen. I'm going to have to call Doctor Herbert and get him to come."

A glimmer of recognition flashed into Zeke's eyes. He shook his head.

"I'm sorry. It's the only way."

Zeke returned to his slumped position against the wall while Noah messaged Habib to call off the search, then rang Leo. Aware that Command recorded all calls, he kept the message short and vague, asking Leo to meet him in Fusion. Leo, equal parts surprised and confused, came within minutes.

"What's wrong?" he said, panting, after he'd rushed through the doorway. He *had* taken the time to remove his shoes. "I'm halfway through my shift."

"I'm sorry, Leo. I didn't know who else to call." Noah moved away from Zeke, gesturing for Leo to fill his space. Leo leapt straight into doctor mode, and Noah filled Leo in on the events of the day as he examined him. Just as Leo was finishing, Zeke made a harrowing garbled sound of agony and vaguely pawed his stomach. Noah's own stomach twisted in terror as he knelt down, cupping Zeke's face with two hands. His eyes fluttered shut.

Leo pushed himself up, and Noah followed. Leo's eyes flicked between Noah and Zeke for a second before he said, "We're going to have to admit him, you know that, right? His organs could be about to go into failure." He crossed his arms and looked at Noah sternly.

"I know this is a lot to ask—"

"—Noah..."

"Please," he said, making his eyes wide and pleading. *Maybe if you'd returned his messages over the last few weeks, he'd be far more receptive to your demands.* "They'll eat him alive in the Hole. He'd die an even more painful death than if we'd just left him here."

Leo sighed, a dark shadow crossing his face. "This could cost me my job, Noah."

A pregnant silence fell between them and he was grateful for the darkness that hid the burning heat on his face. "I'm a dick. I'm so sorry, Leo." Noah hung his head. "It's fine. Let's just admit him then."

Leo turned to face the wall and rested his head against the bricks. "I'll see what I can do."

Noah started. "What?"

"I'll bring him through the back and run some tests. Depending on what I need to do, I *might* be able to keep it on the down-low."

"Thank you," Noah gushed out.

"Don't thank me yet." Leo hoisted Zeke up by one arm, wrapping his arm around his waist, and Noah rushed to support his other side. Leo glanced at the large cupboards, each of them engraved with a religious symbol. "Did he have to get up to his debauchery in here? He's definitely offended at least one god, if not many."

Noah gave a low chuckle. Together, they walked out of Fusion into a thick, misty drizzle.

"I'm sorry I never got back to you about meeting up. Let me know when you're next free and we can do something. As... friends?" He shot Leo a nervous glance. The doctor had been patiently pursuing him for the last four months. In Leo's defence, until recently, Noah hadn't been discouraging it.

Leo's face twisted into a small smile. "That sounds lovely."

They trudged slowly towards the hospital, half-dragging a staggering Zeke.

"I must admit though, I have to question your taste in men, if this is what you're passing me up for," Leo said.

Noah let out a low laugh, praying that Zeke was too out of it to be listening to this conversation. "He's a lot cuter when he's not injured or high."

"I'll have to take your word for it."

ZEKE

"I wasn't trying to kill myself."

Noah, sat at Zeke's bedside in the small private room that Doctor Herbert arranged for him, snorted.

Zeke fixed his eyes on a broken tile on the wall. Every part of him throbbed. His body felt light, like it might float up, out of the bed and through the window at any moment. Beside him, a long tube stretched from his left forearm to an IV. Wolf, curled up fast asleep at its base, snored quietly beside him. "I wasn't. I wasn't really thinking at all."

It had been a moment of panic, of blind desperation. A way to stop seeing Frankie's terrified face as types dragged her off into oblivion. When he first bought the drugs—led to Old Billy by hearing a snippet of a conversation about 'picking up' from two workmen fixing a leaky pipe—he thought he'd just keep them in his pocket to be discovered at an opportune moment. This would lead to the powers above finally realising that he wasn't soldier material and taking him off active duty.

However, once the pills were in his hands, the dark thoughts had started swirling. Visions of Squad E being devoured in front of him while he just watched, motionless—useless—clouded his mind. He'd slipped each little pink pill into his mouth, swallowing them one by one. Maybe he *had* wanted to die. To die on his own terms.

Noah folded his arms and stared at him like he was a misbehaving child. "Do you understand how lucky you are? How hard Leo has had to work to keep this under wraps?"

Zeke gritted his teeth, shutting his eyes so Noah couldn't see him roll them. He didn't want to hear how hard done by Noah's precious *Leo* was. Zeke, mortified by the doctor's involvement, had pretended to be asleep every time he'd checked on him over the last few hours. The only small mercy was that he could barely remember the time that followed swallowing the pills. Even the memory of Leo using the orogastric tube to pump his stomach was fuzzy. Thankfully.

"Zeke?"

Zeke drew his arms around his body, hugging himself. The coarse material of the hospital gown made him itch. "I understand I've terribly inconvenienced everyone. Can I remind you that, according to you, I begged to be left to my own devices?"

"Can I remind *you* that, according to you, you're not suicidal?" Noah said, in a strained voice that tugged on Zeke's heartstrings. "What were you thinking, goddamn you? I'm doing everything I can to help you. What more can I do, Zeke?" Noah, almost shouting now, grabbed Zeke's arm and gripped it, hard.

Looking at Noah's anguished face filled him with icy guilt; hot tears prickled the corners of his eyes. He pressed them shut.

"Sorry," Zeke said, his voice a pathetic whisper. He shrank back into the bed. "I'm sorry I'm such a fuck-up." He pulled the blanket up to cover his face. "It's not you. You've been amazing. It's me. Just send me to the prison, Noah. Then you'll be rid of me." His entire body shook as he became unable to hold back the sobs that he'd suppressed since yesterday.

Zeke felt the blanket being ripped from his grasp. Beside him, the bed sagged with added weight. He froze. Noah's body lay beside him, not touching his own but still radiating heat. When Noah began to stroke his hair, he instantly stopped crying, more out of shock than out of comfort.

Noah's feather-light touches smoothed Zeke's tangled hair out, tucking it behind his ears. Zeke prayed the light was too dim for Noah to see his face, which burned with heat. When Zeke didn't respond—how was he meant to respond to this?—Noah stopped playing with his hair, and cleared his throat.

"Sorry," Noah said, and made to move off the bed.

Reacting on impulse, Zeke reached out and grabbed him. Now it was Noah's turn to freeze.

"Thank you," whispered Zeke hoarsely. He slid his arm down so that the back of his hand was resting lightly on Noah's. "For everything. I don't know why you're so nice to me, when all I do is continue to disappoint you."

"You don't disappoint me, Zeke," Noah said, turning his head slightly to meet his gaze. "I've seen how hard you've been trying. Even though you hate it here."

"I don't hate it here. Honestly, I don't." It was the truth. He hated himself for what happened yesterday, but he didn't hate being a part of Squad E. He hadn't hated it here for a long time now.

Their eyes bored into each other's for a moment before Zeke looked away, overwhelmed.

"Whatever happens, you don't want to get sent into the Hole. You'd be beaten, and... much worse... in a heartbeat."

"But I don't want to be responsible for anyone's death."

Noah fisted his shirt sleeve and used it to wipe away Zeke's tears. Eventually he said, "Nobody died, Zeke. Frankie isn't even upset, or in any way annoyed. You know what she's like. She's more worried about you."

"But Habib—"

"Shh," Noah interjected, pressing a finger to Zeke's lips. Noah's thumb stroked his cheek in soft, circular motions. "Let me handle him."

Zeke blinked. What was happening right now?

A brief knock at the door interrupted them. There was just enough time to spring apart, Noah slipping back into the chair, Zeke sitting up, before Doctor Herbert came rushing in.

"It's three a.m. You'd better sneak him out of here now before changeover. We've flushed it all out. His charts are all good. Just make sure he drinks plenty of water." Doctor Herbert's tired eyes swivelled between them.

"Thanks, Leo. I can't tell you how grateful I am."

"Sure. I'd say anytime, but..."

"It won't happen again," Noah promised.

Zeke squirmed. "Thanks," he muttered quietly, returning his gaze to the broken tile.

"You can thank me by being nice to him," the doctor said, nodding towards Noah. "Don't scare him like that again. He might look tough, but he's a delicate flower underneath all those layers."

"You're too kind, Leo. We both know I look about as tough as a teddy bear, but I'll take it."

Before Leo and Noah could continue their nauseating back-and-forth, Zeke swung his legs over the side and picked up his trousers from the table on the side. Doctor Herbert removed his drip, and they were out in the frigid nighttime air in no time. The eerie silence of Avantis as they walked back to Beech block only compounded his awkwardness towards Noah. Zeke walked slightly ahead of him, unsure of what to say. When they finished climbing the stairs to their floor, Noah caught up with him, grabbing the back of his coat.

"Wait," Noah said, his voice low. "Come into my room to sleep. So I can keep an eye on you. And so you don't wake the others."

Zeke hesitated for a moment, but wasn't sure how to refuse, so followed Noah through his door.

"What the—" Zeke cut himself off, eyes widening as he took in Noah's bedroom. It was in utter disarray. The mountain of laundry heaped messily in the far corner spilled over half the floor—how did Noah even have so many army-issued uniforms? He could barely make out an inch of surface space on Noah's desk and a small paper bin, overflowing from flattened cardboard, sat near a haphazardly made bed, the sheets rebelliously crumpled up in a pile, leaving the bare mattress of the single bed exposed.

"Sorry," Noah muttered, rubbing the back of his neck, sheepish. "Nobody ever comes in here." He set about remaking the bed.

Zeke stepped towards the small desk, a glimmer of reflection from the glass of a framed photograph catching his eye. It captured a bright sunny day. Noah filled the frame, his arm around another man in a position so intimate it could only be Khyan. Both of them were gazing at each other, rather than the camera, smiles etched onto their faces.

He stepped backwards, a sudden urge to escape overtaking him. "I think I'll just go back to my room. There's only one bed in here, anyway."

"You take the bed. I'll nap on the floor. It's only a few hours until dawn now, anyway. Wolf will keep me warm."

After kicking the assortment of items on the floor into a pile to clear space, Noah threw down some blankets for himself, curling into a ball with Wolf beside him, the dog already snoring again. Zeke lay down slowly on the bed, pressing himself against the wall, facing away from Noah. He considered suggesting Noah join him—after all, they had both fit on the hospital bed earlier, just about. But the silence stretched on for too long, and so his mouth remained clamped shut.

Waves of nausea and tiredness from the drugs hit him like a brick. He barely even recalled any blissful moments of oblivion that taking Old Billy's pink pills had given him. What an absolute idiot he'd been. And now his actions meant that they would get a fraction of the sleep they needed before having to face another day battling vicious monsters.

"I'm so sorry I ruined your evening," he whispered into the dark. "I really wasn't thinking properly. Sorry you and Leo got dragged into it. Let me know how I can make it up to you."

"It's fine, Zeke. You can stop apologising," Noah replied. He started saying something else, but hesitated, before finally continuing, "Go to sleep. You need rest."

He pulled Noah's duvet over his head, inhaling its musky, woody, resoundingly *Noah* smell. What would have happened if Leo hadn't interrupted them at the hospital? Various images wrestled their way to the surface of his brain before he forced them down again. He needed to sleep, not fantasise about completely inappropriate, impossible scenarios. *He was just being nice,* he chided himself, as he finally slipped into sleep.

Cold, bright sunlight streamed from Noah's window, snapping Zeke upright with a lurch. He'd overslept. His wristband informed him that it was almost noon. A small piece of torn paper rested on the pillow, a hasty handwritten scrawl that read: *Turned off your alarm so you could rest. We'll be on the field.*

Next to the note was a cheese sandwich. He couldn't help but smile, despite the shame that circulated in the pit of his stomach. He'd caused Noah an absolute headache, not to mention embarrassment, and the guy repaid him with undue kindness?

Promising himself that he'd somehow make it up to Noah, he headed straight to the field. With every step, he battled the anxiety coursing through him in anticipation of his squad's reaction to his reappearance. When he slipped through the gate, Noah was facing away from him, staring at Meredith and Splat, some way apart from the group, training together on the high bars. Splat had clearly said something hilarious—Meredith's body was shaking with laughter. Splat reached over and pulled her patterned headband back into place.

Frankie noticed Zeke first, running to him and scooping him up into a massive bear hug, informing him that the captain ordered that they complete extra training days before their live capture mission.

He waved over to Noah, nervous, hesitant. But Noah grinned, calling everyone to him to form a circle. Everyone smiled warmly at Zeke, as if nothing had ever happened. Was that also Noah's doing?

"What's on the agenda for the rest of the day, Noah?" asked Vitt, huddling her coat close to her chest despite the warm sun.

"Aoife, Meredith and I are going over to the shooting range for an hour with Zeke and Frankie. Then I'm sending them to Habib and Luo for physical combat drills. Splat, you can have some time with Benefici in the armoury making sure you have everything you need." Splat saluted Noah. "When you're not needed, review the local area maps of where we're headed on our live capture. Mark out potential places for the traps."

The plan of action ignited the team with purpose and Squad E marched off in their separate directions. Zeke trailed far behind the others on the way to the shooting range. No amount of extra practice in the world was going to turn him into a soldier, no matter how much he wanted to succeed.

When they arrived, the women headed straight for the moving targets, leaving him alone with Noah. The leaves on the ground became very interesting to look at.

"We need to talk about what happened yesterday," Noah said. "I mean, out on the field, with Frankie," he added.

Was this going to be more or less painful than talking about them cuddling in the hospital bed? Had Noah just conveniently forgotten that part?

"There's nothing to say. Obviously, I messed up."

"You didn't mess up, Zeke, you just... froze."

He almost explained that he'd had some sort of PTSD flashback from that last day in Rye, but stopped himself. He didn't want to give Noah excuses, he just wanted to do better. "I think freezing when your friend is being dragged off by two hungry typeBs is a perfect description of messing up." Zeke turned away from Noah, kicking the muddy ground with the toe of his boot.

"Stop being so hard on yourself. You had a human reaction in the face of danger. That's completely normal, and completely okay."

Zeke shut his eyes. He didn't want to hear it. He didn't want any forgiveness, he just wanted to forget about it and move on.

"Zeke?"

Forcing his eyes back open, he found Noah had moved closer. Very close. His warm breath tickled his nose.

"Promise me you'll stop beating yourself up about this."

He nodded.

He was quickly learning he'd most likely do anything for Noah.

ZEKE

"Zeke!"

Zeke's eyes cracked open before slamming shut again. Surely it wasn't six a.m. already? He rolled over onto his side to Habib's grumbling snores assaulting his ears.

"Zeke!"

He blinked twice. That was Noah's voice. Sharp lines slowly formed in the darkness to reveal the outline of his face.

"What's going on?" he hissed at him, matching his low volume.

"Sorry. I was going to tell you last night but I only got the confirmation from Command approving the swap past midnight." He paused. "Do you still want to go see Zaya in the city today? Happy birthday, by the way."

Zeke, semi-delirious, fumbled for words. Was today his birthday? How did he forget that? "Uh... sure?"

"Get ready and meet me outside."

Making as little sound as possible, he slipped into his casual wear, his coat tight around him. The garment had brought him immense comfort over the last few days. It helped that it still smelt of Noah: of bonfires and woody earth.

Closing the door to the dormitory room, he turned to Noah and said, "What's with the crack of dawn mission?"

"I thought you'd want to make the most of the time. And... I thought the others would respond better to our sudden disappearance if it happened before they got up."

"Our?"

"I'm going to tag along, if that's okay." Noah scratched the back of his head. "I mean, I've got some stuff to do there myself, while you're with your sister."

Joy rocketed through him at the mention of finally seeing Zaya. How was this his luck? But of course, it wasn't luck: it was Noah. Noah, who trusted him enough, even after yesterday, not to be a flight risk?

"Noah," he said, not bothering to disguise his emotion. "This is awesome. How did you even do this? I don't deserve it, after—"

"Don't be stupid," Noah cut in. "I did have to call in several favours though, so be nice to Lowenna and Krish from Squad K when you see them."

Guilt coursed through him, dampening the sunshine that had installed itself above his head. "Sorry."

"It was my choice, Zeke. Anyway, I'm excited for some time away from this place as well. Let's go. Frankie will be fuming if we're not back at a decent time so she can give you your cake. I've never met such a relentless people pleaser."

Where had he found Frankie, and could he please have four more of her?

"You English weirdos are crazy nice to each other on your birthdays," Noah continued, as they dashed through the eerily quiet compound. "In Denmark, *you* have to provide the cake for your own birthday."

"Sounds rough."

"It was. *Mor* died when I was twelve, and my father could barely use the microwave, let alone the oven. We had to make a mad dash to the shops every morning of every birthday to get a cake for me to take to school."

"Better than enduring my mum's awful homemade concoctions. Zaya and I used to suffer through one slice, then sneak it out to the foxes. Luckily, she only ever bothered to make one for us to share."

"Oh, how you suffered!" Noah said, playfully nudging him.

Noah was quiet on the journey into London. He'd booked a compact car for them, impressing Zeke by driving it using manual mode. The warm air from the heater lulled Zeke to sleep again, and he woke to see the sun beaming low in the sky.

"It's a good day to have a birthday," said Noah, smiling over at him.

He sat up. "I haven't even told Zaya we're coming."

"Well... I figured I'll just drop you off and pick you up in a few hours."

"What are you going to do?"

Noah hesitated. "I haven't visited Khyan's grave in a while. I was going to stop by, then swing by to see his parents."

"Okay." He reached for something else to say, *anything* else to say, but his traitorous mind drew blanks.

"And then... I was thinking we could... do something before we head back? Together?"

He flicked his eyes over to Noah, who remained fixated on the road ahead of him. The word *together* ricocheted around his mind.

"What did you have in mind?"

"It's a surprise," said Noah, his voice light and playful.

An electric thrill shuddered through him.

When Noah dropped him outside of Zaya's block of flats, he teetered on the edge of asking Noah to come inside. After all, he *had* said he wanted to meet Zaya. But instead, he waved Noah off as he tore around the corner.

Morning was just getting started on Zaya's road. Only a handful of other residents were awake, walking dogs.

He rang Zaya.

"Hello?" she answered, her voice thick with sleep.

"What's the number one rule about birthdays?"

"What? Zeke? What are you on about?"

"What's the number one rule about birthdays?"

Zaya's groaning voice boomed out of his wristband. "That you're an arsehole that never lets me sleep."

"Wrong. That we always have to spend them together." A dog-walker passed by behind him and their poodle barked a squalling yap.

"Are you *outside*?" she cried.

In response, he pressed her buzzer, hard, for five seconds. Twenty seconds later, the door burst open to reveal Zaya dressed solely in an oversized t-shirt. He scooped her up, clutching her tightly to him as he swung her in a circle. He was home.

He kissed the top of Zaya's dirty-blonde hair, styled in her signature twin braids.

"What the hell?" she said, through a choked sob.

"Surprise?"

"You mean, you just stood there while your only friend was dragged off into the abyss?"

"She's not my *only* friend," grumbled Zeke. "Splat is kinda nice to me, and Noah is..." *One of the best people I've ever met. Gorgeous. Literally my goddamn guardian angel.* "Noah arranged this whole day for me."

"Careful, it almost sounds like you like them. That you like it there."

He and Zaya lay sprawled over a turquoise rug that filled most of the living room space in Zaya's flat. They'd quickly settled back into their childhood position: heads on each other's shoulders, legs pointing in opposite directions. The feel of her body took him back to warm summer childhood nights; their heads pressed together as they crawled together through the bushes of the fields by their house to feed the foxes.

"Definitely not. I'm utter crap, Zaya. Next time we go over the wall, I'm bound to get someone killed for real." He rubbed his hand over his face.

She reached back to slap his chest. "Stop that. I can't even imagine what it would be like if they conscripted me. You're being so hard on yourself."

He couldn't help but hear the echo of Noah's words in what she said.

"Honestly, Zeke." Zaya's weight on his shoulder lifted, leaving the spot cold and vacant. Opening his eyes, he saw she'd twisted around to face him, looking stern. "You've always been so stubborn. You succeed at anything you put your mind to. This whole soldier thing is just taking a bit longer. You'll see. You're the bravest person I know," she said, solemnly.

He scoffed.

"I'm serious." Zaya pulled his arms, yanking him upright. "You're so much stronger than you think," she whispered, blinking rapidly several times. "I've been lost without you. Anyway. Let's not waste the day crying."

He smiled. "Save your tears for—"

"—a rainy day," Zaya finished. On instinct, their eyes flickered to the family portrait on her bookshelf. Their mother was standing in the middle, her arms wrapped around the two of them—ten years old, wearing grins, faces plastered with matching ice cream smears. If Zeke chose chocolate, so did Zaya. Wherever she went, he was always two steps behind.

In a handful of hours, he'd leave her behind again. Every cell in his body ached to stay with her. But, there was also a part of him that wondered what Frankie, Splat and the others were doing right now. Did he... miss them?

They spent the morning in the sun, meandering around the block, then the park, and then around the block again, trading stories and secrets. He told one outlandish tale after another, surprising himself at how much he enjoyed telling Zaya about his squad. Zaya spoke about how busy work was at her architecture firm, who'd been tasked with redesigning supply caches for soldiers over the wall. When she bit her lip to suppress a smile at the mention of a colleague she was meeting later, he teased and tormented her for a solid five minutes.

"Hey, what about you? You're clearly hitting it off with Frankie."

He bellowed a laugh, which ricocheted off the sky-rise buildings towering above them.

"Oh, shut up. Don't deny it. Your eyes lit up when she messaged you a second ago. You forget I know you better than you know yourself. Besides, it's about time you finally met someone."

They rounded the corner, approaching Zaya's building.

"Frankie didn't message me."

Zaya raised her eyebrows.

"It was Noah." He fought to keep his expression straight. He'd never mentioned liking a guy to Zaya before. Zaya knew him better than he knew himself—apart from this particular newfound revelation.

"*What*? Since when have you—"

"Shit, that's him," he hissed, voice low.

Noah leaned against the car they'd borrowed, parked exactly where he'd dropped Zeke off. His pale face, eyes closed, tilted up towards the sun like a flower drinking in the light; statue-still.

To his horror, Zaya gave a low, appraising wolf-whistle. "Say no more."

"Shut up!" He shoved her, hard. She tumbled into a lamppost and the sound of their scuffle finally attracted Noah's attention. His eyes opened, and the brilliant smile he wore when he caught Zeke's eye exploded his world. He was gone. He was far, far gone.

"Hi," Noah said, hands in his pockets. He nodded at Zaya. "Nice to meet you. And happy birthday! *Gefeliciteerd!*"

"Likewise! Zeke's told me so much about you," she said, a wicked glint in her eye.

Zeke fought the impulse to wrap his hand around her mouth.

"Did you want to come in?" she continued.

"No, no," Zeke said. "We've got to go."

Noah looked between them. "Have we?"

Zeke turned to pull Zaya into one last hug. She wrapped her arms around his waist and squeezed so tight it hurt.

"You need to ring me more," she said.

He grumbled and kissed her forehead.

Once they were back in the car, they sat for a moment, silent, as Zeke watched Zaya disappear behind the glass doors and recede into shadow.

"I feel bad for coming back now. You should go up with her for a while longer."

"It's fine. How was… your thing?" Why was Khyan's name so difficult to speak?

"Yeah." Noah tapped the steering wheel. That was all he seemed able to say. "So, anywhere else you need to go?"

"I wondered if we could swing by my flat so I could grab some more clothes."

Speaking about his flat made him instantly nostalgic. He'd considered cancelling his lease a few times—it was now a colossal waste of money—but couldn't bring himself to do it.

"A most excellent idea. Splat has threatened to burn your current outfit at least twice."

"And then… can we quickly stop at my friend Oliver's house?" Zeke grimaced, becoming acutely aware that this was turning into an afternoon of Noah following him around on his errands.

Noah tilted his head. "Your colleague?"

"Yeah, the one who's not replying to me."

"Sure, if you think it's a good idea to appear at his doorstep."

"Well, I'm running out of ideas."

For some reason, Zeke couldn't cope with the thought of Noah in his flat, so left him in the car to take the stairs two at a time to reach his floor. His apartment was exactly how he'd left it, all those weeks ago, when the two strange men arrived to implode his life. He shoved as many clothes and a few random trinkets as he could fit into his large duffle bag. Sliding back into the passenger seat, he found Noah on a voice call with someone. Noah hastily hung up.

"Who was that?"

"Just Habib."

"Everything okay?"

"Yup." Noah's frown as he gripped the steering wheel suggested otherwise. "Right then. To the elusive Oliver."

Oliver was the only person Zeke knew that lived in a proper house. The population of London, which had always been full to bursting, only increased in the last decade as millions of survivors poured into its relative safety. His friend lived in a beautiful yellow Victorian, one of many brightly painted three-story townhouses in an affluent part of town. Noah automatically got out to follow him, and this time, Zeke didn't ask him to stay in the car. He wanted him with him for this.

As they approached the red door, his dread compounded inside him. For some reason, Oliver clearly didn't want to talk to him. He'd left at least ten messages over the last few weeks, all unanswered.

"Hello?" he shouted through the letterbox, when nobody answered the banging from the dragon-shaped door knocker. "Is Oliver home?"

He was moments from giving up when a shadow passed over the frosted glass. The door opened a slither.

"Are you that friend from the lab?" a woman's voice asked. One brown eye, heavily set into lined skin, peered at him.

He nodded. "Mrs Thompson? We've met a few times before. It's Zeke."

Oliver's mother exhaled a long sigh. She unlatched the door and ushered them through. Noah introduced himself as they walked along a narrow corridor. Mrs Thompson travelled around the rectangular island in the middle of the kitchen, folding her arms as she looked between them. Looking at her closely now, Mrs Thompson was not how he remembered her. Usually bouncy curls sat greasy and limp around a haggard, grey face and deep purple patches underneath her eyes suggested sleepless nights.

The woman narrowed her eyes at him. "You look well," she said, strangely, as if it annoyed her.

"Where's Oliver?" He swallowed nervously. A sudden urge to flee gripped him as a foreboding sense of danger seeped through the room. Noah pressed his hand into the small of his back and he leaned back into the comforting touch.

"He's upstairs. Follow me."

Mrs Thompson silently strode off, leaving them to hurry after her. Noah threw him a quick, questioning look as they traipsed up the spiral staircase. The woman didn't knock as she entered Oliver's bedroom.

He knew at once that something was amiss. A sticky, stale, putrid smell hung in the air, even though an open window blew fresh air into the room.

Oliver lay still on the bed, eyes shut. A pale, gaunt face peeped from under his duvet.

"Oliver?" Zeke whispered, but more to Mrs Thompson than his sleeping friend.

"Do *you* know what they gave him?" Oliver's mother was visibly shaking.

He blinked at her.

"Disgusting," she spat out. "You're going to stand here and play innocent, just like that Rebecca woman."

"I-I... have no idea what's going on. Is he ill?"

"Ill? Ha! That's one way of putting it. He's barely spoken in days. The hospital admitted him for a while, but sent him home when they couldn't do anything. The one private doctor I managed to get over here to see him had no clue what to make of it. I swear to God, if they ever let that man out of prison—"

"Doctor Harding didn't do this!" Zeke said, gesturing wildly to Oliver.

A grunting sound came from the bed. Oliver's eyes flickered open.

"Zeke?" came a weak, gravelly voice. He shuffled forwards to linger awkwardly near his bed. Noah stopped pressing against him to move into the corner of the room, and he felt his absence like a lost tooth.

"How are you?"

"I feel like shit," he croaked, while Mrs Thompson rushed to pour him water from a jug. "Are *you* okay?"

"What? Yes, I'm fine. I mean, they've drafted me into the military, thanks to Doctor Harding's arrest, but I'm technically fine."

"Wow. That's... good. I thought you might be like me. You know, since he injected you as well, I mean."

Mrs Thompson and Noah's eyes bore into the back of his neck, prickling his skin. The unwanted truth that he'd been trying to lock deep, deep inside his brain broke free, growing into a tangled vine, wrapping itself firmly around his mind. It wasn't possible. Doctor Harding couldn't have caused this, surely? He wanted to scream, to pull Oliver out of the bed and shake him until he said he was lying, that he was fine and it was just a mistake. He sank to his knees. As they hit the floor, Noah rushed over to him, squeezing his shoulder from behind.

"How do you know it's that?" Zeke said in a strangled whisper.

Oliver shut his eyes. It seemed like he might have drifted back off to sleep, but he eventually replied, "Whenever I helped him out by giving blood, he would say my vitamin B12 levels were low. Then he'd give me a shot of it. But every time, it made me feel weird. And now—now my organs are failing."

"I'm so sorry, Ollie." Hot tears trickled down Zeke's face, but he made no move to wipe them.

"Hey, maybe the crazy fucker gave you some different shit? I'm glad you're okay, Zeke. Really." Oliver started coughing, which turned into a gargling choke.

His mother rushed to sit him up. "You need to leave now."

"Have you contacted the police?" Noah asked. "Zeke said they're building a case against him."

"Of course I have," she spat. "It took weeks for someone to come round. Then I begged them for help, but they said Harding is refusing to talk."

Oliver waved at them feebly through his coughing fit, and all at once, Zeke couldn't face him anymore.

He ran down the stairs, bursting back onto the street, and threw himself into the car. Pulling his knees up onto the seat, he pressed his eyes to them, vaguely aware it was coming up to the tenth time Noah had seen him curled into a helpless ball but powerless to stop it.

Noah shut his door with a click. His quiet, steady breathing steadied Zeke.

"I really need to stop crying in front of you." Zeke forced a laugh.

"You really don't."

Unfurling himself from his ball, he said, "I think I need to ask one more favour from you."

"It *is* your birthday." Noah looked at him expectantly, his kind eyes eager and bright.

He hesitated. Was he really about to ask this?

"I need to see Doctor Harding. He's in Blackhouse Prison."

Noah's eyes widened. He clearly hadn't expected the favour to be this big.

"Please. He might talk to me if I see him face to face. He liked me. Kind of. And I need to know if I'm— If he—"

"So, he really did illegally use the two of you in a study?" Noah asked, his face crumpled with concern.

"He was arrested on charges of child abuse. So I don't think it was just us."

"Shit. What did he do to you?"

"He was only meant to be drawing blood. He was having trouble accessing enough via the blood banks," Zeke whispered.

The smell of the alcohol on the sterile cloth.

The feel of Harding's fingers pulling his skin taut.

Three taps on the palm of his gloved hand.

A short sharp pinch.

The promise Zeke wouldn't see any blood.

Why hadn't he questioned why Harding always drew the blood from them after everyone else had left for the evening, leaving him and Oliver to clean up?

"He was so nice... so *charming,*" Zeke continued, "I guess we were blinded by that. I'm not sure what he did to us. That's why I need to see him. But if it's too much to ask—"

Noah held up his hand. "It's not. There's a friend of a friend of my uncle's that might be able to help. It won't be today, though." Noah reached over to brush the tips of Zeke's fingers. "Try not to worry yourself. You seem fine to me."

"Apart from being a hopeless mess?"

"Well, yes, that." Noah grinned at him, turning his heart to putty and melting the gnawing worry away.

"So, what's next on the agenda? It's definitely your turn to choose the activity."

Noah scratched the back of his neck. "I know this one place. It's halfway back to Avantis. It's really beautiful, even at this time of year."

"Lead the way."

On the way out of the city, a sight caught their eye. A crowd gathered around two men, lying face down on the ground, handcuffed, the shattered remains of a glass shop window scattered nearby. Earlier, Zaya spoke in depth about the state of London. How she and her friends now felt unsafe out after dark. The rise of knife crime, the relentless riots. These events hadn't appeared out of nowhere, but for years, he'd largely remained oblivious, choosing to remain in his sugar-coated bubble. They *would* win the war. Things *would* go back to normal. But now, the world had hurtled past the decade mark with no sign of hope on the horizon.

Thirty minutes later, Noah pulled the car over into a ditch on a quiet road. Turning off the engine, he faced him to say, "This isn't anything spectacular. I think I mainly like it because it reminds me of Rold Forest back home." Noah sounded like he'd merely popped over to England for a holiday, rather than fled a now uninhabitable country.

Finding a wooden farm gate, Noah used one arm to swing his body over it, landing on graceful feet. Zeke, on the other hand, clambered over it with the elegance of a bear, practically falling into Noah as he reached out to grab him. Noah laughed as he brushed the leaves from Zeke's stolen coat. A flash of guilt at leaving all his own coats neatly tucked away in his wardrobe earlier—very much deliberately—struck him.

"I found this place in my first year here," Noah said, as they ambled along. Luscious green trees, littered with tiny budding blossoms, lined a narrow path. The sweet scent of spring made up for the boot-deep mud they battled through. "I was struggling with leaving home. Almost everyone I knew from Rotterdam was gone. I drove and drove until I was as lost as I felt. Then I pulled over exactly where we just did."

Beside them, a trickling stream of water joined a tributary. Noah walked three steps ahead of him, causing him to have to hurry to keep up.

Noah's urgent pace seemed to match his tone of voice as he continued talking. "I walked and walked until I hit this river." He pointed to a spot in the distance before increasing his speed even further, breaking into a jog. He didn't stop until they were at the riverbank. Gushing, murky-green water, littered with sticks, hurtled downstream. "I was going to throw myself into it."

Startled, Zeke's breath caught in his throat.

"Come on."

Noah took off again, following the river up to cross a rickety, rotten bridge that'd seen better days. He almost commented that the bridge looked like suicide before deciding that would be in poor taste.

Another few minutes of more muddy trails, and their destination finally came into view. Noah stopped at the base of a hill, on which sat a small stationary watermill. The tree line almost completely camouflaged the wooden structure that was overtaken entirely by thick emerald moss. Two doves perched on the highest spoke of the wheel. Noah smiled at them like they were old friends, rubbing the tattoo on his wrist. Then he sat down on a nearby boulder, throwing his small rucksack to the ground.

Zeke hovered nearby. "It's lovely here. Was it this that changed your mind about throwing yourself into the river?"

"No. I went all the way up to the mill and found two dead bodies inside."

"*What?*"

"Don't worry, they're not there now. I came back with a shovel and buried them."

"Who were they?"

"A mother with a young toddler. There were barely any remains left to bury. I think they probably hid up there during the first wave. Maybe even starved to death, too terrified to leave to find help." Noah paused, looking up at the building, a dream-like expression on his face.

Zeke threw himself down on the damp earth in front of Noah's rock, daring himself to rest his back against Noah's knees, though it made his heart pound to do so. "Jesus, Noah. This sounds awful."

Noah fiddled with a loose thread on the collar of Zeke's coat, his hand coming distractingly close to his neck. "Anyway, the story is, finding them there reminded me of why I went into the military. My uncle and father were a large part of it, sure. But I guess I've always had this... urge... to protect people. It started with my younger brothers and sister. My parents were away a lot, so it was up to me."

Zeke tilted his head back, so it rested fully on Noah's lap. He gazed at him, upside down, and smiled. "You're very good at it. Protecting people."

A dangerous smirk stretched across Noah's lips. "Thanks."

The light breeze blew a few strands of Noah's hair around his face, and Zeke's hands twitched in his lap. The pair remained frozen in place, neither one averting their eyes until the sudden flapping of a bird taking flight distracted Noah.

"So," Noah began. "I may have lured you out here under false pretences."

Zeke almost choked.

"I've got a paddleboard stashed over there." He pointed to a spot under the mill, where black material covered something large. "Habib and I found it on a scavenging mission a few years back and brought it here. Want to take it down the river?"

Positioning his expression into one that didn't reveal his disappointment, he said, "You're joking! It's December. The water's freezing."

"I thought you grew up next to the ocean?"

"So? We didn't swim in it in sub-zero conditions."

"You'd have hated Christmas day with my family. We went into the sea every year without fail. Without wetsuits."

"You're mad."

"Is that a no to paddleboarding then?"

There was no resisting Noah's sad voice, so he sighed and got to his feet. Noah cheered, and ran to the paddleboard like an excited puppy, dragging the cover off to reveal a large blue and white board and a black paddle attached by a cord.

"It's actually a one-person board, but you can easily fit two on if you're careful."

"If I get wet—"

"You'll only get wet if you're bad at it." Noah grinned. "Or if I push you in."

"I think you've forgotten it's my birthday."

Five minutes later, Noah helped—or rather dragged—Zeke onto the paddleboard after him. Noah wedged it onto a rock so they could board, but it still rocked unsteadily as Zeke found his balance kneeling down behind Noah. His terror caused Noah to roar with delight. When they were ready, Noah used his paddle to push off from the side, and the gentle current pushed them downstream.

"There's not really much paddling in paddleboarding after all, huh?" Zeke said.

"Wait until we turn the corner."

They continued gliding gracefully over the water, Noah's strong strokes propelling them forward even faster. When Zeke lurched to the right, Noah reached back and pulled him further towards him. A sense of déjà vu struck him, and it took him a few moments to place his other memory of his face being so close to Noah's neck—on the back of the motorbike, on his first day with him. He pulled Noah against his chest, closing his eyes to enjoy the closeness of his body, resisting the urge to nuzzle into his shoulder blades.

"Hey." Noah ruffled his hair. "Don't fall asleep on me. We need to land here so we can carry the paddleboard back to the mill."

'Landing' involved several failed attempts to stop the paddleboard by ploughing the paddle into the water in a specific direction, usually resulting in them twisting backwards to travel further downstream. Noah was howling with laughter by the time they finally managed to stop—Zeke resorted to gripping a large handful of rushes on the riverbank to anchor them.

The board was surprisingly light, so it didn't take them too long to walk back up to the mill. As they walked, Noah pointed out birds he could see in the trees, and offered up a fun fact for each one. "Chaffinch. Historically kept in cages and made to compete in fierce competitions."

"To the death?"

"I mean, I think it was more like which bird would sing the longest, but your idea is much more interesting."

They hid the paddleboard under the mill again, and Noah returned to his rock, with Zeke sitting on the muddy earth opposite.

"I have something for you." Noah rummaged through his bag before passing him a postcard, and a small, oddly shaped object wrapped in brown paper. "It's from everyone," he added, a light blush creeping up his neck. "Sorry that it's not a proper card. I was working with limited resources."

Zeke marvelled at the multicoloured swirls of watercolour paint on the postcard, forming human-shaped silhouettes. Ten of them standing in a line. One dog-shaped squiggle sat on the far right of the group.

"It's meant to be us, I think. Frankie did it. I think she was missing her past life decorating cakes."

If he forced it to, he could make his brain assign squad members to the silhouettes. Habib, half a head taller than the rest, muscular arms crossed. Meredith and Savannah, legs crossed, arms outstretched in yoga poses. Noah's ponytail. Zeke's glasses.

He traced the brushstrokes. "Wow."

Noah ducked his head. "It's probably a bit much."

How was it possible for his heart to feel so heavy and light at the same time? He turned the card over to read the inscription, recognising Noah's scrawling, child-like handwriting: *Happy Birthday, Zeke! All our love,* followed by nine hastily scribbled names.

He picked up the package. Unwrapping the thin parcel paper, his fingers brushed soft wood.

The paper fell away.

His jaw dropped open.

In his hand was a wooden fox.

"Did you make this for me?" Zeke's voice shook.

Noah had depicted the fox's fur in delicate, swirling lines, and its pointed snout hung slightly ajar. The wood was a warm, golden-brown colour, polished to a smooth finish. The carving possessed a sense of liveliness, as if the fox was just about to spring into action.

"It's not my best work," Noah said quickly. "I mainly do birds, to be honest, so it was a good challenge. The tail was a nightmare."

"Are you joking? Noah, this is…" He trailed off, unable to find words, distracted by the warm tingles circulating in the pit of his stomach. "I don't des—"

Noah stretched his leg out to kick him. "If you start another self-deprecating speech, you're going in that river."

Zeke laughed as he held the small fox up, turning it over and over. It was already his most precious trinket. "How long did this take? When did you even have time to do it?"

"I had to work on it once we'd gone to our rooms, mostly. Honestly, don't worry about it. It was fun."

He stared at Noah. He knew exactly what he wanted to happen next, but was unsure of how to make it happen. The air grew heavy with unspoken tension. He willed himself to stand up and cross the space between them, but his thoughts paralysed him. *Don't be an idiot. You've got it all wrong. He's just being a good friend.*

But good friends didn't look at each other the way Noah was looking at him now. His hazel eyes gleamed with hunger as his lips curved upwards; the beginning of a tentative smile forming. Wordlessly, Noah slipped down from the rock to sit next to him, startling him for a moment. One hand slid into Zeke's, shakily, to entwine their fingers. The other reached across to fist the edge of his coat.

Zeke's thoughts scattered like autumn leaves in the wind. The world around him blurred as the sensation of Noah's hand in his own overwhelmed his thoughts. *Do something,* his brain screamed.

If there was ever a time, it was now.

Zeke swallowed. "Noah, I don't know how to thank you. Not just for this, but for everything. I would have had such a shit time if I didn't land in your squad. I'm so thankful every day that I did." His cheeks already radiated with heat, but his traitorous mouth continued, "I don't even know what I'm saying now, but you've been so awesome, and I think you're amazing and—"

Noah's mouth pressing against his spared him from finishing his rambling speech.

The kiss was perfectly chaste at first: his lips ghosted across Zeke's as soft as a whisper. But before he had time to think, react, or even breathe, Noah cupped the back of his neck and parted Zeke's lips with a warm tongue. Noah became frantic, needy, as his grip tightened, strong arms pulling Zeke closer towards him. Noah ran his hands down Zeke's arms as if he were checking he was still there as he kissed him again, again and again. Unsure of what to do with his own hands, Zeke feebly pawed at Noah's shirt, bundling the fabric there, anchoring Noah to him.

Zeke became untethered from reality.

His stomach liquidized. His heart raced, matching the frenzied flutter of a trapped bird's wings. He was floating, flying, *soaring*.

Distantly, he became aware of the incessant buzzing of Noah's wristband. Noah drew back, panting lightly, and both of them glanced down at the screen. Five missed calls from Vitt. How long had they been kissing for?

"Hold on," Noah muttered, rising to his feet, and Zeke fell forward from the sudden absence of his weight. "What is it?" he snapped into his wristband, causing Zeke to suppress a delirious laugh. Noah had kissed him. Noah had *kissed* him!

"Finally! Habib said you and Zeke were in the city today?" Vitt sounded incredulous.

"He was visiting his sister on their birthday. I saw Khyan's parents for a bit."

"Oh. Did it go okay?"

Noah sighed. "They're... fine. It was hard."

"I was just ringing to see when you'd be back. Murphy posted all of us at the wall in the end today. We lost five men in the morning, which threw everything into chaos."

Noah paced back and forth, concern etched into his face. "*Five*? Anyone we knew well?"

The whiplash change in energy was disorienting, casting a sense of unease over Zeke.

"Not terribly. I think they were mostly new recruits. Two of them were Brian's. He's pretty beat up about it. I think he would appreciate you checking in with him later. Forewarning, the general morale across the barracks is low." Loud chattering in the background and the sound of water running distorted her voice. "Also, Frankie says hurry up back. She's eager to give Zeke his birthday cake."

Noah ran his hand over his face. "She's relentless. Tell her we'll head back now." He hung up with a promise to see them all soon.

Zeke stared at him. *Can we not just go back to the kissing part?*

But Noah remained standing, and he took that as a cue to move. He sprang up, brushing the dirt off him, following Noah's fast pace back down the river. His near-jog made it seem like he was running away from Zeke.

Something was wrong.

"Are you... okay, Noah?" Zeke called out to Noah's back.

"I'm fine."

Okay... Are we really not going to talk about this?

Noah didn't say anything else on the return walk, leaving him to trail unhappily behind him. Did Noah want to pretend that it all never happened? Would they just carry on as normal? What if Noah regretted it so much, he never spoke to him outside of their shifts ever again? Zeke's thoughts quickly drifted to the five people who'd died today, imagining their faces, imagining what their squads were going through right that moment. His problems certainly paled in comparison.

By the time they'd reached their vehicle, Zeke had prepared a short speech to deliver, which let Noah off of whatever hook he clearly felt he was on. *We just got carried away,* he would say. *I won't say anything to anyone. Please just talk to me again.* But after they silently slid into the car seats, Noah didn't start the engine. Zeke glanced over to find him gripping the steering wheel so hard his knuckles had turned white. Noah stared out of the windscreen, straight ahead.

"Noah?"

He was almost imperceptibly trembling.

After an eternity, Noah reached over him and opened the passenger-side door, pushing it ajar.

"If you follow the signs, you can be back in the city in under two hours."

"What? Why would I want to walk back to the city by myself?"

Noah didn't reply, only continued to stare ahead of them.

"Oh..." Zeke said, as he processed what Noah was suggesting. "Well, that's a stupid idea." His brain whirling, he crossed his arms and scowled over at Noah. "Where would I even hide? Wouldn't you get into loads of trouble? Weren't you the one just telling me not to give up, that I'm not a complete waste of space on your squad?" *Weren't you just kissing me?*

Zeke slammed both fists on the dashboard, and Noah flinched. "Jesus Christ! What the hell, Noah?"

"I don't want you to die," Noah whispered.

The intensity of his words wrapped a fist around his heart, squeezed it tight. "I won't die. You'll protect me. You and the others." Cold air leaked in through the open door. Zeke slammed it shut.

"Just go, Zeke, please." Noah was almost begging now. His chin trembled and his dark complexion had paled.

"Christ, Noah, I'm not deserting the military. I didn't work this hard for nothing. Most likely just to be caught and punished," Zeke replied through gritted teeth.

Noah turned towards him, a frantic look in his gaze. "I have some connections who might be able to help hide you. They'll be able to take your chip out."

Zeke let loose a strangled sound and pressed his palms into his forehead. Why was Noah doing this? Especially now? He paused to consider his offer. He tried to imagine himself living a surreptitious, underground life in the city. Zaya sneaking food into some basement he holed up in. Every day spent twitching at the slightest noise. Not seeing the sun. Every image was devoid of colour, of meaning.

His mind drifted back to the pattern of his old life. His routine of going to the lab each day, then returning to his lonely flat every evening. It now seemed remarkably dull. Why was that? Did he really need to be running around shooting monsters—not that he was even capable of that, clearly—for his life to have a purpose? Yet life without Noah, Frankie, and even the others, now felt rather quiet. Rather pointless. But at least he'd be alive...

"There might not even be that much time left," Noah added.

"Huh?" He stared at Noah. What the fuck did *that* cryptic comment mean?

Noah gave a small shake of his head.

"What do you mean, 'there might not even be that much time left?' You can't just throw that out there and expect me not to freak out!"

Noah ran his hands through his hair with considerable force, then made a frustrated sound. "I'm sorry," he said, in a ghost of a voice. "I shouldn't have said that."

One of Noah's hands dropped its steel grip on the steering wheel. It clutched the other one, fingernails digging in hard, forming four half-moon indents on his flesh. He'd draw blood if he didn't stop. Zeke knocked his hand away, towards Noah's chest. "What are you doing? You're going to hurt yourself." He stared at Noah.

"Everything already hurts."

Zeke, out of his depth, shook his head. He clicked his seatbelt in.

"Drive us back," he said.

And Noah did.

NOAH

It was quickly turning out to be a bad day.

Noah had woken up to a series of sharp-bladed knives twisting themselves into his stomach.

The first, when he remembered it was the day of their live capture mission.

The second, the torrential rainstorm beating against his window. Rain again. He was so sick of rain. It provided less than ideal conditions for their excursion today. Not that Murphy would reschedule.

The third and final thrust, the killing blow—a detailed replay of his last conversation with Zeke. He hadn't spoken to or even looked at him since. Not that Noah blamed him.

He was all smiles with Frankie and the others when they'd joined the rest of their squad at the fire pit, festooned with makeshift bunting, yesterday evening. Frankie beamed when she'd presented him the 'carrot cake' she'd cobbled together in the compound's kitchen, and everyone quickly devoured every slice of the peculiar-looking dessert. Apart from Habib frowning at the pair of them as they emerged from the forest path, there'd been a festive atmosphere to the evening—despite the five deaths that ignited his meltdown in front of Zeke.

He told himself this was all for the best. What had he even been playing at anyway, by caving in and kissing Zeke? It was a stupid, selfish act that was bound to have repercussions.

But when he remembered the feel of Zeke's lips on his, the way he'd trembled at his touch, he found he didn't regret it, despite what happened next.

Now, every member of Squad E waited, suited up in full gear, at the south-eastern exit, for Command to give the order for the first gate to rise. Rain fell and glided off their plated armour like rivers, a constant visible reminder of the weather they were about to battle through.

Briefing earlier was a quiet, sombre affair. They'd met in a classroom, and Noah brought up photographs, videos, and maps on the screen. Murphy, on behalf of a client, was requesting the capture of a specific typeB. Originally a male human, early thirties. Squads were never privy to the complex reasons behind these requests. He could only guess that it demonstrated strange behaviour. Behaviour that needed to be studied further.

After Noah talked for a solid thirty minutes, they left the safety of indoors to become soaked in the storm on their journey to the armoury. Before they even entered the check-point at the main gate, all ten of them were moody and sniping at one another.

But there was one way he could improve this day.

Noah sidled up to Splat, tugging him away. "Splat, I need to borrow you for a second," he shouted over the rain, praying Splat could hear him without using their audio feeds.

"What is it?" Splat replied, wary of his serious tone.

"I've been thinking… We never know when one day will be our last."

Splat shuffled his weight from one foot to another. "Okay… Thanks for the… pep talk?"

"Fuck the standard protocol. If you want to be with Meredith, and she wants to be with you, don't let me hold you back."

Splat took a sharp intake of breath.

"I'm serious." Noah grabbed his arm and looked him dead in the eye through the glass panes. "I don't want anyone to have any regrets. Besides, I trust the both of you to remain professional on the field."

"Absolutely," Splat said. "Thanks, boss. This means a lot."

Noah nodded and increased his pace to rejoin the others. Splat followed, looking shell-shocked, like Noah just told him the secrets of the universe.

A massive weight lifted from Noah's shoulders. He'd royally fucked things up with Zeke, but Splat and Meredith may at least enjoy a sliver of happiness in the messed up world they all inhabited.

The 'all clear' came. Five of them would take three motorbikes, five would ride with Wolf in the transport vehicle. When Noah asked Zeke to get into the van rather than share a bike with him again, he looked for any small sign of reaction. There was none.

It's better this way, a small part of him said. The far larger part ached with anguish.

Noah drove on his bike alone, flanked by two others. Meredith and Aoife rode pillion, their crossbows already positioned on their shoulders.

The journey to the target was relatively quiet, especially considering the low light, which typically drew more types out into the open. Only a handful of types, that ventured onto the path attracted by the noise of their engines, needed to be taken down. The thundering weather must have spooked most of them, forcing them inside.

As usual, the further from the city wall they drove, the worse the driving conditions became. His bad mood only increased when they hit a colossal pile of rubble that blocked their paths. Next to it, a half of a large house remained standing, with the rest of it spilling out into a heap of broken concrete and twisted metal. Splat promised it hadn't been there when he checked the route that morning—it must have finally succumbed to damage inflicted from prior bombings.

"We don't have time to move all that. Looks like we're on foot from here." Noah marked their location on the map, clenching his jaw. They'd have to drag the type an entire kilometre to get back here once they'd caught it. He hoped whatever research came out of this was worth the effort.

Once they'd helped each other over the rubble, they entered their standard V formation and marched through the torrent of rainfall. Water pelted the glass of Noah's visor so hard it created a deafening sound.

Two flashes of sudden light illuminated the dark city ahead of them, followed by a roar of thunder.

"Noah? I don't like this," shouted Vitt.

The wild wind picked up its speed, throwing numerous cans, boxes and a rogue basketball at them.

"Is this technically a hurricane yet?" asked Habib. "I think we should turn back. If Murphy needs the type this badly, she can come and get it herself."

Beside them, telephone poles swayed in the wind, wobbling like pins at a bowling alley.

"Wind speed is seventy-two miles per hour," reported Splat.

"We need to get inside somewhere," shouted Noah. Water trickled down the back of his neck, making him shiver. "Then we can decide what to do."

"Incoming!" came a sudden cry. Splat pushed the drone feed onto everyone's visors. "Two separate clusters. Five and nine o'clock. Orders?"

Noah groaned as his brain absorbed the scene. To their left, four typeAs were jumping out of a smashed, second-story window, pushing and jostling each other. To their right, three others were emerging from behind an upturned car, crouching on hands and knees. Noah swiped at his helmet: the world was increasingly becoming wet blurs of colour.

"Our visibility is too poor," Noah shouted, then pointed to a crumbling brick wall. "Fall back! Backs to that wall."

But they were too slow. Both clusters charged through the storm towards them, jumping to unnatural heights and throwing themselves at the squad. Within seconds, Squad E unloaded round after round, taking the roaring storm to a crescendo. Around him, flashes of light and furious screaming and wailing wrapped him in a distorted bubble. Panic pumped through him. Where was Zeke?

He pawed at the screen on his helmet, trying to wipe the rain off, while scanning the backs of his flock's suits for their names. He found the one he was looking for: Bates. The black Zeke-shaped figure was running off down a side road, chasing after another dark shape—one moving across the tarmac in an inhuman scramble. He charged after him, a stream of expletives running through his head. Why had Zeke chosen now to play the hero? What part of protocol involved running off alone in a storm?

If he's trying to prove something, that's on you.

"Zeke!" Noah shouted as he tripped over a reel of rusty wire, catching himself at the last second.

Ahead, Zeke cornered his target against a high, redbrick wall. The typeA turned to face him, slashing the air with its claws. Noah raised his rifle, but there was no way he could shoot it from here, in these conditions, without risking hitting Zeke.

The type shuffled closer, arms outstretched.

Noah fell into the space between two heartbeats. Zeke was about to die, right in front of his eyes.

Flashes of light exploded in front of Zeke.

The typeA dropped to the ground.

Zeke turned to Noah, staring at the firearm in his hands.

He wanted to cheer, wanted to hug Zeke and spin him around. But there was no time for that. He grabbed him roughly by the arm and dragged him away from the type. "We need to get out of this storm. We're too vulnerable."

"Fine by me!"

"Forrest, Bates, where are you?" came Habib's voice through his helmet.

"Barakat! We're just down a side road. Can't you see us on the map?"

"The si—" Habib's voice cut off, replaced by silence. "—and out. Can—"

The connection ended.

Noah pressed the buttons to reconnect. "Walsh? Shun? Bianco?"

The audio feed on Noah's helmet made a horrifying clicking noise before powering down. Flashing symbols on the side informed him the signal was gone. The drone feed was therefore also down. He used his wristband to switch to the radio setting, but it was no use. That was down, too. They had no tracking, no comms, and no visuals. They were alone.

"Goddamn it!" Noah shouted. To nobody, as Zeke could no longer hear him.

Zeke threw his arms out in an alarmed 'what's going on?' gesture.

Noah shook his head, pulling Zeke back in the direction they were last with the others, while they raised their arms over their visors to keep the worst of the rain off their helmets. The glass was supposed to be water resistant, but that notion currently felt comical. If a cluster swarmed them right now, they were dead. Flashes of lightning sliced through the dark sky and Noah increased their pace, tugging at Zeke when he fell behind.

The space where they'd left the others had been abandoned. It was impossible to guess what direction they'd gone, so Noah picked one at random and ran as fast as he could without slipping, dragging Zeke along with one hand and vaguely aiming his rifle with the other.

Zeke pointed at something, waving his arm around wildly. Up ahead was a small structure, barely bigger than a shed, its tiled roof miraculously intact. Its existence puzzled Noah for a moment before he finally understood what it was: a decrepit bus shelter. An old-fashioned one, mostly found in small villages or towns, made of concrete and bricks. Zeke clutched at Noah's arm, jumping up and down like when Wolf was excited, and dragged him towards the tiny building.

Noah tried to shout at Zeke over the storm, but it was no use. He gestured at the open doorway to the building and put his thumb down.

Zeke pointed to something on the ground and then gestured to the bus shelter. A heavy-looking fence panel—recently ripped from its past life, if the fresh splinters along its right edge were anything to go by—lay on its side on the ground, a handful of steps from the shelter.

Together, they dragged it towards the shelter. It was difficult to manoeuvre, but eventually they positioned it over the gaping hole, sealing off the wind and rain, and the world.

"We're safe for a second." Noah tugged his helmet off, turning the headlight on and placing it on top of a pile of rubble to create a makeshift lamp. Zeke copied him, and soon the small interior, illuminated by their lights, became visible. A rusty saucepan sat glumly in the corner, lying on a bed of shattered glass from the timetable board.

Zeke stepped closer to him, shivering. "Did you see me kill that type?"

He bit back a smile. Zeke's eyes gleamed with pride. Although he really should lecture him for running off alone, he couldn't bring himself to.

"Of course." He slapped him on the back. "Well done."

Zeke's face lit up like a firework and he grinned to himself before asking, "Has this ever happened before? Both audio feeds failing?"

"Don't worry. We'll have the radio signal back again in no time. The back-up generator will just need a kick or two."

The wind howled outside, an angry beast seeking its prey. A pang of worry for Wolf shot through Noah, but he pushed it aside. Vitt would make sure he was alright.

They collapsed on the bench, looking worse for wear with its scaly patches of paint. The awkward tension between them that had momentarily been forgotten made its way back in full force, and an uncomfortable silence filled the air. Noah knew he needed to say something, fix it, apologise. But instead, he picked at a spot of paint, covering his black glove with flakes of blue.

After a while, Zeke reached out and grabbed his hand, stilling it. "Stop that."

"Why? We have nothing else to do."

Zeke sighed, but didn't let go. After fumbling around with his glove's catches, he tugged it off. He grasped Noah's hand gently as he pulled it closer to the light, inspecting it. His behaviour confused him until Zeke brushed his thumb over the pale, small half-moon shaped scars on his skin, noticeable only to someone who knew what they were looking for. Zeke pushed his sleeve up—the inch or so that the material would allow—his face blanching when he found more marks peppering Noah's forearm.

Noah's cheeks prickled with heat. He pushed Zeke off, tucking his bare hand away by folding his arms. "It's never on purpose."

"What does that even mean?"

"You try leading a squad, pointlessly fighting day after day in an impossible war, while mourning a dead boyfriend," he spat. "See if you come out of that entirely sane. Back off, okay?"

His words had the desired effect: Zeke shrank back from him, shuffling away on the bench. He looked almost afraid of him, which drove a nail through Noah's heart. Noah reached for him, but Zeke flinched.

"Don't," Zeke warned.

"What's wrong?"

"What's wrong? What's *wrong*? Are you kidding me right now? How about the fact that yesterday you kissed me, then ignored me, and then immediately tried to get rid of me?" Hurt shimmered in his eyes. "Does that ring any bells?"

Noah's chest constricted. How could he have been so idiotic? So cruel? "I didn't try to 'get rid of you'. I was only trying to give you the way out you've desperately wanted over the last two months." *I was only trying to keep you safe. To properly protect you the only way I can.*

"I've also been working my arse off for the past two months." Zeke's voice shook with anger as he kicked at the ground. "I thought you believed in me," he said. "Then you just... gave up on me."

Noah's heart split in two. "No!" How could Zeke think that? "Of course I believe in you, Zeke."

"Then why did you ask me to run away?"

"Why didn't you *want* to run away? Why did you stay?"

A silence. A heartbeat. A breath held in anticipation.

They surveyed each other in the near dark. Zeke moved ever so slightly closer to him on the bench.

"Because I... like it here? I like our squad. I like being useful. And I'm getting better at it all, slowly. And..." Zeke nudged his leg so that his ankle was brushing Noah's.

"And?" Noah said, in a barely audible rasp, the words sticking to his throat.

Zeke slid across the remainder of the bench, closing the small distance between them, reaching over to tug Noah's body closer to him.

That was all the encouragement Noah needed. He cupped Zeke's face with two hands, then pressed his lips to his.

Zeke gasped. Then gently took Noah's bottom lip between his own.

Noah moved his hands down to Zeke's waist, easily lifting him onto his lap, despite his clunky combat suit. Zeke straddled Noah, his eyes flashing between desire and panic in the dim light. Gently, Noah removed Zeke's glasses, placing them onto the bench. Taking Zeke's face in his hands again, he opened his mouth with his tongue, feeling him melt against him. He pressed hard on Zeke's back, forcing him as close as possible to him, and Zeke responded by wrapping himself tighter against him.

The pragmatic part of his brain screamed at him. *This is a bad idea, this is a* very *bad idea.*

He silenced his inner voice by revelling in the feel of Zeke's body against his. He sucked Zeke's bottom lip into his mouth, nibbling gently on the swollen skin, almost laughing at the cherry lip balm he tasted there.

Noah's hands slid down to Zeke's neck, thumbing gently at his soft skin. Under his fingers, Zeke's pulse thudded faster than seemed humanly possible as he released tiny, breathy moans between kisses. He became drunk on the knowledge that *he* was doing that to Zeke, that Zeke wanted him just as much as he wanted Zeke. Soon he couldn't hear the raging wind, or the rain battering the shelter's roof. He became lost in a fantasy world where it was just him and Zeke. Here and now.

They came apart for air, panting, resting their faces on each other's shoulders.

"For you," breathed Zeke, directly into his ear, tingling every nerve in his body.

"What?" choked out Noah, breathless and half-delirious.

"I stayed for you."

Four little words. Four little words that quickly wormed their way inside of him, destined to stay a part of him forever.

A ravenous fire sparked in Noah's stomach as he pulled Zeke forcefully back towards him, pressing his lips to his once again. Zeke drew back, staring at Noah reverently, liquefying Noah's insides.

"We shouldn't be doing this," Noah groaned, even though every part of his body was saying, *yes, yes, yes.* "I'm your CO."

"I can keep a secret," Zeke said, a bashful smirk forming on his lips.

Noah pushed Zeke's hair back from his face. "I told you to go yesterday because I can't face losing you, Zeke. I think it would be... I think it would be the final straw. For me." He took a breath. "I can't always be there to protect you. Not every time. I wish I could, but I won't always be there. You'd be safe in the city. You'd have to stay hidden, but you would be alive."

"But if I go, then who will protect you?"

Noah tried not to laugh at the absurd idea of Zeke protecting him. He ran his hands down Zeke's arms before squeezing his hands. He brought each one to his lips and kissed them.

"Okay, fine, you have a highly skilled, literal squad of soldiers who'd all die to protect you." Zeke snickered before continuing, "But what if I don't want to be away from you now? What if I'd rather take my chances by your side, than be holed up by myself, hiding in some basement?"

"Zeke..." Noah started, but Zeke silenced his protests with his mouth.

"It's too late," Zeke whispered, his voice rough and sultry. "There's no getting rid of me now."

Zeke's body trembled as he reached up to brush Noah's cheeks with his thumbs. Then Zeke's unsteady hands slid back and upwards to yank on his ponytail with some force—was he was trying to free his hair from its tie? After a final tug, the elastic band snapped, and Noah's hair tumbled down onto his shoulders. Zeke reached straight for it, scratching into his scalp with one hand as he ran Noah's hair through his fingers with the other.

It had been a long, long time since anyone had touched Noah like this. He'd forgotten how amazing it could feel. Zeke continued to comb Noah's hair with his fingers, and a soft moan escaped Noah's lips as he nuzzled into the touch. With the still-howling wind outside, he barely caught it when Zeke said, "I can't tell you how long I've wanted to do that."

Burning flames of heat consumed him. Abruptly, he surged upwards, pulling Zeke against his chest as he carried him across to the other side of the shelter. He pushed him against the wall, hard. "I would tell you how much I've wanted to do this," he growled into Zeke's ear. "But I think I'll show you instead."

Their tongues slid against each other once more as Noah pushed his lower body into Zeke's, the hard shells of their suits clashing against each other. He would give anything for them to be anywhere else right now—anywhere else that wasn't in the middle of a monster-filled war-zone.

Zeke's grip on his hair became tighter and tighter but what should have been painful only served to arouse him further. Since when had he been into hair pulling? He'd been missing out. He moved his hand down to graze feather-light touches over Zeke's groin—buried under multiple layers of material—and his gaze bore into Zeke's as he raised his eyebrows questioningly.

"I'm not..." began Zeke, flushing even redder, averting his gaze and biting his lip. "I'm not t-terribly experienced... not experienced at all actually, in this particular—"

Noah placed a finger over Zeke's lips. He shot Zeke a smouldering smirk. "I've had it said I'm an excellent teacher."

The look of desire on Zeke's face took Noah's breath away. Zeke began tugging at Noah's combat suit, trying to find chinks in the armour to slip his hands into.

This is a terrible idea.

This is a very *terrible idea.*

With a series of well-practiced moves, Noah removed his own chest plate and made quick work of Zeke's as well, then pulled out the springy material of their undershirts, still damp from the rain, from their trousers. Simultaneously, hands slid behind backs, stroking the skin they found there. Noah reached all the way to the nape of Zeke's head, drawing him in close. He nuzzled his cheek for a moment before moving to kiss him again, his lips parting Zeke's.

Noah's fingers slid over the base of Zeke's scalp, finding something there. Something hot and wet.

He froze.

Noah released Zeke so fast that he staggered forwards, confusion in his eyes. Noah held up his fingers to the light. Red liquid gleamed in the light.

He stared at Zeke in horror. "I'm so sorry."

"It's fine," said Zeke, but his voice trembled as he averted his eyes from the blood. "You said we're safe in here, right?"

"I said we were *relatively* safe. We're not safe enough for me to be throwing you against rusty metal surfaces. We need to blue tape it, *now.*"

Noah opened his medical kit before Zeke even had time to sit down on the bench. He thoroughly cleaned the wound—which was just a scratch, really—before smearing a generous amount of blocker all over his neck. Zeke gasped in pain, squeezing Noah's leg tightly as Noah rubbed it in.

"Sorry."

He completed the mission by taping over the cut with triple the amount of blue tape it needed.

"Stop apologising," Zeke said, taking the hand Noah offered to help him up. He kept hold of it, stroking its back with his thumb. "You've just saved my life, again."

A wicked smile crept over his lips, and Noah ached to kiss him again. But outside, the sound of the rain petered out to a slow trickle.

As if on cue, both of their wristbands spluttered to life, alerting them to incoming radio audio. "This is Barakat with Bianco. Radio signal is back up. Requesting rendezvous point, over," came Habib's strained voice.

"This is Forrest, requesting a status report from every officer, over."

Ten minutes later, they were back in their suits, ready to leave the bus station. Noah delayed them by agonising over Zeke's armour, making sure it was perfectly protecting every inch of him. Together, they heaved the fence panel away from the open doorway, and slipped back into the open world.

The *real* world.

The world where you couldn't go around kissing whoever you liked with no consequences. Especially not members of a team you commanded.

But there was no turning back from this. He'd touched the sun, and remembered how good it felt. Now, he would rather burn than give up another chance at love.

As they walked along, side-by-side, he wasn't sure what to say to Zeke, or where they should even go from here. "I'm sorry about yesterday," he said at last. "I freaked out. I know it was a shit thing to do. I think a part of it was me trying to punish myself for kissing you by pushing you away."

Zeke nudged into him. "You're forgiven. I'm sure you can make it up to me."

"So, when you said you weren't 'terribly experienced' earlier, what did you mean exactly?" Noah asked, glad for the barrier of their helmets.

"I... I just meant that I haven't slept with any guys before."

A wave of possessiveness surged up inside Noah as he realised that Zeke's inexperience didn't bother him at all. But he put those thoughts into a deep vault inside his brain, locked it twice. He needed to focus. They needed to regroup with their scattered squad, and there was still a typeB to capture.

"Tango-Quebec-six-seven-nine-eight-seven-two," Noah said, enunciating each word to bring up the mapping program.

Noah and Zeke raced through waterlogged streets that streamed with debris. Drizzle still trickled down, obscuring their vision as they made their way to the meeting point. When they'd turned the final corner, after jumping over several lake-sized puddles, Savannah waved her gun at them under a large oak tree. He scanned the group. Eight soldiers, dressed in black. One soggy dog. Each member of his flock accounted for.

Wolf brushed against him as they joined the rest of Squad E and he allowed himself three seconds of smoothing the dog's ears before he launched back into CO mode. "Status report."

"No injuries. Tracking system popped back up a second ago. Target remains in the same location, approximately ten meters under ground level, half a klick from here," said Vitt.

Noah turned to Splat. "King, do we have visuals?"

"Tech support radioed me a few minutes ago to say support systems were rebooting ASAP."

"Roger. We'll wait for all systems to be live. Then we'll enter the building, locate the target, tranquillize, then bag-and-drag it to the vehicle."

Simple.

Things were back on track.

NOAH

Thirty minutes later, the ten of them gazed up at a large, derelict warehouse. Vines twisted around a metal shutter gate that probably hadn't opened in a decade. Above it, a faded sign proclaimed it the property of the Juicy Orchard Cider Company. Its logo, an apple with a grinning face and legs, possessed a slightly deranged feel. Half the building's grey slate roof had collapsed into itself; several tiles lay scattered on the ground nearby.

"There must be a basement," said Habib. Everyone stared at the map open on their visors, looking at the red flashing dot they were now only a handful of steps away from. "It's still underground."

"Grand," said Aoife, grinning. "With any luck, it's found the cider stash and we'll get down there to find it completely sloshed."

"We can only hope," said Vitt.

"Aww hell, no," said Splat. "Even better if it leaves the cider for us. We're going to need it by the end of this cake and arse party."

They surveyed the perimeter, damp, shivering, and miserable. Eventually, they concluded the types were entering and exiting through the caved in roof. Noah and Splat debated the possibility of blowing up a part of the wall, but Noah expressed concern that it would jeopardise the structure of the building, potentially cutting them off from the target permanently. Splat sulked before eventually agreeing.

"Let's just cut through the shutter," Habib said, already growing bored with the argument. Habib swung his backpack around and produced a small circular saw.

Noah groaned. "That'll take ages."

"It's this, or scale the wall and jump down the hole in the roof."

Sighing, Noah gestured for Habib to go ahead. The squad formed a circle around Habib while he cut the metal shutter painstakingly slowly, producing soft sparks of light. Splat resorted to knock-knock jokes to entertain himself and only stopped when Frankie finally cracked and told him to shut up.

Habib pushed the metal outline of a small archway backwards, and it fell with a satisfying thud. Splat whizzed the drone through. Finding it empty, they sent Wolf ahead to do a last sweep. After he returned, barking twice before sitting down to give the all clear, they all hurried inside, eager to be out of the drizzle.

"Thank the heavens," Aoife declared, perching on a wooden box. It disintegrated under her weight, sending her sprawling downwards. The entire squad howled with half-suppressed laughter before Noah reluctantly reminded them to be quiet.

"Where's this cider at, then?" asked Savannah, peering around at the dim space. Around ten high shelving units divided the warehouse, but it was largely empty. A scattering of rotten wooden crates littered the shelves, some spilling onto the floor. Near the back, two yellow forklifts sat plugged into the wall. Noah gave the signal, and they fanned out in pairs, inspecting the surroundings, taking photographs of everything for HQ. Noah, alone with Zeke for a few seconds, squeezed his hand for a moment before letting go. Even through Zeke's helmet, he caught a beaming smile that sent his heart into a flutter.

Get it together, Forrest. This is not the time, nor the place, to be acting like a lovesick teenager.

"Boss!" Splat called them over to the corner, which housed a door that led to a tiny corridor. "Stairs."

Noah stared down the dim staircase that spiralled around to a pitch-black basement. Splat sent the drone down; it hurtled merrily off into oblivion.

"Listen up. For most of you, it's your first live capture mission. Remember, we are *not* using ammunition down there. Not unless you want Murphy to put a bullet in your head." A small round of nervous laughter circulated. "Sanders, Walsh, and myself are all carrying the tranq guns. Leave it to us, and don't forget it takes ten seconds or so to take effect. Bates, Fleming—I'm leaving you up here with Bianco this time,"—he gave Splat what he hoped was a pointed look—"as I know *she* won't run off and leave you." He grinned to show he was joking.

"Depends if I see any cider or not," Vitt said.

"The rest of us will head down."

"Uhh... boss?" said Splat. He was fiddling with the buttons on his helmet. "The feed's gone dark."

"Don't tell me the drone is playing up again," said Luo.

"It's not like before... it was working perfectly, but now the connection has been severed."

Savannah sighed. "Theme of our day."

They watched the few seconds of footage the drone recorded. It had flown down the staircase before sweeping the basement with an illuminating spotlight. No types in sight, but plenty of industrial clutter. Suddenly, the camera dipped, like something knocked it, and then, blackness.

"We'll have to presume fatal error. Count it out of our strategy," said Noah. "Intel suggests that we're only expecting the one type down there. This shouldn't be a difficult mission." So why was he himself looking at the staircase like it led directly to hell?

The seven of them loaded their weapons—in case of surprise guests—before creeping down the staircase. Noah's stomach lurched at leaving Zeke, even though he would be twenty times safer guarding the top floor than he would be in this godforsaken basement.

Light from their helmets darted around the space as the soldiers scanned the room at the bottom. Rows and rows of stacked metal barrels, glass bottles, and wooden crates lined the walls in the cavernous space.

He lifted his hand, signalling them to stop. It was quiet. Deathly quiet. Was there even a type down here? Usually it would have charged towards them by now, drawn by the noise and the need to feed. He glanced at his map. The tracker—shot into the type by a previous team—flashed red. It was only accurate to ten meters, but they appeared to be almost right on top of each other.

"Let's keep going," he said.

As one, they crept forward.

An unusual arrangement drew him to over to the far wall. A camp bed was set up in the basement's corner. An oil lamp lay nearby, on its side. Someone hiding out here in the first wave perhaps, a decade ago? But no. This felt... more recent. But types—even typeBs—didn't set up beds, did they? Surely it was some brave—or stupid—person trying to exist outside of the city walls?

A few scraps of paper near the oil lamp caught his attention, and he knelt to get a look. Certainly, someone had written something on them, but it was meaningless scribbles to Noah. If there was a code to the vague symbols, he couldn't decipher it.

"What's that?" Meredith asked, pointing to something running up the wall. The combined light of all their headlamps lit up the space. Three metal brackets—shelfless now—adorned the otherwise plain wall. Three metal brackets, and one long piece of metal wire...

Curious, Noah reached out to touch it, but Meredith slapped his hand back. The wire, which ended in a coiled pile near the camp bed, stretched up through the ceiling into the room above via a small hole.

"Bianco, I need you to look for some wire on the ground floor. It's poking up through the basement to your level. About forty steps to your left if you're facing away from the stairs. But don't touch it."

Vitt struggled for a few minutes, cursing under her breath, before finally announcing, "Ah ha! You were way off-piste. Found it to the right of the stairs."

"No..." Noah said, frowning. He may have been wet and tired, but he wasn't at the level where he'd confuse left and right. Yet.

"I can see it. Very thin wire. I'm not surprised we missed it earlier. It goes all the way up through the hole in the roof. But what's it for? It couldn't take any weight, surely..." She paused, and there was some clattering around as Vitt moved things around. "Oh! The wire goes all the way across."

"Okay... just go back to Bates and Fleming now. Stay with them. Thanks."

"What's going on, Noah?" said Habib, arms crossed.

He examined the wire again, but there was nothing else to see. "I'm not sure. But I know I want to find that typeB. I want to find that typeB, *now*."

"Shh!" hissed Luo, cupping his palm near his helmet, gesturing for them to listen.

Noah could hear it. A scratching sound. Subtle, but definitely there. And the sound of light, raspy breaths. Coming from—

In a grotesque parody of every childhood nightmare, two scaly arms shot out from under the bed, grabbing and clawing at the nearest human legs: Meredith's.

A single terrified scream from Meredith ricocheted through the basement before she caught herself. The type's claws missed her leg by millimetres as she jumped back.

In its haste to get to its prey, the typeB flipped the bed over, sending it flying across the room. It picked up the coil of wire and yanked hard. Noah frowned. What was it doing? No wonder the research team wanted to study it.

"Don't kill it," Noah shouted. Even though all he wanted to do was to sink six bullets into its brain, this would all be for nothing if it ended up dead. He signalled for Wolf to get behind him and stay there, not wanting to risk him in the carnage. Wolf gave him a small huff as he trotted off.

He raised his tranquilliser gun, and Aoife and Meredith did the same. Each of the three guns was loaded with six small darts. He fired off two, both narrowly missing the monster to bounce off the wall.

Noah became aware that Vitt and Zeke were asking a series of concerned questions through the audio feed, but he tuned them out.

The typeB furiously bounced between the seven squad members, who darted, ducked, and dived away from it. If they were only trying to kill it, their mission would have been over in seconds. Habib and Luo threw as many objects at it as they could get their hands on, slowing it down. It roared, revealing a too-wide jaw and far too many sharp teeth. TypeBs were supposed to be the more human ones, but to Noah right now, it looked every bit the monster from hell he knew it was.

"Fuuuuuuuuuck!" shouted Habib. He looked down at his calf, then at Aoife. "You shot me, you idiot!"

Wolf whined in distress and Noah's blood ran ice-cold for a moment—but they weren't shooting actual bullets. Only the sort that will put you to a deep, comatose sleep.

Habib collapsed onto the floor, groaning.

"Circle him!" Noah shouted.

"Noah? What's going on down there?" said Vitt.

He could barely hear her over the commotion in the room. Luo was attempting to throw glass bottles of cider at the typeB's head, but most missed the target, splattering sticky liquid all over the floor. Reaching the end of the bottle supply, Luo rummaged in a box beside him and started throwing, of all things, rolls of sticky labels at the creature.

Gritting his teeth, Noah said, "Bianco, down here now. Bates and Fleming, stay put. Keep your eyes trained on the hole in the roof. If there's even a hint of movement, shout. That's an order!"

He turned back to assess the scene. At least ten yellow darts lay useless on the floor. They didn't have many more chances left. If they didn't hit the target soon, he'd have to face a very embarrassing meeting with the captain.

The thin rags the typeB wore flapped in the air as it jumped, frog-like, eight feet across the room, towards Luo, who staggered back. Out of the corner of his eye, Noah saw Vitt reaching the bottom step, rifle at the ready.

It's no good. He raised his crossbow. *I'm not risking anyone's life over this.*

The type raised its left claw, powerful biceps flexing as it—

A strangled cry of shock came out of its warped mouth. It turned around, a yellow dart embedded in its cheek. It tried to swipe it away, but couldn't coordinate its movements. Already, it was swaying. Then it sank to the floor, howling softly, just a few steps away from Habib's unmoving body. Finally, it stilled.

"*Porca puttana!*" whispered Vitt, running to Habib and grabbing his wrist. "He's breathing and stable. Which one of you twits shot him?" Vitt pulled the dart out of his leg, looking up when nobody answered her.

"Not important right now," said Noah. He turned to Meredith, chief medic and miracle worker. "Can we wake him up? There's no way any of us can carry his weight."

Luo and Aoife set about rolling the typeB into the black, multi-handled carry bag.

Meredith rummaged around in a med-kit. "The fact that he dropped down cold is not a good sign. They're not calibrated for the human body. Let's get Command on the line, pronto."

Noah reached for his wristband, but paused when he heard an almighty crash coming from above them. Stomach lurching, he was at the bottom of the staircase within seconds, the sound of his squad's footsteps following close behind. He emerged into the light of the ground floor to find Frankie and Zeke standing by a toppled over shelving unit, rifles trained on it. Wolf circled the metal structure and bared his teeth.

"Is there a type under there?" Noah asked. "Alive?"

"Yes, and unsure. We pushed it over," replied Frankie.

Zeke turned to Noah. "Sorry. I panicked. I didn't think about the noise."

Noah and Luo pulled up the unit slightly, the strength of Luo's bionic doing most of the work.

"Looks pretty dead to me," Vitt said.

They let the unit drop back down.

"It came from the roof," said Frankie, using her rifle to point to the gaping hole.

Noah squinted. There was the wire Vitt had described earlier, a tiny silver sliver, reaching up, out of the gap to... where? On instinct, he used the collapsed shelving unit as a springboard to jump onto the second-to-top shelf on another set of racks. He groaned as he pulled himself up onto the final level. Where was Habib when you needed him?

"Forrest?" Vitt shouted.

"Ring Command and request back up, now."

He had to see, pronto, where the wire led, and how much danger they were about to be in. The jump to the edge of the caved in roof looked precarious, but he only hesitated for a second before leaping upwards, fingers scrambling for purchase on the slabs of slat.

For one horrible second, he slipped backwards, and imagined his bones breaking in all sorts of sickening ways before his other hand grasped onto a steel chimney tube. Pulling himself to his feet on the roof of the warehouse, his eyes traced the wire. Pulled taut by invisible weight, it geared off to the left, into a tree that brushed up against the building. The tangled branches easily hid it from them when they surveyed the perimeter earlier.

Noah lay flat on his stomach, lifting a branch and peering down. He could only track the fine silver thread for another few feet before it became lost in the foliage. He frowned. Was this strange set up the work of humans, potentially many years ago? Or typeBs? The latter idea made his skin crawl. What could it possibly be for?

Straight ahead of him, a small flock of birds erupted from the vegetation, snapping him back to reality. He was on his feet within a heartbeat, rifle aimed and ready to fire.

"Activity. North-west, less than half a klick," he said. He drew in a sharp intake of breath at what he saw next.

Dozens of them. Tonnes. *Hundreds?*

Too far away to say for sure if they were typeAs or Bs, but hurtling towards them at full speed, nevertheless. Together, they formed an enormous writhing beast, almost tripping each other up in their close, tumbling desperation to reach the warehouse.

"Everyone up here, now!" he shouted. He wanted them off the ground. "There's many more coming and we need the height advantage. King, bring whatever you can carry from the bomb kit."

"I'm still with Habib in the basement," said Savannah. "We injected him with adrenaline, but he isn't lucid or mobile yet. What's going on?"

A string of explosive curses filtered through his mind as he struggled to form a plan. Should they all hurry back to the basement, and bottleneck the types as they came down the narrow staircase? *But there are so many.*

"Forrest?" came Vitt's voice. "I've requested backup. It's not going to be anytime soon, though."

"Roger," he said, eyes trained on the army of monsters charging towards them. Behind him, he heard several squad members making their way onto the roof, grunting.

As his squad surveyed the scene, the round of gasps they made alarmed him. He needed them ready and focussed.

An unadulterated scream burst through his feed, distorting his senses. Was that Savannah?

"There's more," Savannah said in a hoarse whisper. "In the basement. I can hear them."

This was too much. Far too much.

"Noah!" came his name again, but this time, not through the feed. He turned to find Zeke, face distorted in panic. Zeke grabbed his hand, squeezing it tight. He locked eyes with Noah, eyes boring into him.

He turned to his flock.

"Walker, Bianco is coming down there to help you get Habib out of there. Then the three of you grab Wolf and get out of the building. There's a clear path if you head south down the road. The noise from our firearms should attract most of them towards us. Try and find somewhere safe while we take most of these down."

Vitt didn't waste a second; she turned and disappeared back through the hole.

"King, I want all the ET-MPs we have ready in two minutes."

"I couldn't carry my whole box up here, but I've got enough material for something," Splat replied, and set to work.

Noah scanned the expectant remaining soldiers and the weapons they shouldered. Six rifles, three snipers, two light machine guns.

"While we wait for the grenades, Walsh, Sanders and I will snipe as many as we can. Fleming, Bates, Shun, get ready with your rifles for when they're close enough."

"Can't we just run?" stammered Zeke.

Noah shook his head. "There's too many."

A twinge of pride coursed through him as his flock created their formation, gliding between each other like water through fingers. The oncoming horde surged forwards, jumping over puddles, machine wreckage, and each other to get to their destination.

At least it's stopped raining. He fought back an absurd giggle.

"Mostly typeAs with a sprinkle of Bs," announced Luo.

"Take out the Bs first," Noah ordered.

Squad E crouched in position, bracing. Noah lined up his shot and began to snipe. With the amount there was, he was sure to hit more than he'd miss. Indeed, a handful of types did fall to their feet, to be trampled on by others. But most carried on, now closer than ever to the warehouse.

"Alright, begin with the rifles!" Noah said, at the same time as Splat's voice spluttered through his feed.

"Forrest! Over there! Six o'clock!"

Noah turned to find Splat—numerous coloured wires and all sorts wrapped around him, attached to his belt and spilling out of his pockets—pointing in the opposite direction to where they were facing. He ran over to Splat, whose grim gaze focussed on the surrounding countryside. Another horde, the same size as the other if not bigger, ran across a muddy field.

It was over.

They were all going to die.

Noah shook his head.

He remained motionless until Splat whacked him on the back of his helmet with his fist, hard. "Don't do this to us now, Noah."

"Forrest!"

Can everybody please stop saying my goddamned name? It's not going to do you any good. I can't save you.

But the cry came again, distinctly Zeke-sounding, and Noah found that his legs were sprinting over to him. Zeke waved his rifle, pressing down on an unmoving trigger—jammed—in Noah's direction with wide eyes and shaking hands. Noah whacked it against the tiles of the roof. The same trick had worked once before. He tested it, unloading a round at the closest type—*they're so close now*—thanking a god he didn't believe in when it fired.

He thrust the rifle back into Zeke's hand before ordering Meredith over to Splat's side.

"Brace! First explosive in position, southwards. You've got five!" Splat cried.

Noah pulled Zeke and Frankie back from the edge. Two seconds later, a booming, deafening roar came from behind them, heat warming their backs. Both new recruits turned to look, but Noah slapped their arms, gesturing for them to continue firing, even through the wisps of smoke the bomb produced.

Beside him, Luo reached the end of his clip and paused to reload. Catching Noah's eye, they shared a look that said, *Is this really it? Here? Now?*

Commotion behind him. Splat was back over to their side. The types were about a minute from breaching the perimeter. Splat dropped to his knees, programming his next explosive. "Ten seconds!" he shouted, launching the grenade off the roof, to the far side of the car park, into the thicket of the pulsing mass of types, now so close to the shutter gate they'd sliced open earlier.

A shockwave of power and heat pounded through the air. Zeke and Frankie dropped to their knees, their faces awestruck as they watched types hurtle across the concrete or become devoured by the inferno.

"I'm running out of kit, boss." Splat broadcasted. "And I can't build them fast enough. Can Zeke come help me for a second?"

Noah tapped Zeke's shoulder and nudged him towards Splat.

The car park was ablaze now. Several vehicles burned ferociously, one causing another explosion as the fire tore through it. But through the carnage, a multitude of types remained. Some charged on towards them even while on fire, remnants of clothing or hair fuelling the flames as it blackened their skin.

Noah scanned the horizon for any sign of Vitt, Savannah and Habib, but there was no sign of them. Hopefully, they were safe.

Then something directly below them caught his eye. "They're entering through the shutter gate!"

"Not all of them." Meredith pointed her gun at the closest tree. "I just shot one down from there."

As she spoke, two sets of scaly grey arms pulled up to a sturdy, high branch.

Before there was time to help Meredith dispatch them, Luo dragged him over to the opening in the roof, pointing wildly. "We need to kick the unit down else they'll be up here before we know it!"

"Zeke has activated the third device. South. Five seconds!"

"Forrest, I don't think we have many rounds left."

"Forrest, what's our next orders?"

More demands came flooding through, but Noah tuned them out. He pulled on a memory of Leo's voice, back during the worst weeks of his life. The doctor's calm voice told him: *breathe in, breathe out.*

He nodded at Luo, and together they kicked over the shelving unit they'd used to climb onto the roof. Several typeBs were already at the bottom, jumping out of the way as it crashed to the floor. Hungry eyes gazed up at them as the types snarled and spat. Then, to Noah's horror, three of them began to push the unit back up. One of them—a bulging, fat creature—made a series of grunting noises, which attracted two typeAs to come and join in. The five monsters worked side-by-side, united in their mission.

He made to kick the shelf again as it lurched diagonally towards him, but it was too late. Two other typeAs were already scampering up it, throwing themselves onto the roof from the top of the metal structure far, far more easily than any of Noah's human squad. Noah picked up his rifle and shot them in their heads.

Overlapping screams penetrated his eardrums—Frankie? Meredith?—as he turned to assess the rooftop. Gone was their height advantage—the space was now teeming with types. His soldiers shot bullet after bullet, not always hitting their marks.

"Spray their feet!" he ordered, desperate to turn the tide. The squad was seconds away from being overwhelmed; more and more types were climbing up through the hole, some were even scaling the outer walls. Their numbers were the greatest he'd ever seen. Where had they all come from?

He couldn't stop his eyes darting over in Zeke's direction every few seconds. But both Zeke and Frankie held their own better than he could have ever imagined, dispatching monster after monster as they flung themselves at them.

"I'm all out of juice," Splat shouted.

Every muscle in Noah's body went rigid. If Splat was out of ammo, the rest of them wouldn't be far behind. Noah ran over to Splat, who unsheathed his dagger. He slashed out at a type, plunging it through its rib cage with an audible cracking sound as he twisted the knife. At the same time, it bent its neck and bit deep into Splat's forearm.

As he heard Splat's shocked cry, Noah knew he was too late.

He lunged forward. Sharp fangs dragged themselves across naked flesh, making deep lacerations.

Noah cut the typeA's throat with his dagger before sending it flying off the roof with a round kick.

"Where... what...?" Noah said, staring at Splat's arm, where the black protective fabric of his undersuit should be.

"It tore it a few minutes ago."

"But Stephen said it didn't need replacing," said Noah, as if that would magically fix everything. Their conversational tone masked the unspoken truth neither of them wanted to face.

Splat pulled something from his belt. His last bomb. His shaky hands clipped it to a chain wrapped around his stomach.

"Splat..."

By this time, the others surrounded them. Luo, Frankie and Zeke formed a defensive semi-circle, firing their last few rounds at the relentless wave of types. But Meredith dropped her weapon on the roof and stared at Splat's arm, shell-shocked.

"I'm going to get as close to my kit box as possible," said Splat, his voice even. "The rest of the gear in there should create enough of an explosion to turn this joint into a small crater for you guys. I'll set it up so Zeke can detonate it when you guys have cleared the area. Let's aim for sixty seconds max, Zeke. There won't be much left of me after that, and you'll have types leaving the feast to come after you." Splat pressed something into Zeke's hand before pulling his helmet off his head and throwing it to the side.

Meredith dropped to her knees, eyes downcast and Splat scooped his arms under her armpits, pulling her up and to him. Then Splat reached under his chest armour and removed his metal chain, his dog tags glinting in the light. He pressed them into her hand.

There was a moment of fuss where Meredith fought to get her helmet off and Splat fought for it to remain on her head. Eventually, she won, and Noah grabbed her helmet as Meredith threw her arms around Splat, burying her face in his neck.

He whispered something into her ear. She pulled back, lifting his chin up with her palms to gaze into his eyes.

Noah almost turned away. The look of pure love—twinged with regret for what could have been—that was passing between them was so intimate and intense it burned his soul.

It could have been a lifetime of happiness, of shared jokes, of Splat pulling on Meredith's braids, of Meredith rolling her eyes at him.

But instead, it was this.

It was Splat stepping back.

It was Meredith pressing her knuckle to her lips, biting down, hard.

It was Splat crying out, "Sixty seconds!"

Splat teetered on the edge of the gaping mouth. He raised his dagger to his already injured arm. With a single slash, he created one long, grim, red line in his flesh, then jumped into the pit of hungry, frenzied monsters.

Meredith's anguished scream only added to the pit of nausea that threatened to overwhelm Noah as types wrenched the armour from the body of one of his closest friends using brute force, like a starving man desperate to get at the flesh of a crab.

A small, faraway part of his brain told him, *fifty seconds.*

Splat's blood now attracted every nearby type into the interior of the spacious warehouse. Hissing, grunting and snarling sounds rose from below them as the hungry beasts fought each other for a taste of his flesh. Zeke gripped his arm, swaying—woozy from seeing Splat's blood?—as he pulled him towards everyone else, who were already at the edge of the roof. Luo wrapped his arm around Meredith, dragging her to the precipice.

"We have to jump to that branch," Luo said, and Noah nodded. A jump at this height onto the concrete was risky, even in their suits.

Noah urged them all forward, moving to the very back of the queue. There were no types on the roof now—the angry sounds of the beasts told him they were preoccupied below.

He watched each one of his squad scramble to grip onto the rough bark before making the fifteen feet drop to the ground. Once he'd reached the floor, they hurried off, pushing and pulling each other away as fast as they could. Noah's eyes scanned for further clusters, but found none.

"Ten seconds." Meredith stole Splat's line in a choked, out-of-breath whisper. The six of them sprinted through the foliage like their lives depended on it.

Noah watched as Zeke lifted the detonation device—a palm-sized electronic rectangle—out of his pocket and pressed various buttons on the interface. Noah knew the moment Zeke had finished, as Zeke reached out for Noah's hand, gripping him so hard it was as if Zeke was trying to break it.

Splat's bombs always were reliable, and his swan song was no exception.

The thunderous boom created a powerful blast that shook the ground, the trees, and Noah's soul. He turned to look at the blazing inferno that now consumed the warehouse. Further quieter pops and bangs erupted from the building. Noah wanted to close his eyes, to take a moment, but he still had a flock to lead.

Noah turned to Zeke to say, "Well done." Even though Splat's fate had been out of Zeke's control, it couldn't have been easy executing Splat's plan under so much pressure. "You did great."

Zeke leaned heavily into Noah, legs wobbling. "I can't... I can't believe..." he managed to get out, before Frankie scooped him away from Noah, into her arms.

"We're on our way over to you."

Vitt's voice through his feed sounded so normal, so calm, Noah wanted to scream. The smell of smoke and burnt plastic assaulted his nose. Thick, dark grey smoke billowed over to them, obscuring his vision. Avoiding inhaling it became impossible, even through the filter on their helmets. It stung his eyes, causing them to stream while his lungs filled with ash. He attempted to scan the tree line for the wire setup that possibly caused the tsunami of types to materialise from every direction, but he couldn't find it.

Once they'd cleared enough space from the warehouse, they waited for the other three to find them. When they arrived—Habib walking groggily but un-supported—he thought for a brief second he was going to have to explain Splat's absence, but one look into their harrowed eyes told him it wasn't necessary. Wolf whined pitifully as he pressed himself against Noah, looking up at him with large, brown eyes. *I know, boy. Me too.*

In the distance, he heard the roar of motors speeding towards them. The cavalry had finally arrived. He almost laughed. He almost sank to his knees, ready to rip off his own helmet and give up right then, right there.

Instead, he walked in the direction of the car park, ready to brief whoever Command sent to save them.

ZEKE

The hours that followed were the most difficult of Zeke's life.

As soon as they returned to the compound, Murphy's Command minions ushered them into the HQ building. Meredith returned separately to them in an isolation van—Splat's proximity to her in his last moments had triggered this protocol—resulting in Savannah and Vitt kicking up an almighty fuss when they weren't allowed to accompany her to an isolation booth.

What felt like hours and hours of questioning began, with official-looking administrators asking a barrage of questions, documenting everything Zeke said. He spaced out several times, distracted by the looping memories of Splat jumping to his death, him pressing that final button on the detonator, and Noah's desolate expression on the journey home. The ache in Noah's stare had mirrored the ache in Zeke's heart.

The interviewers were particularly interested in the wire at first, but stopped that line of questioning when it was obvious he didn't have a clue about it. The line of inquiry then moved on to asking questions about Noah's decisions. By the end, he'd been a stuttering, quivering mess. What incriminating things had he accidentally revealed?

When they finally released him, he expected to see the rest of his squad waiting for him outside, but he found no one. His aching body, combined with sympathetic looks from passers-by, made the journey to Beech block difficult. Opening the door to their room, his stomach gave an unpleasant lurch when he saw it was empty.

"I'm over here."

He turned to find Luo slumped against the wall. He'd pulled Splat's drawer onto his lap and was staring down at it, face completely aghast. He looked every bit the empty husk Zeke felt himself.

Long before he joined the military, he often wondered how they coped with losing the people they loved.

Now he knew.

They didn't.

"If you take that drawer, you know Splat's ghost is going to haunt you for the rest of your life, right?" Zeke said.

Luo's mouth twitched with the tiniest hint of a smile.

"Where is everyone?" Zeke asked, even though there was only one person he wanted to see.

"Hab and Aoife have gone to Fusion. Vitt and Savannah are camped outside Meredith's isolation booth. Frankie's run off somewhere. I think she needs some time alone."

"Noah?" He couldn't keep the desperation from clouding his voice.

Luo shrugged and returned to staring at Splat's drawer.

He left Luo to race down the corridor to Noah's room. He raised his hand to knock, then paused. What if he also wanted to be left alone? But the memory of Noah's blank expression and haunted eyes as they escorted him off to a separate interview room earlier swayed him. He wasn't sure he trusted Noah to be alone right now. He knocked twice. Hard. When there was no reply, he twisted the handle to find it locked. He continued banging, swallowing as images of what Noah could be doing alone in the room overwhelmed him.

Behind him, a door creaked.

"What's go— Oh! Zeke. Are you looking for Noah?" It was Krish, one of Noah's friends from Squad K. He gave Zeke's arm a squeeze. "I saw him in the upstairs bathroom a few minutes ago. He... I'm not sure if..." Krish stared at him as he trailed off, scratching his neck.

He wasted no time replying. He reached the bathroom, heart hammering in his chest, to find it deserted—bar one shower cubicle, steam pouring out from under the gap in the door.

"Noah?" he said tentatively, knocking lightly.

The silence spoke volumes.

He slid onto the damp floor, peering under the door, expecting to find feet. Seeing Noah's face instead, he flinched back in shock. Noah was curled up sideways on the floor, eyes open, fully clothed in his black hoodie, the water from the shower streaming over him. He stared right through Zeke as if he weren't there.

"Let me in."

Noah continued to stare, unblinking, his face an expressionless mask.

Seeing no other choice, he removed his glasses and dragged his slender frame under the door, instantly saturating his clothes as he lay in the puddle created by the water. This prompted a reaction from Noah at last and he furrowed his eyebrows, as if Zeke had confused him. There was little floor space now, forcing Noah to sit up. He pulled his knees to his chest and cast his eyes downwards as the scorching-hot water continued to pour.

There was a long pause as Zeke searched for words. "Noah... it's going to be okay."

This was definitely the wrong thing to say. Noah gave him a scathing look, as if he was an utter fool.

"It's going to be... *okay*? How is it possibly going to be *okay*?" Noah's volume increased to a manic shout.

Zeke flinched, moving away from Noah to press his back against the wall. The Noah before him was not one he recognised, or knew how to handle.

"What the *fuck* is even the point of all this?" Noah said. His haunted hazel eyes bore a wild, crazed look.

"Noah," he choked out, swallowing. His throat constricted, and he struggled to breathe in the humid air.

Noah leaned back, his head now against the tiled wall. He lifted his head slightly, and Zeke thought he was going to say something, but then he let his head drop against the hard ceramic. *Bang.* He repeated the motion, slamming the back of his head even more violently. *Bang.*

"Stop!"

Noah did not stop.

"Noah, you're scaring me!"

Zeke's words did nothing to halt Noah's determined movements, forcing him to reach over, placing his palm between the tiles and Noah's head. He cried out in pain when Noah's heavy head smashed into his hand. Surely that would stop him? But Noah only pushed him away, moving forward to bang his forehead on another tile.

"Enough!" he roared. He lunged at Noah, manoeuvring behind him and pulling him towards his chest. He used his thighs to squeeze Noah's torso, pinning him in place. Noah unleashed a wail of fury as he thrashed against him, screaming so loud everyone would likely hear him on the below levels. "I'm not letting you go until you calm down," he said, but it was useless. Noah wasn't listening. He threw his head back, smacking Zeke in the mouth. His lip collided painfully with his teeth. "Ouch!"

Noah stopped moving, going limp in his arms before twisting around to face Zeke. He brushed his fingers over Zeke's bottom lip, staring at the faint smear of blood on his fingertips when he pulled them away. The water thankfully washed it away, but after the sights from earlier, the sight of his blood barely affected him.

"I'm sorry." Noah's face dissolved into an almost unrecognisable crumple of its usual shape. "I'm sorry. I'm so sorry. I'm—"

Zeke reached his arms around Noah, pulling his face against his chest. Noah collapsed against him, sobbing so hard the vibrations shook his own body. Zeke stroked Noah's wet hair. "It's okay," he whispered. "You don't need to apologise." He lowered his head to kiss the top of Noah's head, pressing hard so he could feel it. He kissed him again and again, as if each kiss could wipe away his pain.

"You're going to die. You're all going to die. I'm going to lose *everyone*," Noah said, his voice barely audible over the pounding shower. His breathing became a series of short, sharp, gurgling gasps and tremors shook the entirety of his body.

Zeke's frantic brain scrambled back in time to when Zaya used to suffer from panic attacks, when they were first evacuated to London after the first wave.

"Do this for me." Zeke sucked in a massive breath and expelled slowly, humming a low note.

Noah's head tilted in confusion, but he followed the instructions.

"Hold it for as long as possible."

Several choked sobs cut off Noah's first attempt, but by the third he made the sound continuously, and the shaking of his body subsided.

Zeke squeezed him even tighter to him. "Who should I call? Habib? Vitt?" He raised his wristband. "Leo?" he added.

Noah shook his head against him, pushing Zeke's wristband down. "I don't—" he choked out, between wheezing short breaths, "want anyone else." Noah grabbed Zeke's hand and squeezed hard as he fought to take control of his breathing.

Many tense minutes passed. While attempting to sooth Noah by rubbing his arms, he wrestled with whether to call one of the others anyway, but finally, Noah's breathing became more regular. He still clutched at his chest like it pained him, however. He needed to continue to calm down in a safe, and preferably dry, place.

"I think we need to get out of this shower before we shrivel into prunes," Zeke said.

Noah laughed weakly and let Zeke drag him to his feet.

Thankfully, there was no one around to witness them marching through the corridors sopping wet on the journey to Noah's room. Wolf was waiting by the door, his sleeping form curled into a ball. Noah dropped to his knees, gathering the dog up in his arms and squeezing him tight. "Good boy. Such a good boy," he murmured into his fur.

Zeke coughed, not wanting to push their luck with being discovered in this state. Noah swiped his wristband to unlock the door, and they hurried inside. The chaotic mess from the other day remained unchanged, and Zeke nearly stumbled over several items as he traversed the room.

Noah fell straight onto the floor to continue to fawn over Wolf, leaving Zeke to find dry clothes for them. Most of Noah's laundry was piled into heaps in the corner, but he found two t-shirts and underwear. Once he'd changed, the too-large clothes hanging off him, he turned his attention back to Noah, who was now shivering in his damp layers.

He tugged at Noah's hoodie, peeling it off for him. When Noah was almost fully undressed, he sighed, and went to complete the job himself, facing the corner.

When Noah turned, Zeke pointedly focussed on his damp hair, that fell in loose black curls around his face, rather than his bare torso. Something distinctly more Noah-shaped now inhabited him.

"I'm so sorry about all that," Noah said, as if he'd just spilled some tea.

"Don't be sorry." Zeke paused, fiddling with his shirt. Questions circled around his mind, but he was unsure of how much to pry. "Are you feeling okay now?"

Noah's mouth twisted into a subtle grimace. "I'll be fine. I've had panic attacks before. That was a pretty short one, thanks to you."

Zeke, leaning against the wall, ducked his gaze. Noah crossed the room to join him, taking his face in both his hands, tilting his head up.

"Stay with me tonight?" Noah's pleading eyes sent his stomach into somersaults.

Zeke swallowed. "Of course." As if he'd say anything else.

This time, there were no pretences about someone taking the bed and the other the floor. Zeke slid across the narrow bed, pushed his back against the wall, then held out his arms. The look Noah gave him before slotting in next to him took his breath away. How had this person—this *man*—invaded his heart, mind and body so completely, in a way nobody had ever done so before? He ran his hand down Noah's bare arm, marvelling at the tsunami of goosebumps he caused.

"I don't know if—" Noah broke off with a sigh. "I don't know if I can lead Squad E anymore. It's... killing me."

Zeke couldn't see a Squad E without Noah as its leader, its glue, its heartbeat. "Everyone knows you're doing the best you can." Zeke pressed a kiss into the back of his head. "But if you want to step down, people will understand."

A few silent minutes went by, punctuated only by their rhythmic breathing, gradually becoming synced. Light snoring drifted up from the floor—Wolf was sound asleep on the rug. Tension seeped out of Zeke's muscles as Noah lay calm and still beside him.

Zeke moved his hand up to the back of Noah's head, parting his hair as he examined his scalp. He found a tiny bump of swollen flesh, and Noah gasped as he pushed it. He let go and grabbed Noah's hands, running his thumb over the patches of skin that he knew housed small indent scars from his nails. "The next time you want to hurt yourself, please come and find me. Or anyone. But I'll be there for you. Anytime. Always."

Noah pushed his face into the pillow.

"Hey. This is important. Also, you should go to see Doctor Herbert tomorrow." Zeke squashed back irrational waves of jealousy, locked them in a box. Noah's health was far more important.

"I will." Noah turned in Zeke's arms, lifting his leg to hook it around Zeke's leg. "Thank you for taking care of me," he said, before pressing his lips to Zeke's. Zeke trembled as they became a tangled mess of sheets and limbs and pillows.

Noah pulled away. "I want to..." he began, groaning as he sifted Zeke's hair with his fingers, tugging lightly. He would happily have him do that all night. "But..."

"Shh." Zeke pressed a finger to Noah's lips. "I know. This is enough. This is more than enough."

They were silent again for a while before Noah said, "Can I tell you about Splat? Stories from before you got here?"

More tears prickled Zeke's heavy eyes. How would the squad ever recover from this great, indescribable loss? How could Noah have endured this so many times before and still carried on day after day?

"Of course," he said. "Tell me."

ZEKE

Sunlight streamed through the window the next morning, warming Noah's tiny bedroom. Sparks of joy rocketed through Zeke as the warm skin of Noah's bare leg pressed against him. But then, memories of Splat jumping through the roof came flooding back, repeated punches in his stomach. Although he tried to contain it, his intense sobbing fit woke Noah. The out of control, manic version of Noah he'd met yesterday was now long gone. Noah calmly kissed away his tears, before suggesting he change into his own clothes before breakfast. He left Noah with a heavy heart; he'd have done anything to stay in his bed with him all day.

Zeke found his glasses waiting for him on his pillow in his empty dorm. He must have left them in the bathroom yesterday. Who'd returned them and did they wonder where he was all night? He hurried to change, figuring the others must have gone for their workout routine, even today.

When he reached the field, the familiar sight of Meredith, Savannah and Aoife in the warrior pose while the others ran laps around them soothed his soul. It *would* be okay. They could get through this. The others already had ample experience with grief, after all.

Frankie gave up running to join Zeke on a bench, confessing she'd spent most of the night crying to her mother on a voice call.

When Zeke asked her how Meredith was doing, Frankie scrunched up her face. "As well as can be expected, I guess. They let her out of isolation at midnight. She didn't say much when she got back to our room."

A sick sensation came over him when his eyes scanned Meredith's puffy face. She and Splat had respected Noah's request for them to maintain a professional distance. Now he and Noah were waking up together and shoving their tongues down each other's throats. If he himself felt bad about it, how must Noah be feeling right now? *Great, another thing for him to beat himself up over.*

"We're off duty today to recover and regroup. Also, apparently Splat's dad wants to talk to us. He's been told what happened, but still wants to hear it firsthand."

Zeke hesitated. "Do you think Luo or someone else who was up there could do it?" he asked. "Noah wasn't in a very good place yesterday and I don't want—I mean, he probably shouldn't—"

Frankie threw him a curious look, questions dancing around in her eyes.

Heat bloomed on Zeke's cheeks. He quickly turned to face the runners. "Well?"

"Sure," said Frankie, smooth as ever. "I'll ask Vitt what she thinks about who should call Splat's father."

Noah didn't join them until breakfast, which was a sombre, quiet affair. It started badly from the beginning, when they quickly realised that it was Splat's mug duty. Then commenced the stream of soldiers coming up to their table to offer their condolences, when all any of them wanted was to be left alone to brood in silence. Near the end of breakfast, Noah announced he had an appointment with Doctor Herbert early that morning. Under the table, he squeezed Zeke's thigh before jumping up, calling Wolf to follow him.

"So, what happens today?" Zeke asked Luo. Everyone had finished eating and was staring down at their empty plates and mugs.

"Aoife has agreed to call Splat's family," said Luo. Zeke nudged Frankie's leg with his foot in thanks. "We get today just to breathe and process. This evening, we'll say a few words around the fire before releasing some sparks for him."

"Before heading straight back out tomorrow," added Meredith, her bleak frown causing deep creases in her forehead.

"If you need more time, Mere, we—" Savannah started, but Meredith held up her hand and shook her head.

Members of Squad E slowly peeled off. Zeke headed back to his room, where he spent two hours on a voice call to Zaya. She did her best to cheer him up, even succeeding in making him laugh at one point. He opened his mouth several times to tell her about Noah, to confess his guilt over Splat and Meredith, before remembering that Command monitored all their communications.

Afterwards, Luo, Frankie and Zeke took a long walk around Avantis's surrounding countryside, the cold yet beautiful winter day distracting Zeke slightly from the depths of his grief. When Zeke saw Noah, with Wolf by his heels, waiting for them at that gate when they returned, his heart jumped to his throat. He wanted to run to him, gather him in his arms and whisper into his ear about how he had missed him. Instead, he settled for a shy smile that he hoped communicated volumes.

That evening, Squad E gathered around the fire pit for Splat's send off.

They sat in a circle, bright clothes and tight smiles. How many times had the other members of Squad E done this? Ten? Twenty? More?

No matter how many deaths came before Splat's, he knew this one was different. Tears streamed down almost everyone's blotchy, swollen faces. Everybody loved Splat.

Although Zeke hadn't known him for long, he'd been one of the friendliest and kindest towards him—after that initial first day—and now his absence was like a missing limb.

Habib began the ceremony by reciting a funeral prayer in Arabic. Vitt and Aoife then shared some of their favourite memories of Splat. Some of them were familiar to Zeke, as he'd heard them last night from Noah. He found himself chuckling feebly along with the others as Vitt acted out the story of when Splat tried to break into the alcohol cupboard in Command, and hid under a desk for two hours until Captain Murphy left the room.

The ceremony was tears and smiles. It was pain and laughter. It was the sense of an ending, but a story unfinished.

"Speaking of alcohol," Aoife said, once Vitt finished her tale, lifting up two bottles of red wine. "So, Squad K was kind enough to share this wine they stumbled upon. And wouldn't you know, they 'accidentally' didn't declare it at the border. Ain't that just our luck?" Aoife shared the dark liquid out between their metal mugs.

A collective, "To Splat!" accompanied the traditional tapping of mugs against one another, the wine sloshing and spilling onto the mossy ground. The fire warmed Zeke's face, and the wine warmed his belly. Further memories were shared until everyone, exhausted, agreed it was time to light the fireworks. Habib lined up twenty-four tiny rockets—not quite far enough from where they were sitting for Zeke's liking—that looked alarmingly homemade. Habib waved a stick into the fire to form a makeshift match.

"Evening," said a familiar voice. The expression on Noah's face could only mean one thing: Tobias Newman.

The intruding soldier stepped into the middle of their circle. "Just came to pay my respects. Splat was such a great guy." His gaze swept over each of them.

Noah tensed, folding his arms.

"This is a private ceremony, Tobias," said Vitt. "Like usual. Thank you so much for your kind words, but we'd appreciate it if you left us now."

"Of course. I just wanted to make sure Noah was doing okay, given how many losses he's now had."

Time froze for a beat.

Then, Zeke jumped to his feet, closely followed by Habib and Meredith. Fury shot through his veins as he prepared to tell Tobias exactly where to go. Habib beat him to it—taking two giant strides towards Tobias, his face a picture of violence.

But it was Meredith who overshadowed the pair of them. On the way to her feet, she'd picked up one of the empty wine bottles. She lifted it high above her head, then smashed it against the circular brick base of the fire.

Smashing glass. Shocked gasps.

"I SWEAR TO FUCKING GOD, NEWMAN," Meredith screamed, brandishing her jagged-edged bottle like an axe, "IF YOU SAY ONE MORE WORD, I'LL CUT YOUR FUCKING TONGUE OUT WITH THIS BOTTLE!"

There was a stunned silence as jaws hit the ground.

Tobias slowly backed away, hands up defensively, eyes wide, as if she was a crazy lady. Right now, she *was* a crazy lady. He disappeared down the dark path, shaking his head and muttering something probably obscene.

Once enough time passed, Vitt started a round of slow applause, which ended up in a crescendo of cheering and whooping. Zeke joined in, but unease settled over him—Tobias wasn't likely to forget that in a hurry.

"To Splat!" someone said, and then they were all tapping mugs again and Habib was lighting the fireworks.

Twenty-four tiny sparks of light whizzed into the air, spinning and flickering before falling to the ground, extinguished.

"Alright," began Noah, the next day, in a ground-floor briefing room in the armoury. "Sorry to get straight back to it, but... you know how it goes." Everyone nodded at him, and he continued. "Murphy's shuffled a few people around."

Zeke froze. That could happen?

"We've got Brodie Campbell joining us from Squad J. Ideally, whoever joined us would have a speciality in explosives, but, turns out, our entire regiment is pretty short on that. So, Zeke, you're scheduled for training to become our official new bomb specialist."

"What?" Zeke's knees weakened. Why hadn't Noah found time to tell him this in private before they met?

"Yep. Sorry for the surprise. I found out all of this ten minutes ago."

"That's amazing!" said Frankie, snaking her arm around Zeke to squeeze his waist. "You're already great at it, anyway."

'Great' was probably an exaggeration, but it was true that Zeke had enjoyed the demolition role when he'd supported Splat. It was an opportunity to play to his strengths: logical reasoning and being far away from the enemy.

"Anyway, the rest of us are stationed at the border for three days while Zeke completes his course. It shouldn't be hard for you though, Zeke, since Splat probably taught you most of it already."

"You better pass the first time," said Habib. "I don't want to be stuck there for any longer than necessary."

Noah's jaw twitched, but he focussed his attention on Zeke when he continued, "You'll have to go away for a few nights at a western compound to train. Someone will collect you in a minute. Sorry."

Noah caught Zeke's eye meaningfully as he said the last word, but it did nothing to stop the pang of anxiety that assaulted him. The others filed out to head to the locker room, but Noah hovered behind, closing the door shut and checking for cameras before giving Zeke a quick kiss on the cheek.

"I'll miss you," Noah said, the lightest smattering of pink blotching his face. "Go get better at blowing stuff up, firestarter."

Zeke could only smile, not trusting his voice not to betray his emotions. Three days away felt like an eternity.

"Zeke Bates?" A young woman, wearing cat-eye leopard print glasses, popped her head around the door and asked that he follow her. Noah took that as his cue to leave, giving Zeke one last small nod.

En route, the woman introduced herself as Eliza Holmes. "Wow. And how have you found military life so far?" she said, after Zeke had shared his background with her.

He pulled a face and blew out a breath of air. "Difficult."

She laughed. "Well, if you take to this role, in a few years you could be training others across all the London regiments, like me."

In the brief silence that followed, the expression 'few years' ricocheted around his brain. Was humanity doomed to be locked in cages, fighting an endless war for the rest of time? Mankind couldn't go on like this infinitely; their resources wouldn't stretch to it. When he worked at the lab at Oakfield, the future had felt more hopeful. Although his team weren't specifically working on a treatment for the RONS virus, they were in contact with many others who were. But this lady didn't seem to think that salvation was coming anytime soon.

"Maybe," he replied, trailing after her in the direction of the gate. *If we're all still here in a few years.*

NOAH

On the second evening into Zeke's absence, a soldier met Noah at the gate on his return from his border duty and escorted him straight to Murphy's office. As he approached her door, he anticipated anxiety, the kind that twisted his stomach into knots, but instead, a cold numbness crept over him.

Two men in smart suits joined Murphy at her desk. As he slid into a chair opposite the three of them, they introduced themselves as government officials. He knew immediately that they were there to talk about his uncle.

He endured thirty minutes of questioning. When was the last time he'd seen or heard from him? *Two months ago.* How had he seemed? *Batshit crazy,* he wanted to say, but settled on '*absolutely normal, ma'am*'. Did Noah understand that he was to contact them straight away if he heard from him? As if they wouldn't be obsessively monitoring his communications.

Any questions he himself posed were instantly shot down, and he left the interrogation in an awful mood to go and hide in his room. Unfortunately for him, Vitt came to drag him to the fire pit with the rest of the squad. The rest of the squad, minus Zeke, who was the only one he really wanted to see.

Now he'd—stupidly?—acted on his feelings for Zeke, he'd opened a floodgate he couldn't close off. He'd forgotten the feeling of being held all night, enclosed in a cocoon of comforting warmth. And now he'd had a taste, he couldn't help but seek out more. Noah tapped out a message to Zeke on his band.

It's regrettable that we're not able to complete the extra training we had planned. We will have to cram in three evenings' worth when you return Sunday.

The reply was almost instantaneous:

> Are you sure that'll be possible? There's a lot to cover. The time constraint will be a challenge.

> If we don't fit it all in, we will have to continue Monday evening. And Tuesday. Perhaps we make it an indefinite daily occurrence. I do think you need the practice.

> It's true I am lacking in experience compared to you.

> Not for long. Please send me updates on your progress at Colne. The welfare of my squad is important to me.

> Yes, sir.

"Who are you sending that to?"

Noah jumped as Habib interrupted him. He was midway through sending Zeke a picture of Wolf, sleeping next to the fire pit. Lies danced over his tongue—should he say Alice, or Leo? Spotting someone familiar entering the clearing from the forest path, he seized the opportunity to ignore Habib's question.

"Voigt!"

Leonie Voigt, dressed in her Black Ranger uniform, caught his eye and beelined towards him, sitting down with her back to the blazing fire.

"Alright?" He eyed Leonie, unsure if she was here with another message from his uncle. She looked far more sober than their last encounter. Thankfully. The woman took a couple of deep drags from her vape, creating a haze of vapour in the space between them.

"Forrest." Leonie nodded to him. "Who's this?"

"Barakat. He's with me."

Leonie raised her eyebrows. "And can he be trusted?"

"On my life," said Noah, and Habib smiled. "How are your eight friends?" he asked, referring to the soldiers who she'd said were 'banked' by types.

"In a very similar position to when we last spoke. That's one of the reasons I'm here."

Habib looked between the pair of them, a wary, deep frown etched into his face.

"How can I help?" Noah asked.

"The Black Ranger's numbers are dipping low. Word's on the street that a few squads from this regiment are being sent up north soon. Near Cambridge. Intel gathering mission. The group of typeBs that nabbed my friends are apparently getting a little too organised for their own good."

"Okay..." said Noah.

"If a few nudges in the right direction result in your squad being chosen, I want you to take some... private recordings."

He stared at Leonie. "If we're being sent to gather intel, surely that means they're planning a rescue, right?"

"I doubt it. We expect the whole place to be drone bombed. They'll declare the humans too injured or too much of a risk to bring back." Leonie's mouth curled downwards as her eyes flashed dark. "It wouldn't be the first time."

"Hold up," said Habib. "What's this?"

Leonie glanced his way before turning back to Noah. "Will you do it?"

"Look, there's no way Squad E will be placed on this mission. We're not exactly in Murphy's favour right now."

Leonie waved her hand. "Don't worry about that part. I just need to know if you'll do it."

"You just want me to take some videos? Don't you want me to rescue your friends?"

Leonie scoffed. "Your uncle wasn't joking when he described you as an idealist. You'll be under strict instructions not to engage with any humans. Sworn to secrecy. If you think you can persuade every officer to directly disobey Command, as well as transport dozens of starving, weakened, critically ill people back to the compound, be my guest."

"And where is my uncle?" He didn't bother to hide his irritation.

"Alive." Leonie stood to leave.

"I'm not committing to doing this for you without talking to my uncle first."

Leonie only nodded. Then, without looking back, she disappeared into the dark of the night.

"What the absolute *fuck* was that all about?" Habib said. He stared at Noah, arms crossed. "Wasn't that Leonie Voigt? The famous Black Ranger? And what's going on with General Forrest? What's happened?"

Noah ground his teeth. "I don't have all the answers. She was even more cryptic the last time we met."

"I hope you're not seriously considering helping her."

He shrugged. "I'm not sure."

Habib let out a low hiss. "Noah. You'll be sent to the Hole. Permanently. We all could be."

Noah considered Habib. He wasn't one for secrets or breaking rules, but he was also Noah's best friend, who'd fought with him side by side for years now.

"I need to tell you something," Noah started, then fumbled for words. Since his uncle's visit, he'd been busy burying what he'd said deeper and deeper into his brain. He wished it could stay there forever. "My uncle told me that London is screwed. Months or weeks away from collapse."

"Bullshit."

"Just listen," Noah snapped. "Take it from someone who's already lived through it once. If London is about to collapse, we need to make an exit plan."

Habib stood, stepping closer to him and hissing in a low voice, "And what about our families? We just leave them to die? This isn't what Squad E needs to be hearing right now, *Lieutenant*. This is the sort of shit that incites mass panic."

He stared at Habib's feet and clamped his lips together. Was Habib right? Was he fucking up yet again? But Noah refused to sit idly by if London really was about to fall. He needed to think ahead, for the sake of his squad.

"Have you guys seen this?" said Vitt, coming to join them. She flashed a tablet displaying a news website at them. "Ten people have just died in a riot stampede outside the Palace of Westminster. At least four of them directly from police push back."

"A few other squads have been called into the city for backup," added Luo.

"Thank God it wasn't us," said Meredith. "Beating up angry civilians is the last thing I want to do right now."

Noah stared meaningfully at Habib, who met his gaze without blinking.

Noah hovered by the gate where Zeke was due to arrive back. His transit van, which was supposed to arrive at nine p.m., was over half an hour late. When it finally came in, Zeke shuffled out of the underground parking lot amongst a small crowd of soldiers. He walked straight past Noah, who reached out to grab him, his stomach a knotted ball of nerves.

Three days felt like a long time. More than enough time for Zeke to come to his senses, and call time on whatever the hell it was they were doing. But Zeke's genuine, beaming smile when he saw Noah was waiting for him catapulted those thoughts out of his head.

"How was it?" he asked, as if Zeke hadn't messaged him updates five times a day.

"It was good! I would have made Splat proud with my timer configurations," Zeke replied, with a sad smile which squeezed Noah's heart.

Noah reached out for Zeke, wrapping his hands around Zeke's forearms as if Zeke might run away if he didn't hold on to him. "It's good to have you back here."

Zeke ducked his head. "I missed you," he said, so quiet he almost didn't catch it.

"Do you want to come up to my room? We've still got that extra *training* to get to."

Zeke laughed, his now-familiar dark blush creeping up his neck. "Sure," he said. "I have three days' worth to catch up on, so we better get started."

As they walked to Beech block in silence, guilt-ridden thoughts swam shark-like around Noah's brain. He shouldn't be doing this. Pursuing Zeke when it put his relationship with his squad in jeopardy. But hadn't he just witnessed Meredith and Splat lose their chance at love? Did he really think Splat would want the same for him? And wasn't London on the brink of collapse? Who knew how much time he had left on this planet? He couldn't waste a single moment on regrets, on not knowing *what if.*

Their pace increased as they grew closer to Noah's room, taking the stairs two at a time to finally reach his door. Noah slammed the door behind them. Then, he turned to Zeke, his heart pounding so loud that Zeke could surely hear it.

Noah froze, not knowing what exactly to do next, not wanting to push Zeke into something he wasn't ready for.

For a few moments, they stood there in the dark room, staring at each other's shadowy outlines.

But then every inch of Noah's soul magnetized towards Zeke. Like a breath of air after being submerged underwater. Like seeing your home again after being lost in the dark. Like Noah's true north.

Zeke let out a loud, unsteady breath, prompting Noah to close the gap between them. He slid his arm around Zeke, pulling him towards him. Zeke collapsed against his chest, almost knocking him off balance. As Noah guided them towards the bed, he tripped over a stray object on the floor, surging them backwards. Despite his best efforts earlier to tidy his room, something had slipped through the net.

As they fell onto the bed, Noah fumbled around in the dark, taking three attempts to turn his bedside table lamp on while still cradling Zeke in his arms. Turning to face him, he found his slightly parted lips were glinting where he'd just ran over them with his tongue. Noah swallowed, his anticipation growing stronger with each passing second.

Hands quickly found Noah's hair, removing the band that held it with far more skill than the time before. When Zeke ran his fingers through it ever so slowly, ever so gently, it sent electric shock waves from his scalp to his feet. One gentle, lingering kiss on Noah's collarbone preceded another, slightly higher, and then another. Finally, their lips collided.

And then it was Zeke's hands pulling Noah's hair, Noah's lips against Zeke's neck, bodies thrashing, hearts pounding. Gone was the nervous energy from their frantic fumble in the bus shelter. Now Noah would savour every last second of this moment; sear Zeke into his mind and body.

Noah tenderly bit down on Zeke's bottom lip. Gasping, Zeke pushed further into him, as if he couldn't possibly be close enough. They broke apart to sit up, tearing off shirts as quickly as possible before coming back together again, lips finding lips, skin finding skin. Noah's head spun: touch-drunk, kiss-drunk, euphoria-drunk.

He sank back onto the bed, lying flat and pulling Zeke on top of him. Zeke's wide eyes looked wild in the low light; his grin lopsided as he lowered his head to find Noah's again. Both of Noah's hands brushed the soft skin of Zeke's back, gentle until Zeke's tongue flicked against his and Noah dug his nails into Zeke as he tried to hold back a moan. For the last three nights, alone in bed, he'd had plenty of time to fantasise about this moment, but the euphoric feel of Zeke's weight pushing him into the mattress was a thousand times better than he could have ever imagined.

Zeke's mouth left his and a needy, pitiful sound escaped Noah's lips before he could stop it. Zeke devoured his neck, chest, nipples as he ran his hands down Noah's torso, travelling lower and lower until he reached Noah's trousers, where his erection was pressing almost painfully against his zipper. Tugging at Noah's belt, Zeke's eyes met his, asking a question.

Noah groaned softly. "I'm supposed to be teaching you, remember?"

"I think I already have a fairly solid foundation," Zeke replied, making quick work of the belt before pulling down both the layers of fabric separating him from Noah.

Noah arched his body up, quickly kicking down his remaining clothes until they hit the floor with a soft thump, leaving his fully erect cock completely exposed. Zeke was clearly fighting hard not to stare at it and his cheeks quickly turned a delightful deep beetroot colour.

"Why are you laughing?" Zeke said, pursing his lips and pulling back.

Noah grabbed his face, pulling back to him to kiss him deeply. In one swift move, he flipped them over, positioning Zeke under him. "Because you're fucking adorable."

Noah's hand reached underneath Zeke's trousers, stroking the skin he found there. "Can we even the score?"

"Seems fair."

After Zeke's clothes had joined Noah's on the floor, he bracketed Zeke's head with his arms, hovering his body inches above him.

"If you want to stop—"

Zeke blinked. Stared at Noah. "Why would I want to stop?"

"I don't know. The sight of another guy's dick might have untriggered your experimental phase."

Zeke's jaw dropped as his eyes became saucers, so wide they reflected his own dark-maned portrait back at him.

"Noah..." Zeke said, his hand cupping Noah's cheek. "You are *not* an experimental phase." His eyes flashed with hunger.

Noah needed no more encouragement. He lowered his body fully onto Zeke's, enclosing him like a blanket, while pushing his tongue back into Zeke's mouth, where Zeke readily parted his lips for him. He began to slowly grind against him, his aching cock desperately seeking some sort of friction.

Low, rhythmic noises of pleasure hummed from Zeke's mouth as Noah kissed him again and again. Noah became all too aware of Zeke's own rock-solid erection pushing into his stomach, and broke off to spit into his hand, before pushing it between their writhing bodies. The sound Zeke made when Noah closed his wet hand around his hard length was one he planned on hearing many, many times.

"God, Noah," Zeke panted, then pawed at Noah's stomach with frantic hands before he finally found what he was looking for.

Noah gave up all attempts to reserve his dignity as Zeke's hand grasped his cock, stroking up and down in quick motions, causing him to cry out as waves of pleasure rocked through his body.

"I'm already close," Zeke said, breathless, quiet, unsure.

Noah released him. "I want you in my mouth," he said, taking immense pleasure at the look on Zeke's face. "If that's okay."

Zeke didn't reply, just gasped and nodded, stroking Noah's hair as he slid downwards. Noah gripped Zeke's hips, then slid his hands under to cup his ass, digging his fingers into the firm flesh. Finally his mouth arrived at its destination. Noah took in a slightly shaky breath before slowly licking Zeke's cock from its base to its leaking head. Then, he peppered it with kisses as it twitched against his cheek.

"Please..." Zeke's pathetic whimper almost sent him over the edge himself.

Noah opened his mouth, taking most of Zeke into his throat in one swift motion. Zeke moaned, a loud, throaty, guttural sound and Noah whacked his thigh, hoping Zeke would understand his signal to shut up. He knew from experience how thin the walls were.

"Sorry," Zeke whispered with a laugh, arching his hips into him.

Noah took him deeper and deeper into his mouth, flicking his tongue up to lick at the velvety skin, relishing its soft feel and the way Zeke squirmed beneath him. Noah dug his nails even harder into Zeke's hips as Zeke gripped Noah's head and began to thrust slightly in his mouth. Every time Noah reached Zeke's head he'd tongue the slit, and Zeke became more and more undone until he was a quivering mess—clawing the bedsheet, writhing, mumbling nonsense.

"I'm..." Zeke said, before lifting a pillow up and smothering his face with it.

Thick, hot liquid filled Noah's mouth. He swallowed.

For a few moments, Zeke lay stone-still, groaning into the pillow. Then he threw it to the side, revealing wild eyes on a flushed, glistening face.

Noah climbed back up to kiss him, more than content to leave it there for today. But within seconds, Zeke had flipped them over, and Noah pressed his erection back into Zeke's waiting hand, slick with spit. Zeke's touch sent him to new depths of elation and heat immediately pooled in his groin as Zeke stroked his dick in time with his thrusts, each of them sending blissful tremors of ecstasy through his body. Now it was his turn to tremble and writhe, tiny moans escaping his lips. This was going to end far too soon for Noah's liking—his balls were already tightening and he was already beginning on float in orgasmic bliss.

When Zeke increased the pace, swiping his finger over the head of his cock on each upstroke, he was done for. He lightly scraped his nails over Zeke's shoulder blade as he pumped Noah's release out of him, coating his stomach in sticky glory. He lay for a few moments, eyes shut, stars dancing on his lids.

Zeke chuckled lightly, relieving some of the tension, drawing Noah to him as he collapsed beside him. He kissed the top of Noah's head, smoothing his hair away from his face before continuing to run his fingers through it.

Noah suppressed a smirk. Zeke was clearly obsessed with his hair. It didn't matter—Noah was obsessed with Zeke.

"I hope that was an... educational experience for you," Noah said.

Beside him, Zeke's body shook with laughter. "Marks out of ten?"

"One hundred."

Noah reached into his bedside table and threw them both a tissue. Then he shuffled their bodies so that his head rested on Zeke's chest. His heart thudded against his ear.

"You'll have to sneak back into your room later," he said, mood sinking at the thought. The morning they'd woken up together, legs and arms entangled in a cocoon of warmth, had quickly become a favourite memory. "There's only so many times you could pretend you got up before the others. Which is an implausible lie, anyway."

Zeke made a grumbling noise. Noah looked up to see he'd shut his eyes. His blonde hair, tousled and damp with sweat, lay sprawled across the pillow.

Noah smiled.

This is what happiness feels like.

Zeke seemed to be on the verge of sleep, but then said, "I meant what I said earlier. This isn't just a bit of fun to me." His fingers traced the small scar on Noah's ribcage that he'd gotten tumbling down onto rusty metal in a scrap yard a few years back.

Noah was a feather, floating out of the window and up into the sky. "Me neither," he said. "So... am I the first guy you've ever been attracted to?"

"I guess if I'm really honest with myself, I probably had a bit of a crush on Oliver, looking back."

"*Oliver*?" Noah said. "Your colleague we visited in London? *Really*?"

Beneath him, Zeke shook with laughter.

"You don't need to be jealous of Oliver." *He's probably about to die anyway,* lingered unspoken between them. "Anyway, you're the first guy I've properly *liked,* if that makes you feel any better." Zeke mussed Noah's hair.

"What about girlfriends?"

"Loads of them. Thousands. Kicking down the door."

"I can believe it."

Zeke laughed. "I've had a couple of casual things. Nothing too serious." There was a beat before he said, "Can you tell me about Rotterdam?"

"Rotterdam?" Noah went rigid, the word a trigger for thousands of memories, not all of them good.

"Only if you want to."

"What do you want to know?"

"About you. Your life there. And what happened in the end? Only if you want."

Noah considered what to tell him. How to summarise a lifetime into a few sentences. "I'm the oldest of five. It's just me now. Well, me and Uncle Nathaniel."

"*Five*? What was that like? Zaya and I struggled with sharing things between two."

"It was... it was pretty great, actually." He must have sounded sad, as Zeke squeezed him tighter against him. "I ended up looking after my younger siblings a lot. But I didn't mind. I enjoyed protecting them." *But ultimately I failed to do that, in the end...*

"What about your parents?"

"*Far* was away a lot—he was a major in our military, with my uncle—so *Mor* raised us, really. But we all loved and respected and idolised our father—three of us followed in his footsteps, myself included obviously. Let me find you some pictures..." Noah reluctantly untangled himself from Zeke to find a tablet, digging deep into folders he hadn't opened in years. Soon Zeke was flicking through decades' worth of beaming smiles.

Noah tore his own eyes away, focussing on the ceiling. All he saw in the photos was loss, pain, lives unlived. His throat tightened.

"I'm sorry," said Zeke, biting his lip, eyes crinkled with concern. He threw the tablet onto the floor.

"It's fine. It's nice to talk about them." He sighed. "To answer your other question. About the last days of Rotterdam. It was fucking *awful*. I can't even put it into words, Zeke."

"Then don't. I'm sorry, I feel bad, I didn't mean to spoil everything—"

"Stop that." Noah stroked Zeke's chest, lightly tugging at the light, downy hair. "It's sweet you want to know about it." He took a deep breath. "We got no warning. One day everything was fine, then one day it was all sirens, fire, types on our city streets and ten bombers in the sky."

"Shit."

"It was, it really was. I was one of the lucky ones. They herded us onto transport flights and brought us across to here. It didn't feel lucky at the time. Most of us felt awful for abandoning everyone. Friends. Family. All the civilians."

A familiar image bubbled to the surface of his mind, the one his mind tortured him with in his darkest moments—Noah, in the cargo plane, looking down at Rotterdam burning as he was lifted higher and higher into the air. The sound of screaming audible even over the engines. Or was that detail only supplied by his imagination?

"There was nothing you could have done."

Zeke was correct, but Rotterdam was a car crash. A blazing inferno of teeth, blood and death. And soon, would London meet a similar fate?

Noah looked up at Zeke, his face haloed by his hair, golden in the light. He looked blissfully happy. What good would it do to tell him what he knew? He was already an anxious wreck on the field. But if London really was falling, he wanted him to be ready.

He opened his mouth. Shut it. Then opened it again to say, "I've got something I want to tell you."

ZEKE

Zeke gazed out of the window from the passenger seat of the car as the world whizzed by, a blur of green and brown. Ahead of them, a marigold-yellow sunrise inked the dark sky. Noah held the steering wheel lazily as he leaned back into his seat, flicking through now ancient songs on the stereo from the time *before*.

It was twenty days since Zeke's return to Avantis, each ending with a *training session* in Noah's bedroom, late at night. Each morning, he'd crept back into the dormitory room before Habib, Luo and their new addition, Brodie Campbell, awoke. If they wondered where he was when they all went to bed, they didn't ask.

"Can you turn the volume up?" Frankie asked from the backseat of the car.

It was already pretty loud, in Zeke's opinion, but he complied.

Frankie had been a last-minute addition to their little road trip. When she discovered her day off corresponded with theirs, and where they were going, she'd practically invited herself. Part of him was glad to spend time with Frankie outside of the compound and was touched at how she wanted to support him today. However, a far larger part imagined all the things he'd be doing if he was alone with Noah in the car right now, like reaching over and grabbing Noah's hand, entwining their fingers and stroking the back of his hand and—

"Zeke?"

"Huh?"

"I said, how are you feeling about seeing him? Your boss? The evil genius?" Frankie cackled to herself like she thought she was hilarious, throwing her head back and giving him a manic grin through the rear mirror.

"He is not an evil genius. Well, definitely not the genius part, anyway. My friend is really sick from what he injected him with." Zeke shook his head to shake away the memory of Oliver entering Harding's office after him, to 'give blood'. Was Oliver even still alive? Surely Becca would have called him if he'd died?

"But you're not, even though you had the same stuff?"

"I'm really not sure what went on. That's the whole point of going today."

"How the hell are we all getting into London's most top security prison, anyway?"

Noah tutted. "*We all* are not. I already told you, Zeke and I are the only ones my uncle's friend could put on his visitor list. Ten minutes, in and out."

Yesterday evening, Noah took a call at the fire pit and slipped up into the allotment, Zeke following close behind. Noah appealed, begged, *pleaded* with the person on the other end of the call for their help. Zeke had lingered uselessly nearby, feeling like a burden.

"Thank you," Zeke said, for the zillionth time. He stared at Noah before dragging his gaze away, praying Frankie was too distracted to be analysing their every movement.

In front of the others, Noah and Zeke had been incredibly careful over the last few weeks, addressing each other in only the most polite and formal tones. There was no point spoiling the illusion now, even though Zeke would have loved to talk to Frankie. He hadn't even been able to tell Zaya yet, thanks to the militantly monitored communication policy.

Shortly later, they pulled up at a security booth adjoined to a tall red-brick wall, rolls of sharp barbed wire adorning its top. Noah made casual conversation with the guard, as if he visited the prison every other day. Their digital passes checked out, and the guard soon ushered them through to the car park.

Leaving Frankie behind to wait in the car, Zeke and Noah walked over to the prison. The main building stood quietly before them, ominous and bleak. A faded sign read: HMP Blackhouse. After a laborious checking-in process, which made the process at Avantis seem like a walk in the park, prison officers escorted them into an empty waiting room.

"There are still cameras," said Noah, nodding to a red light in the corner.

Zeke grinned at him. "I wasn't about to jump on top of you."

Noah shuffled across in the hard metal seats to press his thigh against Zeke's. "Are you ready for this?"

Not really. "Are you still okay with coming in with me?"

"Of course." Noah yawned and relaxed back in his chair. "It's a shame Frankie decided to tag along. It was a nightmare to swap to get this date off together. I thought we could go somewhere after this. Back to the watermill, maybe."

"We could push her into the river?"

"Sounds like a plan."

"Lieutenant Forrest and Officer Bates?"

Zeke's head snapped up. A plump woman in a white coat gestured for them to follow her. Her heeled boots created a *clop, clop, clop* against the tiles. A harrowing, howling scream echoed down the corridor from a distant room.

The woman glanced back at them, frowning. "I don't know who you are or how you've wrangled ten minutes with my patient, but it's going to be *ten minutes* at the absolute maximum."

"Patient?" asked Zeke.

"Albert Harding was transferred over to my psychiatric team a few weeks ago. He's going through the process of being diagnosed. Before you ask, his trial is currently on hold," the woman said, her voice dripping with disdain.

Zeke caught Noah's eye as Noah let out a scoff that he quickly tried to disguise as a cough.

Abruptly, the woman halted her determined march outside of the windowed door. She swiped her lanyard to release the door. "He's through here. The guard will be present in the corner at all times. I'll see you in ten."

Zeke froze in place, swallowing. His fear must have been written all over his face, because Noah squeezed his waist as he pushed him gently through the door, his hand rubbing the small of his back.

"Let's get this over with," Noah whispered. "Whatever he says, we'll face it together."

Zeke steadied himself and allowed himself to be dragged into the small interview room.

Someone was sitting handcuffed to a small table. At first, he almost turned to tell the guard in the corner they'd brought the wrong prisoner. The man—Doctor Harding—that was sitting at the table was skeletal. A dark jumper hung off his body, exposing pale, thin wrists under its sleeves. Gone was Harding's usual trim beard, a straggly grey mess in its place. His gaunt face housed deep set wrinkles.

"Doctor... Harding?" Zeke's voice was loud in the silent space. Noah hung back until Zeke grabbed his hand, dragging him forward towards his old mentor.

Doctor Harding looked up, blinking at them. His glassy eyes took a while to focus. "Zeke?" he said, at last, twisting the handcuffs around his wrist.

Even though he'd spent the last few days imagining this conversation, every word and every rehearsed speech left his brain. Noah tapped his wristband. Time was already running out. He sat down opposite Doctor Harding, and Noah followed suit in the second chair, brushing his ankle against his.

"I'm Lieutenant Forrest, Zeke's friend. We've come to ask you some questions." He nodded at Zeke to continue.

"Zeke..." said Doctor Harding, shaking his head like he couldn't believe it. He cast his eyes down to his cuffs, fiddling with the chain that fixed them to the table. "Why are you here? Where's... Where's Oliver?"

"What? Oliver? He's not with us. He's at home. Sick. He's really sick, Doctor Harding." Zeke stared at him, his brain unable to connect the man in front of him with the man he knew.

"Sick you say? Will he be back in the lab tomorrow, do you think?"

Zeke glanced at Noah, who'd raised one sceptical eyebrow.

"No, he won't be. He's extremely ill. Dying, even." Noah said. "Can you tell us what you injected him with, Doctor?"

Doctor Harding stopped playing with his handcuffs, looking up to meet Noah's gaze.

"I'm sorry," he said, mildly, as if they were discussing the weather. "I think I'm confused."

"Bullshit," snapped Noah, with some force.

Zeke blinked rapidly—Noah so rarely lost his composure. The guard took a hesitant step forward, a warning in his eye.

"Fine, let's skip straight to Zeke. I want you to organise a detailed substance report, and a sample to be handed over, of what you injected inside of him. Today." Noah lowered his voice to the barest of whispers as he leaned across the table. "Or else I'll do everything in my power to make your life a living hell."

Zeke very much doubted there was anything Noah could do to Doctor Harding, considering how difficult it'd been to organise a ten-minute meeting. "Noah," he hissed. "Calm down."

Doctor Harding began to rock. A rumbling cackle erupted out of him, quickly escalating into a cacophonous roar.

Zeke reached for Noah's hand under the table. The man in front of him was not the cool, composed Doctor Harding who'd led Oakfield as efficiently as a well-oiled machine. This man was a deranged stranger.

"Please, Doctor Harding," Zeke said. "If you won't do anything else, just tell me why you did it. You owe me that much, at least." Years of working under the man, and it was reduced to this?

The doctor stopped, stared, appeared to consider his request.

He lowered his voice to say, "The scientific community have long lamented the constraints suppressing advancement in comprehending the intricacies of the RONS virus. A consortium of esteemed colleagues—leading experts from around the world—started working closely together, following a lead on immunomodulators." Doctor Harding's eyes drifted away from him, and his voice became almost dream-like when he continued, "But here in London, The Health Research Authority and their endless regulations were always getting in our way. They were slowing us down. We didn't have time to wait for their approval, not when lives were on the line. Hence, the imperative arose for an assertion of self-reliance."

Self-reliance? Zeke wanted to scream at him, but Noah nodded, likely to make Harding continue rather than agreeing with Harding's questionable moral code.

"We were testing an immunomodulator on subjects and were starting to see promising results. Our methods were controversial, of course, but we believed that the potential benefits outweighed the risks. We were so close... so, so close."

Noah increased his grip on Zeke's hand.

"But Zeke, my boy, you don't need to worry."

"I... I don't? Did I not receive the same batch as Oliver? Is there anything we can do to help him?" The questions gushed out of Zeke like a burst dam.

Doctor Harding leaned forward, as if about to tell them a secret. "You have nothing to worry about because... I never injected any of my staff with anything," he hissed with a sneer.

"You liar!" Noah jumped to his feet, sending his chair flying across the room with a screech.

Zeke flinched away from him. What did Noah hope to achieve with this outburst?

He was saved from suggesting they leave by the guard shouting, "Sir!" with a furious expression etched on his face.

Half a second later, the door to the room swung open, hitting the wall with a crash. Their favourite friend was back.

"We've still got five minutes," protested Noah, quickly silenced by the woman's glare. Zeke took one last look at Doctor Harding. He wore the tiniest of smiles on his lips as he leaned back in his chair, his fingers touching together to make an arch.

"Lovely to see you, Zeke. I hope military service is treating you well."

Zeke opened his mouth to say something before snapping it shut, jumping up to follow Noah out of the room.

"Well, that went well," Noah said.

"Sounds like it," replied Frankie. "Sorry, Zeke."

Noah drove them out of the prison site, his face set in a grim frown. He'd put the car in manual mode and was now pushing the gear stick with aggressive force. "I... lost control for a second in the room back there. I don't know what came over me. I'm sorry if I scared you."

Zeke caught Frankie's eye in the rearview mirror. "He was infuriating, for sure. It almost made it worse when he dropped the insane act."

"I just don't know how we can get you help without information from him."

"It's fine," Zeke mumbled, his head resting against the window. He was done with this conversation and was becoming concerned with how Frankie was interpreting it all. "I'm fine. You already had Leo run every test he could, and they all came back clear. Let's just forget about it and move on."

Noah's mouth twitched. It looked like he was about to press the matter before deciding against it.

They drove for a few minutes in pensive silence before Frankie asked, "Did Zaya get back to you about seeing us? I would love to meet her."

Zeke checked his wristband. Seeing a message from Zaya, his mood instantly brightened. "She said she can meet us for an hour at the park near her house." Noah slowed the vehicle to input the address. "If you guys don't mind?" Zeke added.

Frankie reached over from the backseat to touch his shoulder. "Of course not."

Zaya was waiting for them on a bench when they arrived. He ran the last few steps, hugging her tightly and swinging her around as Noah and Frankie hung back. "Hey Zee," she said. When he released her, a red, raw burn mark on her forehead, partially obscured by sunglasses, drew his attention.

"What's that?"

Her hand shot to the gruesome wound, touching it gingerly. "It happened at a protest the other day." She narrowed her eyes. "It got pretty violent. Several buildings were blown up."

Her words instantly transported Zeke back to the day of Splat's death. His stomach clenched as his mind replayed Splat, bleeding profusely from his forearm, jumping through the hole into the horde of monsters waiting for him, for the thousandth time.

"Shit," said Frankie, stepping forward.

Zeke shook his head as if it would erase the image forever seared into his soul. "This is Frankie."

Frankie hugged her. "Great to finally meet you!"

"Likewise. Thanks for taking good care of this one for me." Zaya ruffled Zeke's hair. "And you, Noah. Zeke always talks so highly of you both."

Noah shuffled forward. "It's a pleasure."

Zaya's eyes twinkled as her lips twitched into a smile.

"I take it things aren't improving in the city?" Noah asked.

Zaya sighed and sat down on the bench, wrapping her plaid jacket around her.

"Were you actually *in* the protests?" said Zeke, trying to keep his voice even.

Rolling her eyes, she said, "It was meant to be a peaceful march. It's not my fault some idiots took it too far."

"Still, you need to be more—"

"Can we not? We've only got a short time together before I next see you God-knows-when."

The four of them walked along the gravel path, Zeke and Zaya trailing ahead of Noah and Frankie. The normalcy of it all struck him: angry cyclists dinging bells at slow-to-move pedestrians; children screaming and running circles around each other; dogs chasing balls.

"So," said Zaya, nudging into him, lowering her voice to a murmur. "How's it going with Noah, then?"

He glanced over to meet Zaya's eyes, her analytical gaze boring into his as she grinned at him, her smile a wide horizon.

"What do you mean?"

"Oh, come off it. His eyes haven't left you since the moment you all got here. He practically snarled at that random guy that pushed into you earlier."

Zeke attempted to suppress the hot flush that crept up his neck. His chest felt tight as he stared at the gravel path.

He lowered his voice to say, "Frankie doesn't know. It's sort of a bit awkward with him being our CO. But, it's going well. He's amazing." He kept his eyes firmly on the gravel path.

"Why didn't you tell me you were interested in guys?" Zaya sounded pleasant enough, but he knew her well enough to spot the light drizzle of hurt leaking through.

"It's sort of a recent discovery."

"Well, I'm happy for you. How did—"

Someone barrelled straight towards them on an e-scooter, seemingly unwilling or unable to change their course. The four of them dove to the side of the path, tumbling into each other. The rider—a spotty teenage boy—screeched the scooter to a halt. He scanned their faces, locking onto Noah's. Without a word, he threw a piece of paper at him.

"You dropped this," he grunted, before pressing down hard on his handlebars, zooming off down the path before any of them could react. Noah's eyebrows knitted together as he fumbled to open the small piece of heavily folded paper.

"I hope it's a treasure map," said Frankie, and Zaya snorted.

They crowded around behind Noah's shoulders to read it.

Unit 12, top floor. E17 9HQ. 3 pm. Alone.

- N

There was a pregnant silence.

"Is this from... your uncle?" Zeke reached forward to touch it.

Noah folded the paper and slipped it into his pocket, his lips pressed into a grim line.

"That's miles away," said Zaya. "You'd better leave soon if you want to make it. I'll lead us back."

Noah shook his head, putting his hands in his pockets. "You two stay with Zaya."

"Absolutely not," said Zeke, while Frankie nodded her head in agreement. "I don't care that he said alone. This could be some sort of weird trap."

Frankie's face flickered with confusion. "For what?"

"I have to head back to work anyway," said Zaya. "I'll walk you to your car."

All too soon, the three of them stood looking up at a tall, derelict building on the corner of a quiet street, in an industrial part of East London. They hadn't seen a single soul for the last five minutes of the drive, which hadn't reassured Zeke.

After trying every door they could locate only to find them locked, Noah removed his coat, balling it up in his fist before smashing the glass pane on the door furthest from the street.

"Christ, Noah!" Frankie hissed.

Noah said nothing in reply, just pushed the glass away to lean through to unlock the door from the inside.

There was no power inside the dark building. They climbed the central staircase, eyeballing various debris scattered on each level: a blood-soaked sleeping bag, three scurrying rats, torn cardboard boxes. When they reached the penultimate floor, Noah hesitated.

"We'll wait here," said Frankie, throwing herself on the floor. She, like Zeke, was slightly out of breath. They were still a far cry from the super soldiers they needed to be, but he could only imagine what state they'd have been in if they'd tried to climb the staircase at this pace months ago.

Zeke threw Noah a quick glance. "I think I saw a sign for a toilet on the last floor. I'm going to take a look."

"I doubt it still works." Frankie said. "May as well go and shit in the corner."

"No thanks."

Leaving Frankie on the floor, Noah and Zeke climbed the final set of stairs together. As soon as they turned the corner, Noah said, "You're not coming in with me. I need to see him alone."

"I just wanted a second alone with you." Zeke scanned the corridor for any sign of cameras.

Noah reached to lace his hand with his as they walked. There was only one door on this floor, waiting ominously at the end of the corridor. When they were a few steps away, he stopped them. Pushing him against the wall, Noah kissed him softly for a moment before pulling away to press their foreheads together. He seemed to be delaying the moment he faced whatever was on the other side of that door.

"I'll be right outside," Zeke whispered. "If you shout, I'll come running."

Noah's grimace twisted into a smile, no doubt imagining how little use he would be in any scenario where Noah was shouting for help. Noah kissed his forehead before shuffling back, holding both of Zeke's forearms as he looked deep into his gaze.

"Hopefully, I won't be long."

"Are you guys... okay?"

Noah sprang away from him. Frankie stood on the top step, her eyes wide.

"I thought you were waiting downstairs?" Zeke said, cringing at his evident panic.

"I decided to wait outside the toilet for you. That stairwell was creeping me out." She looked between them, then to the wide space they'd created between their bodies. "What's going on?"

Noah sighed, running his hands through his hair. "I'm about to go in. I'll see you shortly," he said. He opened the door and slipped through, leaving them alone in the hallway.

NOAH

When Noah entered the spacious, empty room, he almost didn't recognise the figure standing near the wide window as his uncle. He couldn't remember the last time he'd seen him out of uniform and his uncle's casual clothes transported him back to childhood weekends when he and his father were on leave. They were often spent at De Biesbosch National Park: early morning jogs along the rivers, followed by pancake breakfasts, his brothers spooning chocolate spread directly into their mouths, to their mother's dismay.

Taking a tentative step towards him, the light streaming through the window highlighted the crow's feet etched deep in the corner of his dark, baggy eyes. His customary service cap was noticeably absent, revealing the streaks of peppery grey that littered his hair.

As Noah met his unwavering gaze, his uncle let out a breath, making the sign of the cross.

"Uncle Nathan." Noah hovered a few feet away from him, unsure how to greet him. Neither of them were one for hugs, but a handshake felt odd. "Where have you been? What's going on?"

"What part of *alone* didn't you understand?" were his first words, although there was no real malice behind them. "You're going to need a cover story for why the three of you ventured over here, if they trace your trackers."

Noah's eyes flickered to his uncle's left arm.

"Mine's been removed," he said. When Noah only stared at him, his uncle let out an unsteady sigh, running his hand over his face. "That kid found you then? I wasn't sure if he was going to take the money and run. I just watched you smash open that door, by the way. Didn't he tell you the key was in the plant pot?"

Noah wasn't in the mood for any more chatter. "Why are we here, Uncle?"

His face looked pained as he replied, "I've... left the military."

"No shit." Noah folded his arms. "What happened?"

"Things got tense between myself and the Chief General. We had several..."—he rubbed his eyes—"*disagreements* that escalated into him issuing an arrest warrant."

"What?" Noah's stomach clenched as a wave of dizziness struck him. He tried to say something else, but words failed him. Murphy's odd interest in his uncle finally began to make sense.

His uncle paced back and forth across the room. "Luckily, a close friend forewarned me. He cut out my chip." He rubbed at his left bicep as if it still pained him. "I've been moving from place to place since then, usually at night. I would have contacted you sooner, but..."

Noah's brain raced to make connections, to make this make sense. "What sort of disagreements? What did you do?"

"Jesus, Noah," his uncle snapped, taking a step back to look out of the window. "Has Murphy really got you so conditioned you can't even entertain the idea that I might not be in the wrong here?"

"Just tell me what's going on and let me make my own judgement on it then."

"I threatened to leak several documents unless we made them public. Statistic reports detailing type-related deaths spiking in the last six months. Attempted typeB border breaches. Data predictions of food supplies running dry by midwinter. Papers detailing the army's updated crisis response protocols."

"But... why? There's good reasons not to do that. London already has massive rebellion problems without inciting further mass panic." Noah's voice was loud enough for Zeke and Frankie to hear in the hallway, but he didn't care.

"Because civilians have a right to know!" His uncle's nostrils flared as red patches flared to life on his cheeks. "Because they have a right to choose. To *live!*"

"But—"

"I heard what happened a few weeks ago. I'm sorry about Cameron King. Splat was an exemplary officer."

Noah flinched at the abrupt change in conversation. He imagined Splat's reaction to being called an 'exemplary officer' and almost smiled.

"I also heard about what your squadron found out there. With the wire? A team went out to investigate it the next day. What was left of the wire anyway, the part that stretched into the trees. I've read the report. It's a remarkable manifestation of the type's evolving intelligence and coordination. It represents a significant leap in their ability to communicate and strategise. It was *nine hundred metres* long, Noah. Their set up utilised specially designed hooks and clamps that securely fastened the wire to the trees."

"How did it actually help them communicate, though?" Noah found himself irresistibly compelled to engage in the conversation, his thoughts consumed by the wire that had lingered in his mind ever since he first laid eyes upon it.

"The scientists say it was designed to emit low-frequency subsonic pulsations when tugged. Infrasonic vibrations or something like that."

Noah's mind reeled. What was next? Types building bombs? Digging tunnels underground?

"What did Murphy tell you about it?" his uncle asked. "And has she asked about me?"

Noah crossed his arms. "Is that why you wanted to meet me? For information? I'm surprised you didn't just send Leonie Voigt again. I'm not following her bullshit secret plan to record things for you, by the way."

"I wanted to see you, Noah, because this is likely my last opportunity. But please, consider Leonie's request. We wouldn't be asking if it wasn't important. If we can get all the information out to the public now, before our infrastructure collapses, we'll be in a better place to save more lives." His uncle's wristband vibrated, and his uncle glanced at it. It was not the standardised army-issued band he usually wore. "We're out of time. Someone is coming to transport me to my next safehouse." He stepped forward to grip Noah's shoulders. "My sources say it could be a matter of weeks before everything falls apart. You need to make a plan. Does everything in the package make sense?"

The package. The one now hidden behind his skirting board. "I haven't opened it."

His uncle made a garbled sound halfway between a scream and a sigh before grabbing his arms to shake Noah. "It was a fluke of luck that got us out of Rotterdam. You won't get that lucky twice. Especially now I'm a wanted man." His hands fell to his sides. His eyes squeezed shut. "I'm sorry about that."

Another stream of vibrations from his uncle's wristband interrupted them.

"I have to go. Open the package. Make a plan." He reached into his pocket and pulled out a tiny data chip. "Here. Here's a copy of all the documents. I'll try to send a message to you a few days before it gets leaked."

His uncle attempted to put the chip in Noah's hand, but he threw his hands up in the air, away from him. "No. I don't want any part of this. They've already interrogated me about you. I'm surprised they even let me into London today. They'll probably search me at the gate."

Why on earth did he allow Frankie and Zeke to accompany him here? He couldn't ask them to lie for him. Should he go straight to Murphy and tell her about meeting him today? Why had Uncle Nathaniel put him in this position?

His uncle shook his head. Reaching back into his pocket, he took out a piece of paper similar to the one the boy on the scooter gave Noah earlier. "You'll be able to reach me on this number for a short time. Memorise it or rewrite it using a cipher." His uncle stepped towards the door.

"Wait!" Noah cried, stepping in front of him to block the way. Words failed him again, so he stood open-mouthed, staring at the man who'd helped raise him for potentially the last time.

His uncle clasped his head with two hands before kissing him on the top of his head, as he'd done when he was a child. "You'll be fine, Noah. You have a loyal squad behind you." He brushed his finger over the glass on Noah's watch. "Your father would be so proud of the man you've become."

Noah blinked, fighting back hot tears.

"*Jeg elsker dig,*" his uncle said. "I'll pray to my lucky stars that we see each other again."

Uncle Nathan kissed his head once more, then left the room without looking back.

Noah's day went from bad to worse, to truly abysmal, when Habib confronted him at the fire pit that evening.

"I need to speak to you." Habib walked off towards the allotment.

Noah picked up his rucksack and trailed after him, walking in silence for a few minutes, until they reached Habib's destination behind the shed.

For a short time, the pair of them stood staring each other down. Habib's face glowed in the small patch of light the lamp attached to the shed offered. Noah waited for Habib to begin, mentally preparing to rehash the prior conversations they'd had since Leonie Voigt spoke to them.

"Right. No bullshit. What's going on with you and the puppy?"

Fuck. Frankie was one thing, Habib on the other hand, was another.

"What?" He blinked at him, attempting a bewildered expression.

Habib threw him an accusatory, irritated look. "Don't even try it. For a start, he keeps looking at you with love heart eyes every time he thinks nobody's watching."

"He does not!"

"So, I suppose he's got some other secret lover that gave him the scratches all over his back?"

Noah's face burned hotter than the fiery pits of hell. The fiery pits of hell he wished would come and swallow him whole.

"I'm not fucking stupid. Obviously, I was going to notice he's never in our room when we go to bed. I just don't understand, Noah." Habib paused, clawing his hand through his hair. He scowled at him with such ferocity, Noah felt physically chilled. "You gave Splat and Meredith that entire speech about why inter-squad relationships are inappropriate, and now you—the *commanding officer*—are messing around with some—"

"Don't insult him, please. He doesn't deserve that."

"I'm sure you won't mind defending his honour."

He'd already had enough. Noah raised his hand. "Listen. We're not 'messing around'. And you don't need to tell me how hypocritical this is." Noah's voice broke, and he took an unsteady breath to compose himself. "I berate myself for it every second of every day."

"Then get him transferred to a different squad."

Words tumbled around Noah's mind, but he failed to string them into coherent thoughts.

"I don't trust anyone else to protect him like we will," Noah eventually said, in a small, yet determined, voice. This was his call, and Habib was going to have to accept it.

Habib raised his eyebrows, his gaze penetrating into Noah's. "If he needs that much protecting, then he's a risk to us, anyway."

"Look, I've already been to Murphy and asked her to move him out of direct combat and it was a flat-out no. There's nothing else I can do. Besides, he is improving day by day. You can't deny that." Noah sighed, running his hands through his hair. "Are you going to tell the others about us?" he asked, and braced for Habib's response.

Habib made a frustrated sound. "No. But I'm not happy."

"I can see that," Noah snapped. "Don't worry, I'm not happy with myself either."

Habib's face morphed, his eyes crinkling in concern. "Hey," he said, his voice far softer now. "Come here."

When Noah remained frozen in place, Habib crossed the small distance between them in two strides and threw his arms around him, squeezing him tight. Noah weakly returned the hug.

"A part of me is happy you finally found someone again, Noah. Really, it is. But this is a lot to take in. We rely on our COs to model the rules we all have to follow. To be objective in the field. What happens if you start to play favourites? Plus, I already watched you be completely destroyed by Khyan's death. There's a massive risk that Zeke could die any given day. I love you, but I don't trust you not to completely lose it if that happens."

Noah nodded against him. "I give you full permission to hold me to account. I can only give you my word that you don't need to worry. My loyalty to our squad will always come first," he said, believing the honesty behind his words.

Habib pulled back, nodded. "I believe you. Just... be careful, okay? And think about how you're going to break this to Meredith. Because you can't hide this forever." He punched Noah's arm before walking off back to the fire.

Anxiety bubbled and boiled within Noah, threatening to pull him under. He sank against the cold metal of the shed. His fractured brain didn't know where to begin to untangle his growing list of problems. Reaching into his pocket, he pulled out his latest whittling project, shaving slivers off what would be a raven's wing in the dim light of the lamp. He'd been at it for a few minutes when he heard footsteps.

Zeke's body slid down next to him. "What was that all about? Or do I not want to know?"

Noah groaned. "Habib knows about us. He's not going to tell the others, but he was sharing his... concerns."

"Shit. I think Frankie suspects as well after she saw us in the corridor earlier. I tried to fob her off, but..."

Noah found Zeke's hand and interlaced his own with it, squeezing it tight. The fast, high-pitched melancholious song of a nightingale drifted down from the trees across from the vegetable patches.

"Do you think he's right to be concerned?" Zeke asked at last.

"I think... I think we need to promise each other that we'll follow protocol in the field. That we won't let this"—Noah gestured between them—"impact any decisions we have to make." *Easier said than done.*

Zeke nodded. "I'll do my best. What are you going to do about your uncle?"

"I haven't decided." Noah sank against Zeke's chest. "I have no idea what to do. The more I think about it, the more it hurts my head."

Zeke pulled back to whisper, "No matter what happens, I'll be there with you."

Noah wanted so badly to believe him. The clouds parted to reveal a bright, full moon illuminating Zeke in a mellow, serene wash of moonlight. Noah traced the shape of his face with his fingertips. How was he so lucky that Zeke had entered his life at just the right time?

Zeke lifted his chin up to kiss him, tentative and butterfly-light at first, deepening quickly into hungry desperation.

"Not here," Noah hissed. It was unlikely that anyone else would venture this far from the fire pit, but he didn't want to risk it. He entwined his fingers with Zeke's and pulled him to his feet before leading him over to the shed door. Hopefully, it would be unlocked—work in the allotment died down somewhat by December, but bulbs were still planted and carrots and cabbage harvested.

The metal door was stiff from rust, but gave way after two hard budges. Earthy aromas of soil and plants filled the air as they made their way inside. The moonlight from the single grimy window danced across the cluttered shelves and workbench, revealing a layer of dust that covered everything.

Noah fiddled with a spade for a moment, attempting to prop it against the door to form a makeshift lock.

"We seem to be developing a habit of locking ourselves into small spaces." Zeke leaned back against the wooden workbench, arms folded, magnetic eyes liquid pools of desire.

Noah crossed the space and placed his hands on either side of him, locking him in place. He pushed up against him, relishing the friction when he rolled his hips into Zeke's.

"Is there something wrong with your bedroom?"

Noah traced the outline of Zeke's jaw with his mouth to whisper in his ear, "Too far away," before nipping at his lobe.

Zeke's hands slid underneath Noah's hoodie, his icy-cold fingers only adding to the sensual experience as he glided his hands up and down his back.

And then they were kissing, pressing into each other so hard it was as if their lives depended on it. A fire ignited in Noah's heart, Noah's essence, Noah's everything as he crushed his mouth against Zeke's, pushing his tongue deeper and deeper in. Breathing was no longer important. Waves of lightheadedness hit him and he could have sworn the pair of them were spinning in circles, wrapped in a dizzying embrace.

The sensation of Zeke's growing erection jutting into the side of his hip only added to his fervour. He broke apart their kiss to nibble at the space above Zeke's collarbone as he rubbed his groin through thick tracksuit bottoms. A low, throaty groan came from Zeke's mouth and Noah felt his hair being tugged free of its band before Zeke fisted it almost to the point of pain.

"Hold on," Noah half-whispered, half-panted, and stumbled away from Zeke—who made the most adorable noise of protest—to open a cupboard in the corner of the cluttered shed. It took him a while to find the pile of burlap sacks he was looking for. After kicking the contents of the floor—plastic plant pots, trowels, packets of seeds—into a pile under the workbench, he tossed the pile of hessian fabric onto the floor, arranging them as best he could in the dark.

Zeke laughed. "These are the sort of organisational skills you need to apply to your bedroom."

"Shut up and come here."

Zeke removed his glasses, carefully placing them by a plant pot, before tumbling to the floor and smothering Noah with his body. His weight comforted Noah like a blanket, and finally some of the stress of the day started to drain out of him.

Noah pushed them back upright slightly, and Zeke pulled off their coats so violently, it was as if the garments offended him.

"You'll be col—"

Zeke's mouth silenced his worries. Their tongues danced together in long, wet kisses before Noah's aching cock couldn't take it anymore. He pulled Zeke's hips towards him and ground up against him again and again, in the familiar rhythm he'd gotten far too accustomed to. Every tiny moan that left Zeke's mouth sent a fresh wave of ecstasy through Noah at the knowledge that *he* was causing his pleasure. Small stones jutted uncomfortably into his back, even through the sack and his hoodie, but it was a small price to pay for the exhilaration of feeling Zeke on top of him.

Simultaneously, they reached for the other's trousers, and tugged them down their legs in a tangle of hands and fabric.

When Zeke pushed his body back on top of him, and started to gently suck his skin just above his collarbone, Noah became lost in a fever-dream of skin and stars. But it was Zeke taking both of their lengths in his hand at once, and moving his hand up and down, that truly wrote him off.

"Hold on," he hissed—reluctantly—because there was one thing that would make this even better. He kissed Zeke on the forehead before leaning past him to rummage through his rucksack. He brought out a small bottle of clear, thick liquid, half full. Zeke squinted at it in the moonlight, taking a few seconds to recognise what it was. He blinked in surprise, then a complicated expression crossed his face. Noah inwardly grimaced. Was he being too presumptuous? Or was Zeke wondering where he got it from?

He wiggled the bottle. "I got it from Leo."

This did *not* have the desired effect. Zeke's face crumpled in annoyance and horror.

"Fuck, Zeke, I didn't *use* it with Leo. Just borrowed it from him." He shook his head and laughed. "Christ, why is this so awkward?"

"Stop talking." Zeke pushed Noah backwards again, pressing his mouth hard against his. He stole the bottle from his hand and clicked open the lid.

A few seconds later, Zeke's hand was back where Noah wanted it most. The feeling of their dicks rubbing together in Zeke's slick, thrusting hand was every-thing, *everything*. Bolts of electricity ran through every nerve as Noah felt himself moving uncontrollably under Zeke. With his other hand, Zeke gripped Noah's hip, pulling him downwards. And then Noah felt a new sensation. Zeke, who'd slowed the pace of his hand on Noah's cock, had positioned his other hand millimetres from another very sensitive part of his body. All Noah would have to do would be to push his hips slightly in the right direction, and Zeke's fingers would be *there*.

"Shall I...?" Zeke began and Noah was absolutely sure that if there was more light, Zeke's face would be his favourite shade of pink. "Do you want me to...? Or do you usually...?"

"I'd like that," Noah said, instead of *fuck yes, please, now.* "Only if you want to, though."

He bit back a needy moan as Zeke's finger teased his crease in answer, the cool sensation sending vibrations straight to his cock, and pressure quickly built at the base of Noah's spine. When Zeke swirled his finger around his hole again and again, Noah thought he was going to have to beg for it after all, but then Zeke finally slipped the tip of one finger inside. Greedy for more pressure, Noah pushed his body downwards, hoping he'd get the hint.

He did. Zeke thrust his finger inside of him in time with the heavenly strokes with which he was still gracing their dicks. The feeling of fullness soon sent him spiralling towards the edge, especially when Zeke started whispering his name like a prayer. That, along with Noah's panting and the wet sounds coming from Zeke's efforts, formed a delightful soundscape that threatened to be his undoing.

"I'm almost there," Noah said, and Zeke leaned in to kiss his neck, sucking lightly on it again as he arched his finger towards the spot inside Noah he'd been looking for. "Oh my god," Noah grunted, praying Zeke wouldn't stop. His entire body vibrated with pleasure as he rocked into Zeke's touch.

When Zeke added a second finger, he clamped his lips together as a scream threatened to erupt out of him. Most nights for weeks now, he'd imagined Zeke inside of him in some capacity, but this was ten times better than anything he'd dreamed up.

"This is fucking amazing," Noah whispered, running his thumb over Zeke's cheek.

He was going to say more, so much more, but then Zeke's cock began to twitch against his own, and a choked gasp came out of Zeke's mouth. Hot cum pulsated out of him, coating Noah's lower stomach and jumper. *Oops.* Without breaking his punishing rhythm, Zeke scooped it up and used it to continue to rub Noah with slick, warm fingers. Zeke's heated gaze met Noah's just for a moment. *Oh, the things I'm going to do to you.*

Unable to hold back anymore, Noah came violently as his arse clenched around Zeke's fingers, which were still massaging inside of him in all the best ways. Noah's muscles tensed as his orgasm rocked through his body, and he closed his eyes, riding wave after wave of sensation. Zeke kept pumping until Noah had released what felt like an infinitely long spurt, until Noah had to push his hand away with a happy mumble, unable to take any more.

Zeke groaned, removing himself from Noah then collapsing on top of him. He ran his hands over Zeke's head, that rested in the nook of his shoulder.

Zeke let out a nervous laugh, shooting him his dorkiest grin. "So, that was okay, then?"

You're amazing, he almost said. *You're amazing and brilliant and mine. When I wake up in the morning, I want to hide forever until I remember I get to see you. I was drowning, but now you're my life-raft. I was lost, but now you're my compass, my true north.*

"It was perfect," he said, instead.

Zeke smiled his blinding wide-toothed smile and Noah kissed him until he almost forgot about his uncle, about Splat jumping into the pit of ravenous monsters, about London on the brink of societal collapse, and their impending doom. Almost.

NOAH

It was eight thirty-five in the morning, and Captain Murphy was uncharacteristically late for her weekly briefing. Noah, seated with the twenty lieutenants, couldn't help glancing at his wristband every few seconds. When the door flung open, the soldiers leapt to their feet to salute her.

Murphy waved her arm as she burst through the door. "Stand down." Hurrying to her chair at the end of the boardroom table, she tapped her tablet a few times to bring her presentation up onto the screen behind her.

"This briefing really will be brief this morning," she began, taking a few seconds to smooth her hair back and regain her composure. "Firstly, Forrest, Newman and Roskilly, I need you to remain afterwards to review plans for a mission next week."

Why couldn't Murphy have waited until the end of the meeting to announce that? He couldn't help but tune Murphy out to run through plausible scenarios that required the attention of the specified three lieutenants. Tobias caught his eye a few times, glowering at him from across the table, further distracting him. By the time Murphy reached the final item on her agenda—government proposals to station armed officers outside any business in the city that sold food, pooling personnel from every regiment—Noah was ready to burst from the suspense.

When the meeting ended, Tobias and Lowenna Roskilly came to sit on either side of Noah. Out of all the other squadron leaders, Lowenna was one of Noah's favourites—Squad E always had been friendly with Squad K. But why, oh why, did he and Tobias have to land together in whatever fresh hell this was?

"We're forming a platoon from your three squadrons," said Murphy, in her usual abrupt manner. "This mission was originally assigned to the Black Rangers, but they're... thin on the ground currently. The three of you will head out next Tuesday. Location is Red Ridge Farm." An area map and several photographs filled the screen. Noah stared at the postcode, the letters and numbers confirming what he'd known deep down all along: this must be the mission Leonie Voigt—and his uncle—were waiting for.

"Initial aim is data collection. Our research team has been gathering evidence of unusual type activity for a while now."

"What type of unusual activity, ma'am?" Tobias asked, sitting dead upright and looking serious, which irritated Noah. The jackass never ceased to be a suck-up.

Murphy tapped her fingernails on the table, swivelling slightly on her chair. Ignoring Tobias's question, she said, "After collecting the evidence required, including the live capture of at least three typeBs, Command will give the order for you to exterminate any type within a kilometre's radius."

Lowenna's jaw dropped open. "An entire klick?"

"Hence the platoon, Roskilly." Murphy's voice frosted over. "You'll have plenty of manpower for the job. You'll be well-supplied with ammunition—within reason—and will have five canine units with you. Your main challenge will be the route to the farm. The roads you will be required to use haven't been driven on in quite some time. Our intelligence team are putting their heads together to decide the best route, but expect a fair amount of road blockages, and to camp out overnight."

Noah's heart sank further and further as Murphy droned on and on, talking them through a variety of images, maps and scenarios. This mission was quickly chalking up to be a nightmare, with or without the presence of Tobias and Squad C.

"Finally, know that anything witnessed on this assignment will be highly confidential. All your squads will go through an intense debriefing, where it will be made explicitly clear to them what they can and cannot share about anything discovered on the farm."

Noah gritted his teeth. From Leonie, he already roughly knew what they'd find there. Clearly, whoever she was working for somehow managed to get them assigned to this mission. Regardless, he didn't want any part in filming surreptitious recordings. He'd complete the mission, stick to the script, and if Leonie popped back up at the fire pit to shout at him, he'd tell her to go to hell.

"Absolutely Captain," Tobias's voice drawled. "We won't let you down."

Inwardly, Noah groaned. How would he get through forty-eight hours side-by-side with this obnoxious arsehole? He caught Lowenna's eye across the table. She raised her eyebrow slightly, her lips twitching. Likely she was thinking the same thing. Perhaps with her in the mix, it wouldn't be so bad. Or so he could kid himself.

As he left Murphy's office, an uneasy feeling came over him. His uncle was seemingly a highly wanted man, threatening to reveal state secrets, and now Murphy wanted to send the nephew of that man on a highly classified mission? Something wasn't adding up, but Noah couldn't quite put the puzzle pieces together.

ZEKE

Z eke became increasingly aware of Noah's mood spiralling downwards each day that passed as their Tuesday mission became ever larger on the horizon. He'd been oddly enigmatic about it when he relayed the information from Captain Murphy. Even when Zeke pressed him for more information later, in private, he'd said very little. His irritable, quiet demeanour and snappy temper rubbed off on Squad E, who quickly gave him a wide berth. By the time Monday evening rolled around, he was intolerable.

"You go talk to him, Zeke."

Frankie, shivering from the light drizzle, leant against a fence alongside Zeke in the training field. A short distance from them, the rest of Squad E formed a tight circle, talking in raised voices with arms crossed. Vitt was gesturing wildly.

They'd been running through low-light target elimination drills when Noah fell into an argument with Brodie Campbell. Apparently, the way Noah did things was too different from his old lieutenant for their new member to cope with. In his late thirties, Brodie was easily the oldest of them, and was not taking well to following orders from a man a decade younger than him. Tensions had risen over the last few days, bubbling over in tonight's cold, damp evening training session. Zeke hadn't actually heard their final blows at each other, only Noah announcing the session was over, storming away from Brodie in the compound's direction, Wolf following at his heel.

"What?" he replied. "Me?"

Even in the fading light, he saw Frankie roll her eyes. "Oh, come off it. You've got a better chance than even Vitt of getting him to calm down."

"I doubt it," Zeke mumbled, forcing himself to keep his expression neutral.

"Come on. You've seen what he's been like lately. With everyone apart from you, that is. He doesn't even bother to look up from his breakfast until you come down. Then he'll at least respond to direct questions." She shook her head. "Just go and try. Tell him Brodie wants to apologise, and he needs to come back and stop acting like a baby. The others aren't going to let this behaviour from our CO slide for much longer. I'm not sure what's going on with him, but we need the old Noah back."

Zeke peeled himself from the fence, flicking his hood up so he wouldn't feel the stares of Squad E as he walked past them, following Noah's path. It didn't take long to find him sitting hunched over on a bench a few metres down from the wooden gate, Wolf curled up at his feet. Noah's eyes widened as he sat down next to him.

"You're making a habit of appearing when I need you." Noah crumpled into him, balling Zeke's coat with his fist.

"What's going on?" He smoothed Noah's hair back in the particular way that comforted him the most.

Noah sighed against his chest. "He just got under my skin. Kept going on and on about how J does things so much better than us. He acts like I personally petitioned Murphy for him to be transferred to us."

"It must be shit for him to be fair. I can't imagine being moved away from you guys."

"Still. He should focus on building relationships with everyone instead of criticising every instruction I give. That's what I was telling him before he started shouting back at me a second ago."

"Write him up then. Show him you mean business."

Noah slumped down further into him and made a strangled noise. His lack of resilience alarmed him. Months ago, Noah would have laughed off Brodie's defiance with quiet confidence. Now, his first response was screaming and storming off.

"I can't go back there. God only knows what everyone thinks now." Noah groaned, burying his face into Zeke's neck.

Zeke pulled Noah back upright. "Noah, you need to get your shit together. Seriously. You need to act like our CO. The others are worried about you."

"They should be. I'm their lieutenant and I'm an absolute mess."

He calculated his reply. Denying Noah's words seemed futile. "Even so, they'd still follow you to the ends of the earth if need be. They love you. Maybe you could try and lay off them a little?"

"We're literally already at the ends of the earth."

"Well, there's nobody I would rather be here with than you." Zeke held Noah's face in his hands. "We're going back to face them, together. By now, Habib's hopefully already threatened to beat some sense into Brodie, anyway."

Noah laughed, albeit a shadow of his usual one. "I hope not, else I'll have to write *him* up."

The others were standing in a semicircle when they returned to the field, with Brodie in the middle, as if they were standing guard of him. Brodie, not meeting Noah's eye, mumbled an apology and agreed not to question Noah's authority again.

"Sir," Brodie added, at the end of his brief speech, likely due to Vitt glaring at him.

Noah looked Brodie dead in the eye. "Campbell, if you defy a single further order, you'll be cleaning the toilets for a month."

Brodie nodded. "Understood, sir."

Noah turned to address the group. "We'll meet at seven a.m. sharp for breakfast tomorrow before joining C and K for briefing. I'll see everyone then." Noah's eyes scanned his squadron, landing on Zeke's for a second too long, its gaze screaming, *I'll see you in my room in about thirty minutes. Please be quick.*

"Can you carry all that, Zeke?"

Vitt's sceptical look made him even more determined to lift both the heavy duffle bags that housed supplies for their mission. The task of transporting weapons, food and camping gear from the armoury into the six vehicles allocated to them was not one he was relishing.

"Hey, I can bench two hundred pounds now."

Vitt raised one eyebrow.

"Well, I can lift it an inch off the ground, at least."

Habib appeared, chuckling as he grabbed the bags from Zeke's struggling arms, throwing them over his shoulder like they were bags of feathers. He surprised him by ruffling Zeke's hair, almost affectionately.

When all thirty of them, plus five dogs, were hovering around in the car park, the atmosphere was bizarrely jovial—like they were about to head out on a grand adventure. Krish from Squad K caught Zeke's eye and smiled, making him feel at ease. At least he vaguely knew one of the strangers that they would spend the next forty-eight hours with. He recognised a few others from border duty, including Lowenna. Noah spoke at length yesterday about his respect for the tall, thirty-something brunette. Her face was stern as she ordered her men to pack and repack the vehicles several times until the arrangement met her satisfaction.

"Hi, Zeke, right? I'm Alex."

Zeke turned to find a tall, blonde stranger beaming at him.

"I've seen you around," Alex continued. "It's great to meet you properly."

He was spared from replying by Noah appearing from thin air, annoyance etched onto his face as he pressed bags into Alex's hand and gave him a long list of orders. Zeke turned so that nobody would see him laugh.

To his dismay, he ended up separated from Noah when Lowenna split them into groups for the six vehicles. Even though she was the same rank as Noah and Tobias, her additional years of experience meant that she held ultimate command of the platoon. Tobias frowned deeply when she started ordering C and E's personnel around, especially when she mixed all three squads up for the journey.

Vitt instantly shotgunned driving the van that she and Zeke ended up in. He hopped into the passenger seat and a handful of people he didn't know climbed into the back, shielded from them by a retractable partition that nobody made any attempt to open. The barrier enclosed Zeke and Vitt into their own private bubble, causing him instant anxiety—he liked Vitt, but had never spent extended time alone with her.

"So," Vitt said, once they were past the gates and on the open road, wide and clear—for now. Their van was at the back of the convoy, the other five vehicles snaking ahead of them like they were all magnetically attached. Vitt put the car in self-drive and turned her wide, freckled face to him. "How's it feel to be at the three-month mark?"

His brain shut down in the classic way it always did when the conversation turned to himself. "Good, I guess."

"You don't look like you're going to throw up, freeze, or run away at the first opportunity anymore."

"I mean, I achieved two out of three things already. A full house would be too much."

"Noah seems pleased with your progress," Vitt said. Was she looking at him like that to keenly observe his reaction?

"I guess," he replied, turning to gaze out of the window at the countryside, where large, bramble-like weeds had long since overtaken manicured fields. He prayed Vitt would change the topic, but alas, no such luck.

"You haven't seen him at his best, to be honest," she said. "He's amazing, the best CO I've ever had, but ever since Khyan..." She trailed off, sighing. "I've known him since he arrived here after Rotterdam five years ago. I've never seen anyone—*anyone*—so broken as he was the day Khyan died."

Khyan. Zeke continued to wonder and wonder about him, late into the early hours of the morning. The question was often on the tip of his tongue, particularly when he saw Noah brush his hand over the dove tattoo on his wrist. *What happened to him, Noah?*

Vitt sighed, tapping her hands against the wheel. "God, they were so sweet together. Sickeningly so."

He swallowed, pushing down his green-eyed monster, reminding himself for the millionth time it wasn't appropriate to be envious of a dead guy.

Vitt looked over at him. "Do you know what happened? Noah won't mind me telling you."

He shook his head.

"Khyan was training three new puppies. He handed them over to go out of the base on their first run—against his will, I think—he was being pressured by Murphy to make them battle-ready quicker and quicker. Anyway, they were spooked by a cluster of types, and ran off, all three of them. Soldiers tracked the dogs using their chips, but they wouldn't let them get close to them, just kept running off. The officers called Khyan, who freaked out. I think he was quite attached to the puppies. He did spend all day training with them, after all. Luo was hanging out in the canteen with Khyan at the time. He says he point blank insisted he leave Avantis to help look for them."

Zeke almost asked her to stop talking. He already knew how this story would end.

"Anyway, Khyan, escorted by a few officers, headed out in the direction they were last seen. He thought his smell and voice would bring them back and he could bring them home. But twenty minutes into the rescue mission, they're jumped by a shit load of types. Khyan and another of the soldiers were taken down almost immediately."

"Wow," he said, fighting back horrific images of the beautiful man in Noah's photograph.

"Noah was at the border. No idea any of this was happening. They called him back when Khyan's body came in. I was off that day so met him at the gate." Vitt swiped at her eyes, blinking rapidly. "He fell to the floor at first, became catatonic. Then he insisted on watching the recording from the helmet cam footage again and again and again, even though we were begging him not to. About twenty times he must have watched Khyan being ripped apart before Habib finally wrestled the screen out of his hands. He went straight to Luo and started screaming at him for 'letting him go'. That fucked up Luo for a while." Vitt stared straight out of the windscreen. "Noah apologised to him a few weeks later," she added. "He was horrified by his behaviour."

Zeke's throat constricted. *Poor Noah*. He'd been through so much. "Sounds like it was tough for you guys."

"It was. Noah was removed from active duty for several weeks. This was before he was made LT, back when Georgia was leading Squad E. She got moved to another regiment. Anyway, Leo was amazing with him, and eventually he found a way through his grief. He'll never be the same, obviously. But after a long while, we had our friend back. Especially over these last few months. Well, until whatever's happened recently. So, what's up with that?" Vitt looked over at him expectantly, and he squirmed. "Come on, we can't help him if we don't know what's going on."

"I think it's some stuff with his uncle. I don't know anything really though, you'd have to ask him."

Vitt clicked her tongue. "If he hasn't said anything to you, then he hasn't told anyone what's going on. Oh, Noah..."

After an hour, they reached the end of the roads the military actively kept clear, and were forced to pause continually every ten minutes or so. At these points, everyone filed out of the vans to clear the road. Sometimes it was just a matter of moving light bits of debris, including window panes, metal railings and, at one point, a giant metal horse from a funfair ride—something that triggered Squad E to become oddly quiet.

When in transit, the vans rumbled along the rough roads, their suspension struggling to smooth out the deep potholes and jagged cracks that marred the surface. As they bounced and swayed, loose stones and gravel sprayed out from under the wheels, adding to the already battered state of the road. Despite the poor conditions, the platoon pressed on, navigating around the worst of the damage and trying to maintain a steady speed.

At twelve-thirty, they hit a large fallen oak tree. They'd been expecting it—Command provided them with detailed outlines of the route—but it was one thing hearing about it and another seeing it in real life.

"There's no way in hell we're moving that," said Savannah. Squad E, after unloading from their separate vans, instantly gravitated back together, like magnetic parts of a well-oiled machine. "We'll have to go back and try another road."

"We're sticking to our orders," stated Lowenna, arms crossed, staring at the tree that came up to her hip.

"Can I suggest that we break for lunch first?" said Tobias.

"I was just about to suggest that myself," Lowenna replied, flashing him a sugary-sweet smile.

At her signal, the officers relaxed and broke apart to sit in small groups. Most of them looked a little green—the turbulent terrain was causing a serious case of car sickness.

Noah disappeared with Tobias to collect the cool-boxes of food from a van, returning to dump them into the middle of the group.

"Are you sure it's just these two?" Tobias said.

"Positive. We've got strict instructions from the kitchen. It's one bread roll and one piece of fruit or a carrot each for lunch."

"Bullshit, Forrest," he sneered. "That can't be right."

A hush of silence swept over the soldiers, who looked between Tobias, Noah and Lowenna with shocked expressions. Zeke had heard from Zaya—and from Noah's recount of his conversation with his uncle—about how bad the food shortages were getting, but never imagined that it would impact the city's military force.

"If you were listening when the kitchen staff were trying to talk to us earlier, you'd have heard the information for yourself," spat Noah, clenching his jaw and shaking his head.

Before Tobias could reply, Lowenna stepped into the middle of them. "*Lieutenants.*" She raised her eyebrows. "Can we focus on the task at hand, please? We're already losing precious daylight hours."

Zeke stared up at the cold sun, which was already beginning its slow descent to the horizon. He shivered.

Tobias stalked off to vape near the tree, leaving some other members of Squad C to sort out their share of the rations.

"It'll be easy to move," said Lowenna, looking at the tree. "Ten minutes, tops."

But it quickly became apparent to Zeke it would not be a ten-minute job. For a start, the three lieutenants spent fifteen minutes surveying the tree—which was buried in a slight dip—calling Command and bickering between themselves while the rest of them stood back, pacing up and down to keep warm in the December chill. Eventually, several chainsaws came out of a van, to be wielded by Luo and Alex.

Once the job was done, a full hour later, Luo collapsed onto the ground, dragging Zeke with him. "Christ, even my right arm aches," Luo said, waving the shiny metal of his bionic limb in the air.

Noah flashed him a grin. "Told you it would be 'easy-peasy' or whatever you guys call it."

Zeke threw back his head and laughed, reaching out his arms for Noah to pull him up and relishing the snippet of contact with Noah's body before he released him.

It was well past three before they reloaded the vans and were ready to drive again. The skeletal trees cast deep, crooked shadows around them as they drove slowly through the rest of the afternoon, pausing frequently to clear the roads. Eventually, the warmth of the heater and the gentle rumble of the engine lulled Zeke to sleep in the passenger seat, despite his best efforts to stay awake for Vitt. He was rudely awoken, however, by Noah's voice coming through the van's stereo.

"All vehicles halt."

NOAH

"**C**heck this out," said Lowenna, holding out a tablet displaying video feed footage.

Noah, Lowenna and Tobias, assembled outside the lead van, leaned in to watch. At first, it was hard to make out what the night-vision grainy recording depicted. Many shuffling forms on two feet—a cluster of typeBs—gathered in a huddle. A huddle around a bright light in the middle. A burning, flickering light. A... fire?

"We *need* to investigate this," said Noah.

"That's a decision for *Command*, not us," hissed Tobias. "But it's cold and dark. We need to be thinking about setting up camp, not gallivanting off on pointless excursions."

"I'm going to call them," said Lowenna. "Wait here." She slid into the passenger side of the van, slamming the door shut.

"Newman, how can you not see how momentous this is? These types have *built a fire.*"

"Definitely not." Tobias crossed his arms and scowled at him. "They must have found it."

"In this weather? You've got to be joking. You don't just 'find' a fire. Sometimes it takes Habib and I half an hour to get the fire pit at Avantis going in the winter evenings."

Tobias scowled. "Please don't tell me you're seriously proposing they have the brain function to light fires, Forrest."

"Hence our need to investigate."

Lowenna hopped down from the van. "All clear to divert route. Orders are to clear the perimeter of every type. We're taking the next right. The drone shows a clear path all the way to the graveyard."

Noah's breath caught in his throat.

Graveyard?

"Would you remind me again why we're feckin' freezing our arses off outside a graveyard in the middle of winter?" Aoife grumbled for the third time, jumping up and down on the spot for warmth.

"It's barely the beginning of winter," Meredith replied. She was twisting a bangle of coloured gemstones around and around her wrist: her standard pre-battle ritual.

"That's not comforting me, Mere."

Noah stood on his tiptoes to gaze through the tall, black iron fence that surrounded the perimeter of the cemetery. A feeling of unease settled over him as he stared through the gaps, surveying the rows of headstones that stretched out endlessly. A short distance away, an old church towered over the graves, its steeple piercing the sky like a knife. On the other side of it, they would find the cluster of types gathered around their miraculous fire.

"Drones all indicate this group are the only types in the area. But be on guard. The dogs will lead." Noah stood in front of the open gate—a gaping mouth ready to swallow them whole—addressing the platoon. Unhappy faces glared at him. Nobody was particularly pleased to be dragged out of the warm vehicles into the frigid air to go off-piste.

Lowenna addressed every soldier through the comms. "Don't get spooked into swapping to firearms too easily. We don't want to risk the noise. In addition, the more rounds we fire, the greater the risk of hitting each other. Walker, Shun and Ranjan have silencers, and will do most of the heavy lifting. The rest of you, use your crossbows and daggers where possible."

Let's get this out of the way as quickly as possible. Noah turned to Wolf and the other four canine units, dressed in their black harnesses that covered most of their torsos, and clicked his fingers before making the hand signal for them to walk forward in formation, staying five metres ahead of the platoon. If there were types lurking in the bushes, they would be the first to sense them—and the first to be attacked.

With crossbows at the ready, the platoon marched in three separate V formations down the path that led to the church. Tall grass and weeds choked the chipped and weather-worn graves, which mostly lay in broken piles of rubble. Noah couldn't shake the notion they were being watched by unseen eyes. Routinely, he glanced back at where Zeke walked next to Frankie, to check he was still there, still alive. He couldn't make out Zeke's expression through the darkness and his helmet, but he imagined him rolling his eyes.

The platoon hugged the cold stone wall of the church as they crept towards the cluster. Noah signalled to the dogs, instructing them to surround the perimeter and make sure none of the types escaped.

Before Noah was ready to face the battle, the platoon turned the corner.

It was one thing seeing the drone footage, but it was an entirely different beast seeing it in real life.

Eight typeBs were sitting around the fire, their palms stretched towards the warmth in an oh-so-human way. But more alarming than that was the low hum of... chanting? Whatever they were saying, it wasn't in any language he'd ever heard; it was more accurate to describe the noises as rhythmic grunts.

It was unclear if the typeB's heard or smelt them first, but it didn't matter. Once one of their heads snapped towards the officers, the others followed suit in a matter of milliseconds. A rumbling growl came from the one nearest to them, but instead of lunging towards them, it ran over to the church's west wall. Beside him, Vitt sharply inhaled.

"Are those wind chimes?"

Noah squinted through his interface, zooming in on the type who'd left the fire. A loud chiming sound echoed through the quiet graveyard before his brain had a chance to process the lines of silver chimes, constructed of bundles of metal keys, dangling from the sloping roof.

"It's a call to battle," shouted Habib, "just like last time!"

"What?" said Lowenna.

Before any of them could reply, the earth erupted from beneath their feet.

Several soldiers jumped back as a gravestone flew several feet through the air, landing near Noah with a thud. From every angle, heavy thumping footsteps charged towards them. A circular stained-glass window at the top of the church tower shattered, raining shards of glass down to the ground. Terrified shouts, combined with the angry, snarling moans of the types who were jumping down from the tower, created a deafening cacophony.

"Why didn't we know there were types *in* the church?" screamed Lowenna.

Brandon Penn's reply—something about the drone not being able to get in through the locked door—was drowned out in the chaos.

"Everyone! Forget crossbows and daggers. Ignore everything I said earlier and fucking take them down. Now!" Lowenna unshouldered her rifle and flicked off the trigger guard to unload two rounds, her precise shots rendering two of the nearest types dead within seconds.

Do not think about Zeke.

Do not think about Zeke.

Do not think about Zeke.

Noah, flanked by Vitt and Habib, charged off away from the church to where types were emerging from everywhere—behind gravestones, jumping from trees, and, most disturbingly, out of marble coffins. Bullets whizzed through the air, finding their targets with squelches and gurgles or else ricocheting off stones with loud cracks. There was no dodging the speed of them. All he could do was pray the officers kept a clear head and didn't get trigger-happy.

Noah, Vitt and Habib always had been the dream team from the first day they served together five years ago. Now, as he felt the awesome power of them beside him, he felt like a god. Like dancers performing a perfected routine, their synchronized movements formed an unbreakable bond, each step executed flawlessly as if they shared a single mind. Their weapons moved in perfect harmony, striking with precision and efficiency. With every fallen type, their confidence grew, fuelling their determination to eradicate the horde.

Noah's combat suit became a canvas drenched in a grotesque tapestry of blood. Methodically, he discharged round after round, each shot finding its mark. The smell of blood in the air whipped the types into a frenzy, and it was hard to relate the creatures in front of him to the ones he'd observed around the fire moments ago.

"I've got three left before reload!" Vitt took another type down from at least ten metres away and pride swelled in Noah's heart. "Make that two!"

"We'll cover!"

Noah and Habib flanked her as she made quick work of reloading. He glanced around. They'd cleared most of this part of the cemetery. But next to the church tower, the carnage was still ensuing.

"Support required!" Krish's voice echoed through Noah's helmet as his interface brought up the area map, showing Krish's location on the other side of the church.

"Habib and I will go," said Vitt. "I can see Brodie over there by himself." Vitt pointed in the distance, at the far edge of the graveyard's perimeter. "He's got himself backed into a corner."

"On it," said Noah. On his way to Brodie, he glanced back towards the fire, and blinked twice, slowing to a halt. What on earth was he seeing? Two typeBs held long, thick, tree branches with thick white cloth bundled onto the end of them. They dipped the cloth end into the fire, igniting the material into a vicious, fiery inferno. Next, they brandished their weapons like swords, swinging them wildly at officers, who jumped back, stunned.

"Holy fucking shit," Noah said to nobody.

Gazing past the fire, something else caught his eye. A familiar, fluffy brown dog was tearing away in the direction of the iron fence, up a steep hill, four types stampeding after him. *Wolf.* His heart twisted in his chest and he forced his gaze back to Brodie. The man was alone, backed up against the corner of the iron fence. Brodie brandished his dagger—was he out of rounds already?—as a stream of types charged towards him.

Swallowing hard, Noah committed to joining him, jogging in his direction while firing to help Brodie take down the ones nearest to him.

But he couldn't resist a quick glance back at Wolf.

His dog had reached the opposite fence now, and stood still, trapped, the four types surrounding him. They slashed out at him in turn with claws, dodging the rapid snaps of Wolf's jaw as he tried to sink his teeth into them. Then, one typeB turned away from Wolf, distracted.

A lone soldier had left the fray by the tower and was charging up the hill towards Wolf. Relief surged through him, quickly replaced by glacial fear.

Because he knew who it was, even before his name flashed up on the screen, next to the sprinting figure.

There were twenty-nine other soldiers with him in this graveyard, but he'd be able to pick out any of his squad in a group of thousands.

Of course it was him.

Zeke.

Noah was forever destined to lose everyone he ever loved.

Brodie called for assistance through the comms for the second time, his shouts ringing in Noah's ear.

He was closest to Brodie.

It *had* to be Brodie.

The commitment he'd made when he took the CO position. His promise to Habib that the squad would always come first. The knowledge he wouldn't ever be able to forgive himself.

He closed the distance between himself and the struggling soldier.

The types were so fixated on Brodie that Noah held the advantage—he took down three with his rifle as Brodie slashed the necks of two more with his dagger. A spray of dark blood coated Brodie's helmet as the types fell to the ground, twitching.

"Thanks LT," he said, panting.

But Noah turned away from him without replying, already moving in the other direction now that Brodie was safe. He flew towards Zeke, stumbling over tree roots, uneven ground and tombstones as he barrelled towards him like his life depended on it. Because Zeke's life did.

He could only watch as Zeke reached Wolf far before he would get to them, raising his rifle at a type that rushed towards him. He missed, stumbling backwards to give himself time to aim again. Even from a distance, the shake in Zeke's rifle was evident.

Please, please, please, please.

Zeke's bullet exploded from his rifle with a bang, and the type went down.

Noah was almost there. He was so close—

The other three types were on Zeke before he had time to react. He hit one on the head with the butt of his rifle—*yes!*—before sprinting off, the types mere inches behind him. Wolf joined the chase, nipping at the legs of the types and dodging out of the way when they lunged for him.

Zeke ran and ran and then... disappeared into the darkness. The types stopped chasing him, falling to the ground.

Noah, just five strides away now, blinked. Were the types... clawing at the ground? "Zeke?" he shouted.

A panicked shrieking sound reverberated through him. But where was it coming from?

Distracted by Zeke's voice, Noah flew off his feet as something shoved him to the ground, a heavy weight pushing him into the earth. His wrist flew back to collide with unyielding stone, resulting in a sharp *crack*. His father's watch! But this was no time for sentimentality. Angry, desperate claws scraped at his torso as the smell of rotting flesh assaulted his nostrils.

"Wolf!" he shouted, as he thrashed in the slick mud, trying and failing to shake the type off him.

A snarl to his left, followed by a bark. Noah felt the heavy weight of the type slip down his body as Wolf dragged the beast off him.

He jumped to his feet. Wolf's jaws were fully clamped around the typeB's leg, allowing Noah to take great satisfaction in shooting a round through its head. The two types that remained leapt towards them. Wolf dispatched one by tearing half its neck out, and Noah finished the remaining typeB with his dagger—his ammo supply was dwindling. One smooth, gurgling slice of his knife through its stomach saw the type falling lifeless within moments. He grimaced as its entrails splashed onto the ground with a sickening squelch.

"Help!" came a weak voice, a stone's throw away. Wolf darted over to it.

And there Zeke was, at the bottom of a rectangular burial pit. Should Noah laugh or cry?

"Holy mother of—"

"I can't get out! The mud is too wet. I can't grip on anything."

Noah darted his eyes around to check there were no more incoming surprises. Most soldiers were now standing around in groups, rifles still at the ready but postures relaxed.

The onslaught was over, for now.

He reached down into the dark pit—Christ, Zeke must be so scared—and pulled the far lighter man out of the hole. Panting, he fell back, Zeke tumbling on top of him. Their hands surrounded each other, Noah pulling Zeke against him as tight as possible, forming their own private bubble while Wolf whined and pressed himself against the pair of them. It was all okay again. Noah's inner compass recalibrated. His true north was back in his arms, and it was all going to be okay.

Noah pushed them back up to a less compromising position. He scanned the platoon, reading off the names that flashed up next to them on the interface, scanning for his flock. When he locked eyes on Brodie's body, he allowed himself to relax somewhat. Ever since promising Habib he would never prioritise Zeke over the rest of them, he'd secretly doubted himself. The immense amount of relief that coursed through him now that scenario had been tested—with Brodie of all people—made him feel giddy.

He turned to dust the mud off from Zeke's body. "What the hell were you doing, going up here by yourself? You almost died!"

"There were four of them trying to get Wolf!"

"Wolf is a canine unit. A dog. I know I don't always treat him like he's one, but he is. Under no circumstances do you put yourself in danger for him. If you do that again, I'll kill you myself."

Infuriatingly, Zeke glowered at him, a small smile visible through the glass on his muddy visor.

"What?" Noah said, scowling. "Why are you smiling right now?"

"You go more Dutch when you're angry."

"*Neuk je.*"

"I'm presuming you just told me you love me very much."

Noah raised his middle finger at him.

"Forrest!" Lowenna's booming voice came through the audio feed. "We need you. There's one casualty."

Every inch of the fleeting moment of joy faded away as Noah crossed the cemetery, jumping over loose gravestones and the fallen bodies of the typeBs to reach Lowenna. *Please not Habib, please not Vitt, please not Frankie, please not us.*

Next to Lowenna, a body lay in the fetal position, neck sliced. Through the cracked helmet, Noah could make out the face of a woman in her early twenties.

"She was the newest member of K. Gracie Bellows," Krish said, his voice flat. "A stray bullet clipped her leg, and she went down. Two typeBs latched on before we even had a second to get there. We had to mercy kill."

Tobias, covered in gore but still recognisable from his cocky walk, stepped towards the body. "I knew this was a bad—"

"Stand down, Newman," snapped Lowenna. "Take half the platoon and sweep the church. Krish, document everything you find and send it to me. After, instruct everyone to set up camp. We're sleeping in there tonight. We need a proper rest and a space to clean up and regroup."

And grieve. Guilty thoughts about being thankful it was one of K and not his flock swirled inside him.

Once they were alone, Lowenna turned to him, stepping close and tapping the palm of her hand three times. Noah stared at her until he finally realised what she was trying to communicate. Noah released the catch at the back of his helmet and pressed the button three times, powering it off. This was standard procedure when officers were about to go off the record. Glancing around to ensure her team had indeed secured the perimeter, she pulled her helmet off her head, so Noah did the same.

"What are you doing?"

"Don't let Tobias contact Command," said Lowenna.

Noah frowned. "What?"

"Let's just say I've told some half-truths this evening. You and I will need to get our story straight before debriefing."

Puzzle pieces clicked into place.

"Are you... working with..." he trailed off, not wanting to say Leonie's name.

She nodded. "Yes. Their influence got our two squads assigned to this mission, but apparently they could only go so far, hence us being stuck out here with *him*."

So many questions danced on the tip of Noah's tongue.

"When I saw the footage, I knew we needed to investigate. I couldn't risk Command saying no. Holy fuck, did you see the ones who made the torches? Terrifying."

Indeed. Everything they'd seen here so far terrified him to the point he dreaded going into the church.

"I'll call some of my team over to help me with Gracie's body. Go supervise inside."

Noah headed over to the church's large wooden doors, which sat under an ornately carved arch. Zeke, waiting for him in the shadows, joined him without speaking. Simultaneously, they lunged for each other's hands, lacing their fingers together before pulling apart.

The interior of the church was dark and musty, the air heavy with the stench of decay. Cobwebs covered the pews and altar, and most of the stained-glass windows stood shattered, letting in icy wind. Dim moonlight lit up a wooden floor littered with debris and the remains of several typeBs, their ruined bodies sprawled out in grotesque poses. Several walls were scarred with deep gashes, as if something tried to claw its way through the plaster. The atmosphere was eerie and unsettling, as if the ghosts of the past still lingered within the walls of the abandoned holy place.

"Lieutenant Forrest!" Krish, with a few others, called him over to the corner. "Come see this."

On the floor, several makeshift beds—wooden planks and cardboard covered in filthy sheets—were divided by lines of rocks. Had the typeBs marked out their own personal territories? Surely not.

Nearby, soldiers gathered around a small red tent.

"Do you think they set the tent up themselves?" Krish asked.

"No way." Habib, looking exhausted, came to stand next to them.

Noah stared at the tent. "What do you think, Zeke?"

Zeke appeared startled to be consulted, then shook his head. "They don't have enough fine motor skills for that. Nor the executive function. I mean, at least, we thought they didn't. These guys have broken all the rules today."

Noah pulled back the flapping door to look inside, shining a light around the small space.

Shock coursed through him like an electric current.

Pieces of paper covered every inch of the groundsheet, and sides of the tent, affixed with tape. Strange markings covered each piece, some crude and indistinguishable, others forming recognisable shapes. Other heads crowded with him in the opening, gasping when they saw the spectacle.

"Is that a map of the church grounds?" Zeke pointed to a piece of paper on the floor.

Noah squinted at the lines that formed rectangles and circles. "I think you're right. I'm going to get Lowenna."

ZEKE

After the excitement died down, Lowenna broke them off into teams to secure the perimeter, remove the typeB corpses and clean up the church the best they could. Zeke, on the cleaning team, fought back several waves of nausea as he scooped up piles of entrails and guts. Eventually, Frankie noticed his swaying body and insisted on taking over so that he didn't faint.

Meanwhile, other soldiers carried in their boxes of supplies from the vans, then set up camp for the night. The platoon spread themselves across the church—lots of people opted to push pews together in the aisles to form beds, but others took over the small kitchen, office and children's playroom.

Noah ordered that the tower, offering an excellent vantage point, be turned into a watchtower, and Lowenna set out a rota, with at least eight officers being on duty throughout the night. Zeke inwardly groaned about being given the last shift—waking up at three a.m. after this hellish evening was the last thing he wanted to do.

The evening meal comprised of tinned food warmed on portable stoves. Some officers combined their tins, going 'all in' to share a meal. Others ate their food straight from the can. In addition, everyone was permitted to take one protein bar from the box.

While most of Squad E sat about relaxing and enjoying the respite, Noah scurried around with Lowenna and Tobias. He smiled whenever he looked his way, but Zeke wished he could pull him down to sit with them, or drag him off to a quiet corner. One of the many downsides to secretly dating your CO, he guessed.

An impromptu talent show of sorts began, starting with Luo performing handstands, putting all his weight on his bionic arm and spinning around. This inspired Aoife to cajole Savannah into performing dance lifts with her. Where they mustered the physical or mental energy from was anyone's guess.

Afterwards, the mood died down again—most of K were fairly subdued, on account of their loss—and small pockets of people gathered in circles to talk or play games. Aoife left their huddle to flirt in a dark corner with Florence Bloomer from Squad C and Habib and Meredith struck up a light-hearted argument about whether she was going to be successful in her conquest and whether they could consider it fraternising with the enemy.

"They're not all pricks," Meredith said, rolling her eyes. "It's just Tobias and his three musketeers we need to look out for."

"That Florence girl seems cool. We helped each other out of a sticky situation earlier," said Frankie. Large clumps of her hair were knotted with dried blood; she was delaying joining the long line for the icy hose-pipe-shower outside that Zeke had endured earlier.

Habib, after licking the packet of his protein bar to salvage every crumb, replied, "I wouldn't trust any of them to have our backs when push came to shove."

"Hey," said a voice, sliding in beside Zeke.

He turned to find Alex's face smiling at him. Smiling at him, as well as pressing his thigh against Zeke's. "Um... hi?"

Frankie burst out laughing at something before turning it into a cough. He glanced behind him to see Noah staring over.

"I saw your epic headshot earlier." Alex said. "Great work."

"Thanks."

A warm hand pressed down on his shoulder. He didn't need to look around to know it was Noah.

"Just grabbing my water bottle." Noah leaned over Zeke to do just that, pushing himself between him and Alex. He crouched low beside him for a moment and whispered, "Down the corridor, second door on the left. Ten minutes."

He was gone before Zeke could question him. His eyes flicked between the rest of his squad, but none of them were paying him any attention, as Avalanche Blitz had begun in earnest.

Struggling to focus on the game or the conversations around him now that he'd been assigned his secret mission, he spent his countdown checking his wristband every five seconds, which *did* attract Frankie's suspicion.

"Got somewhere more exciting to be?"

Apparently, yes, he did.

After nine minutes, he mumbled something about needing to go check something and stood up, leaving the church's nave as surreptitiously as possible. The specified door was ancient and heavy, made of thick oak, dark and weathered with age. The carvers had adorned it with intricate depictions of angels and saints, their gilded features chipped and faded. Taking a deep breath, Zeke pulled on the iron handle. The door creaked open to reveal a spiral stone staircase leading to shadowy depths. *Definitely not creepy.*

Switching on his flashlight, he turned around to shut the door, hoping nobody saw him enter. A giant slab of metal formed a sliding lock and he took a moment to push it across before descending. A musty, damp smell filled the air. Just where exactly was he going? What was—

"Boo!"

He opened his mouth to scream, but powerful hands clamped around his mouth.

Noah's illuminated face jumped towards him, the light framing him like an angel of death.

"Was that really necessary? You've already seen what I look like scared shitless on a number of occasions."

"Did you lock the door?"

"Yep. What's our cover story for— Holy crap, are we in a *crypt*?"

He flashed the light throughout the large circular chamber. Its high, arched ceiling towered above them. The statues of angels, sitting on alcoves carved into the stone walls, glared at them in judgment. A large stone sarcophagus took up most of the space in the middle. As if the situation wasn't odd enough as it was, Noah pulled out from his pocket a handful of tea lights—likely stolen from the candle altar above—and used a box of matches to start lighting them.

"We've got to take what we can get, I'm afraid." Noah set up the line of candles on the edge of the tomb, their soft glow throwing enough light onto the floor to reveal a sleeping bag. Noah shot him a sly grin. "Is this not romantic enough for you?"

He shivered, partly from the freezing chill of the crypt, partly from the look in Noah's eye. "I mean, sex in a crypt wasn't exactly on my bucket list, but whatever floats your boat, I guess."

"The door's locked. We can't hear them, so they can't hear us. The perimeter is secured. The drone footage indicates there's no types for miles. We're both off duty. Let's just steal a few moments for ourselves."

In two quick strides, Noah had banished the space between them, reaching out to pull Zeke's body towards him. His hands instantly flew to Noah's hair, tugging it free of its tie as Noah removed his glasses, sliding them into his coat pocket.

And then it was Zeke tumbling Noah backwards, down onto the floor. It was a frantic mess of legs and arms and mouths. Zeke pushing into Noah, seeking heat, touch, anything, *everything*.

Noah's hands under his shirt burned away the cold as they traced the outline of his ribs, stomach, collarbone. Garments of clothing flew off to the side as they shed them at lightning speed.

Noah grabbed a large fistful of Zeke's hair—grown out longer than ever in the last few months—pulling his head back to nip at the skin on his neck before sucking, hard. A distant part of his mind worried about the mark Noah might leave, but Zeke pushed into it anyway, writhing as Noah's hand travelled down his chest, tugging lightly at the patch of hair at the base of his stomach before finally—*finally*—reaching his now-aching cock.

Moaning as he pushed into Noah's hand, he brushed his lips over Noah's jaw, desperate to find his mouth. Wet lips readily parted as he hungrily drove his tongue inside, running it over Noah's chipped canine tooth as if it was a secret just for him.

Zeke released Noah's mouth, leaning on both hands to raise his body up so he could see his face. Black hair cascaded out around his head like a halo, but the way he looked at Zeke—like he was all Noah wanted and all he would ever need—made *him* feel like the angel.

After worshipping every part of Noah's body in turn with small, lingering kisses, Zeke dragged his mouth down to Noah's dick, already fully erect and begging for attention. He inhaled Noah's heady, earthy scent before taking just the end of the tip in his mouth, probing the small slit with his tongue, savouring the taste of him. With the lightest of touches, he stroked the soft, delicate skin of his shaft.

"God, Zeke, what are you doing to me?" Noah said between pants, bucking his hips up in desperation.

Zeke pulled his mouth away, and inserted a wicked note into his voice to reply, "Do you want me to do something? If you do, you'll have to ask me for it."

Noah half-laughed, half-sobbed as he said, "Fucking hell, I want you to shove my dick down your throat before I put it there myself."

Unable to torment Noah anymore, he obliged, relaxing his throat as much as possible before leaning forward to swallow Noah's length in its entirety. The soft whimpering sound Noah rewarded him with turned his heart to jelly as he moved his head up and down rhythmically, using the little space left in his mouth to lick the underside of his length. Noah's cock pulsed in his mouth as it swelled larger and larger.

Under his hands, Noah's thighs trembled. With each of Noah's moans, waves of ecstasy of his own rolled through him. He was doing this. Noah was moaning for *him*.

"Hold on." Noah sat up, pushing Zeke off of him. "How..." Noah panted twice. "How are you so good at this?"

"I guess I must have an amazing teacher."

He stared at Noah's naked body. The chiaroscuro embraced his figure, a dance of light and shadow that accentuated the contours of his muscular torso, evoking a primal desire to sink his teeth into its mouthwatering form. Raising his eyes to meet the smouldering inferno within Noah's gaze, a symphony of fluttering wings erupted within him as a kaleidoscope of butterflies was freed.

"In that case, I wonder if you wanted to take your training to the next level, so to speak."

Zeke's face burned, and he prayed the darkness of the room would save him. "What do you mean?" *Just spell it out for me.*

"Do you want to fuck me?" Noah all but whispered, as if the creepy angel statues would take offence.

"What? *Here?*" He struggled to keep the edge of panic from his voice as his eyes darted around the crypt. He pulled back from Noah as nerves swarmed his stomach.

Noah's smile dropped, his eyes crinkling in concern as he said, "We don't have to, we can—"

"No." He forced his voice to be steady. "I *do* want to," he whispered into the space between them. He buried his face in Noah's chest so he didn't have to look at him. "I'm just scared of... not being good enough at it for you."

"Hey," Noah said, lightly tilting his head up. "You don't ever need to worry about that with me." He kissed his nose.

"Okay then," Zeke whispered, heart tap-dancing against his ribcage. "But we need to be quiet."

Noah's hand slipped into his rucksack beside the sarcophagus and threw Zeke the lube. Zeke bit back a joke about Noah's clear pre-planning as Noah fell back against the sleeping bag, spreading his legs slightly and arching his hips upwards. Zeke dragged his tongue across Noah's thigh, ever so slowly travelling upwards. By the time he'd reached Noah's crease, he was writhing and crying out adorable whimpers, and Zeke almost forgot they were in a creepy-as-fuck crypt.

"Tell me what you want," Zeke whispered.

"Lick me," Noah panted back. "If you want to."

He obliged, dragging his tongue tantalisingly over the place where Noah wanted it. The gasp that Noah made sent heat straight to his groin, and his own cock became impossibly harder, causing him to grind against their makeshift bed, desperate for friction. He mustered all the saliva he could, soaking Noah's skin. He pulled his mouth away, feeling the spit dribbling down his chin, to tease the soft nub of his hole with slick fingers. Swallowing his nerves, Zeke pushed one tentative finger into the tight space. He began to massage it slowly, crooking his finger as he did so.

"Fucking hell," Noah said, breathless. "Another."

Zeke squirted a great deal of lube into his fingers before wriggling two of them inside of Noah, as deep as he could. With his other hand, he fumbled for Noah's cock, using fast, heavy strokes when he found it. Noah wriggled further and further down the sleeping bag, thrusting his hips down onto Zeke's fingers.

Zeke found the small, firm lump he was looking for and he pushed down, hard.

Noah started to scream: a high-pitched, guttural sound of pure pleasure, before he caught himself.

Zeke stopped. "Do I need to gag you?"

In answer, Noah grabbed Zeke's hand from his swollen dick and inserted it into his mouth, pushing three fingers deep inside and sucking with the ferocity of someone deprived of water in the desert. The quiet noises he made, even muffled by Zeke's soaked fingers, drove Zeke wild.

With even more ferocity, Zeke rammed his fingers inside of Noah again, and again until Noah wrenched his fingers out of his mouth to say, "I need you inside of me. Now."

Heat pooled at the base of his spine. His enlarged cock twitched with hunger at Noah's words, and Zeke prayed he could keep it together long enough to give Noah what he wanted. With haste, he squirted a generous amount of the lubricant onto his dick, making sure it covered every inch.

"Please," Noah said, pulling his legs back and arching his hip upwards. He looked him dead in the eye. This was the hottest thing Zeke had ever seen, crypt be damned.

He gripped one of Noah's hips as he pressed his cock up to Noah's opening. A sudden wave of nervousness made him pause. Although this was what he wanted—he'd wanted this for a while now—he was scared of being subpar, or even hurting Noah. "Tell me if you need me to slow down or stop, okay?"

"Zeke, goddamn you! Stop overthinking and just do it. I know it's going to be amazing."

Noah leaned forward to cup Zeke's cheek, brushing his thumb across his skin. The gesture was so tender, Zeke immediately relaxed. The rest of his nerves dissipated as Zeke pushed the tip of his dick inside, revelling at the unique sensation. It was tight, and the slide of his cock against the smooth muscle ignited flares of desire within him. He pulled out slightly before thrusting in again, further this time, then further again. Once he'd built up a steady rhythm, slow and deep, Noah hooked his ankles around Zeke's calves, then squeezed his shoulders before dragging his fingers down Zeke's arms, grabbing his hands to entwine their fingers. The sight of their joined hands in addition to their bodies did something to Zeke. The moment of connection was so all-consuming, he felt hot tears prickle his eyes.

"So good... Zeke, you're doing so good," Noah spluttered out between feral moans, and Zeke prayed the crypt was as soundproof as it seemed.

A groan escaped Zeke's lips. "I won't be able to last long if you keep saying shit like that."

"Say you're mine," Noah gasped out, in between low moans. "Say you're *only* mine."

The sudden demand made Zeke falter for a second. But what he said next was the easiest thing to say in the world. "I'm only yours. Always."

Noah sat up, clenching his thighs tight as he clutched Zeke to him before twisting them over, pushing Zeke onto his back. He brushed his hand over Zeke's nipples, tweaking them repeatedly as he took control of the pace. Zeke dug his fingers into Noah's hips as Noah pushed himself down again and again, deeper than before. The view of his dick pounding into Noah's body was obscene and made him push up against him even harder.

Zeke placed his hand on Noah's heart to see if it was beating as hard as his was. The rapid *thud thud thud* seemed to merge with his own pulse until he wasn't sure where he stopped and Noah began.

He gripped Noah's slick, rock-hard cock, and after three hard thrusts, hot liquid ropes spilled over his stomach as Noah cried out. Zeke seared the sound he made into his memory, to replay again and again and again. Incomprehensible garbage came out of Noah's mouth as he dragged his nails over Zeke's chest. Then his hands moved down, to lightly grasp Zeke's balls, squeezing with just the right amount of pressure.

"Come for me, baby," Noah murmured, the candlelight exposing the look of pure bliss on his face.

Zeke couldn't hold back anymore. His orgasm rocketed through him, the hardest he'd ever come before, sending his body spasming into euphoric waves as he filled Noah with his own release.

Noah collapsed on top of him, breathing hard, and Zeke, trembling, wrapped his arms around him, securing him, not wanting to pull out of him yet. He stroked small circles on the base of Noah's back, in the way he knew he liked. A light layer of sweat covered every inch of them, but Zeke shivered, the cold bite of the crypt making its first threat.

They shared a few sloppy, languid kisses.

"That was…"

"Fucking incredible?" Zeke suggested.

Noah laughed, and Zeke wanted to devour him, to climb inside his mouth and never leave him. Zeke went to grab Noah's hand again, but his fingers brushed against the edges of smashed glass.

"Did you break your watch?"

"Earlier. When saving your ass."

Zeke gently pushed Noah back, then wriggled out of him to sit up. "Noah… I'm so sorry."

Noah shrugged. "It's just a watch. Your life was slightly more important to me."

"But still…"

Tilting his head up, Noah's gaze bored into him. The flicker from the candles reflected in his hazel eyes. "Do you know how important you are to me?" he said, expression deadly serious.

Zeke swallowed, his tongue turning to sand in his mouth.

"You are everything to me, Zeke," Noah whispered. "*Everything.*"

Hot prickles burned the corner of Zeke's eyes as he rapidly blinked back more tears. Nobody had ever looked at him this way, and he didn't know what to do with the overwhelming feelings that threatened to consume him.

He fumbled for something more profound to say before settling for, "You're everything to me too," while wrapping locks of Noah's hair around his finger.

"Can you help me with something?"

"Anything."

"I still haven't opened my uncle's package."

"The thing he gave you months ago?"

After untangling themselves, they quickly redressed—it really was far too cold to be sitting in a crypt naked—then Noah reached for his rucksack and unzipped an inner compartment to take out the small but bulging brown envelope.

"Why did you bring that? How am I helping you, exactly?"

Noah sighed. "Just by opening it with me. I don't know why I've put it off this long."

Zeke watched as Noah tore open the package, holding it slightly apart from him as if it were a poisonous snake about to bite. Noah seemed to hold his breath; the air around them felt oppressive with silence.

He tipped the contents onto his lap.

A piece of paper, a handwritten note.

A collection of maps stapled together.

A key.

Noah studied the items for a few minutes, holding a tea light to them so he could read.

"It's for a yacht."

Zeke snatched the paper from Noah. The note, in large, scrawly handwriting, was written in a foreign language—Dutch?

"These are instructions on how to find it, and this is a basic instruction manual."

"Where is it?" Zeke felt strange, like he was floating above them, looking down at two people lost at sea, about to be washed away on separate waves. "Is he suggesting you... run away... on a boat?" A small, hollow laugh escaped his lips. The idea was ludicrous.

"Only if things get bad. If London falls." Noah stilled. "Is it such a ridiculous idea?"

"It's December, and freezing fucking cold. Where would you even go? Does it even still work? Have you even ever driven a boat before? And what, you're just going to pack up and leave us all?"

Noah blinked at him, his voice icy when he said, "I presumed I wouldn't be alone on the boat."

Numbness—partly from the cold, but mostly from Noah's reaction—seeped through Zeke's body.

"Noah... I..." Zeke stared at him. "I can't just leave Zaya." The thought split his heart in two. As did the thought of Noah sailing off on some boat to a desert island or wherever the fuck he wanted to go.

Noah opened his mouth to reply, but loud shouts from above their heads caught their attention. Perhaps the crypt wasn't as soundproof as they'd thought. *Oops.*

Then, Noah's wristband vibrated with an incoming call from Vitt.

Noah stared up at the dark ceiling, eyes wide, lips pressed into a hard line. "That sounds like Habib."

NOAH

Within seconds, Noah had blown out the candles and dragged Zeke up the stairs two at a time to reach the main hallway. He was almost glad of the distraction. Zeke's rejection was an icicle shard to the heart, even if the rational part of his brain understood his unwillingness to leave Zaya.

A flash of worry shot through him as they exited the crypt door together, but he needn't have panicked. Most of the platoon were gathered in a circle around their spectacle: Habib versus David Reeves, one of Tobias's most loyal followers. Whatever this was, it wouldn't be good.

Habib, cheeks flushed, a vein bulging on his neck, stepped towards the smaller man. "Are you calling me a liar, Reeves?"

The silent crowd glanced between them, but Noah sought out Tobias. He stood on the periphery, a faintly amused expression plastered on his infuriating face.

"You're either a liar or hallucinating." Reeves further closed the space between them, glowering.

"Where's Lowenna?" Noah snapped, at nobody in particular.

"She went to get something from the van."

Of course she had.

Noah stepped into the circle, with Tobias mimicking his movement like a mirror. "What's going on? This isn't the time for petty playground fights."

"That scumbag," said Habib, waving a finger at Reeves, "stole two extra protein bars from the box."

"Didn't happen," Reeves spat. "I was just moving the box out of the way."

"I literally saw it happen. Then he went over and tossed them to Penn and Moss."

"Didn't. *Fucking*. Happen." Reeves was inches away from Habib now, hissing in his face. Habib's shoulders rolled and Noah tensed—Habib's self-control would only go so far.

"Did anyone else see this?" Noah scanned the soldiers, meeting as many eyes as possible. Everyone shuffled uncomfortably.

"Just look in the box, Noah. There's two missing," Habib said.

"Confirmed." Vitt stepped forward. "There's definitely two less than there should be."

He turned to Penn and Moss—unmoving, eyes averted. At least they had the sense not to smile at him.

Noah, in a calm, detached voice, said, "Fine. You two won't be receiving your breakfast allowance."

Tobias let out a chilling laugh. "Absolutely not. Are you saying your man's word is worth more than mine?"

Noah turned to him, feeling every eye on him.

"Keep your men in line, Newman, and I won't need to do it for you."

Tobias barked a laugh. "Get back in your own *line*, Forrest. If you can find it."

Fighting back a smirk—was that really the best Newman could come up with?—he shook his head and stepped back, deciding the best way to diffuse the situation was to leave it and speak to Lowenna.

Out of the corner of his eye, he caught the end of Reeves making a hand gesture.

And then the fight began.

While Noah would like to think Habib didn't throw the first punch, he'd got to know him very well over the last five years. Habib's patience towards Squad C was now wafer-thin, and they would suffer the consequences.

As the majority of Squad C launched themselves into the fray, Noah dodged several rogue elbows as he dived towards Zeke, frozen motionless in disbelief. He dragged him up the aisle and pushed him to the side.

"Stay there," he ordered, wincing at Zeke's expression of pure fury for a second before sprinting back to the carnage, standing on a bench to survey the scene. Penn had fashioned a weapon out of part of a broken wooden pew and swung it at Habib, who narrowly dodged the attack and countered with a punch to Penn's gut. Aoife, never one to sit on the sidelines, grabbed a battered hymnal and hurled it at Moss, who stumbled backwards but quickly retaliated by grabbing a candlestick and swinging it at her. Florence, the woman Aoife chatted up earlier, grabbed Moss's arm, trying to pull him away.

"Stop!" Noah shouted, but his words fell on deaf ears. Squad K stood gawking in a semi-circle, acting almost like a wrestling ring barrier, enclosing the brawling idiots within. Krish glanced his way, giving him a look that said 'do *something* for crying out loud!'. Tobias—standing to the side, arms folded—watched the scene unfurl like it was something vaguely amusing but not worth his time.

It was only when Frankie, who'd kept to the edge, hit the floor—with Squad C's Gemma Osborne on top of her—that it came to Noah's attention that Zeke had *not* remained where he left him.

Zeke lunged for Osborne, pushing her off Frankie before dragging his friend away from the scuffle.

Goddamn Tobias, goddamn Habib, goddamn every one of these idiots.

Noah dropped off the bench, beelining straight for them, but Osborne got there first, slamming her fist into Zeke's face. Blood instantly erupted from his nose, dribbling down his pale chin and neck.

Noah roared, forgetting his earlier self-restraint, and charged towards Osborne, knocking her to the floor with his shoulder.

The loud crack of gunshot froze the commotion, leaving them in a tableau of chaos.

Of course Lowenna chose to arrive at the exact moment he'd joined the fight, breaking the first and foremost rule of leadership—don't punch your men.

The church fell deathly silent, bar the sound of panting, pissed-off soldiers.

"What in the actual...?" Lowenna started, eyes darting between them. "I left you for ten minutes. *Ten* fucking minutes. And you descend into this... this ludicrous madness. You are soldiers of the Eighth East Regiment. The last line of defence between humanity and the end of everything. *Everything.* We cannot afford this sort of immature behaviour." She shook her head as if they were schoolchildren who'd disappointed her. "Forrest, Newman, with me." Her eyes scanned the crowd. "And you, Krish. I need somebody with more than half a brain cell to explain to me how the fuck it got to this."

Noah risked a glance at Zeke, who was futilely wiping the pouring blood from his nose with his sleeve. Frankie, standing beside him, put her arm around him and nodded at Noah.

He trailed after Lowenna, eyes downcast, as she led them towards the tower. Each step of the spiral staircase further deepened the abyss of his plummeting mood. The cramped and musty space of the bell chamber housed a colossal brass bell suspended from the ceiling. After ordering the watch team to wait downstairs, Lowenna arranged the three of them into a firing line with her glare.

Krish recounted the whole sorry tale—leaning towards siding with Squad E—and stated that Noah at least attempted to stop the fighting, whereas Tobias did nothing.

Tobias listened without interrupting, his bored expression back on his face. He sounded casual when he interjected with, "Sure, Noah tried to stop it. Until he cracked Gemma's head open."

Lowenna's head shot to him so quickly, Noah stumbled backwards.

"What?" he croaked. "I just..."

"You just pushed her over so hard you made her head bleed."

Guilt coursed through his veins. Was Tobias telling the truth? Noah replayed the event in his head, but he'd been so focussed on Zeke and Frankie...

"You're forgetting that Osborne had just absolutely decked Bates,"—Krish glanced at Lowenna—"you know, the little scrawny one? When he was only trying to drag Frankie away from Osborne. It's clear to me that Forrest's behaviour was justified, ma'am."

"You know what's clear to me?" said Tobias, the odd tone of his voice shooting fear into Noah's veins. "That Forrest lost his shit as soon as Bates got involved. I think it's *clear—*"

"Enough."

Lowenna turned away from them all, staring out of the broken window into the black abyss of the night. "This either never happened, or it did. If it did, I will write up every member of your squads even remotely involved. Including you, Newman. If you'd just have disciplined your two men in the first place when Habib reported it to you, we could have avoided all of this. So, I'll ask you once: did this happen?"

"Didn't happen," mumbled Noah, while Tobias grunted.

Sighing as if this horrendous day would never end, Lowenna said, "Dismissed. Forrest, stay here. You're helping me change the duty rota."

Krish squeezed his shoulder on the way out, hissing, "I'll go check on him."

Noah's cheeks warmed. How many others had noticed his affection towards Zeke?

As soon as they were alone, Lowenna turned on him. "Jesus, Noah, what were you thinking? Now really isn't the time to be putting a single toe out of line, what with our covert operation and all."

"*Our* covert operation?" he cried. "I never agreed to be a part of this!"

"Well, tough luck," Lowenna snapped, eyes blazing. "It's time to get down to business." From her pocket, she pulled out a large, chunky wristband, an older-style civilian model. "Krish has transferred all the image files to this via an undetectable direct transfer. I'm about to send them to Leonie Voigt. We'll need to do the same tomorrow with whatever we find at the farm." Her face softened slightly. "Did Leonie tell you what we're likely to find there?"

He nodded. "I hope you realise the effect the mass panic will have if those documents get released. How many civilians will die because of it?"

"If we don't do something, everyone will be dead anyway." Lowenna didn't return his hostility; she sounded sad, defeated even. "Believe me, Noah, this was a last resort. But the government and the military are refusing to take appropriate action. They're burying their heads in the sand."

He couldn't deal with this right now. "I'm going back downstairs." Noah started towards the door, but Lowenna caught his arm.

"Wait. Be careful of Newman. I wouldn't trust my worst enemy with him."

Snorting, Noah said, "He literally is my worst enemy, so..." He shook his head on the way to the exit. In the doorway, he turned back to say, "Gracie Bellows. I can't stop thinking that if we never went off-piste to the graveyard, she would still be—"

Lowenna crossed the small space and gripped both of his arms with hers. "Listen to me carefully. Gracie is my burden to bear, and mine alone. You have nothing—*nothing*—to feel guilty about."

But Lowenna's words did little to comfort him as he travelled down the spiral staircase to find two soldiers of Squad K sprawled in the hallway, their arms wrapped around each other as they sobbed.

As he studied them, Noah's old friend emerged to sit heavily on his shoulders, bringing with it its familiar visceral, heart-wrenching ache.

Grief. His most faithful companion. His darkest shadow on the brightest days.

ZEKE

At breakfast the next morning, Zeke's eyes drooped. He'd finally nodded off to sleep at around midnight—thanks to less than comfortable sleeping conditions on his rock-solid pew—before waking up at three a.m. for his watch-duty shift. Alarmingly, Noah was still awake. He'd been staring out the window when Zeke risked quickly kissing him on the forehead amongst the sea of snoring bodies. Noah gave him the smallest of smiles before promising he'd go to sleep in a minute.

He'd spent his entire night shift brooding over his reaction towards Noah's proposition of sailing off into the sunset with him. He fluctuated between waves of intense guilt—his mind replaying Noah's awful, devastated expression—and irritation. Because Noah's plan was ludicrous. Nothing could be more stupid than attempting to cross an ocean in midwinter in a boat neither of them knew how to pilot.

A warm body slid down onto the bench next to him, thigh pressed against his.

"Here," Noah said, pushing something into his hand. An apple, similar to the one he'd just eaten after Lowenna shared out all the remaining fruit.

He blinked at it, alarmed. "What?"

"You're still hungry. I could tell from across the room."

Zeke shook his head, pressing the apple back into Noah's hand. "Don't be stupid. You'll starve."

"Honestly, I'm fine." Noah dropped the apple onto Zeke's lap. "Please. It'll make me worry less about you if I know you're okay."

He sighed, taking a large bite of the bland, mushy flesh. His stomach growled, eager for more substance. He passed the apple over to Noah. "Fifty-fifty?"

Rolling his eyes, Noah took a bite, and for a while they silently passed it back and forth.

"What's that?" asked Noah, nodding his chin at Zeke's rucksack, where a piece of orange fabric poked out.

Zeke tried to kick the bag under the bench, but Noah grabbed it, opening the flap. He laughed when he saw Zeke's fluffy fox toy.

"I need it to sleep," he mumbled, grabbing the bag back. Shyly, he removed a bundle of fabric from a side pocket and unwrapped it to show Noah the fox carving he'd given him on his birthday.

Noah's eyes widened.

"I wanted to bring this too. For luck."

Frankie interrupted them by throwing herself onto the bench opposite them, dark bags under her eyes. Her hair was still a bird's nest after not being able to wash properly yesterday. Zeke threw her the last bite of the apple.

"There's a team out trying to snare some meat," said Noah. "We'll be able to eat properly later, if we're lucky."

Frankie nodded. "I just saw them haul something through the fence. Two foxes."

Zeke froze.

Frankie burst into laughter that echoed off the walls. "Your face! Just kidding. It was a couple of rabbits. Not gonna lie though, I would happily eat anything right now."

Brodie materialised next to Frankie, sparing Zeke from pretending to find Frankie funny. "LT, can I speak with you for a second?"

Noah raised his eyebrows. "What about? Is here okay?"

Brodie glanced around—to see if any other squads were in earshot?—before saying, "Just went outside to take a leak around the back. Queue for the bathroom is mad. Anyway, I'm going about my business when I hear Newman in a bush—literally in the middle of a bush—talking through his band. Didn't hear what he was saying really, but then Newman notices me and goes apeshit."

"What did he do?"

"He was proper pissed off, and maybe even a little scared? To be honest, I zipped up and got out of there so fast I didn't give him time to do much."

Frankie frowned. "Strange. Maybe he was calling his secret lover."

"Who the hell would be crazy enough to be with him?" said Zeke.

"Ohhh, burn." Frankie laughed again, and the sound of it slowly chipped away at his bad mood. "Didn't know you had it in you, Zeke."

"Thanks, Campbell. Let me know if he bothers you about it. Or just bothers you. We've only got to get through today, then we're done with Squad C. I'll talk to Murphy." Noah sighed, then beelined to Lowenna, who was marching around barking orders.

Vitt, looking more ready and refreshed than any of them, jumped in Noah's grave, smirking. "Luo owes me five mug duties when we get back. Aoife got with Bloomer last night."

Frankie snorted. "Florence from C? When on earth did they find the time? Or place?"

Zeke's own rendezvous with Noah yesterday made him avert his eyes.

"Don't know, or care."

A deep voice from behind Zeke said, "You'll care when they're too tired to save your arse in a few hours."

Habib joined them, disapproval etched into his face.

"Oh, lighten up, Hab," snapped Vitt. "We don't all have adoring families waiting for us at home. We're allowed to stretch our wings once in a while."

"I'm just saying there *is* a time and a place."

Zeke kept his gaze firmly on Frankie's muddy boots.

Aoife herself appeared, prompting Vitt to wolf-whistle at her and wiggle her eyebrows in glee.

"Ah, would ya stop? She's been actin' dead odd with me this mornin'. Like a different person entirely."

"What did you do?" asked Habib.

Aoife scoffed. "Feck knows. It was all grand last night, but since she talked to her squad this mornin', it's like she's a whole different person."

"Newman probably threatened her to stay away from you upon pain of death," said Vitt. "I wouldn't take it to heart."

"Moving out in five!" shouted Lowenna, easily projecting her voice across the church. Zeke gazed up at the weak sunlight streaming through the stained-glass windows.

Showtime.

Three hours later, Savannah reported they were a klick away from their destination: Red Ridge farm. Sprawling over 800 acres, the farm once produced ten percent of the country's pork supply. Or so Savannah told them, anyway.

Their convoy pulled up in a ditch, guarded each other while they stripped to apply an extra layer of blocker, and then set off through some woods.

"Check out the map, guys. Half a mile to our right is an old quarry," Savannah said as they marched through the overgrown terrain.

"Ah, I think we've had our fill of your craic for the day, Sav," Aoife said, nudging her with her shoulder.

"I'm surveying the perimeter."

"Ah, for feck's sake, you're putting us to sleep here."

"Both of you should be focussed on your sight lines," Noah snapped through the interface.

"*I* was enjoying your fun facts, Savannah," Zeke whispered to her. Every bone in his body ached—during his fall into the pit grave yesterday, he'd landed badly on his left leg and he was now suffering the consequences. He'd done his best to hide the injury from Noah—one less thing for him to worry about.

Wolf trotted along beside him on the far right of the formation. "I hope you appreciate what I did for you," he muttered, stroking his soft head.

"Leave the canine units to their job, Bates." Tobias's voice through his helmet made him jump, and his face burned.

In front of him, he saw Noah turn from his position near the front, until Vitt caught his arm and dragged him forward.

Lowenna, leading the charge at the very front, came to an abrupt halt. Her crossbow remained out and ready as she said, "Hundred metres. We're about to breach the perimeter of the farm. Remember our orders and objectives."

Zeke swallowed as the platoon crossed the threshold and found themselves in an extensive field overgrown with wildflowers. Across the grass, a collection of large farmhouse buildings awaited them. An area map appeared on his display: Lowenna was indicating a specific entrance to a large barn. The group crossed the fields slowly, the dogs following various scents they detected in the foliage. Amongst the wildflowers lay a toppled-over silo, its rotten insides spilled out like guts.

Soon enough, they arrived at the end of the field, relieved to be back on concrete where there were fewer places for types to hide. Lowenna had tasked several others with carrying large supply boxes—including blast bombs—and they set them down at once, panting. Zeke eyed them. The thought of trying to detonate anything with twenty-nine others watching made his skin crawl.

"Penn and Williams, you're our exterior guard," said Tobias, pointing to a spot near the metal gate they'd climbed over. "Do not leave your post without permission."

"It's very quiet here." Vitt stretched out her arms.

Habib surveyed the scene with his crossbow, as if he expected a type to pop out at any moment. "Don't push our luck."

Zeke's gaze drifted over to Noah and Lowenna, who pointed up at a fixed metal ladder that led to the roof of the barn. Enclosed within metal rings, time had rusted the fragile-looking rungs. When Noah shook the ladder, it broke free of the wall in several places, showering them with dust.

"Looks safe," Noah broadcasted, sarcastically. "Squad E, we're first, Bates and Fleming at the back."

Beside him, Frankie scoffed. She didn't like being mollycoddled still. He felt for her—Frankie could now hold her own when compared to the others.

Someone set up a surveillance drone, and it hovered over Noah's head as he pried open the door at the top of the ladder with a crowbar. Half-expecting a swarm of types to explode out of the roof, Zeke tensed. But the door swung open to reveal a seemingly empty, dark abyss. They sent the drone through and the live video feed revealed a small space—just enough height to stand up in—containing a sea of wooden rafters, but not a lot else. Squad E didn't hesitate on the dubious rungs. Zeke, following at the very back, tried to match their pace, but winced as he put weight on his injured ankle.

The attic quickly became crowded when C and K joined them. Helmet lights flashed left and right, illuminating small patches with dim beams.

Noah nodded to the other side of the attic, which was open and seemingly fell down to the ground floor. "Permission to lead on, ma'am?"

"Granted. After you, Forrest."

The platoon was at ease as they crossed the floor, taking care to step over the wooden beams. The attic was large enough that it seemed to take an age to reach the other side, and an odd sense of suspense bloomed within the group. He held a fairly good idea of what could be down there, since Noah had filled him in somewhat—although there was definitely information Noah was withholding from him.

"What's that noise?"

"Doesn't sound like types."

Noah turned back to look at him as they neared the edge, trying unsuccessfully to communicate something.

"What?" Zeke hissed.

"Just... be careful," Noah whispered back.

Zeke fought to keep the bite out of his voice as he replied, "As if I would be anything else right now?"

Noah shook his head and removed a heavy-duty flashlight from his belt, casting it over the edge. "No ladder down, so we should be safe."

Almost immediately, everyone formed a line against the drop, many crouching or even lying down on the floor to look at what lay below.

And what a sight it was.

Acid pooled in Zeke's stomach even before his brain had time to process the grisly scene before them. Naked bodies—humans, for certain, as none of them displayed any visible RONS transformations—hung suspended by their arms, chained to raised poles. Dangled above animal troughs, their ruined bodies were displayed almost exhibition-like, patches of grisly raw flesh scattering their skin like blotches of spilled ink.

Around him, Zeke was distantly aware of the noises the others were making, but he couldn't tear his eyes away from the monstrous scene below them. The nearest person—captive? meat slave?—twitched as she became bathed in multiple beams of light. Her eyes flickered open, and she flinched away from the light as if it hurt her. For a fleeting moment, he thought she would not look up at them, that perhaps she was brain-dead.

But then she did.

Recognition shot through her expression as her jaw dropped open.

She began to scream.

At least, she tried to. The woman writhed in her chains, strange, gurgling sounds emanating from her mouth as her face contorted into pure agony. Her raw, throaty cries reduced quickly to animalistic noises.

Aoife murmured a prayer. "What's wrong with her?"

Blood poured from the woman's lips, running down her chin: two tandem crimson rivers that produced a harrowing sound as it hit the metal trough.

"Sh-she's got no tongue," someone whispered. "Did screaming hurt her mouth?"

Zeke dragged himself away from the edge, turning to Frankie and Noah who'd done the same, their mouths pressed in grim lines. "But... why?"

Multiple hysterical babbles of animated conversation began, soldiers shouting over each other to be heard, despite Lowenna and Noah's shushing noises. Had the types chosen the tongue as an easy source of flesh? Or were the types aggravated by their screams? Had they cut the tongue from every victim? Surely most wouldn't have survived the blood loss, even if they hadn't drowned in their own blood?

Zeke stumbled away to a quiet corner, his mind spinning, his pitiful breakfast threatening to resurface.

A firm arm snaked around his back as he curled into a ball. He looked up, expecting Noah, but found Frankie's concerned face instead.

"Hold it together. This is almost over," she said, knocking her helmet against his. Dragging him to his feet, they stumbled back towards the group, with him feeling less than ready.

"So, what's the plan?" Vitt asked, looking to Noah. "Shall we start getting them down while we're type-free?"

Noah swivelled to Lowenna, who still gazed out at the sea of bodies, contemplative in her stance.

"Roskilly?" prompted Noah.

Lowenna eventually tore herself away from the edge to address the platoon. "I... I need a moment with the lieutenants." She shouldered her rifle and shuffled back into the darkness of the attic, with Noah trailing after her.

Zeke's eyes automatically shot to Tobias. He'd taken his helmet off and was whispering something to David Reeves and Sebastian Moss. *Odd.*

A second later, the interface on his own helmet shut down, as if it was out of battery. His night vision vanished, leaving only the handheld torch lights to create visibility. The shocked cries of the surrounding soldiers told him he wasn't alone in this problem.

"What the hell?" muttered Frankie.

A cry of pain echoed across the space. *Noah.*

"Helmets and wristbands off and weapons to Moss. Hands up where we can see them. Now!"

Waves of frantic panic pulsated through the group as everyone tried to make sense of what was happening. Frankie lunged for Zeke's hand, pulling him towards her.

"I said weapons on the *ground*," Tobias shouted.

Zeke darted his eyes between Lowenna and Noah, who stood shellshocked, hands up in surrender. Reeves disarmed them of their rifles, crossbows, daggers and helmets, throwing them into a pile. Every single one of Squad C trained their weapons on various members of E and K.

"You have got to be kidding, Newman," spat Habib. A small red dot appeared on Tobias's forehead. "What the fuck is this bullshit? And, your brain might be too small for basic math, but we outnumber you two to one. Let them go, now."

"You have exactly ten seconds to comply with my instructions," Tobias stated, his face an emotionless mask. What on earth was going on? "Or we shoot Noah and Lowenna."

Zeke tried to make eye contact with Noah, but Noah only stared at Tobias, rage written all over his face.

"Ten. Nine."

When Moss raised his dagger to Noah's throat, Zeke threw his rifle at Tobias's feet so hard it bounced off the floor.

"Good boy." Tobias turned to the rest of them. "Do we need to continue?"

Soldiers slowly peeled off helmets, wristbands and weapons and placed them on the ground, to be collected by Moss.

"Why are you doing this?" asked Vitt, panic and fury duelling for dominance on her face.

"Call it a citizen's arrest. Of sorts. Special orders."

"Our squads have nothing to do with this, Newman," Noah snapped. "Do what you want with Lowenna and I, but the others know nothing."

An icy grip tightened around Zeke's heart as the puzzle pieces locked into position. He didn't know much about Leonie Voigt's conspiracy—Noah had tried to conceal most of the details, in case Command tried to interrogate him. But clearly Command had discovered something was amiss. What had Murphy ordered Squad C to do to them?

Lowenna shook her head. "Noah didn't want any part of this. It's just me, Tobias. Let's go downstairs and talk."

"What are you even talking about?" Luo said. He and Habib were now the only ones not to have surrendered their weapons yet.

Behind him, Zeke felt someone pull his hands behind his back and lock them together with a zip tie. By the time he turned to Frankie, she'd suffered the same fate. He stared at her. *What should we do?*

Frankie only shook her head, fear written all over her face.

"Barakat and Shun," Tobias spat, his face twisted in rage. "We can do this the easy way, or the hard way. Do I need to start cutting off Bianco's body parts to get you to comply?"

Moss pushed Vitt roughly onto the ground, hands bound, in between Habib and Tobias. She let out a small cry.

Habib and Luo dropped their gear.

On Tobias's signal, Moss and the rest of C started herding their captives into a corner of the attic.

"Wait. Keep Bates."

Frankie, pressed up against him, gasped. "Why?"

Tobias laughed.

Zeke's heart sank ever lower as Squad C squashed everyone else into a huddle, caging them with their bodies. Aoife was dragged kicking and screaming, until one soldier must have got bored with the noise—he hit her in the head with the butt of his rifle.

As Zeke watched Moss bind Noah and Lowenna's hands, he fought back burning tears. *He needs me to stay strong.*

"Tobias," Noah said, calm and steady. "Let Zeke be with the others," he continued, as if it was a perfectly reasonable request.

"You never shut the fuck up, do you, Forrest?" Gone was composed Tobias, replaced with a beast that seemed to be quickly losing control.

Lowenna held her head up high. "If you want to be in charge, Tobias, maybe you could start by telling us the plan."

"We'll begin by you handing over your illegal recording device. I'll also need a list of the names of who you're working with. Then we're going to blow this whole joint up."

Every molecule in Zeke's body froze. It now made sense why Newman wanted him. "I won't do it," he said, in more of a whisper than a declaration.

Tobias threw his head back and roared. "As if I need *you* for that. A five-year-old could detonate those bombs."

Flinching away, Zeke fell backwards onto his knees, body limp. A low ringing began in his ears.

Tobias reached his hand out towards Lowenna and Noah, palm open. "Are we strip searching you or are you going to hand it over?"

Lowenna remained motionless, unblinking.

Pain exploded at the back of Zeke's head, and he flew forwards from the force of a blow. Red and purple fireworks flashed across his eyes as his throat made a strangled noise.

He could hear Noah shouting his name, his voice broken and desperate. Rolling onto his side, he saw Moss was physically restraining Noah.

"Newman!" shouted Lowenna. "He's just a kid. Take the fucking thing. It's around my waist."

Zeke pulled himself into a sitting position in time to see Tobias pull up her shirt to reveal a thin black belt bag. Unzipping it, Tobias held up a chunky black wristband, waving it in victory.

"Was that really so hard?"

"Now let everyone else go back to the vans," said Noah.

Hot, wet blood streamed down Zeke's neck as waves of dizziness kicked in. *Don't think about it. It's not there. It doesn't exist. Focus on Noah. Help Noah.*

"Not part of the plan, I'm afraid."

Lowenna gasped. "You're going to kill all of them? For no reason? Surely Murphy doesn't want that. She can't afford the numbers."

Tobias shrugged. "I'm not paid enough to ask questions. Moss, drag Bates over there with the rest of them, then give the signal to Penn outside."

Penn and Williams. Standing by the gate, ready to shoot any of them that escaped down the ladder. The five dogs were with them. Would Tobias shoot Wolf, just out of spite, once he'd blasted them to shreds? He looked back at Noah, trying to say goodbye with his eyes. *Thank you,* he tried to say. *You were everything.* Noah met his gaze, his face twisted in utter devastation.

Moss pushed Zeke away, shoving him down in between Luo and Frankie, who rested her chin on his shoulder. "Well done," she whispered.

"For what?" he said bitterly.

"For all of it." Frankie kissed his cheek. "It's been an honour."

"We're not dead yet, Frankie," Vitt hissed from behind him.

On the other side of the huddle, something was happening.

"I told you to *look* at me," Aoife snapped, her voice laced with fury and disbelief as she shook her head at Florence. "After what we got up to last night, you could at least show me some fecking respect."

Florence's face was blank, but her rifle shook.

In a very, very, quiet voice, Luo said, "I'm going to give us one shot."

"What?" whispered Vitt.

Luo shook his head. "I can snap my tie. I think. If I pull my bionic hard enough. But I'll probably dislodge my other shoulder doing so. Or maybe break my wrist."

A tiny glimmer of hope lit up Frankie's eyes. "And then what?"

"I'm going to shuffle over there to do it." Luo nodded to his right. "I'll grab Austin's rifle and start shooting. It's not gonna be pretty. People will die. I'll try to get his dagger at the same time and throw it at Vitt. I hear she's got mad skills with her mouth." He winked.

Zeke chuckled weakly, desperate to release some of the tension built up inside him. His head throbbed. His heart hurt. But he was determined to do his very best in whatever happened next. Even if it meant throwing himself in the line of fire to protect his team.

Vitt passed the message down the line in a hasty whisper, Squad C thankfully distracted by Aoife's continued verbal assault of Florence.

"Are we ready?" Luo asked.

Zeke looked at Frankie, at Vitt, Habib and all the others. His family. One he never knew he wanted, but now would do anything for.

"Brothers in arms, family for life," Zeke said, nodding his chin downwards at his dog tags.

"And sisters," Frankie hissed, nudging him.

He looked away from Luo as he began the process of ripping the zip tie—and likely his own body—free, partly to not make it obvious, but mostly as he didn't want to see the pain on Luo's face. How was he even meant to shoot Squad C with a broken arm, anyway?

Low grunts told him everything he needed to know. Around him, the others shuffled, covering up Luo's noise.

"I can't do this," came a distraught cry from the other side of the huddle. Florence.

"What?" Moss spat, looking at her as if she were an insolent child.

"This is wrong," Florence said, her voice shaking. Everyone's eyes were on her as she reached for her dagger, unsheathing it and cutting Aoife's bonds in one swift movement.

Bang.

Wisps of smoke filled the air.

Florence's body fell to the floor like a puppet with its strings cut.

Luo jumping up from the ground was the last thing Zeke saw before all hell broke loose. Tobias's angry shouts filled the air, almost as loud as the violent pattering of bullets. A glint of metal flashed as a knife landed near Zeke's lap. At once, Vitt gripped the dagger with her teeth and Habib threw his hands backwards onto it, cutting his wrist in the process. Zeke tore his eyes away from the blood dripping down his arm. Habib snatched up the dagger and freed Vitt and Savannah within milliseconds.

Moss's crumpled body—a hole in the centre of his forehead—fell to the ground, his rifle tumbling with it. Savannah lunged for the rifle and began to fire. How she knew where to aim in this carnage was anyone's guess; everyone was now on their feet and bodies screamed as they pushed into one another.

Around them, weak bursts of sunlight dappled the attic as bullets burst through the roof. Frankie, still bound like Zeke, pushed him out of the fray, towards Noah and Lowenna. But where was Tobias?

"They're here!" Lowenna screamed, and it took seconds for Zeke to realise who she meant. Because they may have been battling Squad C, but they were also in type territory. Specifically, their fridge.

"Guard the ladder!" Noah commanded, but was anyone even listening? "They're coming up that way too!"

Zeke's eyes darted across the attic. A sea of bodies littered the floor, including one with a shiny metal arm. He bit down on his lip to focus himself.

Vitt and Savannah ran past them, carrying Moss's body. Zeke gasped as they threw it off the edge. The sound of hungry, delighted types rose from the ground floor.

Genius.

Vitt slashed at Lowenna's zip tie, then Noah's. Noah lunged towards the weapon pile and threw Lowenna a rifle while Vitt freed Frankie. And now, finally, *finally*, it was Zeke's—

Strong arms threw themselves around Zeke's neck, pushing his body into theirs. Cold, sharp metal hovered on his cheek. Tobias's voice, low and steady, said, "Easy tiger."

Noah bellowed a primal roar.

"Step back," shouted Tobias.

Tobias, using Zeke as a human shield, crept further towards the edge. With his other hand, he swung his rifle in the air wildly. He squirmed against Tobias's firm arm, but between his bound arms and his injured ankle, it was a futile battle. Giving up, he focussed every inch of his being on Noah, wanting to take him in one last time. At least he'd had this time with him, before the end. He wouldn't change that for anything.

"Please," said Noah, sinking to the floor. "Give him to me. I'll do anything you want. I'll—"

But he didn't get to find out what Noah would do for him. Because Tobias threw them both off of the edge, into the type-infested darkness.

NOAH

Noah slammed his fists into the ground so hard bolts of agony shot up his arms.

Picking up the nearest rifle, he made towards the ledge.

Arms surrounded his waist as the light from his flashlight revealed two bodies weaving through troughs towards large metal doors on the other side of the barn. Tobias only needed to shoot a few types—Moss's body distracted the rest.

"Noah," said Habib, broken. "We still need you."

He turned. The fighting was over. Everyone that was still alive was either collapsed on the ground, tending to wounds, or gazing around, delirious. He saw Luo's body, limp and lifeless, curled into a ball. He expected waves of dark clouds to roll through him, but instead, he felt nothing. Nothing but rage.

"Throw down some more bodies."

Tobias reached the doors, Zeke's body still blocking his from gunfire as he pulled on a massive metal bar.

"Do what you can to patch up the wounded. I'll be back." Noah pushed Habib off him as light streamed in from the far side of the barn: Tobias had opened the doors.

"At least go down the ladder." Habib pushed him towards it while handing him his helmet. "Go."

He tugged the helmet on as he jumped over the dead bodies of his comrades. The interface still wasn't operational, but at least it would protect his head.

Distantly, his brain registered Savannah and Aoife pressing wads of cloth into a wound on Savannah's stomach, and Vitt emptying her bottle of blocker onto Frankie as if it was going to do anything to reduce the smell.

"I'm coming with you," said Frankie, but he ignored her, throwing himself onto the ladder and taking the rungs two at a time as he entered the outside world. He blinked, adjusting to the light.

Penn and Williams were not at their post, but he didn't spare a thought for where they'd gone. But where were the dogs? He whistled. Wolf's whistle.

The large dog bounded around the corner, barking.

"With me!" Noah shouted, already running down the side of the barn.

When he reached the front entrance, there was no sign of Newman and Zeke, only a cluster of types headed straight for him. He dispatched two with his rifle while Wolf tore another's neck to shreds. How many clips did he have left? No time to check.

Sprinting across the gravel, Noah charged off blindly in the direction he could only hope Newman had gone. He followed a breadcrumb trail of dead types, their bodies still twitching, through a field.

Luo is dead, they're all dead.

A bloody handprint on the gate.

Zeke is going to be dead.

Over the wooden fence, down the muddy forest path.

They're all dead. They're all dead. Everyone is dead.

Icy droplets pelting his suit. Snow?

He's going to die unless you run. Run, run, run!

Clear footsteps in the mud, brambles snagging on his suit. Movement, about fifty metres ahead of him.

He lifted his rifle.

"Tobias!" he roared.

Charging towards them, he heard branches cracking to his left. Increasingly loud snarling. Types. Lots of them.

The trees began to thin, presenting a clear view of his target. Tobias swung Zeke around, walking backwards while he aimed his rifle at Noah. But there was no way he could shoot properly one handed, while dragging a struggling Zeke.

"Just let him go! We're about to be overrun with types!"

Tobias continued to stumble backwards until he was out of the forest. Noah closed the space between them until he too crossed the threshold, charging out of the dense foliage and into a large, open space. He blinked, unable to process where he was. Savannah's voice from earlier that day burst into his brain. A quarry. They were standing in the base of a quarry.

The rough, jagged walls of the quarry rose up around him, the result of years of mining long since abandoned. The ground beneath his feet was overgrown with weeds and moss, and the air was heavy with the dampness and the musty smell of rusted machinery—bulldozers and crushers lay scattered around the pit, silently watching what was about to come next.

Wolf growled as Tobias backed up all the way to a truck. Zeke, his hair a mess of blood, writhed in his bonds, fighting Tobias's restraint on him with everything he had. *Keep fighting him, baby.* He'd lost his glasses at some point, his head looking naked and vulnerable without them. Tobias's arm came up to Zeke's neck, squeezing hard while his dagger pointed into the side of it.

"It's over, Newman," Noah shouted. "Let him go and you can make a run for it."

Tobias, conflicted, flicked his eyes between Noah and the forest, where the sounds of the coming onslaught grew louder. Only seconds remained.

Wolf growled at the treeline.

Tobias's grip on Zeke loosened.

Noah held out his hand.

Dozens of types burst into the quarry, their snarls bouncing off the high stone cliff.

Noah turned, flicking his rifle to burst-fire and began to shoot.

A gigantic typeB, with a large hanging stomach that jiggled, quickly charged towards Noah, jaws wide and ready to bite. *Bang.*

Two smaller typeAs, jostling each other as they scrambled along on their hands and knees, lunged for him. *Bang. Bang.*

He was down to his last clip. He stepped backwards to reload.

Wolf, a brown blur of muscle and teeth, threw himself at three more types, sending them flying before sinking his jaw into their necks.

"Noah!"

He turned back to Zeke and Tobias to find them surrounded by five more types. Tobias's rifle lay on the ground—when did he run out of bullets?—and he now brandished his dagger.

At Noah's whistle, Wolf bolted towards them, grabbing one type by the waist and sinking his teeth deep.

The other four, however, were inches away, their arms reaching out for purchase.

Noah ran.

Tobias's eyes widened as he prepared for what was about to unfold. Still holding Zeke against his chest, his head darted from left to right.

Tobias planned his move: eyebrows knitting together and lips pressing into a hard line.

He pushed Zeke, hard.

Towards the types.

And ran for his life, sprinting off to the right.

Still bound, hands behind his back, Zeke fell forward, his chin hitting an enormous chunk of granite.

The types swarmed him within a beat of Noah's shattering heart.

He screamed. He open-fired, trying his best to hit only the types—who were frantically pawing at Zeke with their claws while their jaws snapped open and closed. He took two down, their lifeless forms burying Zeke with their torsos, while Wolf pinned down another, finishing it with a bite to the jugular. But not before it raked a large four-clawed hand down Wolf's stomach, resulting in Wolf crying out in a pitiful whine of pain and falling to the ground.

There were just two left now. *Two left, it's going to be okay, it's going to be—*

A burst of agony rocketed through Noah's leg, originating in his right calf. His legs betrayed him and he tumbled to the ground, blood pouring out of his injured limb, an inferno of fire devouring his every thought. From his position sideways on the ground, he saw Tobias in the distance, a silver pistol in his hand. He'd saved a bullet. Saved a bullet for *him*.

Ignoring Tobias, Noah rolled over. He'd *drag* himself over to Zeke if it was the last thing he did.

But he froze in his tracks. Because what he saw in front of him detonated a nail bomb in his chest, ripping his soul to smithereens.

A typeB, its green-grey jaw locked firmly into Zeke's neck.

"No!" he screamed, or tried to scream, because he was no longer in his body. He was rising up, floating above everything, up with the gently falling snowflakes, almost as high as the nearby crane. Wolf dragged himself, whining, next to Noah's stone-still body, as he put himself between the types and Noah, growling.

The other type hissed at its friend, pushing it off Zeke to reveal deep, angry, bleeding marks on his neck. Zeke was motionless—dead or unconscious—as the pair communicated in animalistic grunts. He could only watch as the duo lifted Zeke's arms, as if he were a rag doll, and dragged him off into the forest, lightning-quick.

An eerie silence settled over the quarry, punctuated by Wolf's laboured breaths.

Noah's body shut down. First went his muscles, locking stone-still. Next went his brain and he floated in semi-consciousness, time expanding into seconds, minutes, eternity. His mind was completely absent of all thoughts and it was a beautiful place to be.

A tiny whine broke through his barrier, followed by a wet lick. A single tear escaped his eye, trickling down his face.

Noah wanted to continue to lie very still with his eyes closed forever. But he couldn't. There was still something that needed to be done. He pulled himself to his feet, using tufts of Wolf's thick fur to steady himself. His body was about to experience a lot of pain.

It. Would. Be. Worth. It.

He took one look in the forest's direction, where they'd dragged Zeke off. If he hadn't been shot, or if he hadn't wasted minutes lying on the ground, he might have been able to catch up with them and put a bullet through Zeke's brain.

No, Noah couldn't help Zeke now, but there was something he *could* do.

He started moving across the quarry towards where Tobias had shot him, each light step on his bleeding leg causing fresh waves of torment.

His efforts paid off. He found Tobias on the ground, a dead type nearby, a bloody dagger in his hand, the shallow rise and fall of his chest telling Noah everything he needed to know.

"Noah," Tobias croaked out as he straddled him, unsheathing his own dagger from his belt.

"Newman!" Noah all but shouted. "You sadistic fuck. You fucking killed him. You killed so many people. How could you go along with this?"

Tobias's face twisted. "Murphy said you were going to cause panic. That civilians would die. That it needed to be done."

"So you didn't blink an eye when she ordered the execution of twenty soldiers? Good people? Most of which weren't even involved in Lowenna's shit?"

"She didn't know who knew what. I... was just following orders."

Noah screamed, slamming the hilt of the dagger into Tobias's chest.

"Noah, listen, please—"

He didn't give him time to say anything else. He cut through the skin of Tobias's neck, feeling no joy, no victory, only relief. The knife vibrated in his hand as he sawed in further and further. He shouted. He cried. He cut deeper and deeper into Tobias's mangled neck.

"This is for Zeke, for Luo, for all the soldiers lying dead in that barn, you absolute piece of shit!"

There was blood everywhere. It soaked his hands, his chest, his hair. It covered his ruined calf.

Good. Let them come. Let this be over.

Wolf watched his display with judgment, making soft whimpering sounds.

Noah rolled off Tobias, falling onto the rocky ground and pulling off his helmet, throwing it far. He whispered, "Come here, boy," and Wolf crowded him, pressing his soft body against him. He fumbled with his combat suit, removing it piece by piece. Finally, he found what he was looking for. He wrapped his dog tags around Wolf's collar, making sure they were as secure as could be. Kissing the dog's nose, he said, "Go back now, Wolf. Go back to Vitt."

Wolf howled, nuzzling his snout into Noah's chest. He knelt to inspect Wolf's wound. It didn't look too bad. Meredith would be able to patch him up.

"I know, I'm sorry too." Noah pulled Wolf's head up to look deep into his brown eyes. "You go protect them, boy. They're gonna need you."

Noah whistled a complicated array of tunes, gesturing wildly to the west. Eventually, Wolf barked once, and trotted away from him, looking back twice with sad eyes.

And then he was alone.

But not for long, he told himself. Noah's world had ended. For the third time. For the last time.

Staring up at the cliff in front of him, his plan formulated within him, clear as day.

With each painstaking step on the arduous ascent, a tapestry of memories unfolded in his mind. Habib and Vitt, laughing with him by the lake during his first year with them. Walking with Khyan through the woods, hand in hand. Him at the beach with his family, throwing his younger brothers into the water. And finally, Zeke. Oh, *Zeke.* Zeke, who'd already stolen his heart, even though he'd only known him for a handful of months. Zeke, who'd given him the thing he needed most to keep going: hope. He felt nothing but love in his heart as the top of the cliff hurtled towards him. Why hadn't he told Zeke he loved him before it was too late? But enough of that. It was futile now.

He reached the precipice of the cliff, staring down at the hundred-foot drop. The snowfall, attacking his cheeks with wet bites, obscured his view of the bottom. Somewhere behind him came the short, erratic bursts of birdsong from a nearby warbler.

Noah hovered his bad leg over the edge, a warm glow seeping through his body. As a child, he'd stretched out on the grass in De Biesbosch, looking up at the bluethroats, wishing he could fly away with them.

And now, he would.

He was going to fly like a bird for a few moments.

A few, glorious, peaceful moments.

He stepped off the edge.

NOAH

Noah was falling.

Falling.

Falling.

Falling... backwards?

Staring up into the grey sky, thick with falling snow, he felt powerful arms surround his stomach and drag him backwards, further and further from the edge. *No!*

Someone slapped his cheek with such force his head swivelled to the left.

"You absolute *imbecile*."

After wriggling free of the unwanted embrace, Noah sat up to find a furious Vitt, a disturbed-looking Frankie—her hand pressed against her chest—and finally Wolf, sitting beside them, looking pleased with himself. *Fucking traitor.* He stared at them until Vitt stepped forward, gripping both arms to shake him.

She waved his dog tags in the air. "Aren't you going to say anything?"

Noah, unable to withstand the pain in his leg in addition to the pain in his heart, collapsed onto the cold, wet ground, his body already heaving with heavy, body-shaking sobs. "Did Wolf bring you here?"

"We followed you almost straight away. Then Wolf found us and led us here. He was quite insistent. But Noah, what happened?"

The girls dropped to the ground with him, rubbing his back and holding him close as he recounted the whole sorry tale. Frankie's face crumpled like a paper bag as he detailed the moment a type bit Zeke before they hauled him away.

Vitt peeled back the ruins of his trousers to inspect his wound, causing him to gasp as waves of pain knocked the breath out of him. "Noah, we need to sort this leg out ASAP, like yesterday."

He pushed her away. "Leave it. It's not going to trouble me for much longer."

Crack. The sound of Vitt slapping him again punctuated the quiet of the quarry.

"Snap the hell out of it before I shoot your other leg, you—"

"Vitt!" Frankie interjected, but Vitt motioned for her to be quiet.

He looked at her. Even with her arms crossed and an angry scowl etched onto her face, his heart swelled with love and pride. Spending almost every day together for five years would do that to you.

"You don't understand, Vitt, I—"

She laughed, a high-pitched, bitter laugh that made half of him want to hug her, and half of him want to crawl back towards the precipice and finish what they'd interrupted.

"Noah. My love. I do understand. Of course I do." Vitt's voice became soft as she dropped down closer to him, cupping his cheek with her hand. "I'm so sorry this happened to you. The universe is a big fucking cosmic joke. If anyone didn't deserve to lose the guy they loved twice, it's you, my love."

Vitt kissed his forehead. Hot tears ran down his cheeks. Why, oh why, hadn't he told Zeke he'd loved him while there was still time?

"Did Habib tell you?" Noah croaked out.

Vitt batted him playfully on the head. "He didn't have to. You two were about as subtle as a neon sign."

"Umm, guys? I think we should at least bandage Noah's leg up or something," said Frankie, who was running her fingers through Wolf's shaggy mane.

The throbbing in his calf had reduced significantly. In fact, his entire leg was now quite numb. He looked down, and the sight nauseated him. Thick gloops of blood and other fluids caked his swollen, bruised skin where the 9mm bullet passed through. Should he be grateful for the additional exit wound on the other side, or were the two lesions causing his pain to be doubled?

Vitt glanced up at the increasingly darkening sky. "Right. We need to get out of this soup sandwich. First, we're going to tie up that bleeding mess. Then Frankie and I will drag you back to the others." Her expression shifted. She bit her lip. "We haven't spoken about the other casualties yet."

Frankie shifted uncomfortably. "Maybe we should just get him back first?" she suggested, as if the mention of the other deaths was going to send him hurtling towards the cliff. He couldn't blame her.

"Let me have it."

"K is way worse off than us," she prefaced, sounding guilty. "But we've lost Brodie and Luo." She tensed and eyed him, but Noah only nodded; he knew about Luo already. The grief that already consumed him negated any effect her words might have had. "Sav isn't doing great either. She's been shot in the stomach."

"Are Lowenna and Krish okay?"

"Yeah. I mean, technically yes, but obviously not. I think they're waiting for you to come back so we can do a full sitrep and talk next steps."

Noah shook his head. How was he supposed to think about the future right now?

"Please, Noah." Vitt slipped his dog tags back over his neck. "Our lives are imploding. We need you. *I* need you. I can't do this without you."

In a tremulous voice, Frankie said, "Zeke wouldn't have wanted you to give up."

Noah lay back again, letting the damp seep through his clothes. The thought of taking even one step back towards that damned farmstead made him want to take a long, long nap.

They need you, he told himself. *There are still people to protect.*

"Fine. But there's something I need to do first. I'll need your help. One of you will need to go back down there and find my helmet. And how much blocker and rounds do you have on you?"

"Are you *sure* this is a good idea?" Vitt asked for the millionth time. Noah rolled his eyes and bit his tongue. He'd given them both a clear choice: he was going to find and kill Zeke, with or without them. Of course, it wouldn't be Zeke he was killing. It would be the monster he'd turned into.

They were over ninety minutes into their expedition, following Wolf's nose as he tracked Zeke's scent eastwards, through the thick woods. At least he'd given them a trail of blood to follow. But Noah worried that the increasingly rapid snowfall would damage their chances. *Come on, Wolf, you can do it.*

"I don't understand why you have to do this. Don't you want to remember him how he was? Some things are better left unseen."

Vitt, supporting Noah's left shoulder while Frankie took the right, paused to catch her breath. His leg, bound with Vitt's belt acting as a makeshift tourniquet, throbbed with every step.

He inhaled deeply. "I was never able to do it for Khyan. Find him, after, I mean."

"There was likely nothing to find."

"I don't *know* that though," Noah snarled, flinching at the reaction his words caused. "I'll never know. With him. With Zeke, at least I can put my mind to rest one way or another. We either find his body, or we dispatch the fledgling type he's become. I just want his tags," he said, appealing to her sentimental nature. "I just want to be able to tell Zaya exactly what happened."

It worked: her gaze softened.

"At least let one of us do it if we find him," said Frankie.

"*When* we find him, I'm going to do it."

He squeezed his eyes shut, not wanting to imagine the task ahead of him if they found a type in Zeke's place, his beautiful body mutated into a monster. But it was a task that was his to complete.

Vitt sighed and repositioned her grip on his body before they restarted their awkward, stumbling journey. They slid down muddy banks, crawled through brambly hedges, and climbed over icy trunks—all while battling heavy snowfall and angry, empty stomachs.

At the point where Noah thought he was going to have to insist the girls at least turn back and make for the barn—the others were surely worried by now and they hadn't been able to turn back on any of their comms—Wolf barked three times, sniffing the air. He, at least, seemed to have recovered from his earlier injuries.

Frankie squeezed his arm with a shaking hand.

"You should stay here," he said, but she shook her head.

It was way past dusk now, the light from their helmets providing the only illumination in the dark night. Would the batteries even last for the return journey? If he caused Frankie and Vitt's deaths because of his own selfish mission...

The three of them pressed on, Wolf becoming more animated by the second. Abruptly, he stopped, sitting on his haunches with his tongue lolling out, staring at Noah like he wanted praise.

His impatience bubbled over. "Keep going, Wolf," he commanded, but the dog remained still, sitting by the base of a large oak tree. Wolf looked up, yapping a happy bark. "Wolf, we don't have time for—"

Frankie yelped, her helmet doing little to muffle the sound, and she dropped her grip on Noah. Her head tilted back, her light revealing the branches midway up the tree as she pointed.

"What?" he said, exasperated. There were no types nearby, judging by Wolf's relaxed demeanour. He squinted through the snow to the dark shadows within the tree, which retained many of its leaves despite the season. Something moved within the boughs.

"Don't come any closer," the tree said.

Noah was dreaming. *Surely* he was dreaming. There was no way, no way in hell—

"*Zeke?*" shrieked Frankie.

"Stay away," the voice called down, a hoarse croak.

Vitt whispered various obscenities under her breath, squeezing Noah towards her.

Noah's dry mouth fought for words. "What are you doing up there?" he asked, as if Zeke were a cat he'd lost up a tree.

"I'm trying to get high enough to jump, but it's too wet and slippery and cold so I..." He trailed off.

Noah tried to position his light to get a clear view of Zeke, but it proved difficult. Then Vitt dropped her grip on Noah, causing him to stumble. He swung around to find she'd unshouldered her rifle to train it towards Zeke's voice.

"What are you doing?" he hissed, and pressed the top of the barrel downwards.

"You said you *unmistakably* saw one bite him."

"That was well over three hours ago," said Frankie, her voice thick with confusion. "Zeke, how are you feeling?"

"I can't feel anything," Zeke said. "I'm completely numb. I managed to climb this high, then I froze."

"How did you get the zip tie off?"

"A broken bottle." He sounded miserable. "I tried to cut myself on it. Managed to nick my wrist a bit. But the blood... Turns out I can't even kill myself properly."

Frankie sighed. "Jesus, what is up with this Romeo and Juliet shit today? Get the fuck down here."

"No!" Vitt snapped. "Don't be stupid, Frankie."

"She's right. You need to leave, or even better, shoot me so this can be over with."

Frankie dragged them both a few feet from the tree, lowering her voice. "Vitt, there's no way he wouldn't have turned by now."

"People have turned far later than three hours."

"In an extremely small handful of cases, yes, but each of those started showing symptoms within the usual thirty minutes. He had enough co-ordination to free himself on glass and climb a tree for fuck's sake."

Noah fell to the ground, taking deep breaths to steady his beating heart. This was almost worse than finding him dead, because there was no way he was about to get this lucky. Not when the world took every opportunity to shit on him.

"I'm going up there to look at him," he said.

"Like hell you are," spat Vitt, but he was already on his feet, gritting his teeth against the pain as he staggered towards the tree. Vitt tried to pull him back, but he pushed her away.

"Be careful," Frankie might have said, but he wasn't paying attention to them now. It was taking every ounce of his energy to manoeuvre his frozen fingers on the icy branches.

"Don't!" called down Zeke.

He ignored him too, using the biceps he'd trained for over twelve years and his one good leg to find purchase on icy bough after icy bough until Zeke's murky shape became clear, nestled in the nook of two sturdy branches, his head between his knees.

Noah shuffled over to him, legs dangling over a large limb, a handful of feet away now.

"Zeke," he said. "Look at me."

Zeke didn't move.

"If you don't lift your head up, I'll come closer. Let me see you and I'll stay here."

Zeke heaved a sigh, unburying his head to meet Noah's gaze.

Noah wasn't usually a liar, but this wasn't a usual situation.

At the sight of his broken, scared expression, Noah pulled off his helmet, let himself slide all the way down into Zeke's shivering body, and scooped him up into his arms as best the tree would allow. Zeke shook as he wrapped his own arms around Noah, pressing his face into his neck.

"I love you," Noah whispered. "I love you, I love you, I love you so damned much. Sorry I didn't say it before."

Zeke's body melted into his and hands entangled themselves in Noah's hair as Noah cupped his face, pulling him up to see his eyes.

"I love you too," Zeke replied. "That's why you need to go now."

"Let me see your neck."

Zeke pulled back, and he angled the torchlight towards him. Noah's stomach sank. His hands trembled, shaking the light. Because as much as he'd wanted to be mistaken, there was no denying the line of angry teeth marks clearly adorning Zeke's neck. Bloody, swollen indents that stretched out for ten centimetres below his ear. He ran his gloved fingers over the thick ridges, brushing away the dusting of dried blood.

"How did you even get away from them?"

"Two of the other dogs found us. They took them down, but then ran off."

Noah swallowed. He pressed their foreheads together, and took Zeke's frigid hand, raised it to his lips and kissed it.

"Noah..."

"Shh. It's going to be okay. I'm going to stay here with you. We'll face it together." He didn't think he could face watching him turn, but he would do it. Do it for him.

Zeke exhaled, his hot, shaking breath warming Noah's face. "Only if you kill me at the first sign of trouble."

"Oh, for God's sake, will the pair of you just come down here?" shouted Frankie. She sounded a million miles away. "You need to elevate your leg, Noah."

Zeke's hand moved down to Noah's thigh. "What happened to your leg?"

"Tobias shot me."

"*What?*"

"He's dead now." Noah kissed the top of Zeke's head. "He's not going to hurt anyone ever again."

"Guys?" Vitt shouted. "I agree. Come down so we can assess the situation."

In all honesty, he would have preferred to stay up in the tree with Zeke—pretend they were in their own private oasis, a protected bubble where everything was going to be fine. But he'd already dragged Vitt and Frankie through the dark on a snowy December evening. Leaving them alone when types could arrive at any moment seemed like a pretty poor way to thank them.

Noah forced his frozen muscles into action. Despite being the injured one, he helped Zeke several times as they descended the tree. When they arrived at the bottom, Zeke shuffled off to the side, unable to meet the girls' eyes.

"Frankie," Vitt warned, as Frankie closed the space between herself and Zeke, who flinched away from her.

Vitt inspected Zeke's bite from a safe distance, then paced up and down for a minute before sighing. "I don't know what to say. As far as I know, there are no documented cases where someone with this level of contact with the pathogen has ever come through the other side unturned. But it has been hours and hours now, and he's not showing any symptoms..."

"Could it— Could it possibly be...?" Frankie hesitated.

Noah tensed. He didn't want to hear what she was on the verge of suggesting. His fractured soul couldn't handle the possibility of hope.

Zeke turned away to face the dark abyss of the forest.

"Could it be what?" asked Vitt, cocking her head.

Frankie shot Noah a glance. When Noah didn't react, she said, "You know the doctor Zeke was working for? The boss at his lab? How he was using him and another employee in some shady off-the-record shit? He was injecting them with untested drugs."

Vitt blinked rapidly. "Wow. If that's really the case, then—"

Zeke turned back to them, his expression guarded. "There could be dozens of other reasons I haven't turned yet. The cold weather, somehow. Or maybe it's just taking its sweet time. I've always been a late bloomer."

Noah sidled up to him, slid his arm around Zeke's waist despite Vitt's death stare. "Or, maybe *not*."

"Don't," croaked Zeke. "It'll just make it even more painful when it happens."

"Well, I, for one, am absolutely freezing. Why don't we at least start walking back? Wolf could lead us back to the vans. We can lock Zeke up in the one with the cage built into the back. Sorry Zeke." Frankie gave him a sympathetic smile. "Plus, Noah is bleeding through our make-shift bandage, which is going to attract types sooner rather than later."

Zeke nodded. "I'll go to the cage."

Wolf rubbed himself against Noah. "Lead the way, boy."

ZEKE

Zeke was famished. Starving. *Ravenous.*

As he lay on the hard metal of the cage's floor, waiting for Noah and Frankie to come back, he ran his fingertips over the wound on his neck. The sharp sting of the type bite had reduced to a rhythmic throb. Images of the type's fangs coming towards his face, the rancid smell of its breath assaulting his nostrils, while he desperately attempted to wriggle away, looped around his mind.

Attempting to shift his focus elsewhere, he tried to tune in to his body's every cue. Were the tremors in his legs from the frigid cold, or the RONS virus starting to devour his nervous system? Was his headache from the stress of the day, or a sign he was running out of time? And most importantly, was his relentless hunger for food, or human flesh?

A loud growl reverberated throughout the cage as another round of hunger pangs tormented him, like live mice gnawing at his stomach lining.

How much time had now passed since Frankie and Noah had bundled him into the van and driven it right up to the barn? One hour? Two? Could the others have all piled into another van, driven off and left him to die? Noah wouldn't do that to him, right?

He pulled out the wooden fox carving from his bag, stroking the soft wood, the feel of it instantly calming him. He pressed it to his lips. Noah would be here any moment now, and then everything would be okay.

Feeling sorry for himself, he dragged himself up onto his knees to look out the window, thankful again for the spare pair of glasses from his rucksack. The ground was an ever-thickening blanket of white as the blizzard contin-ued its onslaught. He shivered despite his coat that Noah retrieved for him.

His heart twisted in relief as he spotted Wolf standing guard at the bottom of the ladder that led up to the barn's attic, the dog's fur now a majestic white. They wouldn't leave Wolf behind, he could be sure of that. Wolf's head shot up to the door above the ladder. A lone figure, bundled up in a warm winter coat, climbed down it.

When Noah opened the back of the van and climbed in, Zeke resisted the temptation to snap, "*Finally!*" at him. Despite his hood, his hair was showered in glistening snowflakes, and the way he looked at Zeke—like he'd been counting the seconds away from him—melted any annoyance away.

"Hey," said Noah, poking his fingertips through the tiny squares of the cage. "I brought you some food. It's not much. We need to go get the rest of the vans."

Noah unlocked the door of the cage to throw him a protein bar. Zeke flinched when he shut and relocked it straight away, causing a deep frown to descend upon Noah's face.

"I'm sorry," Noah whispered, poking his fingertips back through.

Zeke swallowed. "It's fine. I agreed to it." He brought his hands up to entwine their hands together as best he could through the grating.

"Ready for the sitrep?"

"Do I have a choice?"

"Do you want the good, the bad, or the very bad?"

"Let's start with the good. I don't think I can take anything else right now."

"Well, the good news is Meredith patched my leg up and gave me enough pain killers that I'm practically high right now."

"Sounds like a sensible state to be facing the end of the world in."

Noah laughed. "Right? Also, more good news: Habib found what was left of Penn and Williams in the woods. Types got them. They're not going to be contacting Command anytime soon."

"And the bad news?"

"The bad news is that we can't go home."

The air grew heavy with unspoken tension. He locked eyes with Noah. On some level, he understood that it was Captain Murphy who ultimately tried to kill all of them off, but he hadn't the brain space to process what that meant yet.

"What... what will we do?" he rasped, his throat starting to constrict. "Will we be able to get back into London somehow? Lay low?"

Noah shook his head, his eyes shimmering as he squeezed Zeke's hand. "I want to promise you that I'll get you back to Zaya, Zeke, I really do. But I can't. I'm so sorry. This is all my fault. Although I never even wanted to be involved in whatever shit show my uncle, Leonie and Lowenna cooked up. Please know that."

"It's okay," Zeke said, even though he felt like he was dying. For the second time that day. "Go on then, what's the very bad news?"

Noah ran his hand through his hair. "I'm about to call Leo from Lowenna's illegal device." He removed the bulky wristband from his pocket. "Savannah's not in a good way so Meredith wants some advice from him. Plus, I need to ask him how to safely remove our chips. Krish and Habib are about to go grab another van and attempt to deactivate the trackers on them, but at the moment, the ones inside us are the bigger problem."

"How is that the very bad news?"

"Because Lowenna could be wrong about this device being unmonitored. Because Leo could run straight to Murphy. But we've decided we need to get a snapshot of what's being said back there, if anything, about our platoon." Noah regarded the view outside the window. "The only saving grace we've got is this damn blizzard, else we'd have drones all over our arses right now. But it's not going to last forever."

Noah dangled the wristband between them. "Ready?"

He stared at it with confusion. "What am *I* doing?"

"Just emotionally supporting me. Feel free to chip in. I'm not going to mention your bite, by the way."

"What? Why?" Asking a doctor about it seemed like a rather good idea.

"In case Command *are* listening. The last thing we need is them using all their resources in order to get access to you."

Tiny prickles of guilt danced across Zeke's conscience. If there was something inside him that could help, shouldn't that be the priority?

The tone rang three times before Leo picked up. "Doctor Herbert?" The connection was poor; his voice crackled through the tinny speaker. "Who is this? This isn't a good time."

"Leo. It's me," said Noah. "Don't say my name. It could flag this call."

Leo was silent, but the background noise of animated voices and people crashing around indicated he was still on the line. "How can I help?" he said at last, sounding wary.

"I'm sorry, because this is about to be a lot. I mean, a *lot*."

"I'll do my best, but it's carnage here. How much do you know?"

Zeke made eye contact with Noah, their eyes widening in a mirror of each other.

"What's there *to* know?"

A door slammed shut and the background noise faded. Zeke imagined Leo hiding in a supply cupboard. "It's fucking carnage. Red alert. Command tried to keep it quiet but two massive hordes, bigger than ever before, are marching in some sort of at least semi-organised fashion towards the North and East Wall. It's like they were waiting for the snowstorm. We've sent out drones but they're near useless, and our bullet reserves are worse than anyone knew about. Every regiment is being called up there as we speak. Plus, did you hear about all those documents and photos leaked to the press? It's bloody mad here. Where even *are* you? Why are you worried about Command hearing you? And did Ze— did your friend see those letters I scanned over to him earlier?"

Noah cradled the wristband to his ear, slumping to the floor. Zeke could practically see the flashbacks of Rotterdam falling flashing through his mind. Wordlessly, Noah unlocked the cage, and climbed in beside him, curling his body into Zeke's.

"Hello?"

"I-I don't know what to say."

"I have literally two minutes left before I have to get back out there. We're packing up med-kits."

"Command ordered all of squads K and E executed by C's hand. No time to explain why. C are all dead. Same with some of our squads. Sav is potentially bleeding out, we need to cut our trackers out of our bodies, and we're at the very bottom of our food and ammunition."

Now it was Leo's turn to be silent. "Jesus. Is Z.B. okay?"

"I hope so," Noah whispered, tightening his grip on Zeke's chest. "Oh, and no to the letters, we've had to keep all bands and helmets offline. What letters?"

"I'll forward them to this number. I can't help with Sav without seeing her, really. What's the injury?"

"Stomach. Embedded rifle bullet."

"Ouch. Your lead medic should only try to get it out herself if she can't control the bleeding."

"We don't have any other choice Leo, we can't come back. What should I tell her?"

"Tell her I said that she's got this." Through the line, someone was calling Leo's name, sounding angry. "I'm sorry, I have to go."

"Trackers?"

"What? Oh. They're designed to be removed fairly easily, as they're swapped out every few years. Use lots of alcohol, and you should be good. There will be blood, so have blocker on hand."

Zeke felt Noah grimace against his shoulder. "Running low on that, too. I'll let you go now. One last thing. Do you want to come with us?"

"What? Where?"

"Unsure."

"Noa—" Leo cut the word off with a grunt. "I can't. I have a duty to do."

"Should we come back?"

A long pause.

"No. Get the fuck away from here. And good luck, my friend. You're going to need it."

The line went dead.

Noah twisted, the air he expelled from his mouth turning into a hazy cloud in the cold.

"Well, that *was* a lot." Zeke attempted a smile.

Three knocks on the back of the van door had them both jumping apart. Noah locked the cage before opening the door to let Frankie in.

Even Frankie, their eternal ray of sunshine, looked beat. "How are you, Zeke?"

He shrugged. "The same."

"Lowenna has decided that K are all going to Birmingham. They know people there."

Noah nodded, like he'd expected it. "I'm coming back up. Need to update everyone. How's Sav?"

She grimaced.

The wristband vibrated in Noah's hand. Noah glanced at it before saying, "Zeke, Leo's sent that stuff he mentioned through. There's scans of handwritten letters."

Zeke shuffled over to the grate to peer over Noah's shoulder. At the bottom of the documents, Leo had written:

I noticed an envelope addressed to Z.B. when I was at the admin office.
I saw it was from the prison, so I thought it might be from Harding.
I opened it to scan it for him in case he wanted it straight away. The
gist of it is that Albert Harding apparently hung himself in his cell with
instructions to forward some letters to him. I haven't had time to look
at them properly. Take care.

Doctor Harding was dead. Doctor Harding was dead, and Zeke should be
feeling something, *anything*, but all he felt was numb and hungry.

"What's all that scribbled nonsense?" Frankie moved her face closer to the
tiny screen, and Noah zoomed in so they could attempt to read it. Harding's
handwriting always was questionable, but the scrawling mess across five
separate pieces of paper was barely legible. He'd scribbled many of the chaotic
notes out, the pen ripping the paper in the process.

"I think it's research notes." Zeke brought his hand up to rub his deltoid
muscle through his coat, remembering how hard he'd fought against fainting
each time Harding 'took his blood'.

"This bit looks like an address." Noah tapped the screen, reading out the
complicated names in a flawless accent.

5 Vørðuvegur, Hósvík 420, Faroe Islands

"Is that Dutch?" Zeke marvelled.

Noah's eyes lit up. "Nope. Danish. I've heard of the Faroes. Group of
about twenty volcanic islands. Home to thousands of seabirds. Lots of rare
ones too, like Storm Petrels, Great Skuas, Black Guille—"

Zeke silenced him with a raised eyebrow. Trust Noah to get distracted by
birds at a time like this.

"Scroll down. There's more under the address," said Frankie.

Noah obeyed, reading out the final sentence. "Find Gurli Kristoffersen."
He zoomed into a series of numbers scribbled after the name. Was it a phone
number?

Zeke sank down to the floor. "Well, that was enlightening."

"We need to ring that number, *now*," said Noah, with an obvious excitement that Zeke didn't share. After what he'd just been through, he couldn't bring himself to dare to hope for good news. But Noah was already typing the digits into the band. After three rings, a female voice answered in a language Zeke presumed was Danish.

"Hello? Is this Gurli Kristoffersen? Do you speak English? Or Dutch?" Noah shouted down the phone, as if the lady could be deaf.

The wristband crackled.

"I am her. Who's asking?" the voice said, in a thick accent.

"You're speaking with Noah Forrest. I'm here with Zeke Bates, who was working with Doctor Harding, who told us to find you."

"Come to me? Why?"

"Zeke Bates was one of Harding's... unknowing participants in his study. A study I presume you were also involved with?"

"Go on."

"Many hours ago, Zeke was bitten by a type. Badly. And now... well he's still here. Displaying no signs of the RONS virus."

The woman took a sharp intake of breath.

"We also have photos of pages and pages of research notes. Well, either that or the mad ramblings of a lunatic. You'll be the judge of that."

"How soon can you get him here?"

Zeke met Noah's gaze. He nodded, slowly.

"As soon as we can. We'll be sailing across in a yacht from England."

Frankie made a small sound of confusion as she looked between them.

"Stay in contact," Gurli said. "And be safe. We might finally be on the precipice."

Zeke's mind raced.

Of a cure? Of salvation? Of the start of the end?

Noah reached through the bars to interlace their fingers. "We'll be back in ten, Zeke, with the others. It's time for a family meeting."

After what was decidedly *not* ten minutes, Squad E—or what remained of it—minus Savannah, piled into the back of the van. Zeke huddled in the corner as they filed in, avoiding every prying eye. He shouldn't be this close to any of them, not when he could still turn at any moment. But their relieved greetings—from everyone, even Habib—made him unfurl somewhat.

"Right," said Noah, once all eyes were on him. "First, from this moment on, we're not soldiers of the Eighth East Regiment. We're outlaws on the run. So, I'm not your LT anymore."

A murmur of dissent rippled through the squad, quietening as soon as Noah raised his hand.

"Our first order of business, however, has to be removing our tracking chips."

Habib removed his penknife from his belt and held a lighter to it, beginning the process of sterilizing it.

"That's no substitute for alcohol," Zeke said, earning him a pointed glare from Habib. Zeke hoped Habib wouldn't be the one cutting the incisions.

Meredith rummaged through her daysack, producing a small bottle. "I'll do it. Vitt can do me though."

"Me?" squeaked Vitt, and Aoife laughed at her.

"You can watch me first. Who wants to be my first victim?"

Nobody seemed ecstatic at the prospect of going first. Eventually Frankie shuffled over on her knees, removing the top half of her combat suit and pulling up her sleeve. Zeke grimaced at the dirty floor and lack of sanitary conditions. They'd likely all end up amputees after this.

"Hold her still," Noah ordered, and Vitt and Aoife jumped up to help. After cleaning the incision site with an alcohol infused cotton pad, Meredith held the small knife near Frankie's skin. She was facing the cage, so Zeke saw her screw her face up in anticipation, her eyes tightly closed.

"I can feel it in there, I *think*," said Meredith, instilling confidence in nobody.

Zeke turned away as Meredith lowered the knife, already feeling squeamish from the mere anticipation of blood.

Frankie grunted in pain.

"Found it. Five more seconds while I pull it out. It's pretty buried in there."

Familiar waves of nausea swept over him.

"Done!"

Curiosity winning over his haemophobia, Zeke turned back to see Meredith wiping the tracker with the used cotton pad before holding it up between her thumb and forefinger. It looked like a large grain of rice made of dark glass.

"A lot of trouble for something so tiny," said Aoife, taking it from Meredith.

"Crush it." Noah looked between the others. "Who's next?"

Habib went next, sparking a factory line of arms being cleaned, incisions being cut, and chips being crushed. Vitt screamed the loudest of anyone, earning her a thump from Habib. Meredith seemed unsure about her choice of surgeon when her turn arrived, but Vitt turned out to be equally adept at the task.

Once everyone was done, eyes darted between Zeke and Noah. Zeke hovered at the cage door. "Hand over the sterilised knife, I'll do mine myself."

"Not a chance." Noah squeezed by Vitt and Frankie, the key in one hand and the knife in the other.

"Noah," Habib warned. "It's not safe. Unless you want to go for my plan with the muzz—"

Noah's face turned to Habib and whatever look he gave him was enough to silence him.

"Go sort Savannah out," Noah said to Meredith.

Meredith bit her lip. "I don't know if any more blood loss is a good idea."

Noah looked pained as he said, "We don't have a choice, Mere."

She nodded and left the van.

The tenderness that Noah displayed in cleaning his arm clued Zeke in to the fact that by now, everyone must know about them. The others averted their eyes, busying themselves by inspecting their guns.

"Hold still for me," Noah said, a low rumble directly into his ear. Noah brushed Zeke's hair out of his eyes, and Zeke wanted nothing more than to grab his hand and keep it there.

The procedure was swift. After being bitten by a type then having his body dragged through the woods, Zeke's pain tolerance had improved remarkably.

"Don't look yet," said Noah, as he cleaned up every drop of blood. He stuck a plaster over the incision—then some blue blocker tape for good measure—before pulling down his sleeve. "Done."

Zeke opened his eyes to find Noah's face taking up his entire vision. Noah pecked him on the lips. Frankie wolf-whistled.

Groaning, Zeke said, "*Please.*"

Frankie looked gleeful, the traitorous bitch. "Can I just say that I'm now owed a fuck tonne of mug duties, thanks to Savannah and Luo's naivety. Well, I would be if we were actually going home. And Luo was still alive."

The van fell quiet.

"We'll have a send off for Luo as soon as we can," said Noah.

Vitt nodded. "Meredith has his dog tags. And Brodie's."

As if summoned, Meredith slid back into the van. "It's done. She's passed out for now. Krish managed to get the bullet out for us. Neither of us think it's ruptured the intestine. We got lucky. I think she'll be okay. We've irrigated with saline and antiseptic and forced an antibiotic down her throat. I don't think we have enough pills for a full course, though."

"We'll just have to pray." Aoife rubbed her cross necklace through the layers of her clothing.

Habib nodded. "Absolutely."

"I've shown K how to get the chips out. They're doing each other now. They're still set on going to Birmingham," continued Meredith.

"And us?" Vitt looked to Noah, and the others followed suit.

"Again, I'm not in charge anymore," started Noah. "But if you're up for it, I've got a plan."

Vitt stood, looking at each of the squad in turn. "Before you tell us, Noah, let me say this. I know I speak for everyone when I say you will always, *always* be our leader."

The others nodded. One by one, they took each other's hands.

Frankie gripped the cage, but Zeke remained in his corner. He stretched his arm out, as if he were about to take her hand. That would have to be enough.

"Thanks guys," said Noah, his voice choked, and Zeke's heart swelled with pride. He would follow this man anywhere. "So, has anyone ever driven a boat?"

NOAH

V ans were packed, plans were made, and injuries patched up as best they could. But before they left the farm, there was one more thing to do.

"We can't just leave them here like *this*," Meredith said, referring to the large amount of bodies littering the barn. Not just the bodies of the Eighth East soldiers, however. In the carnage that had ensued, many of the mutilated humans, hung like meat by the types, were bitten. The remaining five members of Squad K put them all out of their misery. It was all they could do.

What Noah really wanted to do now was get the hell out of there as quickly as possible, but he agreed it didn't feel respectful to his former comrades, even if some of them were cold-blooded murderers. "We don't have time to dig a mass burial pit," he said, exasperated, rubbing his tired eyes.

Aoife stared up at the barn that loomed towards them in the dark. "Let's burn them. Cremate them."

"In this snowstorm?" Habib scoffed. "As if."

"I could do it," Zeke said quietly. He was still in the cage, with the van back doors wide open so he could talk to them. "I could make an incendiary bomb."

All eyes turned to Zeke.

"That would be great, Zeke." Lowenna smiled warmly at him. "Krish will give you a hand with whatever you need."

"I'll have to leave the van, but I'll stay well back from everyone. Habib can train his rifle on me at all times."

Noah said quickly, "That won't be necessary," and glared at Habib, daring him to disagree.

When Noah unlocked the cage, Zeke climbed out tentatively like a wounded bird before dashing around, searching for whatever he was looking for. Vitt and Meredith gathered as much dry wood as they could from the other outbuildings, while Noah and the others had the pleasure of dragging the dead bodies out of the barn and onto the increasingly large pile. Noah tried not to look at their glassy eyes, blood stained skin or vacant expressions, but it was almost impossible. He was thankful when Lowenna insisted on sorting Luo's body, a small kindness that went a long way.

By the time they'd finished, Zeke had acquired a large metal drum and was using their explosives kit to make an ignition system. He'd instructed Krish to siphon whatever fuel or oil he could from the tractors around the farm. Watching him laser-focussed on his task—eyes narrowed, teeth biting his bottom lip—warmed Noah's frigid body.

Once everything was in place, and Habib poked a series of vents into the metal container with some sort of farm tool he'd found, the group stood well back, waiting for Zeke to remotely detonate his bomb. Noah slipped his arm through Zeke's and glanced at Meredith. There was no universe where he deserved her acceptance of their relationship. Hell, he wouldn't blame her if she never spoke to him again. But a small smile danced on her lips as she nodded at them, once. *Thank you,* he mouthed.

When Zeke successfully released the small explosion, everyone clapped him before they turned to watch the intense flames that rapidly engulfed the deceased, tears streaming down faces like rivers.

Noah squeezed Zeke to him, brushing a dusting of snow from his shoulder. "Well done, firestarter," he whispered into his ear.

"Does this mean I'm not completely useless any more?"

"This is just a fraction of what's been burning in you all along," he said, kissing Zeke's forehead.

The further they drove from the farm, the more doubts crept into Noah's mind.

Apart from Habib behind the wheel, and himself, everybody was asleep. Exhaustion swept over them like a tidal wave as soon as they'd said teary goodbyes to Lowenna, Krish and the rest of Squad K that survived Tobias's culling. He'd never see them again. Every inch of his soul told him that. As they drove off in the opposite direction, Noah's worries about his ridiculous plan tempted him to change his mind and follow them to Birmingham. But days after Rotterdam fell, so had Amsterdam. The cycle had to break.

Noah was done. Done with the fighting, the deaths, the endless cycle of grief.

But what if he was leading them all to their doom? What if he was leading them to an empty boatyard? Or one overrun with types? They were in no state to fight a cluster, let alone a horde.

Zeke, nestled into the crook of his shoulder, stirred. The faint glow of the moon through the relentless blizzard illuminated his hair, and Noah ran his fingers through the golden threads. There had been some wariness about letting him sit next to him, but not much. They could all see Noah needed him.

Even with the snow chains equipped onto the tires, it was a slow, treacherous drive. Despite the roads being relatively clear of obstacles from their outbound journey, the ice transformed each country lane and highway into a ski slope. Habib made pained grunting noises from the front each time he lost control and skidded.

A few types took an interest in the van, but not as many as there should have been. Were they all already amassed at the city wall?

Savannah, lying across two seats, pushed herself up, bleary-eyed. Wolf, lying on the floor near her feet, sat up too, like he was waiting for her to wake up.

"What time is it?" she whispered. "Are we almost there?"

"Almost midnight. Thirty minutes. How's the stomach?"

"Feels like I swallowed a hot coal." Her breathing was uneven as she sank back down.

He opened his mouth to reassure her they'd get her proper help as soon as possible, then shut it. Because that wasn't part of the plan.

Against his chest, he felt Zeke's eyes flutter open. "Don't wake up yet." He smoothed his hair. "You've still got half an hour. Rest."

"I should probably see how Zaya's doing." Zeke glanced at his wristband, which he'd turned back on—briefly—hours ago to call her. They'd figured Murphy was too busy dealing with the whole 'thousands of types about to break down the wall' thing to worry about monitoring their devices. Habib had done the same, and now, theoretically, Zaya was driving Habib's wife and child east to meet them at a gate they'd specified. Unless London was on full lockdown and the riot police barricaded them all in.

"She'll find a way," Zeke had said, determination in his eyes. "She always does."

Zeke's wristband vibrated with incoming messages.

"They're on their way," he said, incredulous, as if he couldn't quite believe it. "She's got them both, and they're almost there. They're likely to beat us."

Habib caught Noah's eye in the rear-view mirror. His face relaxed an infinitesimal amount.

Before long, everyone was awake, looking tired, frightened, but alive.

"Tell me we're at least going to wait for the blizzard to stop before we jump into the row boat," Habib called back to them.

"It's not a row boat, it's a yacht," said Vitt. She'd fallen asleep pouring over the paperwork that came with the boat key in his uncle's package. Vitt never came across a puzzle she couldn't solve.

"Yippee fucking doo dah," Habib sniped.

Noah bit his tongue. Habib was only being such an arse because he was nervous about picking up Zainab and Adeela.

The chatter dissipated the closer they got to the gate. This is where the plan got a bit murky. They didn't need to get back in, but they did need whoever was posted there to let Zaya, Zainab, and Adeela out.

"Zaya's gone silent," Zeke hissed into his ear when they were a handful of minutes away.

"Don't panic. They're still going to wait in the car down the road until you ring them, right?"

Zeke nodded. He was terrified.

"This is almost all over," Noah said, even though they were only at the very beginning of a very, very long journey.

Habib slowed the vehicle to a crawl. In the distance, the light coming from the watchtower that controlled the gate lit up like a beacon. "Are we driving right up, Noah?"

"May as well."

Habib urged the vehicle forward before bringing it to a stop directly outside the metal shutters.

"Here goes nothing. Habib and I will go to talk to them. Everyone else, stay in the van. If it goes south, don't hesitate to drive off. The address is plugged in."

Zeke scoffed, and the others shook their heads.

"I mean it. That's an order."

"Aye, aye, sir," Vitt said. "Now go get them."

He shared a long, meaningful look with Zeke before tearing himself away from him, sliding out of the van to meet Habib, tugging his helmet onto his head.

They were only two steps into their short journey when the shutters rose. *Well, that was easy,* Noah almost joked.

A man stepped out of the dark tunnel, in full combat wear, his rifle trained on Noah.

"Identification," the man snapped. "What are you doing?"

Noah's heart soared. He knew that voice. They'd been on the same squad, many years ago when Noah first arrived. They'd spent many nights together back then, his companionship ebbing the stabbing pains of Noah's grief. "Brian?"

"Who— Noah?"

Noah pulled off his helmet. Beside him, Habib did the same.

"What are you doing? Command hasn't—"

"Listen. We're not here to cause trouble. We're just here to pick up two women and a child, then we'll be on our way."

"You mean the three civvies we just caught trespassing?"

Noah grimaced. "That would be them, yes."

Brian lowered his rifle. "What the actual fuck is going on? Is the rest of Squad E in the van? Where are you going?"

"Top secret mission," said Habib. "Need to know basis."

"You're not particularly convincing right now. Tell me why I shouldn't shoot every last one of you for deserting in a time of crisis?"

Noah stepped towards him. "Because almost everyone in London is about to die. And then there will only be a handful of populated cities left in the entire world. And we might have the key to stopping the RONS virus in the back of our van."

Brian staggered back, lowering his rifle.

"You know I wouldn't lie to you, Brian."

Shaking his head, Brian threw his arms in the air. "Jesus, Noah. What do you need?"

"Your three prisoners. Any spare food you have. We're about to sail past Denmark. And any of these medical supplies." Noah passed Brian the list Meredith made.

Brian laughed, a manic, hollow sound. "And what do I tell Command?"

"If there's a Command left to tell, tell them you helped save the world."

After a moment's hesitation, Brian ordered them to wait there, and went back through the shutter.

The wait was agonising. Was Brian about to come back with the women, or the rest of the soldiers that were stationed at the gate?

The shutter began to rise again.

"Habib?"

A woman ran towards Habib, a toddler on her hip. She embraced him with such ferocity, Noah looked away.

Brian, carrying a large sack, stood with a wild-eyed Zaya. He tossed the sack onto the ground.

"Good luck, my friends. I hope you're right. If I have helped save the world, give me a mention in the footnotes."

Noah nodded at him and held his arm out to Zaya. "Zeke's in the van."

Behind him, the van door slid open and someone crunched into the heavy snow.

"Zeke!" Zaya shrieked.

Noah turned just in time to see her throw herself at him.

After a last wave to Brian, Noah ushered them all into the van.

"Onwards till dawn," Vitt said.

The van ran out of power five miles from the boatyard at Leigh-on-Sea.

The warning light had been on for the last twenty, so it wasn't a surprise, but a collective groan still echoed around the vehicle as it crawled to a steady stop.

"No turning back now," Aoife said.

"Guys, I left my charger at home," Meredith replied, and the squad erupted into nervous laughter.

Zainab and Zaya glanced at each other, likely determining what the hell they had gotten themselves into.

The laughter was a welcome break from the tense atmosphere that'd settled over the group as they had driven south towards the coast. Zaya had scrolled through her media feeds, relaying the headlines to them. London was indeed falling. Types, more organised than anybody had ever seen, charged en masse at the northern wall, and broke through the defences an hour after they'd left. Various friends called Zaya, and she'd cried down the line to them, saying choked goodbyes.

But thirty minutes ago, her connection dropped. Radio silence.

Noah turned to address the group. "Well, looks like we're on foot from here. Everyone will need to help carry the gear. No shots without my say so. You know how limited we are on ammo."

Aside from Zainab, who was carrying a worryingly quiet Adeela, everyone loaded themselves up like pack mules. Keeping the civvies in the middle of their formation, they marched slowly on the slippery snowfall, with Noah and Wolf leading the charge.

As he led from the front, each step on his bad leg making him grit his teeth, the ghosts of everyone he lost urged him onwards. Khyan. His parents. His brothers and sisters. Splat. Luo. His uncle, most likely. But no more. He wouldn't lose another single member of his flock. He *couldn't*.

After a while, the snowstorm ebbed to a light flurry. Adeela stretched her tiny hand out to catch them, giggling.

Savannah, supported by Aoife, needed to stop every few minutes, clutching her stomach. Noah kept waiting for the moment her hands came away covered in blood.

"Should be just down here," called Habib. The GPS system on their wristbands was still online. They could only pray that the yacht's would be too.

Frankie, to Noah's left, started singing the tune to *The Final Countdown*. "I hope it has a swimming pool."

"I can confirm it does *not* have a swimming pool," said Vitt.

"Focus," Noah said. "We can chat about swimming pools once we're on the boat."

When a type staggered out from behind a road sign, Zainab screamed.

Noah unloaded a bolt from his crossbow into the middle of its forehead. Bullseye. Walking up to it, he inspected its limp, deformed body. "Looks like it was half starved to death," he remarked, pointing his crossbow at its skeletal ribs and concave stomach.

Habib peered down at it. "Not much food around this time of year. Not many humans even left to munch on either."

Down the road, a faded sign proclaimed that Harbourview Marina was half a mile to their left.

The dockyard was a ghost town. The only movement came from the gentle fall of snowflakes in the starlight. There were no boats floating in the icy depths—likely they'd floated out to sea ten years ago. A long white pier stretched out in front of them, a couple of gulls perching on the pilings and metal railing.

Vitt pointed toward a long line of wooden structures. "According to General Forrest, it's in the last boathouse."

As the group trudged towards the building, Noah built up a fantasy in his mind that his uncle would be inside, waiting for them, ready to set sail. He'd greet Noah with open arms, pulling him towards him, promising that it was all going to be o kay.

The dream soon shattered when they opened the unlocked door and stepped into the dark boathouse, whose sloped ground led directly into the water.

Just one ship lay waiting for them.

A floating palace of opulence, the luxury yacht sat on metal blocking, its hull proudly proclaiming it the *White Dove*. Noah stared at the name until Zeke nudged into him, shooting him a beaming smile.

With a sleek, stylish slimline design, the two-tiered yacht was clearly a high-end model. Noah glimpsed a plush, circular lounge area through the expansive windows.

Frankie, neck craned backwards, said, "There's no swimming pool, but there is a diving board."

"If anyone is stupid enough to jump off it, they're getting left behind." Habib assessed the framework the yacht sat on. He turned to Vitt. "How do we get it onto the boat ramp?"

"No idea. I'm only taking charge once she's all set."

"Over here!"

As one, they followed the sound of Aoife's squeal past the ship to the far side of the boathouse, where she was scrutinizing a dusty control panel.

"It's a boatlift." Aoife pointed at the ceiling with her light. Sure enough, four green metal columns supported a further one that hung horizontally, high above the boat. When Noah looked closer at the hull, he saw it was already sitting in a cradle. All they needed to do was attach the bungee cord pulley system.

It was almost six a.m. when they'd finally figured it out, working with shockingly patient collaboration considering the state they were all in. When the hydraulic gangway unfolded, everyone cheered, even little Adeela, who was now being supervised by Frankie as she ran around exploring.

Wolf bounded forward first, charging up the gangway. *I hope you've got sea legs, boy, because this is about to be a bumpy ride.*

"All aboard!" hollered Noah. "Get your tickets ready!"

"I hope my ticket grants me three course dinners," said Savannah, staggering slowly across the platform.

Noah reached out to help her take the last few steps. "It'll grant you three ration pouches a day, thanks to Brian."

Surreal wonder engulfed Noah as the boat glided away from the slipway. He almost laughed. He was on a boat, a *luxury yacht*, about to travel a thousand miles to the middle of nowhere in the North Atlantic Ocean, trapped in a confined space with his squad. So why did he feel the most free he'd felt in the last ten years?

The last flurries of the snowstorm faded away, leaving them with a calm, welcoming ocean. After they had all removed their helmets, dumping them with the bags on the top deck, the others rushed down the stairs to explore, leaving Noah alone on the bow.

The first glimpse of sunrise painted the beckoning horizon a delicious gold, creating a dazzling display of orange hues on the surface of the water.

A high-pitched chattering of birds above him tore his eyes away from the water and into the sky. Noah gasped. A large murmuration of swallows was following them, likely migrating for the winter now that the snowstorm had faded. The swooping mass of feathers wove in and out of each other effortlessly, dancing steps to a routine only they knew.

Warm fingers slid in between his own and caressed the back of his hand.

Standing like figureheads, Noah and Zeke wordlessly stared out at the expanse of the great ocean.

Noah didn't know what would happen tomorrow, or the next day, or the next. But what he did know was that with Zeke by his side, he would guide his flock through hell and back if he needed to.

He brought Zeke's hand up to his mouth and kissed it.

"Where to, Captain?" Zeke asked.

He smiled. The answer was simple.

"True north."

The End

Acknowledgements

What a journey writing a book is! Monsters within Men invaded my life for the best part of an entire year, and I couldn't have gotten through it without the friends I made along the way.

Firstly, a super massive shout out to my writing partner-in-crime, Lucie Fleury, the first to read an early version of this book. Your feedback helped me shape the novel into a tremendously better version of itself. You are an amazing friend and an awesome writer. Fans of gorgeously written fantasy should check out her excellent Ambrosia series.

Thank you to Kat—your excitement for Monsters within Men helped me push through round after round of edits!

Thank you to W. H. Lockwood, my fellow writer with a weakness for men in glasses, who helped to make this book shine! Thank you for all of your support and for loving Zeke just as much as I do! Fans of paranormal horror alongside morally grey men should head straight to her Percy and Joe series.

Thank you to my other beta readers, CJ, Tia, and Becca—your feedback was all immensely helpful!

Thank you to Abrianna Denae for the excellent proofreading service.

A massive thank you to the @the.ravens.touch for the stunning book cover—you couldn't have done a better job!

And finally, thank YOU for reading this book and giving Noah and Zeke a chance!

CONTINUE THE STORY...

Want to continue the adventure?

To read **Monsters within Men: Aftermath**, a free bonus extended epilogue which continues and concludes the story of Squad E plus some special guests, head over to my website (https://www.tjrosebooks.com/) and subscribe to my newsletter to be automatically sent the link to download the ePub or PDF file.

MORE BY TJ ROSE

Magic... a murder mystery... and more than a little mayhem!

Get ready to delve into an MM romance urban fantasy duology set in an alternate magical world.

Cinnamon 'Cinn' Saunders thought he'd learnt to control his little ghost problem.

That is, until the moment he brings back a malevolent spirit from the shadowrealm, and quickly finds himself unjustly arrested for the murder of four people.

After breaking free of foster care and a stint in juvie, all Cinn wanted to do was keep his head down and work his way up to become a professional chef. Now he's forced to make a choice: life in jail, or allow a stranger to whisk him away to a mysterious institute in rural Switzerland with the promise of learning how to control his terrifying supernatural abilities.

Julien, the French charismatic charmer who is charged with warding over Cinn, also has a problem: the murder of his sister is still unsolved.

He needs help. Help that only Cinn can provide. He'll do anything to get it, including making Cinn an offer that he can't refuse. What Julien doesn't expect out of the bargain is their undeniable connection, which only serves to complicate matters as they navigate uncharted territories together.

Between battling an uprising of deadly creatures that not only threaten the moteblessed community, but the entire planet, and fighting their ever-growing attraction, can this opposites-attract pair overcome their demons to save the world, and each other?

The Shadows Beyond is available now.

ABOUT THE AUTHOR

TJ Rose lives in rural England. A voracious reader from the age of five, she finally started giving life to the stories inside her head.

Her action-packed romance stories contain vivid worlds, colourful characters, sugar and spice, and happily ever afters.

When she's not watching horror movies or dreaming up doomsday scenarios, she enjoys exploring nature and drinking coffee in the sun.

Follow her on social media & sign up to her newsletter to stay up to date:

Newsletter   Bookbub   Goodreads

Instagram   Tiktok

If you enjoyed this book, please consider leaving a review—they are incredibly valuable to independent authors. Thank you!

9 781068 171437